SET THE
NIGHT
ON FIRE

OTHER TITLES BY CONNIE DIAL

SET THE
NIGHT
ON FIRE

CONNIE DIAL

THE PERMANENT PRESS
Sag Harbor, NY 11963

M

For information, address:
  The Permanent Press
  4170 Noyac Road
  Sag Harbor, NY 11963
  www.thepermanentpress.com

Library of Congress Cataloging-in-Publication Data

Dial, Connie—
    Set the night on fire / Connie Dial.
      pages ; cm
    ISBN 978-1-57962-402-6
      1. Policewomen—California—Los Angeles—Fiction.
    2. Missing persons—Investigations—Fiction. 3. Undercover
    operations—Fiction. 4. Suspense fiction. 5. Mystery fiction.
    I. Title.

PS3604.I26S48 2016
813'.6—dc23   2015046226

Printed in the United States of America

Set the Night on Fire is dedicated to those PDID police officers who were willing to accept the challenges and dangers of a deep cover intelligence assignment during a tumultuous time in Los Angeles. They put their careers and personal ambitions on hold to protect lives and property knowing their courage and sacrifice would never be acknowledged or rewarded.

"My dad's generation was called the greatest. They survived the Depression, fought a bloody war on foreign soil, and saved the world from Nazi lunatics. I'm a product of the sixties, the Age of Aquarius. We fought a war too, mostly in jungles and villages I couldn't pronounce and for reasons I never understood, but marines don't need to know why, just when and where. The sixties was a time that saw too many of our heroes assassinated, riots in city streets, hallucinogenic drugs hailed as aphrodisiacs and mind expanders, and everything we believed in questioned and turned upside down—music, clothes, attitudes— a mystery as well as an affront to the greatest generation. I lived through that decade and now I've come to realize that those who didn't not only missed a hell of a ride, but they would never get a handle on what had to come next."

—SERGEANT JON "BRICKHOUSE" MURPHY
LAPD/PDID — 1971

ONE

Los Angeles, California — 1971

It was a peaceful demonstration until it wasn't. Josie got pushed against a storefront window with a dozen other protesters. She'd ducked just seconds before a rock hit the glass shattering it into dozens of large jagged pieces. The police pulled them off the sidewalk and onto the street before anyone had the foolish notion of picking up a knife-shaped shard and using it as a weapon.

The shouting and screaming, ear-piercing sirens, and clouds of tear gas drifted over them from somewhere down the street and polluted the air seconds before uniformed police officers swarmed over the crowd.

Josie thought she understood these people. She'd been a member of the Workers Liberation Movement or the WLM for two years and although they frequently talked about fighting the cops, she didn't believe they'd actually do it unless in the unlikely event they outnumbered them. This morning five plainclothes officers foolishly got culled from the blue phalanx monitoring the march of more than one hundred demonstrators in downtown Los Angeles, and they were immediately attacked with heavy sticks that moments before had held placards demanding workers rights and an end to the Vietnam War. With military precision, twenty to thirty protesters ripped off the stapled posters leaving formidable clubs in the hands of men and women Josie knew had practiced using them as weapons and were eager to do some damage.

The marchers had always been promised by their leaders that if a melee began during any demonstration in this part of downtown, the oppressed immigrants in the garment district would abandon their sewing machines and jump in to help them fight the police. Confirming Josie's suspicions, no one did anything except stand on the curb and gawk at the spectacle.

Most of the demonstrators ran away, escaping through vacant buildings or over walls as soon as police reinforcements in full riot gear arrived, but Josie and about forty others had been surrounded and captured. She was knocked to the ground with a violent leg-sweep and fell flat on her stomach, the side of her face bounced hard against the asphalt, ripping into the skin. Tears were streaming from her gas-singed eyes, as someone dropped onto her back with one knee and her neck with the other, pulled her arms back, and secured her hands with tight plastic handcuffs. There hadn't been any resistance on her part but these cops were pissed and she'd become the object of their anger. She could hardly see; her face, back, and ribs ached but, probably unlike the others, she understood.

She'd graduated from the police academy three years earlier, but her only significant assignment in all that time had been to infiltrate this group as a UC, an undercover officer. Her badge, police ID, department-issued gun, and new blue uniforms were stashed in a duffle bag somewhere in the Public Disorder and Intelligence Division's basement at the old Georgia Street station and she lay there on the ground unable, no unwilling, to explain to anybody that she was one of them.

Her only real fear now was that one of these officers might recognize her, someone who'd been an academy classmate or had worked with her the few months she'd been allowed a glimpse into the world of crime fighting before mysteriously disappearing into this deep cover assignment. Most of these younger officers didn't even know PDID existed and their first reaction in recognizing a fellow cop was to say something. She had worked too hard gaining trust and acceptance from the WLM to lose everything with a careless offhand remark.

When two uniformed officers finally grabbed under her arms and helped Josie stand, her shoulders and wrists were numb, but in a few seconds began throbbing with pain. They pushed her up the steps and into the back of an already overcrowded paddy wagon. The lingering odor of dried vomit from the homeless drunks who usually occupied this convey-ance had mixed with the sweaty smell of too many unwashed bodies in the cramped space. She leaned against a steel pole just inside the door and tried to hold on to it with her hands still cuffed behind her back. When the wagon started moving, there wouldn't be anything except others in similarly precari-ous positions to keep her from falling.

Before the back doors slammed shut, her vision was clearing and she saw an ambulance parked near several offi-cers lying on the street being treated by paramedics. Blood covered their shirts and a few had their heads and other body parts bandaged. Her WLM comrades had done some serious damage during the brief skirmish and she knew her supervisors wouldn't allow her to be released anytime soon. That was the way it worked. She'd go to jail with the rest of the captured demonstrators and wait for PDID to come up with a make-believe uncle to post bail and spring her. In the meantime, her department contact would find a way to meet and get as much information as he could without letting the rest of the group think she was being treated differently.

This wasn't the first time Josie had been in jail since going undercover and she knew what the routine would be before her release eventually came through—the strip search, delous-ing, the one phone call, an uncomfortable overstarched blue jumpsuit, and a stale Velveeta cheese sandwich on day-old white bread that the deputies called dinner. She would go through the motions of being a criminal defendant but was confident that in a couple of months all the charges would be dropped against her and one or two other demonstrators to avoid suspicion, and if anyone was clever enough to check after she was out of this assignment, all the paperwork concerning her arrest would have mysteriously disappeared from the system.

When they got to Sybil Brand women's jail in East LA, she stood in line with dozens of other women by the back gate and looked for Emily, one of the people she'd gotten close to in the group. Josie knew it would be better if Emily somehow managed to get away, and not only because she was young and beautiful with long blonde hair and blue eyes. Emily had the mental acuity of a naive high school dropout—she'd be easy prey in a place like this.

Behind her back, Emily Rice was what the leadership of the WLM called a "useful idiot." She was the wife of the very rich Century City lawyer Burton Rice and had little understanding of, or commitment to, the group's philosophy but seemed to enjoy the romantic notion of revolution. She had posters of Che Guevara prominently displayed in her expensively furnished home office in West LA, but Josie doubted Emily could locate Cuba on a map. Her real value to WLM was her husband's ability to raise and donate lots of money and his willingness to arrange pro bono lawyers among his buddies any time members of the group got arrested. So they kept Emily around and allowed her to dress like a hippie and play at fomenting revolution. For reasons Josie would probably never comprehend, she liked the woman and was constantly trying to keep WLM's exploitation of her to a minimum.

Before being booked, the arrestees were handcuffed to a bench bolted to the floor in a long hallway outside the cells. One by one, they were taken by plainclothes officers to be interviewed and then fingerprinted, photographed, and removed to the cellblock. Josie was one of the last to be processed because she had to be treated first by the jail doctor for the cuts and abrasions on her face and head.

The jail infirmary was a cramped medieval-looking space with a medical team she thought resembled the Addams family from the television show. Even worse, it didn't look as if anyone had recently cleaned or sterilized any of their equipment or instruments. The overworked Dr. "Lurch" was easily persuaded by Josie to avoid stitches and just pin her long brown unruly hair out of the way, wash and disinfect her injuries, and cover the ones that were still bleeding. He also used an eyewash that finally brought some relief from the itching and burning sensation.

There were only a couple of women still waiting when Josie was finally able to sit handcuffed to the bench in the hallway. Every time she tried to move and get comfortable, her body ached as if someone had attacked her ribs with a baseball bat. She didn't recognize the remaining women, but that wasn't a surprise. Manny Contreras, WLM's leader in Los Angeles, always recruited demonstrators from other cities for his marches.

She had closed her eyes and was resting her head against the wall for a few seconds when she felt a sharp kick at her foot. It startled her and she sat up quickly and groaned, not from the kick, but the sudden movement had strained her already sore muscles.

"Wake up. You're coming with me," the big plainclothes cop standing in front of her said. "You're Pastore, right?" he asked, leaning over to unlock the handcuffs from the bench when she nodded, and then reattach them behind her back.

She got up slowly and followed him down the hallway to an office. She was tall and slender but he towered over her. He opened the door and motioned for her to go into the room ahead of him. When they were inside, he closed and locked the door.

"Sorry, kid," he said removing her handcuffs. "Did I hurt you?"

"No, getting pushed face-first into asphalt and gassed did that," she said, sitting on a padded vinyl chair that had seen better days. She smiled at his confusion and figured it was probably difficult for him to deal with her as an equal. Women were treated differently in the LAPD. Her salary, job, and promotional opportunities weren't the same as his, but in this assignment she had the advantage. She was successful because no one expected the police spy to be a woman.

She didn't know the big cop but her contact, Sergeant "Brickhouse" Murphy, was sitting behind a folding table that seemed to be serving as a desk.

"Tell me which copper did it. We'll take care of him," Murphy said.

"Never mind," she mumbled, taking a sip of coffee from a Winchell's Styrofoam cup on the table. "Okay?" she asked holding it up and Murphy nodded.

"I got it for you," he said. "Lieutenant saw what happened to your face. He wants to know who did it."

"Not a big deal. He got a little excited."

"It's a big deal," Murphy insisted. "The chief never wanted you or any other woman doing this stuff."

"I never saw him," she lied. Josie had not only seen the officer's name tag before the gas nearly blinded her large dark eyes, but remembered his badge number too. She wasn't going to make a complaint just to satisfy the department's patronizing upper echelon. The cop did what he thought he had to do or just lost his temper for a few minutes. The protesters were dangerous and as far as that officer was concerned, man or woman, she was one of them.

"Still stubborn as a damned mule. When you get out of this place if you're not healing in a day or two we'll have a sober doctor look at you. So what the fuck happened out there and why didn't we get a heads-up?"

Josie didn't argue about a second opinion, remembering the unpleasant stale odor of alcohol on the jail doctor's breath. "As far as I knew, nothing had been planned," she said defensively.

"You're supposed to be our eyes and ears so we're ready for this kind of shit and nobody gets hurt except the assholes."

Josie could feel her face getting warm as the irritation started to build. Her body ached and she smelled like Gold's Gym on the hottest day in August, but she understood Murphy wasn't really blaming her. He knew policemen had been badly hurt and, like her, felt responsible for not preventing it.

"I've told you," she began as calmly as she could. "They haven't let me into the inner circle yet. It hasn't been long enough; I'm still not completely trusted." Kind of like you and the good old boys in the police department, she thought, but said, "They've got meetings where I'm not invited. Obviously they intended to start something, but . . . sorry . . . I gave you everything I had," but knew she didn't sound sorry. She did her best, which she suspected was better than most of his other deep-cover operatives could've done.

"This shouldn't happen," Murphy mumbled, shaking his head, but they both knew she was right. The leaders of these radical groups weren't stupid. They were aware the police had informants and undercover officers watching them. Their closest confidants were people they grew up with or the ones who'd shared a prison cell for several years. Josie had given PDID a lot of good information and hoped she'd be told more the longer she stayed with this group, but she'd probably never become what Murphy wanted.

She could, however, identify the assailants she'd seen attack the officers today and told Murphy to confiscate the rolls of film Manny's girlfriend, Carla, had stuffed into her jacket pockets and not book them into the woman's personal property. Manny had managed to get away, but Carla had been arrested. Josie had seen one of the protesters who'd been taking pictures throughout the morning give Carla several rolls of film just before she got captured—because she was unable to get her chubby legs over a parking lot wall.

It was good information, albeit after the damage had been done, but Josie hoped the film would produce incriminating and corroborating evidence. When she finished, she watched Sergeant Murphy still taking notes, the pencil almost disappearing in his huge hands, and she thought he looked like a circus bear sitting on a tiny bicycle as he balanced his large frame on a folding chair behind the table. He was a big man with a short temper and had become her PDID contact as soon as she'd worked her way into the WLM. His gruff manner didn't bother her but she'd been warned by her prior contact that most of the UCs had a difficult time adjusting to him.

Murphy was a retired marine who'd fought in Vietnam and he probably knew more about Communism and Marxist radicals than anyone in the department. He called himself a child of the tumultuous sixties and frequently lamented how different the world might've been if King and the "smart Kennedys" had lived. He was an expert on Stalin and Marx and the *Communist Manifesto* and could recite passages from Mao's *Little Red Book* from memory. When selected to work in PDID, she'd been given a brief tutorial on leftist ideology but he was training her and was her reference library when she had trouble making sense out of the confusing and conflicting ideological camps among the radicals.

"Is Uncle Murphy gonna bail me out tonight?" Josie asked when the coffee was gone and there was nothing left to talk about.

"Your Aunt Alice in San Francisco will post bail in the morning. You sure you don't need to see a doctor now?"

Josie sighed. She didn't need a doctor; what she probably needed was to get out. Her mind and body were telling her it was time to leave this assignment. She was almost thirty years old and tired of lying, tired of having friends who weren't really friends, but most of all she longed for a close emotional and physical attachment to a man who knew what she really was . . . something she hadn't experienced in nearly three years. In this assignment, every relationship was intended to manipulate someone to get information or as an introduction to another source.

At first it was exciting, a challenge to see if she could be accepted, fool people into telling her their dangerous secrets, be the one who stopped terrible things from happening and saved Los Angeles from death and destruction. But lately all she could think about was how much fun it had been to do police work. She'd been reading in the newspapers that the chief would soon be forced by the courts to allow women to work in patrol and be promoted like the men. It was another reason to be available when the time finally came and she could sit in a black-and-white and do the job of her dreams.

Riots, demonstrations, and the occasional homemade bomb had become a way of life in the city. Only a few of the extreme groups were really dangerous; most just wanted to tweak the world to fit their unencumbered lifestyle. She'd ferreted out the WLM as a legitimate target, but she missed the real job in uniform and most of all the camaraderie. She wanted to be among her own kind again, to be one of those officers standing shoulder-to-shoulder protecting each other on the street today, going to court, writing crime reports, and drinking beer in the station parking lot at end of watch reliving their exciting exploits. The department wouldn't allow her to do most of those things now but at least she'd be associating with people who actually thought the same way she did and not be hiding in the shadows waiting to catch Manny or one of his crazies attempting to deliver the devastation he'd always promised he could.

The lies and deception had gone on for so long Josie wondered if the core of who she was had been compromised to the point of no return. When she did leave this assignment, she worried she might never recognize or be herself again.

"Did you talk to the captain about my transfer?" she asked, ignoring his question.

Murphy stopped writing and sat back.

"You still want out?"

"You know I do as soon as you have someone to replace me. This division asked for a three-year commitment; I've done that and more."

He was quiet for a few seconds, staring at his hands.

"I've got a candidate lined up but there's something you've got to do before I reassign you."

"Can't the new guy do it?" she asked, already feeling less pain.

"No, it's got to be somebody who's been around and has credibility . . . with history and contacts."

"Tell me; let's get it over with, so I can get my life back."

Murphy got up. It was easy to see where he got the "Brick-house" nickname. His linebacker body seemed even bigger in a confined space.

"Look, the truth is you might be out of here in a few months anyway. If these arrestees go to trial, the old man might want you to testify if that's what it takes to make sure the assholes go to prison for all the damage they did today. If that happens, you'd have to resurface, but . . ." he said, and hesitated before adding, "one of our UCs is missing. I need you to help find him."

"What do you mean missing? Do I know him? How am I supposed to find him?" she asked, but there were a lot of other questions buzzing around in her head.

PDID policy was to keep the undercover officers from knowing each other. They operated understanding there were other UCs but never being told who they were. It was a check-and-balance system to be certain information was accurate and to avoid the possibility of a rogue UC outing another officer. It didn't always work. Cops were inquisitive and keen observers of human nature, so she and others had identified fellow UCs who hadn't quite cleansed themselves of all those telltale mannerisms that come with policing—looking around the room when they first walk in, asking too many questions, never sitting with their backs to a window, and most of all, that piercing "you'd better tell me the truth" eye contact that seemed to look right through a person.

"It's Dave Soriano," he said.

"No way . . . Dirty Dave is a cop?"

"The Young Socialists want him back. One of our contacts says they think the police have captured him."

"But we haven't, so where is he?" she asked.

"That's what I need you to find out. He's disappeared. He's a member of the National Lawyers Guild too and a couple of other innocuous groups." Murphy hesitated before adding, "His contact allowed him to venture into places he shouldn't have gone so it's better if we can find him first and bring him up quietly our way."

"What's your guess? What do you think has happened to him?" Josie asked.

"Cops don't just disappear. He's either changed sides or he's hiding for some other reason. We need to find him and drag his ass back."

Another possibility popped into Josie's mind, but she wouldn't say it out loud. A constant unspoken fear among many undercover officers, including her, was being exposed as a cop. The consequences of such disclosure might range from nasty public expulsion, to assault, even to death depending on the fanaticism of the targeted group. She'd heard Soriano's buddies were extremists and paranoid about police informants.

Josie stared at Murphy who wouldn't look at her and suddenly she realized that by asking to leave the assignment she had become expendable.

TWO

Spending the night in jail was always a depressing experience for Josie. She lay awake on the hard bunk covered with a worn wool blanket that reeked of disinfectant as she listened to the sounds of caged women. She guessed their nightmares most likely paralleled their disappointing lives. Some whined, others swore, most cried, desperate to find a sympathetic ear in the darkness, but all they got were angry words from those hardened inmates who long ago had acclimated to frustration and confinement.

She had been locked up in what appeared to be a holding cell with an older black woman who was either in the early stages of dementia or was demonstrating the aftereffects of some illicit drug. Josie guessed PCP.

The woman paced throughout the night, mumbling to herself, pulling off her jumpsuit, getting naked, and then putting it back on again as if the temperature were fluctuating from below zero to tropical in the warm stuffy cell. She never spoke to Josie but would stand inches from her cot and talk into the empty space above it.

This activity and noise continued until the lights came up in the morning and then everything in the cellblock got eerily quiet. The old woman dropped onto her bed, curled up in a fetal position, and slept like a baby.

Josie was grateful "Aunt Alice's" bail money came through early enough for her to avoid encountering the standard jail breakfast of microwave eggs and sausage floating in grease gravy. She got processed, had her belongings and clothes returned, and was out the steel door before eight A.M.

There was a phone booth in the lobby so she called Emily, who agreed to pick her up. Sergeant Murphy would be expecting a call this morning, too, but she was starving and decided eating would be more enjoyable if she didn't have to talk to him first.

The continuous background noise and her crazy cellmate had kept her awake all night but she probably wouldn't have slept much anyway. Her body still ached from the effects of street justice and she couldn't get comfortable on the hard bunk bed. More importantly, she was excited about the possibility of going back soon to real police work. She tried to think of clever ways to get close to Dave Soriano's contacts, but couldn't help dwelling on what Murphy's real motive was for choosing her to find the missing officer. The more she thought about it the more irritated she got. She had given Murphy valuable information over the years, but he was obviously frustrated that she might be leaving soon. Her conclusion was he didn't care if she got exposed or worse because she'd be gone in a few months anyway and of no further use to him.

It was disappointing. She'd heard a lot of UCs felt used and discarded at the end of their assignments because no one would ever know what they'd done. She never needed recognition or accolades. However, ingratitude and cold-hearted indifference were another story. She resented being treated like a disposable asset. Josie decided she would find Soriano and get away from Murphy and this bizarre life as soon as possible.

Emily picked her up in front of Sybil Brand about half an hour later. She was driving her husband's new black Mercedes, but was dressed in shabby jeans, a tank top, and a beaded headband.

The woman hasn't got a clue, Josie thought, but said, "Thanks Em, I really appreciate this," as she slid in to the passenger seat.

"Why didn't you call Burt last night?" Emily asked. "Oh my God, your pretty face . . . it's so bruised . . . does it hurt? You didn't need to spend all night in that horrible place."

"Thanks, it wasn't that bad. Is everybody out now?" Josie asked. She didn't think Emily was privy to a lot of confidential information, but her husband was, and he talked about everything in front of her. She wasn't clever but could repeat his conversations the way a teenager might gossip about things she really didn't understand.

"Burt talked to Manny this morning. He's worried about some film Carla had."

"What film?" Josie asked, knowing the department's lab geeks had probably developed it by now and had black-and-white prints sitting on the PDID captain's desk.

"Oh, some stuff WLM's photographer was going to use in the national newsletter."

"What happened to it?"

"He thinks the cops got it. You hungry?" Emily asked.

Finally, Josie thought, and suggested they go to the Denny's restaurant near her apartment in Venice. The word apartment might've been a generous description. It was converted living space in a garage—one room with a bed, bathroom hidden by a curtain, and a hotplate. She was three blocks from the ocean in a run-down, high-crime area that catered to artistically inclined dropouts and drug dealers. Luckily she didn't have anything of value there because most of her furniture and clothing were in storage waiting for the time she could resume her real life again.

They sat in a booth near the front window at Denny's. The waitress smiled at Emily, but avoided looking directly at Josie. She'd borrowed Emily's compact in the car and had tried covering some of the injuries on her high cheekbones with face powder, but it didn't help. She never used makeup because she was lucky enough to have big brown eyes with long thick lashes and an olive complexion, but nasty bruises always trumped natural beauty. Her long dark hair was frizzier and more out of control than usual this morning because of the harsh jail soap and her clothes still had the combined aroma of sweat and drunk tank. She couldn't blame the waitress for avoiding her and couldn't wait to finish eating, go home, and get under that contraption her landlord, with a straight face, called a shower.

"Why don't you stay with me for a few days . . . in the guesthouse?" Emily asked tentatively as Josie was finishing the restaurant's biggest breakfast combo.

"Do you think that would be okay with Burt?" Josie asked, knowing Emily's guesthouse was a palace compared to the garage. Her painful dirty body desperately wanted a soft bed and a real shower with hot, not tepid, water.

"Sure, it's clean and my cook will make sure you eat right and you can rest, heal. That garage is drafty and so . . . you know," she said, blushing. "It will be fun . . . please."

"Okay," Josie said, knowing Emily thought of her as a girlfriend. She felt bad not just because they had nothing genuine in common, but much like the WLM she was using the gullible woman.

EMILY PAID the bill and drove in the direction of West LA. The two women were about the same size, tall and skinny, so Emily offered a change of clothes from her wardrobe. But Josie insisted on stopping at the garage, which was just a few blocks away, to pick up her only other pair of Levis and a clean shirt. Her conscience wouldn't allow her to push this friendship any further than necessary.

She knew Burt Rice didn't spend much time at home, but he did have an office there. If Emily went out during the day, she might have an opportunity to go into the main house and look around. It was tricky because he was a lawyer and everything related to his clients would be confidential, but she wasn't looking for attorney-client information. Since WLM was still her responsibility, she wanted anything she could find on them.

Emily parked in the four-car garage and they went through the side door to the guesthouse. It was actually a wing of the main house but had a separate entrance and a covered carport. Josie left her 1968 orange VW Bug parked out in front of her garage apartment, but didn't have to worry about anybody stealing it. The car looked like junk with old accident damage, rarely started, and had a habit of stalling at the most inopportune times.

The guesthouse was big with lots of windows. It had a king-sized bed, nothing like the piece of board covered with an inflatable air mattress Josie slept on in the garage. She had decided to pamper herself at Emily's expense for a few days before beginning her search for PDID's misplaced cop.

As soon as she was alone, Josie undressed and stepped into the shower for a long wonderful scrubbing, but that didn't feel like nearly enough, so when she finished. she filled the tub and soaked her bruised body until her skin was wrinkled and the water got chilly. She came out of the bathroom wrapped in a towel and found a folded nightgown on the bed. Emily must've come back, but she'd gone again. Josie slipped on the soft cotton gown, lifted the bedspread, got between the sheets, and immediately drifted into a deep dreamless sleep.

Unlike her apartment in Venice where people gathered outside on the streets and sidewalks day and night on their way to and from the beach, or gangbangers shot indiscriminately at each other over dope deals or territorial disputes, the guesthouse was secluded and completely quiet. Josie slept undisturbed for hours and woke with stiff muscles, but feeling more like herself than she had in months. It was getting dark outside and she knew Murphy would be pissed about not hearing from her all day. She'd have to think of an excuse to get to a phone booth and call him, but before she could get out of bed, Josie noticed Emily standing outside the bedroom's sliding glass door under the security light.

"How do you feel?" Emily asked, as she slid open the door and stepped into the bedroom.

Josie sat up and was surprised how little she hurt now.

"I'm much better . . . hungry," she said wondering how long Emily had been waiting out there for her to wake up.

"Linda, our cook, is bringing dinner; you just stay in bed," Emily said, straightening the bedspread around Josie.

"Actually I thought you might take me to get my car after I eat, if you don't mind. I hate to leave it on the street in that neighborhood too long," she lied, but needed an excuse to get away and make a phone call.

"I can have the help bring it here. You don't have to get up," Emily said, frowning.

"I'd like to move around a little. You don't have to come with me, just have someone drop me off and I'll drive right back here."

"No, I'll take you. I don't mind," Emily said and added, "but you do need to get more rest."

Josie smiled, but couldn't help thinking this might've been a mistake. She wanted to take advantage of Emily's hospitality and pamper herself, but it might come with a price. She feared the needy woman would smother her with attention like an overbearing parent, which could make doing her job a bit complicated for the next couple of days.

A few minutes later, the cook delivered a tray with prime rib steak, baked potato, and creamed spinach, which Josie devoured, and then got into her clean clothes. The smelly, bloodstained outfit she'd worn the day before had already been laundered and sat freshly pressed and folded on the dresser. Josie wondered how many people had been in and out of the guesthouse while she was in the shower or sleeping.

Emily drove her back to the garage in Venice. Josie persuaded her it wasn't safe at this hour to leave her expensive car on the street while she collected a few things from the apartment and called her ailing sister. She watched until the Mercedes was out of sight before stuffing her toothbrush and some underwear in a paper bag and throwing it in the backseat of the VW.

There was a phone booth barely a block away and the dog walkers were out in force, so she felt comfortable going there. She preferred to use one of the phones on the boardwalk but her abused body and the late hour told her this one closer to the apartment would do for tonight. She called the PDID switchboard, gave the detective on duty the phone number in the booth, and asked him to tell Murphy she needed him to call. It rang a minute later. She answered and waited until the sergeant finished his tirade about her failure to contact him earlier. Finally she got an opportunity to explain and he calmed down.

"Manny Contreras trusts Burt and tells him everything. Burt talks in front of Emily and she tells me," Josie said, trying not to touch anything in the filthy phone booth. "I'm hoping he'll have names and bank account numbers somewhere in that home office and I'll have an opportunity to find them."

"Good, but don't waste too much time on WLM now. Keep tabs on them but concentrate on Soriano. He's your priority. Have you had a chance to do anything yet?"

"No," she said. The question bothered her. She'd been beat up and out of jail only a few hours; he should've understood she wasn't in any condition mentally or physically to start looking. "I'll get on it in a day or two when I'm feeling better."

"Meet me tomorrow," he said.

"I'll try, if Emily lets me out of her sight."

"Find a reason to go downtown . . . alone . . . I'll be in the back room of Little Joe's in Chinatown at one."

She didn't argue. Brickhouse had spoken and he wasn't the sort of supervisor who'd negotiate if he wanted you to do something.

"I've gotta get back to the house. I'll see you tomorrow," she said and hung up.

The VW started on the first try and kept running all the way to West LA. Maybe her luck was changing. She parked in the carport and used the key Emily had given her to open a side door leading to the kitchen of the guesthouse. All the lights she'd turned off when she left were on again, and she heard voices coming from the living room. She didn't have any real experience as a street cop, but her instincts were good enough to believe late-night visits from this group probably didn't bode well for her.

"Josie, you're back," Emily said cheerfully, jumping up from the couch to greet her.

Manny, Carla, and two burly men she didn't recognize who were sitting on either side of them were gathered around the coffee table, drinking Corona from the bottles. Burt Rice was there too, but he was standing beside the wet bar and had what looked like a whiskey glass in his hand.

"Drink?" Burt said, holding up the glass.

"I'll have whatever you're having," Josie said. She was lingering in the doorway, still holding the paper bag with a toothbrush and clean panties, waiting for someone to explain why everyone was hanging out in her temporary living room, looking so grim.

Burt gave her the drink, and she took a long swallow of a great whiskey.

"We need to talk to you," Burt said, moving a chair closer to the others. He gestured for her to sit, but Josie hesitated trying to estimate from their expressions and body language how much trouble she might be in. It was a long way back to her car and she wasn't in any condition to run so she thought "what the hell," sat, and finished her drink.

"What's up," she said with as much bravado as she could muster.

Everyone turned toward Manny. He put his beer bottle on the coffee table and moved a little closer to the edge of his chair.

"We been watching you," he said with just a hint of an accent, finally looking up and staring at her with bloodshot eyes. Josie's stomach did a double flip and she set the whiskey glass on her lap to keep her hand steady. His voice was raspy from a lifelong addiction to alcohol and cigarettes. He was a thin, middle-aged man with light brown skin, clean-shaven with shaggy black hair. Manny always told members of the WLM he was from Mexico and his wiry frame and hard weathered look came from years of picking strawberries in Oxnard, California, but Brickhouse had done a thorough background on him. He was born in San Salvador, escaped from one of their worst prisons, and got into this country as a political refugee. As far as PDID could determine, since crossing the border Manny hadn't labored at anything except demonstrations and passing out leaflets. He was a political organizer who recruited a lot of ex-cons and parolees and although he always had plenty of cash, he didn't seem interested in earning money or improving his personal lifestyle. His passion was violent dissent.

"Okay," Josie said, hoping nobody noticed the slight nervous elevation in her voice.

"You did good yesterday. Em says you stood up . . . didn't let cops push you around."

Josie turned toward Emily and wondered what demonstration she'd been watching . . . unless standing up meant stupidly getting trapped in the crowd and then captured and beat to the ground by overzealous cops.

"Thanks, Manny," Josie said, trying to sound sincere, but waiting for the other shoe to fall. She knew beneath his calm exterior Manny was a mean sonofabitch and his compliments usually came with a nasty "but."

"I decided I'm gonna make you part of my security team. Alex here," he said, pointing at the tattooed heavyset man to the right of him who had the muscular physique of a man who had spent many hours on a prison weight stack. "He's gonna train you . . . at the camp when you feel better."

Manny didn't wait for her to say anything. He stood and the two bookend bodyguards got up with him. He shook hands with Burt and gave Emily a quick peck on the cheek. His girlfriend, Carla, hugged Emily and everyone said good night, leaving Josie and Emily alone in the living room.

"What the hell just happened," Josie whispered.

"They like you," Emily said.

"Great," she said, but had a feeling something wasn't right. "What if I don't want to be on his security team or go to any camp?"

"You can't say no. Manny has to trust you."

"So this is a test?"

Emily was quiet for a few seconds and then said, "They're always careful, but I told them you were my friend; you're all right. You'll see it's going to be okay . . . get some sleep."

She gave Josie a hug and left.

Josie waited a few minutes then locked the door leading to the main house and the front door. She put the security lock on the sliding glass door in the bedroom and closed the drapes. It was unlikely Manny or his minions would do anything tonight, but she was tired of people coming in and out while she was sleeping or in the bathroom. Maybe Manny really did trust her enough to suddenly allow access to the security and planning meetings, but she was naturally suspicious and worried her cover might've somehow been compromised during the demonstration and arrest, and the real purpose of this "camp" was to get her away from the protection of the LAPD.

These groups had their spies inside the criminal justice system and throughout the city's civil service positions. They knew a lot about the way police operated. Josie had seen staff members from several city council offices and even a woman who worked with one of the police commissioners at planning meetings for demonstrations. She found out later they were participating on their own time, which wasn't a problem, but she wondered who in the city knew about her activities and was privy to information that might inadvertently, or intentionally, reveal her identity.

Worrying about the ways she could be exposed always gave her a headache and it was a waste of time and energy, so she poured another shot of Burt's whiskey, finished it, and went to bed. Her sixth sense was pretty reliable and she had inherited her emotionally challenged mother's trait of never really trusting anyone, so it was unlikely she'd get into any real trouble. She'd stall Manny on the security training unless it was done in a place that felt safe and until she was confident she wasn't being set up.

She had a five-shot revolver hidden in the door panel of the VW, and that sixth sense was telling her that tomorrow she should begin keeping it closer.

THE NEXT morning, Josie was up early and out of the guesthouse in an attempt to avoid Emily's inevitable questions about whether or not she was ready to begin training with Alex. She felt rested and practically pain free and was thinking more clearly now. She put the paper bag with her possessions on the backseat of the VW and her only regret in leaving was not having the benefit of Linda's cooking or Burt's endless supply of expensive whiskey.

Since the WLM had become her second priority, she wasn't going to risk exposure by sneaking around Burt's office. Manny's unexpected gesture last night, giving her a foothold among the trusted few, came too suddenly and didn't feel right. Everything she'd learned in the last few years warned her she was most likely being set up . . . but the tricky question was why and also what had triggered it. Regardless of their motives, she'd decided to keep a safe distance between her and Manny's followers.

She drove around the block trying not to go past the front of Emily's house. Josie knew she couldn't avoid the woman, but she wanted to be back living in her garage when the encounter happened. It only took a few minutes to drive to Venice where she parked her car in the street in front of her apartment. The door was locked but very quickly Josie realized someone had been in her room. Things had been moved. The blanket covering the air mattress wasn't the way she'd left it the night before and a couple of drawers in the antique dresser hadn't been pushed in all the way. The mini-blinds on the only window were down and closed. She never closed them unless she was working on a report for Murphy.

It wasn't a problem. Whoever had been there didn't find anything that could compromise her. She'd been taught not to leave any items even remotely connected to the police department in her apartment. She'd memorized all the phone numbers of her contacts and never kept a copy of any report she'd given to Brickhouse. Other than clothes, books were the only personal items she kept here. The books were an impressive collection of socialist, communist, or women's-issue readings as well as Updike's *Rabbit Redux* and Forsyth's *The Day of the Jackal,* two new novels she'd taken out of the library.

Josie didn't like the idea of anyone going through her under-wear drawer, but since they hadn't found anything it probably wouldn't happen again anytime soon, and she was just grate-ful she hadn't been here asleep when they sneaked in.

Before leaving, she straightened up the room and arranged a few well-placed intruder alerts—furniture and other items left in strategic places to tell her if the "creeper" had come back.

There was still time before she had to meet Brickhouse in downtown LA's Chinatown, so she drove to the most bohe-mian part of Venice where the Midnight Special Bookstore was located. It was a hangout for many of the active politi-cal groups and stocked the sort of reading material a serious radical couldn't find among commercial stacks, items such as *The Anarchist Cookbook*, etc. The bulletin board was a cor-nucopia of upcoming events, meetings, demonstrations, and reading groups, and the bookstore's small café served decent coffee and donuts . . . her favorite meal.

It was a place to meet like-minded people, so Josie had hung out there when she first went undercover as a way to start identifying possible targets. She'd met Emily there, actually worked hard to befriend her as soon as she realized the pretty woman's unlikely connection to WLM. It wasn't difficult. Josie liked her and they quickly became close, as close as she could get to someone she lied to about practically everything.

This morning she wanted to talk to Debbie who usually worked behind the counter in the café. It was common knowledge she'd been dating Dave Soriano. Whenever Josie stopped by for coffee, Soriano was hanging around sitting at one of the tables. She thought he was an odd, nerdy guy who looked at least thirty years younger than Debbie, and she could never understand why the woman wasted any time on him. Josie would never have pegged him as a cop, which was probably why he was chosen for the assignment.

"Hey, Deb," Josie said, putting a dollar on the counter. "Large coffee, please."

Debbie was a middle-aged hippie with long red hair combed into a messy ponytail that hung down to the middle of her back. Her complexion was ruddy and her skin showed signs of gentle aging, but like Josie she never used makeup. She wore jeans and a baggy, oversized top and had stopped wearing a bra long before it became fashionable and politically correct.

"What happened to your face?" Debbie asked, staring at what now was a light yellowish blue canvas of bruising but no swelling.

"It got dragged on the street."

"Still hanging around those loony tunes, huh? I heard about that brain-dead fiasco downtown . . . not real smart to attack cops with puny sticks."

They chatted for a few more minutes. Josie was grateful it was a slow morning. No one came into the café and Debbie pulled up a stool behind the counter, seeming to welcome the company and conversation. Josie complained about her nonexistent love life hoping Debbie would open up about her and Soriano, but she didn't.

"Where's Dave? Seems strange, him not hanging around pestering you," Josie finally asked when she realized subtlety was getting her nowhere.

"Yeah, don't it though," she said, glancing around the empty room as if she were expecting someone. "Guess he's got something better to do." She reached under the counter, produced a hand-rolled cigarette, and offered it to Josie.

"Dave? Doubt it," Josie said, shaking her head. She never found it difficult to refuse drugs. Most people accepted her excuse that alcohol was her chosen addiction.

Debbie swallowed a laugh and mumbled, "Got that right." She lit the cigarette and took a long drag holding it for several seconds before exhaling a puff of grey smoke with that sweet odor of marijuana. She took Josie's empty cup and filled it again before saying, "I heard Quentin's been asking around, looking for him." Another drag and she added with a nervous whisper, "Don't know why."

Josie shook her head. Quentin Barnes was one of Dave's more fanatical associates. She wouldn't be surprised if he was the one who'd spread the rumor about the police capturing Soriano.

"You'd think Quentin would know. They're always to-gether," she said, trying not to sound too interested.

"They had a falling out . . . over a girl . . . not me," Debbie said. If she was upset, Debbie was hiding it really well behind those glassy eyes.

"Sorry," Josie said. "You okay?"

"Just dandy, want another donut?"

It was getting close to the time she was supposed to meet Brickhouse, but Josie kept talking, deliberately picking at the woman's wounded pride like an open sore, hoping she'd volunteer more information on her ex-lover's new girlfriend. The conversation bounced around for nearly forty-five minutes while Josie consumed donuts, drank coffee, and gathered enough pieces of the soap-opera puzzle from the increasingly mellow woman to identify Kate Sparks as the "bitch" who stole Debbie's man. She also confirmed that lately Kate was hanging out at O'Farrell's bar and pool hall off the Venice boardwalk.

As soon as a couple of customers drifted into the café from the bookstore and Debbie got busy, Josie slipped away. It wasn't much but at least now she could tell Murphy she had a place to start.

THREE

Late morning was the best time to drive from the beach into downtown LA. Rush hour was over and commuters wouldn't start back in the other direction for several hours. There was talk of gas rationing, so Josie was grateful her VW Bug could go almost a week before she had to fill it up again.

She had called Emily from the bookstore and thanked her for a pleasant night away from the garage and apologized for leaving without saying good-bye. Josie lied about having a job interview that morning and said she would tell her about it later. It wasn't entirely a fabrication since she'd found a part-time job at the local Catholic thrift store. She hoped this would be the last in what had been a series of low-paying employments she'd held during her undercover years, just to have a viable explanation for how she financed her meager lifestyle. Her police paycheck went directly into a savings account, so she wouldn't be tempted to spend more than she should've had. The upside, her savings account had lots of money—the downside, her current living situation wasn't much better than the squatters' on Venice Beach.

Downtown traffic was as bad as usual, but Josie found a parking space on Broadway about two blocks from Little Joe's. She always wondered how an Italian restaurant got situated in the middle of Chinatown, but it seemed to do a booming business surrounded by dozens of places offering dim sum and pan-fried noodles. Her father and a lot of relatives were Italian, so she'd grown up eating pasta and knew this place had great food.

The restaurant was busy, and no one paid any attention as she walked past the front counter, around tables, into the back room. It was a banquet room but they sometimes used it for overflow lunch crowds. Murphy was sitting in a corner in one of the booths with a woman Josie didn't recognize. They were the only ones in the huge cold space. Some of the lights were on but it still looked as if no one really wanted them there.

"You're late," Murphy said before introducing the woman as Detective Julie Carlson. She looked to be about Josie's age, maybe a little older, but she wasn't much over five feet tall and couldn't weigh 100 pounds. Her short blonde hair was perfectly coifed, not a strand out of place. "Detective Carlson is Soriano's new contact," he mumbled with a mouthful of garlic bread.

"New?" Josie asked, sitting in the booth across from them and holding out her hand. She noted that Carlson was hesitant to shake hands. It didn't seem to be something she enjoyed doing.

"Current, she's taking over for the other team," he said.

"I'm up to speed on Officer Soriano's past activities and associates and I'll be handling his debriefing," Carlson said, and added under her breath, "If and when you find him."

Josie told them about her conversation with Debbie at the Midnight Special.

"I'll go by O'Farrell's tonight, try to talk to her," Josie said.

"It's a start," Murphy said, clearly not impressed.

They ordered lunch and the conversation shifted away from Soriano for a few minutes. Julie Carlson was quiet and serious. She never looked at Murphy and answered his questions with as few words as possible. Josie told them about her encounter with Manny Contreras the night before and had Murphy laughing as she described the two muscular bodyguards and how she decided to consume a large glass of whiskey rather than attempt an escape.

"It doesn't feel right. All of a sudden, they're paying too much attention to me, so I'm wondering if something happened during the arrest to make them suspicious. Maybe a cop recognized me, said the wrong thing . . . one of them heard it . . . I don't know."

"Try to keep some distance from Manny for a while. Tell him you're busy. You can socialize with the others but don't do any of the political stuff, especially the security training if it's outside the city or someplace we can't protect you," Murphy said, stuffing a forkful of spaghetti into his mouth.

"I start working a part-time job tomorrow so it will be easier to make excuses not to participate in some of the stuff. Was Carla's film any good?"

"It's great, probably enough to get a few of them convicted with or without your testimony, but . . . the chief's not inclined to yank you out of the field just yet . . . not until this Soriano business is done."

"Do you have a gun?" Carlson asked.

Josie glanced at Murphy. She knew he preferred his UCs not to have guns, but she didn't care. There was nobody watching her back 24/7 except for her and she wasn't about to be at Manny's mercy.

"Yes."

"Good, carry it if you're with any of Soriano's crowd," Carlson said. "Do not go near them or talk to any of them from this moment forward unless you advise me."

Josie could see the color drain from Murphy's face. His undercover officer in the WLM had practically been appropriated from under his nose and there was nothing he could do about it. Soriano was a priority, and Detective Carlson had unceremoniously pushed his WLM group to the back burner.

He finished lunch quickly without another word, put money on the table, and worked his big body out of the booth.

"You still need to let me know what's going on with WLM. Keep an eye on them while you search for this cop," Murphy said. "I can't get anybody in there yet, so for a while it's up to you. They're too dangerous to leave unattended."

There wasn't an opportunity for Carlson to disagree because he turned and walked away.

Carlson didn't seem to care what Murphy thought or wanted and barely seemed to notice that he'd gone. She finished her cheese ravioli lunch and jotted an address on the back of her business card.

"Memorize this address and meet me there in an hour," she ordered, showing Josie the card for a few seconds and then putting it back in her purse. "It's Soriano's safe house. He goes there a few days at a time to get away. None of his associates know about it, and he doesn't think we do either."

"How can you be sure?" Josie asked. "If he's turned, he might've told them, even brought them there."

"I'm positive," Carlson said. "It's clean, but there might be something inside that will help you locate him."

"What's the matter?" Josie asked. Carlson had been staring hard at her face for several seconds. She wondered if one of her scrapes had begun to bleed again.

"You're older than most of the UCs. Did they take you out of the academy?"

"No, but I was just off probation."

"The captain's impressed with the way you've managed to infiltrate a hardcore group. I've been told some of the UCs aim lower at the easy targets . . . flower children, drop-outs . . . you know. A few buy into their lifestyle, get too comfortable, and start to believe the dogma. What about you? Do you ever think maybe they've got it right?" she asked, her eyes narrowing a little as she waited for an answer.

Josie smiled. She didn't. It was her job to make them think she was a true believer and while she worried that lying about practically everything every day for years might eventually damage her, she never for a moment bought the doctrine. She definitely liked the freedom and openness of their lifestyle, but she was too old to change her basic conservative beliefs. "No" was all she said.

"Good," Carlson said, putting enough money with Murphy's to pay the bill. "See you in an hour."

Josie waited a few seconds before following her. She watched Carlson march from the restaurant's back room like a tiny soldier in a grey pantsuit, all business, no emotion, no nonsense and wasn't certain she didn't like Murphy's volatile personality better. There was never any doubt what Murphy was thinking. He told her as loudly and colorfully as possible. Carlson was cold and analytical. The job would most likely get done, but they definitely weren't going to have any fun.

Soriano's safe house was in the San Gabriel mountain foothills in the city of Monrovia. It didn't take Josie long to memorize the address because she knew exactly where it was. She had grown up in the adjacent city of Duarte. Although it was only twenty minutes from downtown Los Angeles, Monrovia was a taste of rural life in the suburbs. Coyotes, bears, and other wildlife came down from the mountains and roamed in the huge backyards, raiding chicken coops, foraging for garbage, or dining on small pets. Some of the roads were still dirt, and sidewalks were a luxury. The missing UC could go there and feel comfortable that no one would easily find him. Josie's brother had sold their family home in Duarte years ago or she might've spent time there away from the craziness of LA and her job.

The small house was on a cul-de-sac backed up against the mountains. As soon as Carlson arrived, she told Josie it was a rental Soriano had leased with phony ID provided by his former detective contact. An aboveground prefab pool filled with smelly green water sat on a concrete slab in the backyard. There were empty planters and weathered patio furniture around it but no grass. The front lawn was overgrown and besieged by patches of weeds and dirt. Other houses on the block were pretty well maintained with fresh paint and manicured lawns. She figured the neighbors wouldn't be disappointed to hear Soriano might not be leasing the neglected eyesore any longer.

They entered through the back door. Carlson had a key and had been inside or talked to someone who had because she knew where everything was and pointed out Soriano's bedroom as the first place Josie should look.

"I'm betting you've already searched this place, so why do it again?" Josie asked, confident she was right.

"You know these people better than I do. There might be something important here that just doesn't mean anything to me."

"Right," Josie said, not concealing her sarcasm. She wondered if the woman thought UCs communicated in some sort of secret code. Although she'd just barely begun her career, Josie knew evidence was pretty much a universal language. "How long have you been in PDID?"

"Let me know if you find anything," Carlson said, walking away and ignoring the question.

"Yes, ma'am," she said and gave a sloppy salute as the sergeant disappeared down the hallway.

Unlike the exterior, the house appeared tidy and clean inside. There wasn't any clutter or garbage thrown anywhere; even the bed had been made. Expensive-looking suits were hanging in the closet with freshly laundered dress shirts. Josie didn't know much about men's clothes, but thought the two pairs of leather shoes, the briefcase, and wool coat in the closet looked pricey. Her last boyfriend was a photographer who'd been hired by the women's magazine where she worked as an associate editor before the LAPD hired her. He never wore anything except Levis, sweaters, and tennis shoes, so she had no idea if she should be impressed by the labels on Soriano's wardrobe.

She checked the pockets of all the clothes, the empty briefcase, and every drawer in the dresser but didn't find anything with a name, phone number, or address. Soriano definitely would not be wearing any of this stuff while he was working. These outfits would have been out of place among his funky associates, so she guessed he had another life apart from his group and the department.

"So what do you think?" Carlson said.

She came back into the bedroom as Josie was sitting on the window ledge staring out at the pool wondering what Soriano might've been up to in his spare time.

"Do you know why he had this wardrobe?" Josie asked.

"No."

"Did he have some sort of job as part of his assignment?"

"No, he never worked."

"How can you be certain no one ever came here?" Josie asked. None of this made any sense. If PDID was watching Soriano's movements and knew none of his targets came here, why didn't they know where he was?

"I'm certain. Do you want to look at the rest of the house?"

"Why not," Josie said, getting frustrated with the woman's lack of candor.

They went into every room with the same result. Soriano hadn't left anything revealing or even a clue where he might've gone. Josie wandered out to the garage while Carlson used the kitchen phone to call her office. She was closing the door to a tool storage cabinet when she noticed something stuck between it and the garage wall. Her fingers wouldn't fit into the space, but she found a rusted screwdriver on the workbench and used it to retrieve an empty matchbook cover. It was fairly new and had a picture of the Venice Beach boardwalk in front of O'Farrell's bar and pool hall on the outside, and a phone number written in pencil under the flap.

Josie stuck the matchbook in the pocket of her Levis and went back into the house. She knew she should've told Carlson what she found but didn't. For the first time since she'd started this assignment, Josie felt as if her lifeline to the real world wasn't completely reliable or trustworthy. Although undercover officers were rarely privy to the whole picture, this Soriano matter was different. Josie had a gut feeling that Murphy and Carlson were involving her in something that was very different and a lot more dangerous than what they were telling her. She had nothing solid to back up that hunch, but trusted her survival instincts and had decided to do things her own way for a while.

It took much longer to drive back to the West Side in bumper-to-bumper freeway traffic in a car that wouldn't go over forty miles per hour. Her VW Bug stalled, but she managed to get over into the emergency lane to wait until the engine hopefully started again. She was grateful for her heavy jacket since the heater didn't work and the winter chill kept the car cold enough to keep ice cream from melting. Half an hour later, she got the engine to turn over and drove the rest of the way like an eighty-year-old lady in second gear but got back to Venice Beach. She pulled into her driveway in the dark and was surprised when the car's headlights washed over Emily's thin figure hunched over sitting on the retaining wall between the garage apartment and the house next door.

As soon as Josie turned off the ignition, Emily jumped from the wall and was at the driver's window.

"Where have you been?" she demanded before Josie could get out of the car.

"Out . . . what's wrong?" Josie asked, determined not to let the clingy woman manipulate her.

"Aren't you coming back to the house tonight?"

"No, I feel much better so I thought I'd stay home . . . stop imposing on Burt's hospitality," Josie said, locking the overheated bug and glancing down the driveway, half expecting to see Manny, Carla, or one of their bookend bruisers lurking in the shadows.

Emily looked upset and asked, "Did Burt say or do something? I thought you liked staying with me."

"I do, Em, but I need my space . . . with my things around me. I know it's not much but I like it here," Josie lied.

The look in Emily's eyes said what Josie knew to be true—no one in her right mind would actually like living in this dump.

"If that's what you really want."

"Why don't you come inside while I change my clothes and we can go find something to eat, maybe get a glass of wine or two," Josie said. She really didn't want to go to O'Farrell's alone, and Emily was good company. Besides, she knew it would look better if two women were there together.

Emily's mood immediately lightened after the invitation. She followed Josie into the garage, but insisted the door stay open so she could keep an eye on the Mercedes. A quick look around told Josie she hadn't entertained any more uninvited visitors while she was out. Every marker was still in its appointed place. She quickly changed into her clean Levis, a peasant-style shirt, and dangling earrings, and combed her long curly hair into the southern Italy version of an Afro.

It was just a few blocks to O'Farrell's but Emily hated walking and must have remembered Josie's prior warning because she balked at leaving Burt's new car unattended in that neighborhood. Josie knew the woman's real objection wasn't the walk but the gantlet of drifters, drug dealers, and other undesirable characters they'd most likely encounter getting there. Emily really wanted to try a new expensive seafood restaurant in Marina del Rey, but Josie convinced her they should go to O'Farrell's because it was closer, had the best pizza in Venice, and a decent selection of cheap wine.

It was a cold weeknight on what turned out to be a nearly deserted beach so they didn't have any trouble getting into the bar or finding a table. The place was a hangout for locals because most tourists who were brave enough to visit the area took a quick look inside, saw the run-down interior, walls covered with antiwar, antiestablishment posters and cartoons, heard the loud music, and slipped away before the heavy aroma of marijuana got permanently embedded in their hair and clothing. On many occasions during the summer, Josie had watched them sneak around the doorway with their 8 mm cameras, stare at the young patrons with long hair and shabby clothes, then back-step outside to the boardwalk— indigenous folk were fun to observe and talk about later in the safety and comfort of home, but the traditional family crowd really didn't want to mingle.

O'Farrell's was a favorite spot for political organizers to hold strategy meetings and a haven to argue subversive ideas, then get drunk among compatible folk. When she first went undercover, Josie had gone there regularly to meet people but didn't make any usable contacts, so she hadn't been back for a while. She had realized, after a few visits, that nothing much got organized or accomplished in the bar but remembered that the comradeship and fun always made her feel good. She had enjoyed the time she spent here and wasn't sorry to have another legitimate reason to come back.

Most nights one or two indigent musicians would drift in and play for as long as patrons kept dropping coins in the hat. They'd set up in an area reserved for them behind the pool tables. Some were talented; others just hoped someone in the bar would keep the drinks coming during their monotonous, single-chord renditions of simple, boring folk songs. This evening, according to the fliers taped on the front window, the entertainment would be Kate Sparks.

FOUR

O'Farrell's had added a spotlight and sound system since the last time Josie had been there. As the lights dimmed, the bartender shouted over a noisy background of conversations and racked up pool table balls, "She's here for another night, shut-the-fuck-up and welcome Ms. Kate Sparks."

The spotlight came up targeting the slightly raised platform behind the pool tables where a short, skinny woman in black jeans and sleeveless, sequin-covered grey silky blouse was perched on one of the barstools holding a guitar. She waited for a spattering of claps to fade, then started playing her version of some Bob Dylan song that Josie recognized immediately but couldn't remember its name. The crowd got very quiet as Kate's surprisingly deep and wonderful voice filled the room. It was difficult to make out her features or guess her age under the bright light, but she had long straight brown hair adorned with Janis Joplin-style feathers and played the guitar and sang better than anyone Josie ever remembered hearing in this bar, much better.

Kate finished her set in thirty minutes but the applause convinced her to do another two songs before she stopped.

"Isn't she wonderful," Emily said when the lights came up and the applause finally stopped.

"She's got to be a professional. I wonder why she's playing here," Josie said.

"Favor to the owner."

"You know her?" Josie asked.

"Burt helped her out of a bad situation a couple of years ago . . . actually kept her out of jail."

Before Josie could ask what happened or if Emily would introduce her, Kate was standing at their table, grinning like a rhinestone-covered Cheshire cat. Emily jumped up and gave her a long hug, invited her to sit with them. Josie couldn't believe her good luck. She hadn't devised a plan or plausible way to meet the woman and now thanks to Emily it wasn't necessary.

"You have an amazing voice," Josie said, sipping a glass of whiskey. The singer only drank whiskey, so Emily had started ordering rounds for all of them. Up close Josie could see Kate was older than she appeared to be on stage, maybe in her late thirties or early forties. She was a chain smoker too and kept a pack of cigarillos on the table, lighting one pencil-thin cigar off the dying embers of another. Her left inner arm had dark lines nearly hidden under a colorful Chinese dragon tattoo, but there was enough light for Josie to be fairly certain she was looking at a heroin user. She'd been around plenty of addicts since making her home in Venice and had become something of an expert in recognizing the signs. Kate had the droopy eyelids, drowsy appearance, and pinpointed pupils that should've been as large as saucers in the dim light of O'Farrell's, but most of all there were those telltale track marks peeking from under the dragon on her arm.

They talked and drank for almost an hour before Soriano's name finally came up in the conversation.

"So how's your handsome Dave?" Emily asked in her innocent girlish way.

Kate crushed a half-smoked cigar in the ashtray. "Who the fuck knows," she said, coughing and taking a gulp of Jack Daniel's.

Most people couldn't get away with asking the sort of personal questions Emily did, but she acted so childlike in her persistent probing that the object of her inquiries rarely became angry or defensive. Unlike Josie, Kate apparently hadn't developed any skill in deflecting the woman's inquisitiveness or maybe it was the whiskey or opiates, but she was very candid about her relationship with Dave Soriano. Josie sat quietly and listened. She didn't try to participate in the discussion and turned slightly away as if she were disinterested and preferred to watch the pool games nearby. It was raucous and noisy in the bar, but Kate's gravelly voice was loud enough, even when she tried to whisper.

She confided in Emily that Soriano had abruptly stopped coming to her apartment and wouldn't return phone calls. He had a one-room bachelor pad in Mar Vista just east of Venice, but she'd gone there and had seen junk mail overflowing in his mailbox. The landlady claimed she hadn't seen him for at least a week. Kate convinced the woman to use her passkey and look inside just to be certain something hadn't happened to him. He wasn't there and Kate thought the apartment looked abandoned—no clothes, food, or other signs that anyone had been living there.

The fact that Soriano had the apartment didn't surprise Josie. She'd been told several UCs had places they maintained as an address they could give their targets, but they actually lived somewhere nicer. Soriano had the house in Monrovia so his apartment was probably strictly for appearances or a clean location he could bring members of his group which explained why none of them seemed to know about the place in the San Gabriel Valley; however, not having any clothes or personal items in Mar Vista seemed odd to her if he wanted anyone to believe he actually stayed there.

"Quentin is convinced Dave's been arrested, but if that happened why wouldn't he call me?" Kate whined, lighting another cigar.

"Maybe he just took off for a while . . . maybe he needs some time alone," Emily said, rubbing Kate's arm. "Men are funny that way, aren't they? Sometimes Burt is gone for days," she said, her voice trailing off. Burton Rice had a reputation as a lady's man and all of them, including Emily, knew when he disappeared he most likely wasn't spending his time in solitary reflection.

"I'm pissed . . . but I'm worried too. Quentin says he'll find him . . . he's got contacts," Kate said, giving Emily a faint smile.

"What sort of contacts?" Josie asked, abandoning her intention not to become part of the conversation. She had met Quentin Barnes and knew he and Soriano spent a lot of time together. Quentin sounded like an anarchist and a conspiracy theory guy. He had his personal 8-mm copy of the Zapruder film of JFK's assassination and showed it at every opportunity, the way some people did movies of their last vacation. Although he'd never served in the military, he usually wore camouflage pants and jackets and saw government plots everywhere. He claimed to have contacts in nearly every branch of the military, state, local, and federal governments and even the CIA, but most of his associates seemed to be petty criminals or dedicated dropouts. Last summer he started a rumor that the LAPD had bugged every pay phone on Venice Beach. Josie asked Murphy about it and the sergeant laughed. His exact words were, "The department can't get the damned phone system in police headquarters to work right. You think we have the technology to bug dozens of public pay phones?"

Kate didn't answer Josie's question right away. Her bloodshot, watery eyes seemed to be trying to focus on Josie's face.

"People," she said finally. "He knows people in the right places."

They talked awhile longer but Kate didn't have any more to say about Soriano. She alluded to friends Quentin had in the police department who might be willing and able to help locate her missing boyfriend but wouldn't reveal names or anything specific. Josie was convinced the woman had no idea where Soriano had gone. Quentin, however, had apparently made it his mission to find his missing buddy or at least that's what he wanted Kate to believe. Josie figured it might be productive if she could find a way to get closer to the man just in case he wasn't a complete fraud and could help locate the missing officer.

Shortly before O'Farrell's closed at two A.M., Kate got up to go to the restroom but never came back. A recording of Creedence Clearwater's "Proud Mary" blared from an overhead speaker as Emily paid their tab, and a few minutes later they were back in the Mercedes headed toward the garage apartment.

"I'm going to tell Burt to help," Emily said five minutes later as they sat in her car in Josie's driveway.

"What can he do?" Josie asked.

"I don't know . . . maybe pressure the cops. I feel bad for Kate."

Josie had never known Emily to feel bad for anyone except maybe herself and thought it odd how determined she had been in badgering Kate about her lost lover. It even went beyond her normal irritating inquisitiveness.

"Did you ever think maybe Dave doesn't want to be found?" Josie asked, not really wanting Emily's husband stirring up a lot of publicity about Soriano's disappearance.

"Why?"

"I don't know," Josie said, opening the car door. "But it's possible."

Emily grabbed her arm before she could get out.

"Can you come to the Kremlin about three tomorrow? Alex's got security training set up to get you and a couple others started before the camp."

"I guess . . . but I'm still not sure I want to do this."

"That's okay, just come anyway. See if you like it. I'm going."

Josie agreed and got out. The Kremlin was actually the Salazar Community Center, a neighborhood meeting place in East LA that had earned its Russian moniker among the radical lefties because of all the Marxist study groups that regularly met there. The building was actually an abandoned church renamed to honor Ruben Salazar, a news editor for KMEX, who was struck and killed by a tear-gas projectile at an antiwar protest about a year earlier. Although it was an accident, avenging his death had become a rallying cry for many of the more radical groups.

The center was one of the busier spots in that part of town offering free hot meals for the homeless, legal aid, invitation-only Marxist study groups, as well as having a gym with a basketball court for kids and martial arts classes. She'd go because Manny and his friends weren't likely to do anything sinister to her with that many people around.

As soon as Emily had driven away she took the five-shot revolver out of the VW and put it under her pillow, so that might've contributed to her feeling of well-being in the drafty garage. The blow-up mattress wasn't in any way comparable to Emily's guest bed, but she had so much alcohol in her system that sleeping on the concrete floor wouldn't have kept her awake.

There was little incentive to get out of bed the next morning. The portable floor heater was on but the room wasn't well insulated and at night the small space stayed just slightly warmer than the winter weather's cold gusts of wind off the ocean. She lay there under two heavy blankets for a few minutes but had to get up because it was her first day at the thrift shop.

She got dressed and made a pot of coffee, almost drinking all of it to wash down a slice of toast and scrambled egg. The hot plate worked fine as a source of heat and for a simple breakfast but her other meals were either fast-food takeout or sitting at the counter in one of the cheap diners on the boardwalk.

The Catholic thrift store was about two blocks away on Washington Boulevard. She wore a sweater under her blue pea coat and walked there. She promised the Sisters of Charity that she'd work at the shop three mornings each week, which would give her enough money to pay the rent and have a little left over for food and gas. It wasn't a difficult job. She took in bags of donated clothing and a few household items, cleaned them up, and stocked the shelves. The morning went by quickly and she enjoyed the work. Picking through the piles of discarded clothes, she took some of the nicer things for a young woman she'd seen living on the beach who always wore a patched-up threadbare dress and sweater. Josie knew the homeless girl—who was about her age but mentally impaired—would never venture far enough from the familiar surroundings of the boardwalk to find this store. Social services wouldn't force her into much needed institutional care; Josie had asked them. The girl seemed to live off what she found in trash cans and Josie wouldn't allow herself to imagine how she'd been abused by those predators who roamed the boardwalk at night looking for easy victims.

When her shift ended, she located the girl sitting on a bench in the Venice pavilion watching a toothless man, wearing a red and yellow jester hat, juggle tennis balls. When the man finished performing for his audience of one, he wandered off, and Josie put a clean dress, a pair of sturdy boots, and a practically new wool coat on the bench beside her. She stared at Josie a few seconds, then took everything, and walked away talking to herself. Josie wanted her to have the warm clothes and shoes but wouldn't be surprised if in a few days she discovered those very items on the ground or in one of the trash bins along the beach. Like too many people in Josie's neighborhood who called home a cardboard box in some filthy alley behind a storefront, the girl was incoherent most of the time, and Josie had learned crazy could be very unpredictable.

She stopped at a food truck in one of the parking lots and ate a hamburger before driving to East LA to meet Emily at the Kremlin. It was early but she wanted to check around the area a little and be certain Manny wasn't hanging out anywhere nearby. His sudden interest in her was bothersome. He'd never taken a personal interest in anybody in the group except Carla.

Lunch had just been served in the center but the large cafeteria was nearly empty. There were about twenty people sitting on benches at picnic-style tables. They included mostly seniors, a few homeless men, and mothers with young children. The wonderful aroma of homemade stew and fresh baked bread wafted through the building conquering the smell of moldy hallways and ancient sewer pipes, and Josie could feel her stomach tighten at the thought of how good the food probably tasted. Her diet was definitely going to change as soon as she got out of this assignment and could cook on a stove again. In the meantime, she intended to get a bowl of that stew before she left.

The gym was open and about half a dozen men were standing around talking. Two of them, probably the instructors, wore the traditional white Gi outfits with black belts. She knew Quentin Barnes was the shorter one. He was a nervous wiry little man with no sense of humor and long thinning hair that never seemed clean. She hadn't met the other one but recognized him as one of the regular security people who had protected demonstrators at a rally in Century City just a few weeks ago. He turned to watch her approach as he continued talking to the others.

Emily hadn't mentioned that Quentin would be here, but Josie knew he represented himself as a martial arts expert and had organized security for many of the bigger demonstrations. She figured this would be a great opportunity to interact with him, get to know him better, and maybe find out what he knew about Soriano's disappearance.

A few minutes later, Emily and then Alex, one of Manny's bodyguards, arrived and by the time the lesson started, there were twelve people participating, most of them connected to WLM, and a few who looked as if they'd be more comfortable with a gun or knife in hand. Quentin introduced the tall blond instructor as Charlie Jones, a former marine with a black belt in karate who had returned from Vietnam several months ago. He was a student now on the GI Bill at Santa Monica College and helped Quentin train whenever he had the time or inclination.

Throughout the lesson, Jones took a special interest in Josie, trying to help her master the simple moves he and Quentin were teaching. She suspected his interest in her went beyond perfecting the karate front kick. She didn't mind his help, but kept trying to get Quentin's attention and engage him in a conversation. They did talk a little but Quentin wouldn't reveal much. He was by trade a short-order cook, but he attempted to take on the demeanor of a quiet warrior. Josie figured he was aiming to be seen as mysterious and dangerous, but as far as she was concerned he came across as dull and weird.

"Kate is really worried about Dave . . . have you had any luck locating him?" she asked, after cornering Quentin during a break. They were resting on the first row of the gym's bleachers. Emily was sitting nearby and immediately took up the interrogation.

"There's nothing I can talk about," Quentin insisted, cutting them off.

"Can't you at least tell Kate something?" Emily asked. "She's really upset."

He didn't answer, but got up and motioned for Jones to walk with him away from the group. His body language said they were annoying him. Emily pouted and was clearly disappointed for the moment with his indifference, but Josie knew it wasn't in her nature to stay focused on problems for very long.

"Guess he's not going to tell us anything," Josie said, shrugging and pretending she really wasn't that interested, but she was beginning to question if Quentin actually knew anything relevant.

The lesson resumed ten minutes later and Josie didn't bring up the subject of Dave Soriano again. She didn't get a good feeling from Quentin and decided that pursuing him as a possible source would be too difficult; besides, she suspected that given his tendency to exaggerate he might not know as much as he wanted them or Kate to believe.

On the other hand, Jones was personable, intelligent, and seemed to have a close relationship with Quentin. She had a better chance getting any information Quentin actually did have through his friend who'd made it very clear he wanted to know her better. Not to mention it would be easy to spend time with Jones. He seemed a lot more mature and stable than most of the men she'd met in the last three years, and she liked his easy manner and sense of humor. By the end of the class they were laughing and joking and he asked if she would go to dinner with him. Josie agreed but gave him an excuse to put it off for a few days so she could check with Detective Carlson first. She didn't want to step on another UC's toes if someone in PDID was already watching him, but had to admit if that were the case she'd be disappointed and not just because of the missing officer. Other than his choice of friends and politics, Charlie Jones was exactly the sort of man she wanted to meet in her real life. But Josie understood that as soon as she resurfaced, she'd never see or talk to him or Emily again, and if they ever found out she was a cop, their friendship, such as it was, would probably turn immediately to hate. She swallowed hard and was starting to think it was a miracle that a lot more of her fellow UCs hadn't bolted.

Alex participated in the class but the big man didn't do much instructing. He assisted the WLM people, except Josie. Jones's constant attention never gave him an opportunity to interact with her. The WLM bodyguard was overweight but clearly had been formally trained in the martial arts, and despite his size, skillfully mimicked every move Jones demonstrated . . . with a touch of machismo flair. There was noticeable tension between the two men. Even Emily noticed and commented on it, and although Jones didn't back down he seemed intent on avoiding any confrontation. When the class was over, Alex cornered Jones and challenged him to a friendly match in front of everyone. The two men were about the same height but Alex had to be one hundred pounds heavier. At first, Jones joked and declined to fight him, but the bigger man persisted and baited him until he reluctantly agreed.

"Are you sure you want to do this?" Josie asked Jones as they waited for Alex to change into a Gi.

"No, but he is."

"Don't do it . . . walk away. I've heard this guy's been in prison and is stupid mean. He enjoys hurting people."

Jones laughed. "Is there a smart mean? Look, I've fought before. I just didn't want to hurt him for no good reason."

Josie thought that sounded not only a little arrogant but delusional as she moved away from the area where they were about to fight. She'd been told the volatile bodyguard frequently challenged men he wanted to prove weren't as good as he was or anyone he believed had slighted him in some way, and he'd broken a lot of bones. She wanted to leave so she couldn't see how badly Jones was about to get beat up, but just like watching a terrible traffic accident, she wasn't able to move or stop looking.

Josie barely knew Jones and shouldn't care what happened to him, but she did. She looked around for Quentin, but he had disappeared so there wasn't anyone else who could step in and stop them from fighting.

"This is going to be awful," Emily whispered in her ear, more excited than worried. Josie guessed her friend had expressed what everybody in the room, including her, was thinking.

Before Josie could come up with any viable maneuver to stop the fight, it had started. When the two men faced each other on the mat, Alex attacked but he assaulted empty air as Jones had stepped quickly to his right. Jones came up with a roundhouse kick to Alex's midsection, which caused him to bend forward into an oncoming punch to his right cheek. A second punch quickly followed to the right side of Alex's jaw. The big man crumpled like a marionette with its strings cut, and his head hit the mat with a thud. All this took three seconds and Jones had used the simple techniques he'd taught all afternoon, except the speed and ferocity of his counterattack was blinding and deadly accurate. It happened so fast everyone stood quietly as if trying to figure out what they had just seen. Finally Emily moved to help Alex who was barely conscious and struggling to get up, his rubbery arms and legs refusing to function properly.

The other students quietly dispersed and in a few seconds Josie, Emily, and Jones were the only ones left standing around the wobbly man, waiting for him to get his balance and ability to walk. He finally did get upright with Jones's assistance, but didn't say a word or look at any of them. He stumbled out to change his clothes, and Josie saw him leaving the center a short time later with his arm around Emily's shoulder, still a little unsteady. She almost felt sorry for him.

"Can I buy you a drink?" Jones asked when they were alone.

Josie wanted to say yes but knew she shouldn't. She didn't like the idea of her name showing up on another UC's report and would rather wait until Murphy and Carlson knew what she was doing.

"Not tonight, I can't, but maybe another time."

He didn't seem disappointed and walked with her toward the front of the building.

"I'm starving," he said, stopping at the dining hall doorway. "Want to get a bowl of stew before we leave? They're still serving."

He was standing in the dining hall now waiting for her to decide and it didn't take long for Josie to make up her mind. She was hungry and had already pretty much decided she wasn't leaving without tasting that stew. They went to the serving line where no one was waiting and a man wearing a clerical collar and an apron over his black suit gave each of them a full bowl of stew with several pieces of fresh bread. Most of the tables were empty now, so they picked the cleanest one. A few minutes later, Josie had finished the meal and was ready for another helping. It was the best food she'd eaten in months, even better than the more expensive meal Emily's cook had prepared.

"How do you stay so skinny eating like that?" Jones asked after she'd emptied her second overflowing bowl.

"Nervous energy."

She had intended to leave after dinner but they stayed in the empty room and chatted for almost another hour while volunteers cleaned up around them. It was a strange conversation. They talked mostly about Quentin and Soriano. She tried to find out what he knew about Quentin's search for the missing officer, but she felt as if he was pumping her for information too. There was none of the personal information that usually got exchanged when a man and woman have their first conversation. On her part, that was intentional. She didn't want to lie to him, but couldn't tell him the truth, so she didn't reveal much about herself.

Jones mentioned his military service and a brief visit he'd made with members of the Venceremos Brigade to Cuba but avoided telling her where he was from or anything about his family. She was a little disappointed because the only explanation had to be that he didn't trust her and was trying to get details about her life that could be checked and verified for Manny or someone else. Regardless of how much she liked him, Josie was savvy enough not to give him anything that could possibly link her to the police department, her family, or real background.

He did provide her with enough information about his activities for Josie to realize he was a legitimate target who should be watched by the intelligence division. He seemed to have connections to most of the high-profile radical organizations in the city, some of them underground, and had done security work at most of the biggest demonstrations. She would talk to Murphy about him, but couldn't believe the division didn't have someone already watching his activities.

Josie left him at the center and drove back to Venice. She parked in front of the apartment and walked to her phone booth near the beach to call Murphy. Reaching in her pocket for change, she found the matchbook cover she'd discovered in Soriano's garage with a phone number written inside. It had a downtown area code, so she put some change in the phone and dialed it, not expecting much. The phone was answered after six or seven rings.

"David Jacobson's office, may I help you?" a young female voice asked.

"Is Mr. Jacobson in?" Josie asked, not certain what she'd say to him if he was.

"He won't be back until morning. May I take a message?"

Josie hesitated and then said, "Oh, I'm sorry. Have I called his private line?"

"Yes you have. If you wanted his clerk or the bailiff, I'm afraid they've all gone home. Court is dark until tomorrow morning," she said and then quickly added, "May I ask how you got this number?"

"Switchboard must've made a mistake . . . sorry," Josie said and hung up.

She stood in the phone booth for a few seconds, pondering who David Jacobson might be. He had to be a judge . . . who else would have a court clerk and bailiff. A better question might be, why would an undercover police officer have a judge's private number?

FIVE

Murphy was still in the Georgia Street station when Josie called. She told him about the security training and her encounter with Charlie Jones. He assured her that PDID was fully aware of Jones and his activities and the division already had someone watching him. It was a little disappointing because she felt Jones could give her access to some of the more active radical types, opening those doors that might lead to the missing cop, but now she'd have to back off and let another UC deal with him.

"Do you think this Quentin Barnes is credible?" Murphy asked.

"He's a bullshitter, but at one time he was Soriano's closest friend and pretty much the best I've got at the moment unless you let me take the lead with Jones. He seems to know everything about everybody."

"No, I told you Jones is covered. Back off him," Murphy said, sounding a little testy but then asked, "What about Kate Sparks?"

"Wasted . . . heroin addict . . . doesn't know anything important, but she's got a great voice. Did you know about Soriano's apartment in Mar Vista?" she asked.

"Dead end, Detective Carlson already checked it out."

"Would've been nice if somebody had let me know," Josie said. "I hate wasting my time finding stuff you already have." Everything about this Carlson woman was annoying her.

"That's not the way it works, Pastore. I've told you before; information flows up the chain. You tell us. We don't tell you."

"You know a judge named David Jacobson?" she asked, not interested in arguing with him.

"Why? What about him?"

"Nothing just heard the name and was wondering . . ."

"Heard from who?" Murphy asked, interrupting her.

"I don't remember, some guy in the bar last night. You know Jacobson?"

"If it's the same man, he's a Superior Court judge downtown. How did his name come up?"

"This guy had a prelim or something with him, wasn't happy . . . you know," she lied. "Just wondering what his reputation was."

"What difference does it make? He's a judge, that's all. Forget about him and concentrate on finding Soriano. How bad did Jones injure Manny's bodyguard . . . what's his name . . . Alex?"

"Bad enough. Jones didn't wanna fight him but Alex is a lot like Manny . . . the whole macho thing. He wouldn't back down, kept pushing until Jones had to fight."

"Have you talked to Carlson?" Murphy asked.

"Not yet."

"Do it, so she knows you're working on this."

"Sarge, what's really going on here? I've got this nagging feeling you're not telling me the whole story," Josie said. She was tired of them pushing her to find this cop but not letting her in on everything.

"I've told you what you need to know. Give us something to work with before . . ." He hesitated and then said, "Just do your damned job and find him."

She called Carlson next and gave her the same information. It was a short one-sided conversation. Carlson didn't ask questions or give her any direction.

Her last words to Josie before hanging up were, "Call me when you've got something important."

Josie stared at the phone before gently placing it back on the cradle. She should've been bothered by the woman's dismissive attitude, but wasn't because calling her had been a formality. It was Josie's investigation, and she was learning not to expect much from either Murphy or Carlson. She would do what had to be done, tell them what they needed to know, and find their missing cop, so she could get the hell away from both of them.

On a cold winter night, the beach was nearly deserted except the usual contingent of bums, hookers, and drug dealers huddled in doorsteps or around the lifeguard towers looking for protection against the bone-chilling ocean breeze. Josie remained in the phone booth for a few seconds after hanging up with Carlson, but still thinking about her conversation with Murphy. The idea of walking away from a quality source like Jones didn't sit well with her, but then Murphy might've been right. Any decent undercover operative should be able to get whatever information Jones had. If that led to Soriano, it might be less complicated for her and she'd be out of the assignment . . . so why was the prospect of losing Jones still bothering her so much.

The walk back to her apartment only took a few minutes, but Josie had an uncomfortable feeling she wasn't alone. She didn't actually see anyone but was always so careful about being followed that she paid attention to every noise and was constantly looking over her shoulder. When she left the phone booth, there had been that odd shuffling sound behind her of sand grinding against asphalt on a seemingly deserted bike path, and then the glimpse of shadows moving quickly away from the street lights. She was tall and alert, not the typical victim type, and her clothing told the world she had nothing worth stealing, so she wasn't worried.

Whoever it was kept his or her distance, and when Josie reached the garage she waited near the door watching for signs of anyone skulking in the darkness. A few months ago this street would've been crowded with tourists, prostitutes, and locals double-parked, partying to and from the beach, leaving empty beer bottles, condoms, and other assorted debris at the curb, but tonight it was eerily quiet, too cold for even the most diehard street people.

She removed the revolver from its hiding place inside the driver's door panel of the VW and brought it into the apartment. It would stay close to her again tonight.

It wasn't the possibility of someone watching her that kept Josie from sleeping most of that night, but the feeling she was running out of ideas on how to find the missing cop. She planned to go back to O'Farrell's every night because that's where Soriano's last love interest, Kate, would be, and hopefully he would attempt to get in touch with her.

She could talk to Debbie again at the Midnight Special. That approach wasn't very promising, but then she didn't have many options. Charlie Jones would've been a valuable connection to Quentin and other radical leaders, but as of tonight the former marine was off-limits . . . maybe. Josie had almost convinced herself someone else could get as much from Jones as she could but after several sleepless hours she'd discarded that thought and knew she wanted to be the one who found the missing cop. She decided it would be worth incurring Murphy's wrath if keeping in contact with Jones meant she could do that. In three years, she rarely did anything Murphy or any other supervisor ordered her not to do and even now thinking about intentionally disobeying him made her a little nervous, but not enough to change her mind.

A few hours before dawn, she finally fell asleep. Loud banging on the side door of the garage woke her from a dream that had made her feel happy but she was unable to remember it as soon as she sat up. She pulled on her Levis and looked out her only window at Emily standing on the doorstep. The revolver was still under her pillow, so she dropped it in her shoulder bag before opening the door.

"Did I wake you?" Emily asked, nudging past her to get into the room. "It's almost lunch."

"I was being lazy, no work today," Josie said slipping her nightshirt off over her head. She took a sweater out of the dresser, put it on and began brushing her thick hair.

"What did you and CJ do last night?" Emily asked with a smirk.

"CJ?"

"Charlie Jones, I could tell he likes you."

"Nothing . . . ate stew at the center and I went home. How's Alex?"

Emily shook her head and whispered in her girlish voice, "I thought he was going to get his gun and kill the dude. Burt had to calm him down."

"He's the one who started the fight."

"Yeah, but CJ could've really hurt him . . . wouldn't be the first time . . . anyway you don't know how crazy these guys . . ." She didn't finish her thought, but shook her head as if what she knew shouldn't be discussed or had gotten lost in the urgency of some new idea. "Can you come to a planning meeting for a coalition march?" Emily asked, quickly changing the subject.

"When . . . what march?"

"In about an hour at the Kremlin, Manny's organizing a protest against police brutality for what they did to us downtown. He said he wants you there."

"Okay," Josie said, but she didn't believe it was okay. Once again, Manny Contreras who'd pretty much ignored her for years wanted her involved. Her self-preservation antennae were fully extended now. She'd go because it would be a good opportunity to interact with several other groups and maybe pick up gossip about Soriano. If it was a coalition, the march should be big which usually required experienced security to keep it manageable, so Jones and Quentin most likely would be there.

Emily drove them to the center in less than an hour despite Josie insisting they stop at Winchell's for coffee and a breakfast donut. They arrived just as the meeting was about to begin. The same gym where Quentin and Jones had held their karate class the day before had been transformed into an assembly hall half filled with rows of folding chairs. Josie recognized activists of varying political ideologies, most of them far left of center, scattered throughout the room in small noisy groups. There was never much interaction among the few extremists groups; however, the majority of participants, those without the radical political beliefs, did mingle and drink cheap beer provided by the center. They enjoyed the entertaining aspects of transforming society and although they vigorously promoted civil rights and other social causes, for the most part they would rather party than deal with those scarier factions who talked of revolution and violence.

Manny was pacing at the front of the room holding a microphone, attempting to get the energetic gathering to stop talking. He waved at Emily and Josie, but seemed frustrated that no one was really listening to him. His gestures reminded Josie of a new kindergarten teacher trying to get a roomful of five-year-olds lined up for a fire drill.

As soon as he managed to get their attention, a lesbian from the Lavender Liberation Front stood and got into a shouting match with a young black man from a Citizens Fighting Police Abuse group in South Central LA, over whether or not gays faced as much discrimination as his race did. He was shouted down by a large contingent of gay men who insisted they were just as oppressed and their cause should have equal representation in the demonstration. After a lengthy and loud discussion, a vote was taken and the lesbian won the majority's recognition of gays, lesbians, and transgenders as legitimately oppressed groups. A handful of black activists immediately got up, right fists in the air, and walked out, visibly disgusted with the outcome.

Josie wasn't surprised by the disruption. Dissension was a big part of planning any demonstration and it always happened this way. Every group had outspoken members who wanted to be heard on their particular grievances—overthrowing the ruling class, police abuses, Vietnam War, women's rights, gay rights, workers' rights, civil rights. Regardless of the targeted objective, they would talk and make their point. She had learned over the years to sit patiently, mentally sifting through the verbal antics of different speakers until she found that nugget of relevant information. Many of the splinter groups in LA had been formed according to personal relationships. Their motives and loyalties were shaped more by whom they slept or drank with than any political belief. Josie understood this was a complicated and dynamic world she'd inhabited the last few years, but she also knew when to sit back, drink a beer, and just enjoy the show.

Finally Manny was allowed to get around to the specifics of the demonstration. As usual there hadn't been much real planning except for the security team. Jones outlined the route of the march up Los Angeles Street to the front of the police administration building and he described how the security teams would operate. He was concise and sounded as if he knew what he was talking about. He and Quentin talked for about half an hour before Manny took back the microphone and read a list of committees that would be needed to make placards and do all the prep work. He passed around sign-up sheets and emphasized several times the overall theme of the march should be a protest against police brutality.

His closing words finally caused Josie to sit up and pay attention.

"At all costs we will protect the integrity of this march. If you can't commit to that you don't belong here. Fucking pigs can't tell us where we walk . . . damn sure can't take away my bullhorn," he shouted, too close to the microphone, causing a high-pitched, ear-piercing feedback. He paused for a moment and then said calmly, "If they try, we hurt them . . . bad."

The room got quiet. In the diverse gathering, not everyone had Manny's taste for bloody confrontation. One of the few groups that might've supported him had already left. There was polite applause and a few halfhearted shouts of agreement, but Josie figured the march was destined to be WLM supporters and everybody else. No one would vigorously challenge Manny today, but she suspected the turnout would lack coherence with every group doing its own thing regardless of Manny's direction. Nevertheless it would still be a decent-sized demonstration and with Manny's input it was destined to be a problem for downtown police.

With so many different groups participating, she knew there had to be several undercover officers besides her attending this meeting, so PDID should have ample warning this time. She was sitting in the back of the room with Emily and made a mental record of everyone she knew. It was a skill developed over the years, so later on when she wrote her report Josie could list practically everyone who'd been there. Any new names were associated with someone she knew to help her remember them later.

She spotted Alex standing near the hallway with Manny's other bodyguard. The two men watched the crowd with the intensity of Secret Service agents protecting the president. Alex had bruises on his neck and face and Josie caught him staring at Jones several times during Manny's disjointed presentation. From what Emily told her and what she knew about Alex, she guessed the big man wasn't likely to forget or forgive his humiliation at the hands of Jones.

The meeting was winding down when Quentin stood and asked if he could address the participants again. He began by telling them his friend David Soriano was missing and asked if anyone had information on the man's whereabouts. When no one responded, he offered several theories including abduction or killing by the police. Josie got up while he spoke and moved around the room as if she were stretching her legs but she was watching faces, hoping to see someone's reaction to Soriano's name, hear some offhanded remark.

"We should carry posters with his picture, demand cops tell us where he is," Quentin said, turning to Manny.

"Carry whatever the fuck you want," Manny said, shrugging, and before shutting off the microphone added, "Committees can meet now." He walked away and left Quentin standing alone, but it didn't matter because most people had taken Josie's cue and were up milling around the room, talking, and not listening anyway.

From past experience, Josie knew very few of those attending would volunteer for committees or anything, and even if they did, the same one or two die-hard regulars would do all the work. She always helped a little, but Murphy had warned her not to take too much responsibility. He said most cops couldn't control their take-charge personalities and he didn't want one of his undercover officers becoming a leader in any group. Josie knew he was right because she was always fighting the urge to step in, stop the endless, pointless political discussions, and just get things done.

The center's kitchen staff had provided lunch for participants in the dining room and Josie never missed an opportunity to eat. It wasn't very good this time, but it was free and filling. She was finishing an egg-salad sandwich and laughing at something Emily said when Quentin sat on the bench between them.

"You guys were at the training yesterday, right?" he asked, but added before they could respond, "Manny told me he wants you on the security team for this."

Josie had a mouthful of eggs but looked at Emily and they both nodded. She edged closer to the end of the bench to put some distance between her and Quentin. His breath had an unpleasant fishy odor, his clothes reeked of marijuana, and it wasn't mixing well with a stomach full of hard-boiled eggs. He was probably in his thirties but was balding and seemed permanently irritated. What hair he did have was too long and reminded her of one of Charles Dickens's sinister characters.

"Yesterday was our first lesson," Emily said. "Is that enough?"

"Yeah, sure, you'll do great," he said, interrupting her. He got up, adding as he walked away, "CJ will tell you what to do."

"Maybe nothing will happen," Josie said, noticing a slight tremor in Emily's hands that at first she thought was fear but realized was anger. For some reason her make-believe friend was pissed off.

"We haven't really learned enough. I'm going to tell Manny we're not ready," Emily said.

She doubted Emily could dissuade the WLM leader. He might change his mind about Emily but Josie guessed he had plans for her. She wasn't certain why, but it was becoming pretty obvious he wanted her out front with a security band around her arm.

"Just tell him. He won't make you do anything you don't want to," Josie said, emphasizing the "you."

"Aren't you worried?"

"Sure, but Manny seems to think I'm ready."

Emily took a deep breath and exhaled. "Well, if you can, I can," she said, leaning back, crossing her arms and giving Josie a big, confident smile.

Josie forced a smile back. She knew with her police training, and growing up with a big brother who encouraged her to be a tomboy, she could take care of herself but doubted Emily could, so she cautioned, "Give it some thought . . . talk to Burt and definitely don't do anything just because of me." The last part of the warning was pointless because they both knew that's exactly why Emily was doing it.

Whatever Manny's motives in selecting her, Josie figured this security team would be an opportunity to spend more time with Quentin and Jones. As she talked to Emily, she watched Quentin standing outside the dining room talking with Alex. They appeared to be having a heated exchange that stopped abruptly when Jones joined them. Quentin pointed in her direction and a few seconds later, Jones was at their table.

"Guess Manny thinks you guys are good enough to jump into the fray," he said, sitting next to Josie.

"So we've been told," Josie said.

"You're with me," he said, nodding at her and taking a couple of stale potato chips off her dish. "Emily, you're on Quentin's team."

"But I want us to stay together," Emily said.

"Not my call. Talk to the man in charge."

"Who's that?" Josie asked.

"Quentin."

"Why aren't you running security? From what I've seen you seem to know more than Quentin or Alex," Josie said, hoping he would offer some insight on who was really making the decisions.

Before he answered, Jones glanced at Emily and then said, "Two reasons—first, nobody asked me; and second, even if they did, I don't want the job."

Josie wasn't convinced. It seemed this guy was a natural leader. She'd seen a few of them during her career as an editor and in her short time out of the police academy. They were the calm confident ones everyone, including bosses, turned to for direction or advice when things got out of control. There had to be another reason he'd be willing to allow lesser men like Quentin and Alex to take the lead.

"Do we meet or practice before the demonstration?" Josie asked.

"Nope, show up at eight A.M. at the Grand Central Market, Fifth and Broadway, Saturday morning, on-the-job training," he said and added quickly, "Want to go to a party tonight?"

"What?" She heard him but wanted a minute to think.

"Party . . . you know drinking, dancing . . . fun . . . some lawyer's house in Brentwood," he said.

Emily perked up, for the moment forgetting her disappointment in being separated from Josie. "Burt and me are going to that party. You have to go, and it's not just any law-yer's house. He's a deputy district attorney," she said.

As soon as Josie heard district attorney, she knew she would go but allowed Emily to persuade her so she didn't appear too eager. Jones offered to pick her up and she agreed, not wanting to depend on the VW to get her there.

By the time Emily drove her back to the garage, Josie only had a couple of hours to call Murphy, update him, take a shower, and get ready for the party. She'd type her report later that night and get it to Murphy first thing in the morn-ing. Having a police report in her apartment always made her nervous. On more than one occasion she had to flush pages down the toilet when someone showed up before she'd had a chance to finish or deliver it. Murphy offered his house as a safe place to write but Josie always felt uncomfortable sit-ting at his dining room table while his wife and kids tried to pretend she wasn't there. Mrs. Murphy never complained but had made it clear in other ways she wasn't really pleased with that arrangement—slamming doors and talking too loud on the phone about her inconsiderate husband seemed to be two of her favorites.

An older sergeant had warned Josie's all-female class in the academy that officers' wives never liked their husbands working with young attractive physically fit policewomen. The dangers of police work brought partners close, sharing a professional intimacy that a spouse could never experience, understand, or hope to achieve. Josie decided it was less complicated and better for Brickhouse's marriage to take a chance and do the report in her garage in the middle of the night.

Jones got to her apartment about twenty minutes early. She opened the door and he stood outside for several sec-onds surveying the room. He was wearing a black sweater with his Levis, boots, and green sport coat. His dark blond hair was combed back and she thought he looked a lot better than she did.

"Am I presentable for this thing?" she asked, moving aside for him. Faded jeans were acceptable just about everywhere these days, but she also realized this party was in a very upscale neighborhood.

"You look great, probably overdressed for that crowd. You live here alone?" he asked, stepping inside and walking around the cramped space, touching a bistro table and examining bookshelves she'd retrieved from the alley behind the main house. "This is nice."

"Thanks, it's all mine . . . very cheap but clean."

She had straightened up the bed a few minutes before he arrived and covered the wooden platform with a comforter. Pretty lace curtains she'd discovered in the thrift shop decorated her only window, framing the miniblinds. Josie didn't tell him, but all her furniture had come from the alley she'd labeled her homeless Sears store. When she moved into the garage three years ago, she cleaned, sanded, and antiqued those discarded items and was surprised how functional and durable they had been.

"I'm looking for a place like this near the beach," he said, sitting on the corner of her bed.

"Where are you staying now?" she asked.

"I'm renting a room at Quentin's place off the strand but his girlfriend's moving back . . . that's not gonna work."

"Who's his girlfriend?"

Josie was doing her best imitation of Emily—just keep asking a lot of personal questions as if you have no idea how intrusive and inappropriate they are.

He hesitated before saying, "You know her, Dave's ex, Kate."

"Kate Sparks is moving in with Quentin?" She hadn't intended to say that out loud or sound so surprised. Fortunately she didn't blurt out everything she was thinking about Quentin's sleaziness in taking advantage of Soriano's addicted lonely girlfriend.

"It's not such a shock. She only got involved with Dave about a week before he disappeared. She'd been with Quentin for years before that."

"If you were living with them before she hooked up with Dave, why move out now?"

"She says she won't come back if I'm there."

"Oh . . . why?"

"Long story . . . ready to go?"

"I thought Quentin and Dave were friends. There had to be some hard feelings when Kate walked out on Quentin," Josie said, locking the garage side door behind them.

"Quentin blamed her, not Dave," Jones said. He had parked his white MG sports car in her driveway. It was a tight fit with the top up but she managed to contort her tall body into the passenger seat.

"But now Soriano's gone and he's taking Kate back," she said as soon as he got into the driver's side. "That's peculiar."

"Looks that way," Jones said in a tone that told her he was done talking about it.

"How did you get invited to a party among the Brentwood elite?" she asked, changing the subject because she'd probably pushed as hard as she could without annoying him or making him suspicious.

It worked. Jones seemed to relax and said, "They're actually Quentin's friends. His father is Anthony Barnes, one of those writers that got blacklisted in the McCarthy era. He's a kind of cult hero in that crowd."

He told Josie that Quentin's father never really did amount to much as a screenwriter but got famous for defying the committee. He'd earned a lot of money in real estate and lived in Brentwood on the same street as the deputy DA, an NFL player, a couple of Hollywood stars, and other rich celebs. The deputy district attorney thought of himself as a progressive thinker and wanted Quentin's father and other fringe characters at his parties. His intent had been to foster lively intellectual debate, but Jones admitted most of his get-togethers turned into drunken orgies.

"He has expensive liquor and the food is great," Jones said. "And there's a game room with a professional pool table . . . it's fun, but the discussions are usually just bad-mouthing conservative politicians and the cops."

When they arrived, the party was well underway. The street in front of the house and the circular driveway were crowded with parked cars. Lights from inside and around the exterior of the mansion could be seen from blocks away. Josie suspected the wealthy neighbors probably weren't entirely pleased with the Las Vegas-style illumination and circus atmosphere coming from the lawyer's estate. Groups of people stood talking and drinking on the expansive front lawn and the odor of marijuana hung thick in the air. It was a chilly night but the front door was wide open with partygoers spilling out from the entryway onto the porch.

Jones led her into the kitchen and introduced her to their host, Larry Clarke, the deputy district attorney, who at the moment was overseeing the creation of a potent bowl of punch. With his loose shoulder-length grey hair, Clarke and two older women who were pouring bottles of alcohol into a huge cut-glass bowl reminded Josie of the three witches in *Macbeth*. They playfully chanted names from each bottle's label as they stirred their concoction with long wooden spoons. "Two cups toad juice rum . . . one part bat blood whiskey . . ."

He was a friendly man who'd obviously been testing the punch and had a head start on the festivities. He tried to grab Josie for a hug but she skillfully slipped away.

"I'll catch you later, my pretty," Clarke said, slurring his words trying to imitate the evil witch from *The Wizard of Oz*.

"Sorry about that," Jones said, as they left the kitchen.

"He's drunk."

"Most of the time," Jones said. "I think his last memory of sobriety was graduation day from Harvard."

"This place looks like a hippie convention. Who are all these people?"

Jones smiled. "Some are old lefties, armchair revolutionaries, a few are a little more sinister, most just want to eat and drink at Larry Clarke's expense."

"What do you mean more sinister?" she asked.

"The ones who come to Larry's parties to meet money men or celebrities easily separated from their piles of do-good cash."

"How does he live like this on an LA County paycheck?"

"He doesn't. His old man owns Clarke Motors in Beverly Hills and about a dozen other showrooms from San Diego as far north as San Francisco. He gave Larry this house, a place in Tahoe, and that new Porsche in the driveway."

Jones introduced her to several people he knew, most of them appearing to be his age. She had asked how old he was and was surprised to find he was twenty-seven, a year younger than she was, but acted older. Most of his acquaintances were friendly, easygoing like him, and good company. There was an area on the closed-in back porch where they could sit, talk, and drink Larry's best whiskey. This was another day at work for Josie but to her surprise she was enjoying herself, mostly because she was comfortable with Jones. He was still pretty much a mystery but he was also smart and funny. They laughed about the same things and seemed to have similar taste in movies and books. Their politics sounded compatible, but then Josie was lying about what she really believed. She liked him and thought in another life she could've seriously considered him a friend . . . maybe more. But as long as she stayed in this assignment nothing in her world including his friendship was real and for the first time in three years she regretted that.

From the patio, Josie had a clear view of the backyard including the swimming pool and tennis court. The floodlights revealed people scattered everywhere on the sprawling estate. She immediately focused on Quentin and Kate Sparks sitting at a table near the pool's waterfall. Kate's guitar was propped against a chair nearby, so Josie figured she'd been asked to be the live entertainment. The sooner the better, she thought, tired of listening to the grating Joan Baez music blaring from the sound system. Larry Clarke was standing near them talking to an older well-dressed man, one of the few men at the party in a suit and tie. The man was tall and trim with short striking white hair.

"What are you looking at?" Jones asked, leaning closer to see her view of the yard.

"Who's that old guy talking to Larry?" she asked.

"Some judge . . . lives in the neighborhood. I've seen him here before."

"You know him?" she asked, immediately thinking about David Jacobson's number on the matchbook cover.

"Nope, why?"

She didn't answer because she saw Emily and Burt walking from the house, and they sat down at Quentin's table. Larry and the judge pulled chairs from another table and joined them.

"Wanna go outside?" Jones asked, waving his hand in front of her eyes, trying to get her attention.

"Sorry, I just noticed Burt and Emily. Maybe we should say hello," she said. Actually Josie wanted to know the judge's name and knew Emily would tell her.

Jones looked out, then sat back and exhaled. "You should probably do that alone and I'll catch up with you later."

"Why, what's wrong?"

"Don't think Kate wants to see me. I'm not in the mood for one of her druggie meltdowns."

He got up and went toward the bar. She watched as he stopped to talk to a very thin, attractive woman who was a bit glassy-eyed and who had to reach out and touch the wall to keep from stumbling. Jones helped her get to a cushioned loveseat where she immediately curled up and seemed to fall asleep. Josie recognized the woman from several old movies, but couldn't remember her name.

When Jones was out of sight, she got up and went into the backyard. She hadn't gone more than a few steps in the direction of Quentin's table before Emily jumped up and pounced on her with a hug. She pulled Josie toward the table and demanded that Burt find another chair. No one introduced the older man who was sitting next to Quentin, so Josie held out her hand to him and introduced herself.

"Pleasure, Miss Pastore . . . David," he said with a tight smile.

"It's Josie. Are you with the District Attorney's Office too?" she asked.

"No, afraid not," he said and turned to answer something Quentin had asked him.

She didn't have another opportunity to talk with him because he, Burt, and Quentin got up and walked away to have a private conversation a few yards away.

Larry was flirting with Emily, but he got bored when she didn't show any interest and he joined the other men.

"What a creepy little man," Emily whispered when he was gone.

"Rich and creepy," Josie said.

"His money is the only reason most of these people have anything to do with him," Emily said, slurring her words a little. There were three empty punch glasses in front of her. "Manny refuses to come here but he gladly takes his money."

Kate seemed to be asleep sitting up. Her eyes were closed, and her chin almost touched her chest. Every few seconds, she'd straighten up, look alert, and then her eyelids would slowly close again. It was a classic heroin symptom and Josie knew the woman heard and would remember every word that was said even though she appeared to be drowsy or asleep.

"Manny knows Larry Clarke?" Josie asked. She was finding the tentacles of WLM seemed to go everywhere.

"Of course, Alex works as Larry's bodyguard, driver too," Emily said, snorting a little.

Josie sat back and after a moment asked, "Does Larry know Soriano?"

"He should; Dave works for him."

"Doing what?" she asked, knowing an undercover cop working in the District Attorney's Office had to be PDID's worst nightmare on a million different levels.

"I think Burt said he was some kind of intern at the office before he disappeared, but he's been gone so long he's probably lost that job by now."

"Aren't their interns all law students or paralegals?"

"He's enrolled at the People's College, so it's the perfect job."

Josie knew about the People's College of Law and Justice. It was a funky unaccredited operation that took in hundreds of dollars from well-intentioned students committed to creating the impossible dream—an army of altruistic lawyers. She'd heard its teaching staff was mediocre and graduates rarely if ever passed the California Bar. Neither Murphy nor Carlson had mentioned that Soriano might have been a student there or that he was working in the District Attorney's Office.

Attending that particular college wasn't an issue, but working undercover in Larry Clarke's office was unethical and probably unlawful. She wondered whether Soriano did it on his own, or if he'd been told to go there.

"What's the matter?" Emily asked, moving closer to Josie. "You look a little upset. Are you worried about Dave? We all are," she said, trying too hard to sound sincere.

"I'm worried sick," Kate said, opening her eyes for a moment.

"Has there been any news? Has Quentin found anything?" Josie asked, glancing over at him and the others still huddled out of earshot in animated conversation. "Who's that white-haired good-looking guy?" she added, pointing at the group and noticing Burt wasn't with them any longer.

Emily hesitated as if either trying to decide how much she should say or remember what the man did. "Don't know for sure. I think he's a judge downtown somewhere. Did you hear Quentin just found out Dave has another house in the San Gabriel Valley?" she asked, quickly changing the subject. "Isn't that strange? He can afford to keep two places but he's always borrowing money from Kate or that redheaded hippie at the Midnight Special."

"That is odd. Anything else?" she asked, but was thinking, "Tell me something I don't already know."

"Nope," Emily said shaking her head, but she put her hand near Josie's ear and whispered, "Kate blames your Charlie."

"Blames him for what?" Josie asked, looking at the sleeping woman.

"Making Dave run away," Emily said, shrugging. "She thinks he's hiding from Charlie," she whispered.

"Why would he hide from Charlie?"

"They had a huge fight . . ." Before Emily could finish her sentence there were two piercing screams from inside the house. She stopped and looked up at the only window on the second story where the light was on. Her expression hardened and she murmured, "Not again."

No one in the backyard moved or seemed interested in finding out what was happening, but Josie got up, hurried inside, and quickly climbed the stairs to the second floor. The hallway lights were on and several people were huddled outside a room with the door open. She pushed her way past them and stepped inside in time to see Charlie Jones punch a very drunk, belligerent Burt Rice in the face and drag him off someone who had fallen between the bed and the wall.

"I told you to get off her," Jones said, depositing Burt's limp body on the floor near Josie's feet.

He went back to the bed and reached over to help the actress Josie had seen earlier crawl out from the tight space. She was shaken and crying but kept thanking him for helping her. Up closer, Josie could see she was very attractive but older than she appeared in the dim light downstairs. The woman straightened her dress and pulled up her panties before sitting on the bed and covering her face with both hands. Her hair was disheveled; she had red marks around her neck, and her left eye was beginning to swell and close.

Josie knelt close to her and asked, "Do you want me to call the police and an ambulance?"

"No," the woman said emphatically and glared at Josie. It was more than embarrassment; she was angry. "Do not do that," she ordered. "I'm fine . . . he didn't . . ." She slid awkwardly off the bed and they helped her locate her shoes, fur coat, and purse. She was unsteady but asked Jones to assist her out the back door to her car so she could leave before anyone else saw her. The sleeve of her dress had been torn and the mascara on both eyes was smeared. Despite Josie's urging she refused any help.

Jones escorted her out of the room and was gone only a few seconds before coming back alone.

"Larry will get someone to take her home," he said, standing over the barely conscious Burt Rice.

Emily's husband rolled over on his back and was groaning as he attempted to sit up. Jones roughly grabbed the front of his shirt helping him stand. Burt's belt was undone and the zipper on his pants was down. He had to hold on to his pants to keep them from falling. The left side of his face was bruised and turning the color of the movie star's eye. His mouth was bleeding and a cut over his left eye was dripping blood like a tiny faucet down the front of his expensive shirt. Apparently Charlie had hit him a few times before Josie got there.

"We should call the police," she told Jones while watching Burt's glassy eyes try to focus and comprehend what was happening around him.

"Waste of time, she'll never cooperate with the police. I gave this pervert all the punishment he's going to get," Jones said, pushing the shaky man out the bedroom door. "Go home or I'll put you in the hospital," he said as Burt stumbled into the hallway.

"Did he?" Josie started to ask, but Jones interrupted her.

"Rape her?"

Josie nodded.

"I don't think so. She says not, but she's beat up pretty bad. Sandra's in pretty good shape but she's got to be over fifty. One of these days that lowlife's going to jump the wrong woman and some guy's gonna geld him."

As soon as he said the name Sandra, Josie remembered who she was—Sandra Collins, an actress who was a lot more famous for her political antiwar rants than her movies. She'd made a lot of appearances in some popular films in the sixties and had been married to a wealthy hotel owner who dumped her when her politics got too much negative attention. The divorce settlement left her rich enough to give money to her favorite causes, and her celebrity status had helped raise funds and bring attention to every new cause she supported.

"Poor Emily," Josie said and Jones shook his head. "What does that mean?" she asked as they stood in the hallway, watching Burt cling to the railing, slowly working his way down the stairs.

"She knows what her husband's like. Trust me this isn't the first time that guy's done this or worse." Jones paused for a second as if he were deciding whether or not he should say more and then added quickly, "I know this will probably ruin any chance we have of becoming friends, but your pal Emily isn't as naive or innocent as she pretends to be and you should watch yourself around her."

"Thanks, I can take care of myself," she said. Emily wasn't her pal and would never be more than a source, but she couldn't tell him that. At this point in her life, Josie didn't have real friends, and after her apartment had been searched, no one needed to tell her Emily might not be entirely what she seemed, but she wasn't anyone Josie saw as a real threat either.

SIX

It was after midnight by the time Jones drove her back to the garage apartment. She was grateful he didn't seem interested in coming inside and she didn't ask. He walked her to the door and gave her a robotic peck on the cheek before getting into his MG and driving away.

There wasn't any time to ponder his apparent lack of romantic interest in her because she still had to write a report and call Murphy. Although she wouldn't have encouraged an intimate relationship with him, she had to admit it was a little disappointing to her ego that he didn't even make a halfhearted attempt or signal he was interested in trying. Just thinking that way confirmed her belief she needed to get back to telling the truth and start dating again before celibacy and lying made her as weird and horny as Burt Rice.

It was late and normally she'd wait until morning to call Murphy, but Josie decided the information she had was important enough to make the call tonight, but that meant she'd have to walk down to the phone booth on the bike path. No problem, she thought, grabbing her purse with the revolver.

The phone apparently woke Murphy, which didn't do anything to improve his usual bad mood. To make matters worse, Josie could hear his wife chipping at him in the background as they talked. After she explained what she'd learned about Soriano's internship and told him about the demonstration scheduled for the weekend, he got very quiet.

"You still there?" she asked after several seconds of silence.

"I told you his supervisors allowed him to go places he shouldn't have."

"Did you or Carlson know where he was working?" she asked.

"No, of course not."

Josie could hear it in his defensive tone; he was lying. Murphy was a terrible liar. He hadn't had much practice because for the most part he didn't care what other people thought, so good or bad he usually told the truth. But this was different. Knowing meant culpability.

"I'd say his supervisors have some serious explaining to do," she said, with as much sarcasm as she thought he'd tolerate.

"I'll handle the supervisors. Just find Soriano."

"Can you think of any reason he'd need or want to be in that office? Could Larry Clarke be a target?"

"Absolutely not. Why would we be watching a deputy district attorney?"

"Why not? Are guys in three-piece suits off limits? At the moment, I'm pretty sure I've got a superior court judge and a deputy DA in the big picture. Soriano seemed to have connections everywhere, so if you want me to find him then everybody's fair game."

She decided to tell him about the matchbook cover and seeing David Jacobson at Larry Clarke's party but left out the disturbing scene with Burt and the aging movie star. Getting the police involved might've damaged her cover and certainly would've changed her relationship with Emily, so it was a survival instinct that kept Josie from calling the cops. But she still felt guilty about not putting Burt in jail where he belonged. Jones's revelation that it wasn't Burt's first or worse assault didn't improve her already guilty conscience.

Before Murphy asked his next question, Josie heard a door slam in the background on the other end of the line, and she could no longer hear his wife's verbal sniping in the background.

"So you're saying Manny's bodyguard . . . Alex works for Clarke too? Why would a deputy DA need a bodyguard and why would he use one connected to WLM?"

"Don't know," she answered truthfully. "But you need to ask Soriano's supervisors what he thought was so important that he'd risk his career and theirs by working undercover in the DA's office."

"I don't have to do anything, Pastore. Just do your job and stop worrying about things that don't concern you. Detective Carlson and me will deal with the supervisors."

She wanted to argue, but didn't. If the supervisors were aware of Soriano's activities they would probably lie about it and no one could contradict them until Soriano surfaced again . . . if he surfaced again.

"Fine," she said. "I'll get my report to you before I go to the thrift shop in the morning."

"Meet me at eight in that bar on the Redondo Beach Pier where we met last month. I'll buy breakfast," he said. "Don't call Carlson. I'll fill her in after I meet with you."

Josie agreed and hung up. The food at his favorite bar was good, but the place was a damp mice-infested shack that smelled like dead seaweed and catered to dedicated alcoholics, mostly Vietnam War vets. Murphy liked it because it was close to his house and far enough from LA and Venice that they weren't likely to run in to anyone she knew. She suspected he spent a lot of his time there when he wasn't working. He appeared most comfortable among men who'd shared his war experiences . . . everyone else he just tolerated.

The walk back to the garage felt good. She'd had several drinks at the party and was worried about staying awake long enough to finish the reports, but the cold ocean breeze cleared her head. It was odd but she seemed to recover more quickly from whiskey than wine, and Jack Daniel's didn't seem to cloud her thinking as much as cabernet. When she worked at the magazine, she and her ex-boyfriend would finish a bottle of wine between them almost every night. It usually took half the next day and a gallon of coffee before she was fit to work. I'll have to thank Kate for changing my drinking habits, she thought, laughing to herself as she reached the side door of her apartment.

Josie turned on the porch light and when she pushed open the door, glanced down at the reflection off a small gold cross and chain on the concrete step. The jewelry didn't belong to her and she doubted it was Jones's or Emily's. They were the only other people except her burglar that she was aware of who'd been around the apartment recently. Emily was an atheist and the chain was too delicate for a man. Besides she was pretty certain it hadn't been there this morning. She picked it up and saw the clasp had been damaged and wouldn't close. The cross was lovely, brushed gold with a tiny piece of glass in the center that could've been a diamond. She took it inside and put it on the bookshelf thinking if it was valuable someone would eventually come to claim it.

She made a pot of coffee, removed the typewriter from under her bed platform, and checked to be certain the blinds were closed and the deadbolt was engaged. The reports were finished in less than two hours. She wrote the first one about Manny's meeting at the Salazar Center and surprised herself that without notes she could recall not only the entire agenda but the names of more than fifty people who had been there. The report for the party at Larry Clarke's house was much shorter with fewer people attending and less happening. Again she left out any details of Burt's assault, making only a vague reference to a disturbance in the bedroom between the lawyer and movie star Sandra Collins. She did note that Jones had intervened and "physically controlled Burt Rice," then said out loud, "That's a euphemism for beat the crap out of the miserable bastard."

At four A.M. she got to sleep, but kept the reports and the revolver in her purse near the bed. The alarm woke her at seven and she took a quick shower, dressed, and was on her way to Redondo Beach thirty minutes later. The VW was running fine this morning. She suspected Murphy had gotten the Shadow to work on it when she'd gone out so he didn't have to hear her complain constantly about not having enough money for repairs. She didn't know the Shadow's real name but heard he was a sergeant in the PDID office who was a jack-of-all-trades and something of a legend in the stealth world. He had a closet full of disguises and could sneak into any place, fix anything, and had sources for every odd piece of equipment they needed that the city wouldn't purchase. He was at every major demonstration and got great surveillance photos, but no one ever saw or recognized him. The Shadow reported directly to the captain and no one seemed to know when he worked or who was responsible for him. Josie didn't care. Her car was running again.

She parked in the public garage and had to walk a short distance to the end of the pier. There wasn't any name outside to identify the bar, just the address, which could help explain the lack of any new business. The marine layer hadn't cleared and Josie could feel the dampness in her hair and on her face. She took a deep breath and inhaled the strong odor of kelp and salt water mixed with the aroma of fried fish and chips from the only food stand open this early. The pier was deserted and quiet except for the sound of barking seals and hungry seagulls crowded close to the docks where restaurants and fishermen dumped scraps of food and fish guts. She liked the solitude, being there alone in this place in the early morning fog away from the underbelly of Venice Beach. For a few minutes life was clean and simple.

Murphy was waiting inside, sitting on a barstool having a breakfast beer with a mountain of a black man behind the bar. The man was taller than Murphy, had a full Afro, a bushy beard, and tattoos covering both massive arms. He was dressed in a worn green T-shirt and camouflage pants and stared at Josie until she sat at the bar. She stuck out her hand and introduced herself, and he did the same.

They ordered breakfast and moved to one of the booths across from the bar. She gave Murphy the reports and waited for him to start the conversation. After a few minutes of silence, she said, "Thanks for getting my car fixed."

"No problem," he said, finishing the beer.

His expression hardened as he stared over her shoulder. Josie turned to see Detective Carlson come into the bar and walk toward their booth. She sat beside Murphy and looked unhappy.

"We aren't making much progress, are we?" Carlson asked, not bothering with any sort of greeting or other nicety. She had an accusatory smirk and was looking at Josie.

"I don't agree. I think I'm doing an amazing job of show-ing how fucked-up Soriano and his supervisors have been," Josie said as sweetly as she could.

"Your job is to find him."

"Finding him might be a hell of a lot easier if I had some clue why he disappeared," Josie said, and then waited while the bartender put a plate in front of her and refilled the coffee.

"I'm gonna do something we've never done," Murphy said, chewing on a bite of toast. "I'm not sure it's right or smart, but we've got to locate this guy."

Josie stopped eating the eggs and sat back.

"What?" she asked, uncertain she really wanted the answer to that question. She could see in Carlson's expres-sion that whatever Murphy was about to say, she didn't agree.

"I'm gonna introduce you to another UC. He's got more time undercover than you and he wants to come out too. You can work together until you find Soriano."

"Who is it?" Josie asked.

"This is not a sound idea," Carlson said before he could answer.

"You got a better one?" Murphy asked. "Soriano's your problem, but if you don't find him soon, it could bring down the whole intelligence division. It's pretty clear Pastore can't do it alone."

Carlson didn't respond. Her face flushed and she was obviously upset, but she folded her arms and was quiet.

"He'll be here in a few minutes," Murphy said.

Josie didn't say anything either. He was right. She needed a partner but wondered who it was going to be.

"Do I know him?" she finally asked.

"Yes," Murphy said, sliding out of the booth. He went to the bar, poured another dark beer from the tap, and began a conversation with the bartender.

"Too many things can go wrong when UCs know each other," Carlson said, shaking her head and looking down at the table.

Josie finished her breakfast. She wasn't really interested in what Carlson thought and was concentrating, trying to figure out who the UC might be. It was a man, but she'd met hundreds of men since going undercover. Carlson mumbled something she couldn't quite hear.

"What?" she asked.

"I said Soriano's supervisors did know he was working at the DA's office," Carlson said a little louder. "He told them he had to be there to get details on something big."

"And did he?"

"He'd overheard threats."

"Heard what from who?" Josie asked, annoyed that this woman still insisted on giving her piecemeal information.

"Quentin Barnes."

Carlson was still talking but Josie had stopped listening. She watched as Murphy got up from the barstool and went outside. Her view from the window was blocked by a wooden storage shed that had been set against the front of the building, so she stared intently at the door waiting for Murphy and her new partner to come back inside. When someone tapped her on the shoulder, she stood and turned awkwardly, pulling the tight muscles in her neck and shoulders.

They'd come in the back way and were standing behind her.

"No fucking way," she whispered, rubbing her neck.

"Sorry, didn't mean to startle you," Charlie Jones said.

SEVEN

It took awhile for Josie to reconcile the idea of Jones being a cop with everything she'd heard and known about him. He had the reputation as a disgruntled Vietnam vet who'd taught activists how to fight against the war and protect themselves from the police. He'd been to Cuba with the Venceremos Brigade, and Emily told her he'd helped smuggle guns to revolutionaries in Central America. His arrest record was impressive, much worse than hers, and rumors about his lawless adventures were endless.

She and Jones sat across the table from each other, avoiding eye contact while Murphy explained how he wanted their joint venture to work. Josie felt uneasy and not certain how to relate to someone she had always known as "one of the bad guys."

"You need to watch each other's backs because no one really understands what we're dealing with here. Internal Affairs is looking at Soriano's supervisors. They knew their UC was in over his head and they left him out there," Murphy said. "I won't do that."

"I don't get it," Jones said. "His supervisors only knew what Soriano was telling them. How can anybody blame them?"

"They not only knew Soriano was working in the DA's office but they were aware Quentin Barnes and maybe others had threatened him," Carlson said. She seemed to be focused and her brusque self again.

"But didn't Quentin threaten him because Soriano was sleeping with Kate . . . wasn't that the reason?" Josie asked.

"No," Murphy said before Carlson could answer. "From what we can find out, Soriano uncovered something involving Quentin that sent him into hiding . . . from him and us."

Jones exchanged a quick look with Josie and then asked, "So are you saying there was someone in the police department or PDID he didn't trust?"

"I don't have a fucking clue, Charlie. All I know is he was supposed to meet with his supervisors last Friday night to give them, in his words, 'a bombshell,' but he never showed. Nobody's seen or heard from him since," Murphy said. He closed his eyes and rubbed his temples for a few seconds before sitting back and adding, "The old man says he's gonna make a statement to the press next week about Soriano being missing if we don't come up with him or his whereabouts by then."

"But what if he's still working for us and just can't make contact," Josie said. "Outing him that soon without knowing for sure one way or the other is really dangerous."

"You think I don't fucking know that, Pastore. He's the chief; he gets to make that call and he won't wait, so find the sonofabitch before next week."

It took nearly an hour, but Murphy assured her and Jones that he and Carlson had now disclosed every detail they knew about Soriano. The two UCs left their supervisors in the bar and walked silently together to the end of the pier.

By late morning, dozens of fishermen had positioned themselves along the railing with their lines cast every few yards. They were surrounded by buckets of bait and an assortment of plastic coolers filled with ice ready for the morning's catch. Pelicans had also staked out their territory on rooftops waiting for either the careless toss of a fresh mackerel that missed the cooler or easier pickings in an unwatched bait bucket.

As they leaned against the railing watching the rolling waves splash against the concrete piles, Josie tried to organize all the questions running through her head but was surprised how difficult it was to talk to Jones when she didn't have to lie.

"I knew there was something wrong about you," he said, breaking the silence.

"What do you mean?"

"You always seemed too smart to be hanging out with Emily and those nut jobs at WLM."

"Thanks," she said, not ready to admit she'd actually liked Emily. "I completely believed everything I heard about you . . . never would've suspected you were a cop."

"It's not all bogus," he said and smiled at what was probably her confused expression. "You can't fake some of this stuff. You just gotta dig deep enough inside to get where guys like Quentin live."

Josie nodded in agreement but realized he'd given this undercover assignment a lot more thought than she had. She was good at her job, not really understanding why, but it was true most people, even Manny Contreras, had needs and desires. Tapping into them was the secret to a UC's success.

"So what's our game plan?" she asked.

"We've got a couple days before the chief blows Dave's cover. If he's dead, it won't matter. If not . . ."

"There's a chance he will be when they find out he's a cop," she said, finishing his sentence and adding, "Quentin's our key."

"And the best way to him is probably through Kate. Unfortunately she hates my guts."

"Why is that?"

"She thinks I'm the one that told Quentin she was cheating on him."

"Were you?"

"Yep, always willing to do my part to keep things unsettled . . . if you make them worry about the small shit, there's no time to plan chaos."

"Emily said you fought with Soriano. Is that true?"

"Uh huh, the guy's a knucklehead."

"Did you know he was a cop before all this?"

"I kind of wondered if he might be first time I met him, but didn't know for sure."

"How . . . I mean did Brickhouse say something?" she asked.

"No, I thought it was pretty obvious for lots of reasons I can't explain, but he was so squirrelly nobody else ever suspected him."

"What did you fight about?"

"He was taking too many chances . . . letting Quentin drag him around by the nose. He told me to mind my own business, so I told Quentin he was screwing Kate."

"Aren't you afraid Quentin might've done something to him?" she asked, thinking men do kill each other over women.

Jones shook his head and said, "Quentin's a weasel and talks a lot but he hasn't got the balls to kill."

Josie didn't argue because she didn't know Quentin as well as he did, but she had a suspicion even weasels would kill if they were lunatics or pressed hard enough.

THEY DECIDED to go to O'Farrell's that night so Josie could try talking to Kate again, maybe push her a little bit more. She was late for work at the thrift shop and arranged to meet him at her apartment a few hours after she finished her shift.

"Take this," she said as he started to leave, tossing him the spare key to the garage. "It's my apartment; if you still need a place to stay, you're welcome to share it until you find something else. I picked up an old army cot in the alley; you can use that."

"Thanks," he said, after staring at the key for a few seconds. "I'll get my bag from Quentin's place . . . promise to get out of your hair as quick as I can."

"You're welcome," she said, but he was already walking away.

JOSIE FINISHED her shift, working a little extra to make up for being late, and Mother Mary Margaret, who ran the shop, gave her forty dollars for two days work before she left. She would put most of it toward the rent and use the rest to buy bread, milk, and a few other staples at the little market on the corner of her street.

There was enough time before Jones arrived to put away the groceries and drag the cot out from behind the garage where she'd stored it. She dusted off the spider webs and layer of dirt with a whisk broom, and covered the cot with a clean blanket and her extra sheet. She only had one pillow so he'd have to improvise.

After arranging the cot a couple of ways, she decided it fit best in the corner under the window. When it was finally in place, she sat on her bed and looked around. The space was a little more crowded but it would work if he stored his bag under the cot.

She was weary from the busy morning and stretched out on her bed to rest a few minutes. She shook her head thinking that under normal circumstances she'd never allow a man she hardly knew—even a cop—move in with her, but this period of her life was anything but normal. In a lot of ways it reminded her of the six months she'd spent traveling in Europe after college when she lived in hostels, sharing things that had no permanent value with strangers who entered her life and disappeared without expectations. Life was like that now. Nothing was permanent or familiar. Jones would be her partner. They would work together and sleep under the same roof until they found the missing cop . . . nothing more. "Hmmm," she said out loud and rolled over onto her side.

"Josie."

The sound of her name and a gentle shake of her shoulder woke Josie from a sound sleep. She opened her eyes and sat up quickly. Jones was standing in front of her with his duffle bag over his shoulder.

"What time is it?" she asked attempting to break through the grid of cobwebs in her head.

"Six, I knocked but you didn't answer so I used the key . . . sorry, didn't mean to scare you again."

Her hands and feet felt like ice cubes. She wrapped herself in the blanket and tried to get warm enough to bring some feeling back to her limbs.

"Not scared, frozen. It's so cold in here. Can you plug that in?" she asked pointing at the floor heater.

He did and asked, "Would hot coffee help?"

She nodded and watched as he put his bag on the cot and opened it. He began pulling items out including a small coffee grinder and bag of coffee beans, arranging everything neatly on the counter near the sink. While the coffee was brewing, he put his clothes into the two dresser drawers she pointed out had been emptied for him, then he stuffed his bag under the cot.

The aroma of fresh ground coffee filled the garage and by the time he brought her the steaming mug she was aching to taste it. She worked her hand out of the blanket cocoon, took the cup, and drank as quickly as she could.

"This is wonderful," she said, letting the blanket fall back on the bed. The combination of heater and coffee had begun to defrost her body.

"We need a cover story for why I'm here," he said, pulling a chair over to sit closer to her with his mug of coffee.

"We've become friends. You needed a place to stay. Let their imaginations fill in the rest."

"Good enough. You ready to go?" he asked.

They finished their drinks and Josie splashed some water on her face and combed her hair in the closet-sized bathroom designed by a Rube Goldberg wannabe—with a large drain in the middle and tile everywhere including the ceiling. The shower, sink, and toilet were in such close proximity that all of them could be used at the same time without moving her feet and when she took a shower the entire room got drenched. She warned Jones to leave his towel and clothes on the hook outside the bathroom curtain when he used it.

"That's okay," he said, examining the tiny room. "I run every morning. I'll probably just shower at the beach or the gym."

"Lucky you."

"You could come with me."

"No thanks," she said, wondering why cops had such an attraction to running. During the police academy, she hated those daily treks through Elysian Park and donated her Nike running shoes to Goodwill as soon as she'd graduated.

"If you don't jog, how do you stay in shape?" he asked when they had nearly reached the bike path.

"Alcohol," she said joking.

He didn't seem amused and said, "Quentin will probably be there. Kate won't want me around so I'll take Quentin aside to talk about the demo tomorrow. That will give you some time alone with her."

THEY ARRIVED at O'Farrell's just as Kate was finishing her first performance. The handful of patrons gave her polite applause, but from the few minutes Josie heard, she figured the singer's voice wasn't working well. The raspy hoarseness that had enhanced her songs and made them so special the last time had deteriorated into a throaty off-key sound.

Quentin stood and motioned them toward his table as soon as he spotted Jones.

"Hey CJ, you and your lady come sit with me," he shouted, reaching behind him for another chair. "Jackie, right?" he asked, sliding it over for her. His glassy eyes and slurred speech told her he'd gotten his share of whatever Kate had taken.

"Josie," she said, sitting across the table from him.

"Isn't she something?" Quentin asked, frowning and pointing at Kate with both hands as she walked unsteadily toward them. His sarcastic tone made Josie think maybe life with Kate wasn't all he had imagined or hoped it might be.

"Wonderful," Josie said as Kate held on to the table and leaned over to hug her.

"Hi, Emily's friend," Kate said.

Josie was surprised the woman remembered her at all since she was so stoned and drunk every time they got together. She could smell the whiskey and cigars on her breath and the stale odor of dried perspiration on her costume. It was the same outfit she had on the last time, and Josie suspected it rarely got cleaned.

Jones ordered a round of drinks, whiskey for everyone. They drank and talked for about half an hour before he convinced Quentin they needed to go somewhere quiet to discuss the next day's security plan. Kate nodded off a few times but she seemed a little more alert than she'd been the night Josie had met her.

"How are you doing?" Josie asked as soon as the two women were alone.

"I'm good," Kate said, squinting in the smoke-filled bar. "Where's Emily?"

"She's not here. Have you had any news about Dave?"

"Nope," she said, trying to get another drop out of an empty glass.

Josie went to the bar and ordered two more drinks. Walking back to the table, she looked around the room and saw Jones and Quentin standing in an alcove near the back door talking. She put the whiskey in front of Kate and sat next to her.

"Where's Soriano, Kate?"

"Gone."

"Where?"

"Who knows," Kate mumbled, snorting as she sipped the drink with her eyes closed.

"Quentin knows," Josie said, trying to sound as if she actually had proof that was true. "You need to tell me."

Kate put her glass down and scooted her chair closer to Josie. "Quentin says not to worry . . . he's safe."

"Is Quentin hiding him?"

"Shhh . . ." she whispered, holding her index finger to her lips. "Can't tell." She leaned even closer until her shoulder was rubbing against Josie's. "He's taking me there."

"I don't understand. Where is he taking you?" she asked, catching a glimpse of Quentin and Jones moving quickly back in the direction of the table.

"You'll see," Kate said, her head nodding forward.

"Kate," Josie said sharply and loud enough in her ear for the woman's eyes to pop open again. "Where are you going?"

"The desert," she whispered with her hand covering her mouth.

"What are you girls cackling about?" Quentin asked, sliding over Kate's chair so roughly she almost fell off and moving another one so he could sit between the two women. He stared at Kate's face for several seconds as if he were searching for something. From his cold emotionless expression, Josie couldn't tell if it was anger or disgust, maybe both.

"Gotta get ready," Kate said, grunting and getting up slowly. "Time to sing for my supper."

She walked unsteadily past the stage, pushing through the sparse crowd and into the restroom.

Quentin looked at Jones and shook his head. "Fucking junkie can't piss without taking another hit . . . should've thrown her fucking ass out on the street and let you stay," he said, sounding almost sober before he got up and went to the bar.

"What an asshole," Jones said as soon as he and Josie were alone. "Did she have a chance to tell you anything?"

"I think she said Quentin's taking her to the desert . . . maybe to Soriano . . . but then she's high as a kite so who knows what the hell she's talking about."

"Okay, we'll tell Murphy and maybe he can put a tail on Quentin or get CCS to do it."

"What's a CCS?" she asked. She'd gone undercover so early in her career there was a lot about the LAPD she didn't know.

"Criminal Conspiracy Section, sometimes they work with PDID. Let's get out of here. I've had about enough Quentin Barnes for one night."

They walked from the bar along the bike path to Josie's regular phone booth where she called Murphy and told him about her conversation with Kate. The sergeant agreed that a surveillance team should watch Quentin. Normally it would take a day or two to get them authorized and on the road. But he assured them that for a missing cop, the chief would tell everyone to drop what they were doing and make it happen.

On the way back to the apartment, Josie stopped and looked behind them at the empty sidewalk and street. She had that feeling again someone was watching her.

"What's the matter?" Jones asked, turning and staring into the empty darkness.

"Nothing . . . thought I heard footsteps."

When they reached the garage, he had his key out and opened the side door. Josie started to go inside but saw something shiny on the step. She picked up a pendant; it was a cameo of a young girl's face set on what looked like agate and framed by gold filigree. At first she was confused and then angry at what someone obviously thought was clever, but was becoming annoying.

"What's that?" Jones asked, turning on the lights inside.

"I think I've got an admirer . . . stalker. Whatever it is I don't like it."

He took the cameo from her hands and examined both sides.

"This is old; the stone's chipped, and it's got initials on the back. There's sand stuck in the gold . . . see," he said, showing her as he brushed a few grains off the back. "I think somebody must've picked it up on the beach."

She took the gold cross and chain off the shelf and gave it to him.

"This was on my doorstep yesterday."

"Either somebody has you confused with the lost and found or you have a very strange admirer," he said, putting everything back on the shelf.

"On my next shift, it's all going to the thrift shop," she said, turning on the heater. The room had turned icy cold again in the short time they'd been gone. She kept on her coat and searched the cupboard over the sink for a bottle of Rémy Martin she'd stashed in there. Expensive cognac wasn't practical on her budget but it was the best way she'd found to cut through the chill on a winter night in a place without insulation. "Want some?"

He did and she poured a little into two ancient brandy snifters she'd bought for a dollar at a yard sale next door. They sat at the table as close as they could get to the heater, drank brandy, and talked until it got warm enough to take off their jackets and go to bed. She had prided herself on developing skills for extracting information from people, but Jones remained guarded about his personal life. He did say he had a brother and mother who lived in Texas and that was his escape location when his undercover assignment became too intense or he needed a few days by himself. The trip to

Cuba did happen, but she was surprised to learn he'd gone there with Quentin and Sandra Collins, the movie star who'd been assaulted by Burt Rice.

Although Josie hadn't known him long, she wanted to believe she could trust him and didn't hesitate to talk about her family or what was left of it. She had a brother who was a cop too, but her mom, dad, and older sister were all gone. She told him about her ex-boyfriend who'd abandoned her as soon as she joined the police department.

"He said he didn't want to live with a woman who carried a gun and wanted to do such a depressing job."

"I think there's something sexy about a woman with a gun who knows how to use it," Jones said, grinning. "I'm going to bed."

He took off his coat and emerged from the bathroom a few minutes later, wearing shorts and a T-shirt. She slept in sweatpants and a baggy pullover sweater. Not glamorous, but warm, she thought. She was tired but couldn't drift off for a while. His gentle snoring was so close it reminded her how long it had been since a man had shared her bed, and she had to admit how much she missed the sweaty, wonderful intimacy of sex, the security of falling asleep in her lover's arms. She had to force herself to think about something else or knew she'd be awake and miserable all night.

They were up at dawn. Jones woke first and the smell of scrambled eggs and coffee brought her back to consciousness. While he went for his run, she cleaned the kitchen, showered, and was ready to go by the time he got back. He'd showered at the gym and as soon as he changed his clothes, they left. This time it was his MG that wouldn't start but thanks to the Shadow's mechanical handiwork, she was able to get them downtown in the Volkswagen.

They arrived early in front of the Grand Central Market on Broadway, but Manny Contreras and several of the WLM people were already there and had stacks of posters attached to thick sticks waiting on the sidewalk. Manny's bodyguard, Alex, didn't approach Jones but glared at him from a distance.

Josie had learned to be patient in waiting for any demonstration to get organized and the march to start moving. The stated beginning time was always just an estimate. There was a joke among liberal groups about "leftist time"—just add half an hour and that's what you actually meant.

About an hour later, the Coalition to Fight Police Abuse was out in full force with some fifty demonstrators wearing matching T-shirts, huddled around their own mound of placards. The committees for or against a dozen or more different causes had their contingents with signs demanding everything from gay love and equal justice to an end to the war and protestations against poverty, the coming nuclear winter, and starvation throughout the world. She watched as Jones tried to settle a dispute between one of the outspoken Young Socialists and a Hispanic lawyer. He was calm and rational and managed to make both parties back down enough to prevent any serious confrontation.

Jones mostly ignored the marginally stable loners who'd begun to infiltrate the crowd. These fringe protesters had an assortment of grievances only they understood. General Hersheybar was in his Halloween costume military jacket decorated with phony patches, medals, and plastic airplane epaulettes attached with heavy black Velcro and even bigger planes glued around the brim of his military hat. He was distributing newspapers with fake headlines about Richard Nixon. Josie also spotted a man she'd seen at a number of demonstrations who always wore a green camouflage bag over his head and a rope with a hangman's noose wrapped around his shoulders, but never explained what message he was trying to convey. There was a simple explanation for Tiny Tina's appearance. She was a pretty dwarf stripper, an exhibitionist, who liked to dance in front of crowds. Josie thought her skimpy costume and suggestive gyrations always brought an uncomfortable mix of levity and sadness to any event.

Long hair, Afros, patched-up military shirts, and shabby Levis were the dress code for the day. Josie always wore Levis and was grateful for her long, naturally out-of-control hair that gave her a ready-made rebellious appearance. Jones had tied a red band around her left upper arm. It was identical to his so the other marchers could identify her as security. In a rough count, she estimated that nearly two hundred people were milling around ready to participate in the march . . . although some of them might've been early shoppers who'd wandered out of the Central Market just to gawk at the protesters.

WLM had at least forty members there, but Josie hadn't seen Emily yet. Manny was in the street testing his bullhorn and shouting orders to mostly indifferent participants. Josie knew the majority of these people didn't want or believe in leaders. They made their decisions by consensus and frequently the outcome resembled Medusa on a bad hair day.

The marchers were starting to move eastbound when Josie finally noticed Emily and Quentin standing across the street with the bodyguard Alex. It was an odd scene. Emily was pointing her finger at Quentin and appeared to be scolding him like a child. Quentin let her finish, then stomped away as if he were very angry but wasn't going to argue with her. Alex followed him without saying a word, but he had a noticeable smile and, behind Quentin's back, winked at Emily.

Josie pushed through the wall of demonstrators and got to Emily just as she was starting to walk away.

"Hey, Em, you all right?" she asked, touching Emily's arm. The other woman's face was flushed and for a moment a hint of anger and confusion flashed in her eyes before she realized it was Josie.

"Hi, yes, of course," she said, her expression softening. "Guess I'm a little hyper, but I'm liking this adrenaline rush. Where have you been?"

"With Charlie, where have you been?"

"Wishing I was with you," Emily said, tugging at the red band on her arm. "Quentin's such a jerk. I don't see why Kate stays with him."

Josie wanted to say Kate stayed with Quentin because she was an addict who'd go anywhere with anyone who could score a hit of smack and obviously he was a guy who could do that for her, but instead she said, "Who knows."

"I gotta go. I'm supposed to stay near the front. See you later," Emily said, giving her a nervous kiss on the cheek then disappearing quickly into the crowd of noisy marchers.

The demonstrators moved slowly, erratically, like an unattended herd of cattle across Broadway away from the market on Fifth Street toward Parker Center, the police administration building. They chanted out of sync with Manny, but mostly they talked, laughed, and passed around joints as they walked. Some drank beer wrapped in paper bags, a red flag to the skid row population. It was late morning; the homeless were up, moving around, and thirsty but their broken cardboard boxes, shopping carts, blankets, and other debris still cluttered the sidewalks putting obstacles on the route.

Josie tried to stay on the periphery with Jones and his other security people, but that meant walking closer to the commercial buildings and filthy doorways reeking of human waste and early morning vomit. She wrapped the end of her scarf around her nose and mouth to act as a filter until she had passed Main and turned the corner onto Los Angeles Street. It wasn't much better there but at least the air was tolerable. As a rule, the police department kept the bulk of the transient population south of Fifth Avenue and away from the more upscale civic center, but the biggest homeless shelter was a block from where they'd made their turn. On the weekends the heart of LA became a virtual ghost town and since there was no one to complain, most footbeat cops let the bums roam freely until Monday morning.

It was a dreary day and the mood of the marchers was changing to match the weather as they realized the homeless and hordes of police were the only ones standing around paying any attention to them. Josie saw scores of uniformed officers along the route, some standing on the sidewalk, others in the alleys and on rooftops. Murphy and Carlson were waiting on the corner of Third Street in front of a Japanese restaurant with a dozen other plainclothes officers. Little Tokyo took up the block between Third and Second Streets and a block east. Josie could smell the familiar odors of fried fish, soy sauce, and tempura mixed with the more pungent smell of boiled cabbage from the only Korean place inside the mall. Little Tokyo was one of her favorite places to eat downtown and she could almost taste those little custard pastry tarts from the bakery around the corner.

The dirty-grey stone, Italian-styled steeple of Saint Vibiana's Cathedral had just come into Josie's view as she approached the block where the New Otani hotel and garden were located. She stopped and stepped up onto a retaining wall and could see Manny at the head of the march about a half block from Parker Center. The marchers were mostly on the sidewalk but the police were allowing them to spill over onto the street. Josie guessed it was a concession to shorten the time it took to clear streets and let traffic flow more freely, although, this morning traffic consisted primarily of black-and-white police cars.

She had just crossed First Street and saw squads of uniformed police officers in the southern parking lot of the administration building. Murphy and the other PDID officers had moved and were standing with the officers on the other side of a chain-link fence. Josie noticed there was one television cameraman in the street taking pictures and a few photographers and reporters walking among the demonstrators. If a skirmish broke out today, there would be several members of the media in a position to document every blow.

The comforting thought that they had reached Parker Center without incident was passing through her mind when it happened. At first it sounded like backfire from a car and then she worried it might've been gunshots. Josie had never heard live fire off the shooting range or without ear protection and didn't really know how it sounded. The bullhorn went silent and worried whispers washed over the crowd before marchers began shouting, a few screaming before dispersing in every direction, at first slowly and then running in a panic. Some tried to go back in the direction they'd come, pushing and nearly knocking her down while others ran across the street or north toward the Hollywood Freeway. The media people immediately sprinted with their equipment toward Parker Center.

Manny tried to restore some order by shouting high-pitched confusing commands for everyone to remain calm, run for cover, and then not to run. After a few minutes, when the police sirens drowned him out and there were only a dozen or so marchers remaining in the area, most of them his WLM members, he gave up, but Josie could see he was fuming. He shook his fist at a captain and the lieutenant from Press Relations who had come out of Parker Center to talk to him, and he accused the riot police of shooting at the demonstrators.

Before he could finish his tirade, several fire trucks and a paramedic unit with sirens blaring pulled up in front of the Federal Building across the street just north of the police headquarters. Firefighters ran up the stairs and into the building. Several squads of uniformed police officers ran across the street to join them and Josie saw Murphy and Carlson in the middle of a sea of blue.

"I'm sorry sir, but you'll have to vacate the street immediately. We have an emergency. This march is over," the young captain said to Manny without emotion, but it was clear his order was not open to discussion.

Manny started to argue anyway, but Burt Rice grabbed his arm and pulled him aside. Josie was surprised to see the lawyer. She hadn't noticed him when the march started and Emily, who was nowhere in sight at the moment, hadn't mentioned he'd be there. Josie moved closer with one or two others from WLM so she could hear what Burt was telling Manny.

"You need to do what he says. I'll explain later," Burt said in a panicky whisper, sweat running down his face. "Trust me; you don't want to be anywhere near this place when they come out of that building."

EIGHT

After the confusion and disruption caused by the loud blasts and panicked protesters, the few remaining WLM members had gathered around Manny for guidance, but at Burt's urging everyone followed the lawyer back to the Grand Central Market to the same corner where the march had begun. Burt was pale and seemed tense and distracted as he walked. He didn't respond when Josie asked where Emily was. She repeated her question but still didn't get an answer.

Josie had lost sight of Jones too but hoped he'd eventually work his way back toward the market. She was pretty certain now what she'd heard were explosions and knew she'd feel a lot more comfortable as soon as she saw her partner was still in one piece.

When they got back inside the market, it was late morning and all the stalls were open and crowded. Noisy shoppers spilled out onto the sidewalks carrying bags or pulling carts filled with produce, meat, or an assortment of cheaply made tourist bait, aka souvenirs. She gingerly stepped onto the concrete floors covered with a mix of sawdust and discarded scraps of vegetables and other garbage as she followed Burt, Alex, Manny, and the others to an empty space behind one of the stalls where a row of poorly plucked dead chickens hung by their feet dripping blood into a wooden trough covered with caked blood, feathers, and bird shit.

The small group was hidden from the view of shoppers by a wall of stacked wire crates filled with frantic live chickens cruelly positioned to watch their inevitable fate.

"What the fuck just happened out there?" Manny asked, having a difficult time catching his breath. The brisk walk from Parker Center had exhausted the unhealthy man. His skin had a sickly yellow tinge and he was sweating profusely on a cold day. He coughed several times, trying to clear the thick congestion in his lungs.

Burt took two of the sturdier empty crates from among those stacked against the wall, gave one to Manny to sit on and he used the other one. Manny was obviously sick, but Burt's hedonistic lifestyle had left him flabby, out of condition and unable to catch his breath long enough to speak. His pudgy face was flushed and he used a handkerchief to wipe away endless drops of sweat. Everyone else including Josie just stood around patiently waiting for his explanation. No one had asked her to leave so she intended to stay and test her new status in the group.

"We've struck the first blow," Burt finally said with that stupid grin he got when he thought he was being clever.

"We who?" Manny demanded, not hiding his displeasure.

"Us, you, me, WLM. I told you this march would be remembered."

"Make fucking sense," Manny said, shifting his weight on the uncomfortable crate. "I didn't tell nobody to do nothing."

Burt looked around at the circle. It was just a blink but Josie saw the hesitation. The lawyer was having second thoughts about being candid. It might've been her or someone else in the group, but he wasn't going to say more.

"Not now," Burt said, glancing at Alex who helped him get Manny on his feet. "If you can walk, we need to get as far as we can from downtown."

Josie let them leave without her. She lagged behind, pretending to be preoccupied with the dead chickens and a table covered with miniature piñatas. No one seemed to notice or care that she hadn't followed them out of the market. She needed to locate Jones and find out what had happened in the Federal Building. Getting information from Burt wasn't going to happen and she doubted that even if they trusted her they'd be inclined to reveal much. They were infatuated with intrigue and conspiracies. This event was most likely a bigger deal than the usual Molotov cocktail but she was certain in their minds it would become the equivalent of bombing Pearl Harbor.

There was a hamburger stand near the front of the market where she ordered fries and a beer and sat at a high table on a stool facing the street. It took less than twenty minutes before she spotted Jones standing on the southeast corner of Broadway and Fifth with Quentin and Emily, waiting for the signal to change. They were talking and hadn't seen her yet. Emily put her arm around Jones's shoulder and whispered something in his ear; he smiled at her. It was a quick but intimate moment, and Josie knew immediately these two were a lot closer than Charlie Jones had ever admitted. When they reached the middle of the street, Emily spotted her and waved, and they came directly to her table.

"What happened to you?" Quentin asked accusingly, and sat next to her.

She explained and added, "Manny just left with Burt and Alex. He seemed pretty upset." She was watching Emily's face for some reaction, but there wasn't any. "What happened at the Federal Building?" she asked, looking at Jones. He didn't answer but turned to Quentin.

"Somebody left a pipe bomb in there and put another one under a pig car parked on Temple," Quentin said, grinning.

"Anybody hurt?" she asked.

Quentin shrugged, but Jones shook his head and said, "No, don't think so. The ambulance went away empty."

"Did WLM do it? Is that what Burt meant?" she asked and saw Emily's expression turn dark.

"What did he say?" Emily demanded, more focused than usual.

"That WLM was responsible," Josie lied, although, it could've been a reasonable interpretation of what he didn't say.

"Fucking moron," Emily mumbled, staring at Jones as if she were finally upset enough to deal with her less than perfect husband. Josie recalled how Jones had warned her about Emily. Her facade of simple innocence had eroded a bit this morning; her voice was strident with a nastiness that seemed too comfortable to be newly acquired. Josie had to keep herself from smiling because she was thinking maybe Emily and Burt did deserve each other after all.

They talked a few more minutes before Emily got up abruptly, gave Josie a one-arm hug, and walked away. Quentin followed without a word, leaving Josie and Jones alone at the table.

"So who planted the pipe bombs?" she asked, watching them cross the street to the parking lot.

"They won't admit it, but I'm pretty certain Emily put the one inside and Alex shoved the other one under the black-and-white," Jones said.

"What's so funny?" she asked, noticing that he kept looking at his hands and was having a difficult time trying not to smile.

"Alex must've panicked and didn't secure it so the one under the police car fell off and rolled into the gutter . . . blew up a couple of really big sewer rats . . . the one in the first-floor bathroom of the Federal Building killed a toilet."

"We were lucky nobody got hurt."

"I know," he said. "But it's so typical . . . rats and toilets . . . and they think they've sent a message."

"They just have to get lucky one time and somebody is gonna get hurt or killed."

"There's a chance they'll get prints off pieces of the bombs and with any luck the security cameras were working at the Federal Building, but for now we need to call Murphy and let him know Quentin's leaving town tomorrow night."

"With Kate?" she asked.

He nodded and said, "He just told me his father was driving them to Palm Springs."

"To see Soriano?" she asked, hoping this was the desert trip Kate had mentioned.

"Didn't say, but Murphy needs to have a team follow them. Come on, let's find a phone," he said, finishing the rest of her beer.

They had to walk several blocks west of skid row to locate a functioning phone in a place the bums hadn't used as a toilet. It was inside a Mexican bar but reserved for drinking patrons, so Jones bought them a couple of cheap whiskeys and called Murphy.

"He said CCS would tail him to the desert and stay with him until he gets back," Jones said, sitting beside her at the bar as she'd finished her drink.

"What took so long?" she asked.

"He was a little testy about the pipe bombs . . . thinks one of us should've known it was going to happen."

She pushed away her empty glass and asked, "Did one of us know?"

He stared at her for a moment with those impenetrable blue eyes and said without a hint of emotion, "Of course not."

NINE

Josie didn't sleep well that night. She had a nagging suspicion her new partner knew exactly what was going to happen earlier that day at the Federal Building. That look he gave Emily when they were standing on the street said as much.

Although Jones swore he didn't know, Josie's instincts as well as her reliably sensitive gut warned her he was lying, so she was beginning to wonder who this guy really was . . . a dedicated police officer or a clever double agent. Was he searching for Soriano to return him to the LAPD, or did he and Quentin have other plans for the missing cop? And more importantly, did he just send a department surveillance squad on a wild goose chase to Palm Springs?

Those thoughts bounced around in her head most of the night as she listened in the darkness to his rhythmic snoring from across the room while at the same time wondering why she had allowed him to move into her shabby little sanctuary. By the next morning she had almost talked herself into giving him the benefit of the doubt. Besides, she didn't have any solid proof to back up her suspicions and she believed Murphy was too careful and clever to be fooled by him. It was, after all, just a reaction she'd had to his behavior, but she needed some reassurance.

She waited until Jones went for his morning run then got up, dressed, and walked to the corner to call Murphy.

Although she hadn't explained why, Murphy agreed to meet her in half an hour at his bar in Redondo Beach.

He was sitting on the same barstool talking with the same burly bartender who'd been working the day he put Josie and Jones together. There was an empty bottle of Budweiser in front of him and another nearly full one in his hand.

"Breakfast?" she asked, pointing at the bottle and then sitting on the stool beside him.

"What do you want, Pastore?" he asked, in a strong, annoyed voice.

She convinced him to buy her breakfast hoping he might order food for himself, but her meal came with another cold beer for him. He looked tired, close to exhausted. His day-old beard and wrinkled clothes told her he either hadn't been to bed yet or slept badly.

"I think Charlie knew about those pipe bombs and may have even helped Emily put them there," she said, after eating most of her eggs and toast in silence.

"I think he did too."

Josie sat back and pushed her plate away. "You're okay with him knowing and not warning you?"

"I don't think it was an accident that they didn't do much damage."

"He had something to do with that too?"

Murphy sighed, swallowed the last of his beer and shrugged. "I don't know what he did or didn't do, but I do know those bombs went off and nobody got hurt; no property got seriously damaged, but suddenly the right people are talking to Charlie Jones. He's on the inside."

"Great," she said sarcastically.

"You got a problem with that, Pastore? You said it yourself. These people have to trust you and if they trust Jones then it was worth a few dead rats and an overpriced federal shitter."

"He got lucky. Somebody could've been hurt."

"This high-stakes game too much for you . . . you want out?" Murphy asked too loud, exhaling the stale odor of beer and cigarettes into her face. "Just say the word; I'll take you off the street, put you behind a desk where everything is legal and squeaky clean."

He leaned toward Josie as he spoke and probably expected her to back away, but she didn't. Her older brother always tried to intimidate her that way. Tony was a marine and a tough cop like Murphy, but Josie had learned the hard way if she gave an inch, it meant defeat. She lost a lot of battles when they were kids but her brother knew getting his way wasn't going to be easy, so eventually he must've figured it wasn't worth the trouble and stopped trying to bully her.

"Sergeant Murphy," she said calmly, leaning on her elbow to get even closer to him. "I'm not going anywhere until we find Soriano and we both know it."

"You're a pain in the ass, woman," Murphy said with a grunt.

"Why, because I believe it's better to play by the rules?"

"We all believe that, but sometimes you have to stretch the rules, or the assholes—who by the way don't have rules—will win and life in the big city will suck even more than it does."

"I trust you, but if we do enough stretching pretty soon there aren't any rules and we're making it up as we go."

"You're giving me a headache, Pastore," he said, vigorously scratching his shaved head with both hands.

"Did Angela throw you out again?" she asked, recognizing the signs of him sleeping in his clothes, probably in the dirty storeroom of this no-name bar. His wife regularly locked him out of their house because of his carousing and long hours at work leaving her to take care of their four young sons.

"None of your damned business. Are we done here? I've got to get some sleep," he said, rubbing his bloodshot eyes.

Before she could answer, he was staring over her shoulder with a peculiar expression. She turned and saw Carlson who had entered the bar but was lingering near the door as if she had stepped into the wrong place. She seemed confused for just a moment and then regrouped and joined them.

"Sorry, Jon, I thought we had a meeting this morning," Carlson said.

"We do," he said and quickly added, "Get out of here Pastore. Go earn that paycheck you're stashing away in some big bank account."

She didn't bother to say anything to Carlson who was pretty much ignoring her too, but there was something odd about their behavior. It was Sunday. Except for UCs, who has meetings in a bar on Sunday? Carlson called him Jon, not Sergeant Murphy, and he seemed even more unsettled as soon as he saw her. It didn't take a genius to realize there was something going on between them, but Josie had a difficult time imaging the robust, earthy Murphy ever wooing the rigid, uptight little detective.

JONES WAS back at the apartment by the time she arrived. He had finished his run and showered at the gym.

"I went to see Murphy," she said before he could ask.

He was standing over his bunk digging through a canvas backpack she hadn't seen before and mumbled something but all she heard was, "Okay."

"He thinks you knew about the pipe bombs but didn't report it," she said, sitting on her bed. Murphy didn't exactly say that but she knew it was the truth. He didn't respond, so she kept talking. "If we're going to work together, Charlie, you've got to let me know what's going on or, like most cops, I'm gonna start imagining the worst . . ."

Jones straightened up and tossed the backpack on the bunk.

"Sorry, you're right; I should've told you," he said, finally looking at her. "There were only five of us who knew so I had to let it happen or I'd be burned. They'd never trust me again."

"Emily, Burt, Quentin, you, and who else?" she asked.

"Alex, but I got the Shadow to turn off the cameras and move the bombs at the last minute so they didn't do any real damage."

"You know the Shadow?" she asked.

"Sure he's always around . . . just have to figure out which dumpster or tree he's hiding in."

"What's he look like?"

"Hard to say, it's always different."

"If Emily and Burt were in on it, why didn't Manny know?"

"Burt doesn't trust him anymore. He says Manny's sick. His mind's slipping and he'll probably be dead in a few weeks anyway . . . then WLM in Los Angeles is dead too."

"But yesterday Burt was bragging to Manny and the others that WLM's going to get all the credit for what happened."

"More like take all the blame . . . Quentin's trying to get LAPD's attention away from him and the others. He claims the Federal Building was a test run . . . see how the police would respond. He wants the cops to blame WLM so they leave him alone. That's why Emily was so upset. She and Quentin didn't want Manny to know yet."

"Okay, I get it. You and Murphy let them blow up a toilet and some rats so they'd trust you, now what?" she asked.

"Officially Murphy didn't know anything because there wasn't anything to know," he said, looking intently at her as if waiting for her to agree.

She didn't respond right away but eventually without much enthusiasm said, "Right."

He had the identical expression Murphy had had before the sergeant threatened to pull her out of the field. Jones was clearly saying he was disappointed she didn't seem as committed as he was to playing the game to win.

"Good. You need to pack some winter underwear and a change of heavy socks and clothes. We're leaving in about twenty minutes."

"To go where?"

"Sarge didn't tell you? You must've already left the bar. We're meeting Quentin in Bouquet Canyon when he gets back from Palm Springs. The others won't get there until tomorrow but I want to go tonight and set up."

Jones explained that he, Quentin, and the security team had a spot deep in the canyon in the middle of hundreds of acres of open county land where they frequently set up camp for several days and practiced shooting and other military maneuvers. It was far enough away from civilization that they could shoot hundreds of rounds of ammunition without anyone even knowing they were there. The land had heavy vegetation, streams, and walls of rock that served as a backdrop for their targets absorbing the sound of assault rifles and other weapons.

"They agreed it was okay for me to be there?" she asked, emphasizing the "me."

"This is the camp Manny told you about, but Quentin's the one who actually runs it. Manny wanted you to go and now that you're with me everybody sort of expects it."

"How do they know we're together?" she asked.

"I told them."

"Are Murphy and Carlson okay with me going?" she asked and he nodded. "It's going to be freezing up there. Isn't Bouquet Canyon north of Santa Clarita Valley?"

"Yep, a couple of hours drive from here," he said and smiled. "Quentin saw some Russian documentary and now he's got this romantic notion about surviving in the wild and becoming this superhuman revolutionary soldier."

"So he gets to indulge his fantasy while we freeze our asses off. How does any of this get us closer to finding Soriano before the chief blows his cover?"

"I need to get Quentin away from Kate, his father, and the rest of that West Side crowd . . . he's different when we're out there. I think I can get him to talk to me," he said, holding up a bottle of Christian Brothers Brandy before stuffing it in the backpack.

"Has Soriano ever been to that camp?"

"Couple of times . . . he isn't very good with firearms and isn't all that physically fit. At the time, I didn't know for sure he was a cop but I could never understand why Quentin wanted him there. The guy's a genius but what a klutz. I don't know how he made it through the physical part of the police academy. You could probably take him in a fight."

"Maybe he was smart enough to take care of business without fighting," she said, knowing the comment was intended as a compliment but nonetheless a bit insulting.

"Maybe," Jones said. "But sometimes there's no other way." Now he had a look she'd seen more than once on a policeman's face. She knew it meant, "Do I really have to qualify everything I say around you?"

"Sorry, didn't mean to pounce on you, guess I'm a little sensitive about guys complaining I'm not macho or big enough for police work," she said, not wanting him to think she was just a whiner.

"From everything I've heard you can do the job better than most men. It's never about size; it's always heart, and Murphy's convinced you won't quit," he said, turning to finish his packing.

Josie didn't know why having Murphy's confidence and approval was so important to her, but it was, and Jones would probably never understand how much his offhanded comment had just improved her world.

She dug out an old backpack stored inside her suitcase on the top shelf of the only closet in the garage apartment. She found two pairs of thermal underwear and heavy wool socks in a bottom dresser drawer, then got into her hiking boots and jeans, and zipped her parka over an ugly but warm ski sweater she hadn't remembered keeping after the last thrift shop run. Jones gave her a wool cap that would cover and protect her ears. The revolver fit in the side pocket of her backpack where it could be easily retrieved, and she saw

Jones put what looked like a semiauto holstered gun in his waistband.

Both their cars were unsuitable and unreliable for the long drive north, but they decided to use the VW because it had more storage space. Jones filled most of the backseat with the parts of a large folded tent and their sleeping bags. She didn't ask where he'd been keeping everything because he certainly didn't have it in the cramped apartment, and she could smell that musty odor camping gear got after it had been used and then stored awhile.

"Why do you want to get there before everybody else?" she asked, as he was trying to arrange their backpacks to fit on top of all the camping equipment.

"I don't like surprises. I'll set up the tent, check around the area, and be able see everyone as they drive in."

"Any chance Soriano might show up?"

"Don't know. Quentin's not saying much except he wants to be ready because that big thing that's gonna happen is getting close. Even though he tried to give WLM credit for the bombings, he thinks the police are still watching him twenty-four-seven, bugging his house, so that's partly why we're meeting out there," Jones said, getting into the driver's seat.

"He's paranoid."

"Says he hired a PI and found a bug in his dad's house."

"Is that true?" she asked, thinking there wasn't any logical reason for police to be bugging Anthony Barnes. Quentin didn't live there and his father was a real estate broker now. His subversive writing and HUAC days were well behind him, and even if he were a Communist or Marxist, nowadays who cared.

"It's hard to believe anything Quentin says, but just when you're sure he's full of shit, he comes up with a couple of homemade bombs. We're running out of time and beside Kate, he's our only real connection to Dave."

They didn't talk much during the next couple of hours. With too many people returning from weekend trips, Jones, who was familiar with the route, was forced to concentrate on fighting traffic most of the way to the Santa Clarita Valley. She was quietly struggling with a troublesome, admittedly unfounded, suspicion that trusting this man was going to be one of her more costly mistakes. She normally would've called Murphy or Carlson to confirm what Jones told her and make certain her supervisors were okay with her going to the remote training camp. His flattering, supportive remarks at the apartment had put her off guard and she did something she had rarely done since going undercover—failed to corroborate. Jones was a cop and his word should have been enough, but there was still something inexplicably off about him, an itch she couldn't quite scratch. Besides, he wouldn't be the first operative to change sides, or like Carlson said, "Buy the dogma." She tried to relax and put those thoughts out of her mind, but couldn't.

By the time they got off the main highway and onto the dirt road, Josie had convinced herself all she could do now was be alert. There was no means of communication out here and without him she was practically alone except for her closest, dearest, and most reliable friend, Mr. Smith & Wesson.

It seemed as if they'd driven several miles along an unpaved road, deeper into the heavy vegetation, until finally Jones turned off onto a small clearing where he parked the car. They made two trips to get the tent, camping gear, and sleeping bags through a row of trees down an embankment to a valley blanketed in mud, brown grass, and mostly dead bushes. The open flat area faced steep rocky mountain slopes on two sides with a stream running along the base. Jones told her he was surprised by the amount of water, claiming it was double the normal runoff for that time of year.

Josie's face was stinging from the cold wind as she stepped over patches of muddy slush and ice dotting the ground. In late spring or summer she imagined this location might be lush and beautiful, but today it was not a place she wanted to spend the night.

They found a dry area and had the tent up and secured before sunset. It was big enough for both of them with room to spare. Josie tossed in their sleeping bags and most of the gear, crawled inside, and zipped the tent closed. She used a small foot pump to blow up the mattresses while Jones went off to find wood or anything that might burn for a fire. She wore hiking boots but her toes ached from the cold as she used the pump.

The longer she was inside the tent away from the wind, she could feel her body starting to warm. She arranged the mattresses and the sleeping bags and waited for Jones to return. Her backpack was sitting near her bed where she could easily reach the revolver, but she decided to put the gun in her jacket pocket, not for protection from human predators but from those howling animals, whatever they were, she heard every few minutes.

After almost an hour, she unzipped the tent and went outside. It was colder and barely light enough to see in the moonlight, but there was no sign of Jones. She had a flashlight but wasn't going to traipse around unfamiliar terrain and maybe have to waste ammo on one of those animals that sounded really hungry or really pissed off.

She called out to him, but there was no answer. Keeping the tent in view and within running distance, she walked out a few yards and shouted his name again with the same result. Returning to the tent, she stubbed her toe on something and shined the flashlight on a piece of log that someone had sawed off and left. She thought it would make a perfect table for the propane lantern so she carried it back to the tent, after cleaning off most of the dirt and bugs, and placed it between the two sleeping bags.

Another twenty minutes and still no sign of Jones—her suspicions were growing and she felt foolish for coming to the middle of nowhere with a man she didn't completely trust. Then she saw the tent zipper start to open from the outside. She took off her glove, put her hand in her pocket, and grasped the hard rubber grip of the .38 revolver.

"Don't shoot, it's me," he said, crawling through the small opening. He sat with a loud grunt on the floor of the tent and asked, "Can you help me carry the rest of the firewood from the tree line?" His face was wind burned, rough, red, and dirty, and he looked exhausted. The last place she wanted to go was outside the tent, but agreed to do it for two reasons: First, she was relieved he had returned, and it didn't seem as if anything sinister was about to happen; and second, he looked so miserable she didn't have the heart to refuse.

They followed the lighted path from his flashlight over the muddy field to the place where he had gathered a pile of wood and dragged or carried as much as they could back to the front of the tent where he'd already started a sizable stack. It required several trips but when they finished she thought there had to be enough fuel to last a month. She felt filthy and wondered how many bugs and spiders were crawling all over her body and making nests in her hair.

Jones started the fire a safe distance from the tent and in minutes she'd forgotten about creepy critters and howling animals and was enjoying the warmth and tingly feeling that had returned to her fingers and toes. She was surprised how much of their stockpile had been depleted to make a decent fire. But as they sat together on a blanket as close as they could get to the flames, she didn't care how much work it took to get more wood. She wasn't going to spend a night in this place without a fire.

"This is stupid," she said, when her teeth finally stopped chattering. "There must be a better way to get him to talk than freezing in the middle of nowhere."

"You'll see. Quentin's a different man away from the city. I think he feels safe here and talks too much. Are you warm enough?"

"Getting there," she said, loosening the scarf around her neck and scooting back on the blanket a little. "Do you have any idea who else is coming?"

"Not sure . . . there's a dozen or so regulars. It's Quentin's thing; he invites whoever he wants; some of us are military or into martial arts . . . few gun nuts with impressive firepower."

"What are we supposed to do here?" she asked, trying to see his face in the fractured yellow glow of flames.

"Practice shooting . . . a little karate . . . strategize . . . argue a lotta bullshit politics, drink, smoke grass . . . the usual."

"So basically it's the Salazar Center in a meat freezer with guns."

"Yeah, pretty much."

They sat outside the tent and told stories about Murphy and other supervisors they had worked with, drank a little of his cheap brandy out of the bottle until the fire burned down, and then crawled into the tent and zipped it up for the night. She took her gun out of her pocket and put it under the backpack she intended to use as a pillow, and watched him take the semiauto from his belt and place it on the log between them. As soon as he put out the propane lantern, she bundled up in her sleeping bag, fully dressed except for the boots she'd replaced with two pairs of heavy socks.

Josie was warm enough and physically tired but didn't feel sleepy. She listened to his familiar soft snoring and envied the man's ability to adapt. It was difficult to believe she could've found a bed less comfortable than the one in her garage apartment, but she had, and regardless of her position, some bony part of her body ached.

Sometime during the night she fell asleep and woke to find Jones and his semiauto gone. She could smell the fire mixed with the aroma of coffee and wiggled out of the sleeping bag, pulled on her boots, and stumbled out of the tent.

Chunks of grey charcoal were all that was left of last night's blaze but the air still had that wonderful burned juniper wood smell. Jones was kneeling near a small camping stove set close to the tent and holding a coffee pot and a mug. He poured the steaming dark black liquid and offered it to her. It was too strong but she thought it might be the best coffee she'd ever tasted.

"I've got some warm water in the bucket over there if you want to clean up while I make breakfast," he said.

She finished the coffee and rummaged through her backpack to find a hairbrush. He'd left a bar of soap and one of the hand towels from her bathroom near the bucket. A quick glance at his shaving mirror hanging on the tent pole told her why he'd suggested she clean up. Her face had dark smudges of dirt from last night's wood-gathering trek and when she removed her gloves her hands and arms were filthy. The hairbrush had difficulty going through her thick hair, so she dunked her head in the bucket and washed that too. When she finished, Jones gave her another towel he'd taken from her bathroom. She only had four of these and wondered how many he'd stashed in his backpack.

The reconstituted eggs and instant oatmeal tasted awful, but they were filling and hot. She felt clean, well fed, and ready to face whatever was in store today. By the time she finished washing the breakfast dishes in the stream, the others had begun to arrive. Alex and two WLM security people Josie recognized, but didn't really know, got there first and set up their tent as far from Jones as they could. Burt and Emily came with Deputy DA Larry Clarke who was driving a Chrysler Town and Country station wagon, the color of pea soup, with fake wood-panel siding and an overloaded luggage rack on the roof. The DA's grey hair was tied back with a rubber band in a funky ponytail, the ends sticking out like exploded fireworks, but the biggest surprise got there later in the day. About noon an RV, driven by a handsome blond young man, bounced and rocked into the valley over rough terrain not intended for vehicles, and he parked close to the stream. After a few minutes, the side door opened and the aging actress Sandra Collins emerged dressed in tight jeans, knee-high white boots, and a white fur jacket with matching hat.

Collins didn't introduce her driver, but it didn't matter since he never ventured more than a few yards away from the RV.

"Sandra's got a new plaything," Emily said, as Collins slowly, carefully made her way around the muddy puddles toward them.

Josie was standing with Emily watching Burt and the others put up tents and make their nests for the night. Alex and the other two WLM men had an enormous tent, big enough for their three bunk beds. As they removed guns from their trucks, Josie watched and tried to identify the different weapons, but couldn't. She just didn't know enough about assault rifles, but she saw Jones walk over and talk to Alex. They spoke quietly for several seconds and she held her breath waiting for the gun battle to erupt between the two, but when they finished, Alex patted Jones once on the back and walked away. During their conversation, the other two men had carried at least five rifles into the tent in front of Jones.

He walked back in her direction, and from his wink she guessed he had identified every one of those rifles.

"You've got a new plaything too," Emily said to Josie, startling her. She'd forgotten Emily was standing there.

"He's a great guy. I really like Charlie," Josie said, trying to sound as if she were in a genuine relationship.

"Sandra likes him too," Emily said, raising one eyebrow. "She dumped him, of course, but doesn't enjoy sharing her discarded toys."

"The woman's old enough to be his mother."

Emily snorted and said, "True, but when we're shooting today, don't turn your back on her."

Josie smiled but could see she was dead serious.

Within an hour, Jones and Alex had paper targets set up in front of the mountainside and had laid out a course for tactical shooting, but it got so cold and windy by late afternoon, that removing their heavy gloves for even a few seconds to pull triggers was unbearable. When the icy wind started blowing away the targets, the weapons were unloaded and put away; all the men except Larry Clarke and Burt, who were sharing a bottle of bourbon and some marijuana in the front seat of the Chrysler, gathered more dry wood and everyone crowded around the fire.

The biting cold chased them into shelter pretty quickly. Sandra Collins invited Jones into her RV, but he declined, so she asked Clarke who was happy to go but he asked if Burt and Emily could join them. Apparently he hadn't heard about Burt's vicious assault on the movie star but most likely guessed something had happened when Collins said she'd gladly let Burt come in and get warm if she could "hack off his balls and pathetic little dick and feed them to the wolves first."

Josie stayed in the tent with Jones until morning. She didn't worry about anything happening during the night because it sounded like a blizzard outside, and the temperature felt as if it had dropped below freezing. They moved the log table, pulled the sleeping bags closer together to stay warm, and decided even if Quentin showed up they would leave the next morning since any meaningful communication with him or the others was almost impossible under these conditions. Although she could feel him near her sleeping bag, Jones wasn't as talkative as he'd been the night before and seemed preoccupied. After they made their decision, he turned his back to her and got very still and quiet, but she knew he wasn't sleeping. She'd listened on enough nights to know if he wasn't snoring he wasn't sleeping.

The next morning, Josie was awake at dawn even before Jones started to stir. She got up and pulled the tent zipper partway down then quickly slipped back into her sleeping bag to watch the sun come up over the mountains. It was so beautiful she was willing for the moment to forget the miserable cold and her stupidity in agreeing to come out there. All this trip did was confirm her belief that these people were impractical dreamers, but it hadn't brought her any closer to finding Soriano. Jones's intentions might've been good, but he couldn't draw any information out of Quentin if the man wasn't there.

She wanted to change her thermal underwear before they left, but the thought of removing warm layers of clothing and the heavy coat convinced her she didn't smell that bad and it could wait until they got home. When Jones finally started stirring and got out of his sleeping bag, they crawled out of the tent to discover the storm had passed and it was sunny and warmer. There was a light dusting of ice on the ground, but it was quickly melting into brown slush.

As soon as she moved away from their tent, Josie discovered Quentin had finally arrived. She wasn't surprised to see him perched on a small folding camp seat outside Alex's tent holding court with the others. The only one missing from the gathering was Collins and the young blond man.

Following Jones, she walked over to Quentin who stood to shake hands, then gave her a hug. That sign of affection was a first between them and it was much closer than she ever wanted to get. She could smell the blended odors of mothball and marijuana on his parka and felt the sandpaper roughness of his unshaven face rubbing against her chapped skin.

"Where've you been?" Jones asked and didn't sound pleased. His demeanor from the night before hadn't changed. He'd been quiet and moody all morning, barely speaking to her before they left the tent and now he was clearly irritated with Quentin.

"I've got some bad news," Quentin said, ignoring his grumpiness. "I was getting ready to leave yesterday when I heard, but by the time I got confirmation from my source it was too late to drive out here and tell you."

"Just fucking tell them," Emily said. She seemed to be in a bad mood too.

"We found Dave," he said.

Josie swallowed hard and glanced at Jones. His face was expressionless, but he wouldn't look at her.

"Where is he?" she asked.

"Don't matter, he's dead."

TEN

Josie's first thought was to find a telephone and call Murphy, but she needed to hear what Quentin had to say. She and Jones sat beside Clarke on a rotting log that someone had moved closer to the fire last night. The others wiggled uncomfortably as they sat on rocks, car fenders, or other items scrounged from around the camp to use as chairs and they all waited for Quentin to tell the rest of his story.

His source in the police department had told him that Dave Soriano's body was discovered by a couple of bums two nights ago; it had washed up on Venice Beach. The initial finding by the coroner was he'd been dead in the water several days. That was it.

"I saw his name in the *LA Times*. The story was only this big," Quentin said, holding his thumb and forefinger about an inch apart. "I can't believe I even spotted it. So I call Mitch right away . . . describe Dave, his age, all that stuff. It's him. Everything matches."

Josie tried not to react. Despite the disturbing news, she realized Quentin had carelessly given them the first name of his contact in the department.

Quentin kept talking but didn't have any more relevant information. He didn't know how Soriano died, if it was natural causes, homicide, or suicide. But more importantly, he never mentioned the word cop. He didn't seem to know the dead man was a police officer.

Josie sat quietly wondering if he got it wrong again. Quentin's information was always suspect and rarely reliable . . . or he might be testing her or one of the others to see how they might react to the news.

"I'll see what I can dig up in the office when we get back," Clarke mumbled when Quentin stopped talking. The attorney looked terrible, dark circles under his eyes, puffy sallow complexion, tremors in his hands, and this morning his messy grey ponytail was sticking straight out over his left ear. Josie figured his condition had more to do with the bottle of bourbon and recreational drugs he and Burt had shared last night than any bad news he heard this morning. Why he was hanging around this crowd was a mystery to her. He didn't like shooting guns and never contributed much in the way of political rhetoric. Larry Clarke was a wealthy dedicated party animal, but Quentin treated him as if he were a critical trusted player.

She'd been watching Emily as Quentin spoke and it was pretty clear Burt's wife was displeased with more than Soriano's demise. Josie had been around her long enough to recognize the signs when Emily was on the verge of losing control. For most of their relationship, Josie believed her tantrums were simply childish hysteria, but she was learning the woman could turn mean and bad-tempered without much provocation and rarely tolerated not getting her way. Why Quentin's news triggered so much displeasure was a little puzzling.

Although he provided no proof, Quentin said he was convinced Soriano had been killed by the LAPD or the feds.

"And what possible reason would they have to do that?" Josie asked. She had intended to sit and listen but had challenged him mostly out of frustration. His unsubstantiated ravings seemed to become more annoying as she got closer to leaving the assignment. Before he could come up with an answer, she asked, "Does Kate know yet?"

"I left her with my dad when we got back from Palm Springs. She won't come home until tomorrow . . . I figured she might take it better if you or Emily . . . you know," he said, not looking at either of them.

"Shouldn't we make certain it's him first?" Clarke asked. "Maybe this, this source of yours is full of shit . . . why traumatize the poor woman if he's got it all wrong."

"He gets his info from inside the chief's office and he's never wrong," Quentin said, standing and stretching. "Let's practice some drills while the weather's good so tonight we can move on with the next step. We gotta go without Dave, but he left a few notes so it shouldn't be a problem."

His demeanor changed so quickly no one moved. The others seemed to be absorbing the sudden loss of someone they knew who was a part of their small group. Quentin apparently had decided the mourning period for his comrade was over.

He quickly organized the training by assigning Jones to oversee hand-to-hand combat while he took charge of the shooting scenarios. It required hours to set up the targets and remind everyone how to safely load, manipulate, and discharge the assault rifles. Josie could see that other than herself, Jones, and maybe Alex, none of these people should've been anywhere near a firearm, especially Quentin. The rest of them were definitely not the gun experts or military vets Jones had told her about. They were negligent in handling the weapons, didn't get the concept of not pointing loaded guns at each other, and couldn't comprehend the value of using a gun's front sight if they actually wanted to hit something.

Josie's brother was an avid hunter and taught her how to handle guns at a very young age, so she'd been around them most of her life. When she realized Quentin was watching her move through the scenarios, she made an effort to be as accurate as she could and hit a lot more targets than the rest of this sorry group . . . which wasn't difficult.

However, having a well-developed sense of self-preservation, she stopped shooting after thirty minutes, certain either one of them was going to accidentally shoot her, or a very hung-over Sandra Collins might do it intentionally. Several hundred rounds of ammunition were fired by everyone except Clarke, who sat in his car with the engine running and the heater turned on.

After watching awhile, Josie calculated the safest place in camp had to be directly in front of the targets. Jones must've realized how dangerously unprepared most of these shooters were and probably to prevent casualties he stayed to help. He couldn't allow Quentin to watch them alone, so he had to abandon any attempt to teach the combat fighting and it became strictly a target-practice day.

Before the training was over, Clarke came out of his station wagon and sat on the log beside Josie, a safe distance from the shooting area. He offered her a drink from a silver flask he was carrying, but she declined. He took a long swallow before screwing the top on and sliding it into his jacket pocket.

"I have observed you are a remarkably good shot, Ms. Pastore," he said, sounding steadier than he had earlier that morning.

"Thanks, my brother taught me."

"I'm deathly afraid of guns."

She smiled and, pointing at the line of shooters, said, "And yet you spend your time around all this."

"I like to think I contribute to the cause in other ways."

"Money?"

Now he chuckled. "That's subtle and a little insulting. The revolution will require soldiers on many different battlefields."

"Is that what we're doing here, preparing for the revolution?"

"It's a start. For obvious reasons we can all hope the outcome won't be decided in a gun battle," he said, as a round from Sandra Collins's rifle hit a mound of dirt three feet from any designated target flinging debris in all directions and causing anyone standing near her to duck for cover.

"You have a lot to lose when the proletariat rises . . . sharing that enormous wealth your family has accumulated," Josie said, grateful to have someone to talk with who didn't take all of this so seriously.

"Maybe, but then again someone must always be in charge of the zoo . . . don't you think," he said, grinning and sipping from the flask.

"All animals are equal, but some are more equal than others," she said, citing the only quote she remembered from George Orwell.

Clarke put his head back and seemed to laugh but didn't make a sound. He struggled to push himself off the log but couldn't get up. He sighed, took another sip, and leaning slightly toward her, whispered, "You and I are destined to be great comrades, my pretty."

"I'd like that," she said and decided to test their newly formed bond. "You must be shocked by the news about Dave. He worked for you; didn't he?"

"Good man . . . but Quentin's probably got it wrong . . . again."

"I hope so. Why would anyone want to kill Dave Soriano? It's too crazy," she said and waited. He stared at her and she wasn't certain if he was contemplating what he wanted to say or if those watery, bloodshot eyes were telling her he'd become lost in the dense forest of his own whiskey-soaked thoughts.

"Not so crazy," he blurted out.

"What do you mean?"

"Dave's job . . . oh, let's discuss something less depressing."

"Didn't he work for you?"

Clarke shifted his weight on the log as if he were trying to find a comfortable spot and mumbled, "More or less."

"What did he do?" she asked when he finally stopped squirming.

"An excellent question . . ." he said and immediately seemed to lose his concentration.

"What did you hire him to do?" Josie knew she was pushing hard but hoped his intoxication would keep him from becoming suspicious.

Clarke didn't answer but this time managed to lurch forward, lifting his body off the log. "Do hope to see you at the next house party, my pretty," he said, waving over his shoulder with his back to her as he stumbled away in the direction of his car.

She watched him crawl onto the backseat again and curl up before hooking his foot under the handle and pulling the door closed. It was odd Clarke wouldn't know what Soriano did in the DA's office or that he would be reluctant to talk about it. He might've been too drunk to think clearly, but she had a feeling he either didn't know or had some reason not to tell her.

The target practice ended before lunch. Jones looked exhausted, but he'd managed to get everyone through the potentially deadly session without an injury or fatality. Before the weapons were put away, Emily asked him to take her picture holding one of the AR-15 assault rifles, and then she insisted everyone get together for a group photo with their weapons. It was Josie's 35mm camera and she knew as soon as the film could be developed, Murphy and PDID would be as happy as Emily to get their copies of the pictures.

The news about Soriano had put a damper on the enthusiasm in camp, and what was supposed to be an event not only to train, but to build camaraderie. Everyone was cold and tired and ready to pack up and head home when the shooting was done, but Quentin insisted on one final gathering. Josie helped Jones break down his tent and pack the VW with all their belongings before the meeting got started. She tried to have a conversation with him but he was still sullen and gave her one-word answers or didn't respond at all.

"What's the matter with you?" she finally asked, after he tossed the last piece of camping gear into the backseat of the car.

"Nothing."

"Is it Soriano?"

He gave her a look that said of course it was Soriano, then glanced around to be certain no one was close enough to hear and whispered, "A cop is dead."

"We need to talk to Murphy before I'll believe anything Quentin Barnes has to say. For all we know it's not even Dave," she said. She figured Soriano's death might've affected Jones but also knew his irritable mood had started long before he heard Quentin's news.

Jones shook his head but didn't respond. His body language told her he didn't want to discuss it anymore.

Everyone finished packing their cars and gathered around Sandra Collins's RV where Quentin was waiting. Her driver had moved the mobile home closer to the other vehicles in the clearing then walked away just far enough not to hear what was being said.

"This'll be quick," Quentin said, when everyone was quiet and standing around him in a circle. Josie leaned against the RV next to Clarke while Jones sat on the vehicle's steps with Collins as close as she could get to him without sitting in his lap. The others seemed anxious and eager to get back on the road, but Quentin waited a few moments for dramatic effect before announcing that the event they'd been training for the last few months would occur in approximately two days. "The target will remain classified until we are en route, but I'm gonna pick our team tomorrow . . . no more than six of you, probably less," he said. One of the WLM men started to ask a question about Manny, but Quentin interrupted him saying, "That's it. No discussion, no questions. I'll be in touch."

He marched away like a little general in a worn parka, got into his faded blue Studebaker with ugly primer spots, and drove out of the clearing toward the dirt road. The others filed out like a funeral procession, an obedient little caravan. Josie allowed Clarke to give her a quick hug before he got in to the backseat of his station wagon. Wisely Burt and Emily wouldn't let him drive.

Josie turned to say something to Jones just as Collins pounced on him, grabbed his head with both hands, and passionately kissed him on the mouth. He'd been attempting to get up off the stairs when the aging star attacked like a hungry spider on a fly. It was done so deftly that Josie laughed, mostly at the surprised expression on Jones's face. He couldn't extricate himself from the clingy woman until the pretty blond boy mercifully started the mobile home.

Josie had no idea how to get onto the main highway and didn't feel like driving, so she offered to pay for gas if Jones would get them home. The ride back to Los Angeles in the VW was slow and boring without either of them making any effort to engage in conversation, and after trying unsuccessfully to find a radio station without static, she gave up on breaking the silence. She wanted to tease him about Sandra Collins but wasn't certain he was in the mood to see much humor in anything. When the traffic completely stopped moving, Jones pulled off the highway in the Van Nuys area just north of downtown LA and parked in the back of a small bar in a run-down strip mall. He said he remembered the bar from his weekends out of the academy when he'd been assigned to Van Nuys patrol and was certain it wasn't a cop hangout. He told her they could call Murphy and wait in there until the rush hour traffic died down.

"I HAVE bad news," were Murphy's first words to her.

Josie told him that Quentin had already told them and what else he'd said, and she finished by asking, "Did they really find his body on Venice Beach?"

"Yes."

"How did he die?" she asked, taking a sip from the glass of whiskey Jones had placed in front of her.

Murphy hesitated before saying, "Coroner doesn't know yet . . . I guess he'd been in the water awhile."

"Do you know who Quentin's contact Mitch might be?" Josie asked, trying to wipe the picture out of her head of what she imagined Soriano's bloated dead body looked like.

"I think so. Lieutenant Mitchell is the old man's Press Relations guy, second in command under Captain Moore. We'll leave him in place with round-the-clock surveillance; see who else he's blabbing to about department business."

"I'm guessing Mitchell didn't know Soriano was a cop," she said.

"Nobody except PDID and the chief know that . . . for now."

The next question was problematic for Josie. She needed to know but had an uneasy feeling she wasn't going to like the answer.

"What about Charlie and me?" she asked. "You've got Soriano. What happens to us now? What happens to me?"

"Both of you meet me at the Redondo Beach bar tomorrow morning at eight," he said and hung up.

She placed the receiver back on the cradle and pushed the phone back toward the bartender. He put it under the counter and she waved her hand over the whiskey glass before he could fill it again.

"Well?" Jones asked.

Josie told him everything Murphy had said and finished the few drops left of her drink before asking, "What's wrong with you?"

"What are you talking about? Why do you keep asking me that?"

"Something's bothering you and your pissy attitude is really starting to annoy me."

"It's not you . . ."

"I know it's not me, but whatever it is knock it off. Either talk to me or deal with it on your own but stop your damned moping."

"Sorry," he said sheepishly. "I didn't realize I was doing that. It's not an excuse but I didn't do very well on the sergeant's test and it's been bugging me. I can't stop thinking about it."

"What?"

"Three months ago, I didn't go for my Saturday run. I went to a nice lady's house in East LA. The department had arranged for me to take the sergeant's test in her kitchen. I found out a couple of days ago my score was too low to make it right away. I really want to be a supervisor."

Josie laughed but stopped when she saw his hurt look. "Sorry, I was thinking it was something so much worse. It's a relief that's all."

"A relief my career has come off track?" he asked, motioning for the bartender to fill his glass again.

"No, of course not . . . a relief you didn't kill somebody or blow up another toilet."

He almost smiled, "It's important to me; I planned to leave this assignment as a supervisor and then make lieutenant as quick as I can."

"From what I've been told as long as you get on the list you have a chance. You might not make it on the first transfer . . . just hope a lot of guys retire. If you keep drinking like that I think you'll fit right in on any homicide table," she said as he downed his whiskey in one gulp. Trying to be sympathetic was difficult because she believed doing police work on the street had to be the best job in the world and why anyone would be in such a hurry to promote away from it was a mystery to her.

"What are you going to do when you come up?" he asked, ignoring her comment.

"Unlike you, I don't have a lot of choices, not enough time on the job to be a detective, and I'm not allowed to work patrol. It's either the women's jail or something like Vice."

"Vice could be fun."

"I refuse to sashay down Sunset Boulevard dressed like Cher just so some slimy geezer can talk dirty to me, then be out of jail before my end of watch . . . it's a stupid game."

"There's always Juvenile Division."

"I hate kids."

Now he laughed. "Sorry, but that sucks."

"Any day now the courts might force the chief to train women for patrol and I'll be first in line."

"You'd do that, go through the academy again, all that running you claim to hate, just to sit in a black-and-white?"

"You can bet your commie ass I would," she said, staring at him.

"I think Murphy's right about you, but you might have more heart than brains."

ELEVEN

It was late, nearly midnight, by the time they got back to the garage in Venice. Neither of them wanted to unload the car but Josie knew leaving valuables where they could be seen was an invitation to transients populating the boardwalk to break the windows and take everything. Life near the beach was wonderful but she'd learned that any property that wasn't bolted, chained, or stored safely behind a locked door got stolen.

The lights in the house next door came on as they dragged the heavy camping gear on the ground and tossed it into her living room. Josie knew they were making too much noise for the late hour but she was tired and just wanted to finish as quickly as possible and get to bed. Even the warm shower she'd been dreaming about for days was out of the question.

After she locked the front door, she wrapped her heavy bedspread around her shoulders and fell onto her mattress fully dressed. Before drifting off, she watched Charlie, still wearing his parka and boots, turn off the lights and curl up on his cot.

They were up early enough for him to go for a run and for her to take a long shower. She put the smelly camping clothes in the hamper and got a good look at her wind-burned skin. It was red and a little rough, but she liked the color in her face. Her shift at the thrift store was scheduled for this morning but she knew the meeting with Murphy meant she'd be late again. The nuns liked her so she hoped it wouldn't be a problem. Besides if Murphy was true to his word, she shouldn't need that job any longer.

As soon as Jones returned, he took a quick shower, changed his clothes, and they left in his car for the drive to Redondo Beach. He was in a more talkative mood today and seemed to have forgotten or come to grips with his disappointment about the promotional test.

"I've got a feeling Sarge is going to tell me today I'm out of the program," she said, watching him to see what his reaction would be. There wasn't any.

"Is that what you want?" he asked, turning onto the San Diego Freeway.

"Yes."

"What about Quentin? We don't know what he's up to yet."

"The deal was I stayed to help find Soriano. He's found. I'm out. I don't want to live this way anymore."

"Can I have your apartment?" he asked, attempting to look serious. "Sorry, I was kidding . . . just wanted to see your face. You've gotta lighten up, Pastore."

"I will as soon as I can walk into a police station again without wearing handcuffs."

"You'll miss this."

"Lying, getting beat up by the men in blue, pretending Larry Clarke and the rest of them are sane . . . I don't think so."

"Aren't you curious to know what Quentin's gonna blow up this time?"

"Not enough to stay under. Anyway, he'll tell you, you'll tell Murphy, and it'll never happen . . . I hope."

They were quiet for the remainder of the trip. She stared out the window trying to imagine how normal her life was about to become.

Murphy was waiting for them on the pier as they left the parking structure. The weather had warmed up again and he was pacing near a food stand without a jacket drinking coffee.

"You're late; follow me," he ordered, as soon as they got close enough to hear him over the roar of waves crashing against the rocks.

He led the way past the bike path to the rear of a row of businesses. Stacks of crates and boxes filled the alley between the back of the buildings and a six-foot block wall with barely enough room for them to open the door and squeeze through. It was difficult to get her bearings from this location and the roundabout way he got them here, but she estimated the funky establishment was probably a few doors down from Murphy's favorite no-name bar. The place reeked of cinnamon and vanilla. Her first thought was a candle or incense store.

They entered a stockroom with strings of beads hung in a doorway leading to the front retail space. Josie got a glimpse of the shop through multicolored sparkling pieces of glass. Some light came through the front window and she could make out floor-to-ceiling shelves overloaded with candles, books, and decorative bottles. Crystals hung from a ceiling fan and a fat black cat was curled up beside a register on the counter near a jar of burning incense sticks.

"What is this place?" Jones asked, peeking through the beads.

"Specialty store for witches, but Satilla won't be back for a few days," Murphy said, pushing Jones's hand away from the hanging beads.

"Magic potion conference?" Josie asked.

"Jail . . . she gave me the key so I could feed the cat."

She and Jones exchanged a quick look before Murphy opened a door to their left that had "Private" written in big, black letters. This space seemed larger than the rest of the store. There was a round table in the center of the room with Detective Carlson and four men Josie didn't recognize seated around it. Two of them wore business suits; the other two were in LAPD police uniforms.

Although she'd never met him, the four stars on his collar told Josie all she needed to know about one of them. He had to be directly under the chief of police and the highest-ranking officer she'd ever been this close to. The other one wore captain bars and Carlson introduced them as Captain Williams, PDID's commanding officer, and Assistant Chief Perez, who was in charge of the Office of Special Services or OSS. The older civilian was the district attorney for Los Angeles County, Larry Clarke's boss, and the other man was introduced as another deputy district attorney, Jake Corsino.

Josie stood next to Corsino and could smell his cologne or maybe it was his shaving cream. Clean-shaven men were a rare thing since she'd gone undercover. He was a little taller than her with an olive complexion, short grey hair, and big dark eyes. He nodded and pulled out a chair for her.

Murphy pointed to another chair for Jones but he and Josie continued standing. The assistant chief kept nervously pulling on his short grey sideburns while scrutinizing some papers on the table in front of him.

"Sit down," Murphy ordered.

"What's going on here?" Josie asked, as she and Jones stood side by side. She had a bad feeling about this high-profile gathering.

"Please, have a seat and we'll explain," the DA said. He was a quiet-spoken man with a blanket of tiny purple veins protruding from his cheeks and large nose, but he had a nice easy smile, so Josie did what he asked and Jones followed her lead.

Chief Perez cleared his throat and recited a short speech without a hint of compassion, "As you know Officer Soriano is dead. He's been murdered, shot in the chest at close range with a .38-caliber weapon, and we're fairly confident his body was thrown near or off the pier in Venice." He glanced up for a moment as if to be certain he had everyone's attention before continuing. "His death may jeopardize the future of PDID, putting an end to a very valuable and essential resource for this department."

"Not to mention fucking up any plans Soriano had for the rest of his life," Josie mumbled. She'd been struggling not to say what she was thinking out loud, but everything about this pompous toad was grating on her nerves. She didn't look at him but heard Corsino muffle a laugh.

Although the DA and Perez looked irritated, Captain Williams interrupted his boss and said, "We all believe what happened to Dave Soriano was a tragedy and our first priority is, of course, to find the young man's killer. That's why we wanted to meet with you today."

"I'm not sure what you think we can do," Jones said. "Isn't RHD handling the homicide investigation?"

"Two very trusted Criminal Conspiracy Section detectives will have the lead on this one, but you two are in a unique position to help," Carlson said.

"Why haven't you told the press he was a police officer? Wouldn't that help bring witnesses forward," Josie asked, not liking where this conversation was going.

"We didn't want the killer to panic and run," Murphy said. "Nobody except the chief of police, CCS, and the people in this room know Soriano was a cop. His killing most likely had something to do with his assignment and we need your help."

Josie sat back. This wasn't the deal. "But you promised me . . ." she started to say.

Murphy didn't let her finish and said, "I know I promised I'd put you on the transfer when we found Soriano, but his murder changed all that."

"We can't keep you, either of you, here if you want to leave, Josie," Captain Williams said, giving Murphy a look that warned "let me handle this." "But I can assure you the chief won't forget your personal sacrifice, and he can be very generous in rewarding loyalty. I guarantee at the very least you'll both be allowed to work any division you choose if you help us out."

She looked at Chief Perez who was nodding like a bobble-head dog in the back window of a Chevy Camaro, but he wouldn't make eye contact with her.

"I still don't understand what you think we can do," Jones said.

Josie was smart enough to pick up on his subtle threat. She figured the other side of the loyalty coin in LAPD would be getting screwed for the rest of your career if you refused their request and pissed off someone with bars or stars on his collar. Their real choice was to do what these people wanted or be on their shit list forever . . . no promotions, no good jobs, no chance to work patrol when the time came to pick the first female candidates.

"The same thing you've been doing," Carlson said. "Find out as much as you can about Soriano's friends and enemies. Keep your eyes and ears open and give CCS a lead, a place to start."

"Aren't you worried somebody will discover he was a cop and make a big deal out of the fact the department kept it a secret?" Josie asked. "We all know there's at least one major leak in the chief's office."

"Let us worry about that," Carlson said. "The chief has allowed CCS forty-eight hours before he issues a press release."

"My deputy, Jake Corsino, will be available for warrants or any other legal advice you might need," the district attorney said. "As you can tell from who's sitting here, finding Officer Soriano's killer is very important and not just to your chief of police, so don't be hesitant to ask for Jake's help."

"Do you work with Larry Clarke?" Jones asked Corsino.

"Of course," Corsino said.

"Great," Jones said sarcastically.

"Look, I don't know why one of our attorneys is involved, if he is, but I promise I will personally handle anything related to this case . . . not a secretary, not some intern in the office . . . me," Corsino said, responding to Jones's comment but looking directly at Josie. "I'm also assigned to your court case from the arrest downtown, Josie, so I'll coordinate that with your public defender and get in touch with you later."

She gave him a half-hearted smile and asked, "Is that all?"

"For now," Murphy said, grunting as he got up. "Come on, I'll walk you back."

She could tell from his voice and body language, Brickhouse was not pleased, but he was quiet until they were out of the alley and walking across the pier.

"I don't know what the hell's wrong with you," he said, stopping and glaring at Josie. "This is your job. If you don't want to do it then say so, get the fuck out, and live with the consequences," he said, pointing at the parking structure. He turned to walk away, made a circle, and came back. Jones tried to step between him and Josie but Murphy gently nudged him aside. "Fuck! That's what I hate about this damned program," Murphy continued, his face getting flushed as he became more animated. "We take you out of uniform before you understand discipline or duty, leave you on your own to play spy games, and you think you know everything. You haven't earned a tenth of the respect due any cop sitting in a black-and-white every day who by the way would kill to have your job. What we're asking you to do is important. A real cop understands that."

There was a long silence. Murphy stared at the ground until Josie asked, "Feel better?" She'd been standing with her arms folded watching quietly until he finished his tirade. This was more than letting off steam. He was frustrated and shouting was his way of dealing with it. After two years, she got him.

"A little," Murphy said, much calmer. "Sorry about the black-and-white comment. That's not your fault. I really hate supervising women."

"Better get used to it, Sarge," she said. "The world is changing."

"Look, I know you'll do your best . . . both of you, but take some advice, especially you, Pastore. At least try to make the brass feel like they're in charge or I guarantee you're not gonna survive when this is over. You can trust Jake Corsino, work with him. He's been the DA on a couple of my cases. He's not afraid to stand up to the system."

Murphy didn't wait for her response. He patted Jones on the back and walked away in the direction from which they'd come.

"He's right you know," Jones said when they were out of the underground parking and driving up Pacific Coast Highway toward Venice. It was the long way back, but unlike the freeway route they had a view of the ocean for most of the trip. She looked at him but didn't ask "about what," the obvious question, so he continued, "You won't last a day when you come up from this assignment if you don't respect and defer to rank."

"I give them the respect they earn," she said.

"Not in the LAPD you don't. If you don't agree with them, then promote and you can make the decisions. That's what I'm gonna do."

"They won't let me promote, remember."

"Then you're fucked," he said and shook his head at the absurdity of her situation.

"For the present what's our game plan? They found his body in Venice. It would help to know how long he'd been dead; chances are he was killed at the beach or close by," she said, thinking she'd rather concentrate on the investigation than dwell on her diminished career prospects. It was frustrating. Josie knew she could do this job as well as, or better than, anyone, but as a woman in the LAPD male-dominated world she also knew she'd be expected to prove her worth practically every day of her career. If they'd just give her a chance, she was willing to do that.

"Quentin and Kate were closest to him, but they really don't seem to know much about his disappearance unless Quentin's a better actor and a lot smarter than I think he is. What about Larry Clarke?" Jones asked. "What he told you about Soriano working in his office didn't sound right to me."

"I thought so too. I can probably get more from him, but forty-eight hours isn't anywhere near enough time. What did you think about that Corsino?" she asked.

"I don't know . . . seems okay. Have to trust somebody. I have a feeling he'll do whatever you want."

"What does that mean?" Josie asked, but she knew.

"The guy spent the whole meeting staring at you."

JONES LET her out in front of the thrift shop, after they had discussed all their options and had decided to visit Clarke at home later that evening. He knew the attorney had an open house most nights, and, as usual, always welcomed unexpected visitors with food and a well-stocked bar.

He told her he was going to browse in the Midnight Special Bookstore until she was finished with her shift and try to pick up any of the local gossip. Everyone on the left talked to the owner, Debbie, and she rarely kept anything a secret. The activist community knew she and Soriano were inseparable before he abandoned her for Kate, so any information or rumors about him or his demise would likely filter through her store. From a few of the comments Jones had made, Josie suspected he might've had a brief fling with Debbie at one time. He'd been undercover longer, but unlike Josie, he apparently appreciated and had taken full advantage of the free-love movement from the sixties. She wasn't into casual sex but had to admit smart, handsome Jake Corsino might cause her to reconsider.

The thrift store was busy so the four hours seemed to pass quickly. Someone had dropped off a new blanket that was heavy but not too large. Josie saved it in the back room intending to locate the homeless girl and give it to her. Before leaving, she put it in a canvas tote with some underwear and wool socks.

During the day the beach was warmer, but at night the temperatures could drop and Josie believed the girl always slept outdoors. She stopped in one of the beach parking lots at a food wagon she knew had decent hamburgers and put an order of burger and fries in the tote before searching for the woman.

Josie spotted her sitting near one of the trash cans on the sand not far from the weight stacks where several grotesquely muscled men and women in skimpy bathing suits entertained onlookers by challenging each other, shouting, and grunting as they lifted weights or danced to rock music playing from a portable AM/FM radio on the concrete retaining wall. The girl was digging in the sand, creating different-sized mounds, some decorated with an assortment of bottle caps and other debris. She stopped only to wave her arms to the music or point at moving objects only she could see.

Josie trudged over the sand and dropped the tote near her and she immediately reached in, retrieved the burger and fries, and started eating as if she hadn't eaten for days. The woman never acknowledged her but Josie watched for a moment as she ate and thought she appeared to have lost weight. Up close, she could see the girl's skin was the color of tanned leather, her sun-bleached blonde hair thinning in places and her breathing labored as she devoured the meal. She was wearing the dress and boots Josie had given her. They were filthy, a little too big, but still without holes or patched spots.

"Do you want another burger?" Josie asked, as the girl handed her the empty greasy wrapping. The girl shook her head. Josie asked her name.

Sitting with her bony legs crossed, the girl looked up, using her hand to keep the sun out of her eyes, but didn't answer. It was difficult to tell whether or not the question had registered behind those beautiful, empty blue eyes.

"I've got to go now," Josie said as she turned to leave and thought she heard the girl mumble something but wasn't certain if the inaudible comment was directed at her or anyone in particular. It didn't matter; she kept walking. There wasn't any need to communicate. Josie knew the girl was real and needed help. It was important that her concern for this young woman wasn't a lie or manipulation because it kept her grounded at a time almost everything else in life seemed out of her control.

Jones was sitting outside on the doorstep to the garage as she walked up the driveway. She sat beside him and he handed her a keychain with several keys.

"Yours?" he asked and she shook her head.

"Where did you get them?" she asked, giving them back but not before noticing they were caked with sand.

"The Venice Beach lost and found," he said, pointing where she was sitting.

"This is ridiculous."

"Recognize this one?" he asked, holding it up.

She took them back and examined the key. It only required a quick glance to identify it. The 999 key would open the back door to any station in the LAPD including Parker Center, the department's main administration center.

"You found these on my doorstep?"

"It was bugging me but I finally remembered where I'd seen this keychain before." He held up the small round plastic disk with a painted picture of a sickle and fist. "I was with Soriano when he bought one of these at the Midnight Special."

Josie stared at him, looked down at the keys, and tried to make some sense of what he was saying.

"I don't . . . how would his keys . . ." She stopped mid-sentence because she was beginning to understand. It had to be whoever left the other trinkets found the keys in the sand and brought them to her, another gift.

"The necklace, the pendant, and now these . . . some admirer or stalker is leaving you stuff. We need to find that guy, ask where he found these . . . he might've seen everything or at least seen the killer dump the body. Maybe he can even describe him."

"You're sure these are Soriano's? Other people must've bought these key chains."

"Positive, look," he said, and took his keys out of his pocket. He matched one of his to one on the other ring. "This fits Quentin's place. I saw him give it to Soriano. And Dave always drove an old Ford T-bird," he said holding up a car key with the Ford insignia.

"Where is his car?" she asked.

Jones looked puzzled and shook his head before saying, "I don't know. Nobody's ever mentioned it. I know it's not at Quentin's or at the apartment in Mar Vista. You didn't see it at the house in Duarte?"

"No, the garage was empty. Is Kate driving it?"

"She doesn't drive."

"Let's ask Murphy to run the plate and see if it's been impounded for some reason," she said. "Did you pick up anything interesting at the bookstore?"

"Not really. Debbie says Kate's in pretty bad shape . . . she's guessing it's because Quentin dumped her."

"So where is she staying."

"Some hype crash pad . . . nobody seems to know," he said, getting up and offering his hand to help her off the step.

They went inside and while he dressed she lay on top of her bed resting for a few minutes. He wasn't shy about changing clothes in front of her and she realized they were acting more like a brother and sister every day. He had become important to her but to her surprise not in a romantic way.

She figured he kept his emotional distance and a professional attitude because he felt the same way about her. Trusting him hadn't come easy but all those doubts had dissipated and Josie believed Charlie was developing into a real partner and friend.

She changed clothes too and they were ready to make an appearance at Larry Clarke's house, but on the way to Brentwood they stopped at a phone booth to call Murphy. The sergeant was able to check the Department of Motor Vehicles and get the information on Soriano's car. It had outstanding warrants for several unpaid parking tickets but hadn't been impounded. Josie decided not to tell Murphy about the keys. She knew CCS would be upset if they discovered she'd found them and hadn't said anything, but she wasn't ready to give them up yet. She hoped with Jones's help she'd have a better chance of solving this case than anyone working from inside the department, and those keys might be helpful.

The lights were on and the front door was open at Clarke's house. It was a smaller, less rambunctious party than the last one she'd attended, and the crowd seemed pretty similar, except middle-aged intellectuals outnumbered the college students, dropouts, and hippies. Josie was thankful the dress code hadn't changed—Afros and beads. The music was less protest and more jazz; the smoky haze smelled more like tobacco than weed.

Anthony Barnes, Quentin's father, was the center of attention in the spacious foyer as he discussed the Soviet Union with Judge David Jacobson. A few of the older crowd had gathered around them as Barnes extolled the virtues of Communism and Jacobson insisted repeated failure was not a virtue or a selling point.

"It's been an oppressive disappointment everywhere they've tried it," Jacobson said. He was a tall, imposing figure with his striking white hair and military-like posture.

"But we could make it work this time in this country," Barnes argued.

The judge put his arm around the older man and gave him a hug. "That's why I love you, Tony. You're a good man who will never understand the limitations and true nature of your fellow human beings."

"You only see the worst in people. You think the whole world is like those social misfits who pass through your courtroom," Barnes said.

As they edged slowly into the living room, the two men were followed by the small group who seemed drawn to their discussion. Josie kept watching and listening too and she surmised from their tone they were close friends who disagreed on politics and probably had this debate many times as an intellectual exercise, without any expectation of changing each other's opinion. Jacobson was deferential to the older man, even supporting his arm as Barnes stepped up into the larger living room.

The tenor of the gathering changed drastically with the appearance of their host. Larry Clarke stumbled in like an ill wind from the direction of the kitchen holding a glass of what looked like whiskey in one hand and his other arm around the shoulder of an unsteady Burt Rice. Clarke's face was bloated and flushed and as usual he was too loud and visibly intoxicated. His expensive clothes were disheveled and Josie thought if it hadn't been for this pricey location and his tailor he could've been mistaken for an ordinary bum who'd wandered in off the street. She knew getting him to make any sense tonight was going to be a challenge.

Jones skillfully guided Burt away toward the game room so Josie could move in and command Clarke's full attention. She steered him toward a loveseat near the fireplace where he plopped down with a loud sigh.

"Thank you, my dear," Clarke said in a surprisingly clear firm voice.

"For what?" she asked.

"Saving me from that perverted bore . . . whatever does our lovely Emily see in that lout?"

"You tell me," she said.

"He's rich . . . not as rich as me. He does however humor the woman's fantasies."

"What fantasies?"

Clarke stared at her for several seconds before asking, "Are you attempting to pump me for gossip?"

"Yes."

"I adore you, my pretty," he said, swallowing a laugh and touching her face. "Miss Emily imagines justice in violence and like a petulant child desires to destroy . . . everything for her cause."

"What cause would that be?"

"Let's say revolution . . . She sees herself as Madame Defarge sitting in the front row seats with a basket waiting to catch the heads of the ruling class as they roll from the guillotine, then lighting the fuse to burn down this corrupt government and start again with the pure of heart . . . blah, blah, you know the study group rhetoric," he said, resting his head on the back of the couch and grinning at her. "You are very pretty."

"Okay, I get what Emily wants, but I don't think I'll ever understand what Soriano had to do with her or Quentin," she said, moving a little closer to him. "Dave wasn't a revolutionary. He was dedicated to fun and women, nothing to get killed for."

"Ah, but then you never really knew the faithful little soldier, did you? Few people did. His efforts advanced the primary target."

"Target . . . what target and what does any of that have to do with him working in your office?"

"Not allowed to disclose all the gory details," he whispered with his index finger over his lips.

"Not allowed by who?"

"By whom."

Josie shrugged. "Never mind, I understand. Quentin doesn't want anyone to talk about it."

Clarke laughed, spilling some of his drink on the couch. "Quentin? Quentin Barnes is a messenger boy."

"He acts like he's in charge," she said.

"Acting indeed, the boy does what he's told."

"By you?"

"The world should be so lucky."

"Did Soriano know the gory details . . . Is that why he's dead?"

"Casualties are inevitable when challenging the order of things. It's evolution . . . evolution of the revolution," he said laughing at himself. He turned his head away from her. "I don't feel well . . . just close my eyes for a moment."

Josie didn't need to look. He began snoring immediately. Well, that was pretty much a bust, she thought and sat back, then glanced around the room searching for Jones. Instead she made eye contact with Jacobson who was sitting on a piano bench directly across from her with his back leaning against the keyboard of the baby grand. He motioned for Josie to come over and join him. She hesitated for a moment but only because his invitation was unexpected. Up to this point he'd pretty much ignored her. There was no sign of her partner so she got up, walked around furniture between small groups of partygoers, and sat on the bench beside the handsome judge.

"Don't you think Larry is the perfect host?" Jacobson asked, as soon as she was beside him, but before she could answer he continued, "He has tons of gourmet food and expensive liquor and then he passes out and doesn't have a clue how much you eat or drink." He introduced himself and she did the same. "Haven't we met?" he asked, studying her face. "I've been sitting here thinking I know you from somewhere."

"Can I ask you something?" she said, ignoring his question and feeling a little miffed at being so unmemorable. "You seem out of place at these parties. You're too . . . establishment. Why do you come?"

"I live in the neighborhood; many of these people are old friends. I might ask you the same thing. It can't be for Larry's charm," he said, pointing at Clarke who was still on the couch snoring with his mouth open.

"No, but he does have interesting friends and lots of good food. How long have you known Anthony Barnes? I was eavesdropping on your conversation in the foyer."

"Most of my life. Have you met him?"

"No, but I know his son."

Jacobson nodded and pursed his lips as if he'd just been forced to swallow something distasteful before saying, "How nice."

"You don't like Quentin."

"I don't believe he's inherited his father's best qualities."

"Why, because he talks about overthrowing your government?"

"No, because he thinks he can do it with homemade bombs and terror while under the influence of illegal drugs. Now, on a more pleasant note, tell me what you think of this," he said, turning around to face the keyboard. He began playing a blues rendition of a song she recognized from an old 78 rpm record her father used to love. The background noise around them lowered considerably and a few people moved to stand closer to the piano. Josie sensed they'd been waiting for him to settle in and start playing. She could understand why. The judge was really good. He seemed to relax as he became further engaged in the music and although he looked up occasionally to smile at her, she felt as if he'd mentally gone somewhere else and it could've been anyone sitting beside him.

She listened a few more minutes and was about to get up when she noticed Jones come back into the room with Sandra Collins clinging to him like a pier barnacle. The actress was wobbly, as usual, and tripped on a coffee table, lurched forward, and nearly sat on Clarke who was still snoozing. Jones gently detached her from his arm and left the woman curled up asleep with her head on Clarke's lap. He came over to the piano as Jacobson was finishing and shook hands with the judge who definitely remembered him.

They talked awhile and Josie was surprised how much she enjoyed Jacobson's company and wit, his easy way of drawing her into his world. He was a realist, an artist, a man of principle who seemed to have a wide tolerance for other people's views, but made it clear that as much as he loved and respected Anthony Barnes, he thought Quentin was foolish and dangerous.

When she got around to asking, he readily acknowledged meeting Soriano, saying he'd talked to the "unfortunate young man" in his courtroom after a preliminary hearing just days before he'd disappeared. Larry Clarke had introduced them, describing Soriano as a temporary intern in the DA's office, and Jacobson admitted he had given him his private number telling Soriano to call if he ever needed advice regarding his budding legal career.

But Jacobson's parting words to her were a little chilling. "I could never understand what that bright young man saw in Quentin as a friend or even an acquaintance. It's a terrible thing to say, but I can't help but believe he'd be alive today if he'd never met or had anything to do with Anthony's son."

Now she had a reasonable explanation for the phone number on the matchbook cover, but it was becoming clear Deputy DA Clarke hadn't been candid about his relationship with Soriano. If Clarke had introduced Soriano to the judge, then he lied about not having any close contact with the undercover cop.

"Do you have Soriano's keys with you?" she asked Jones later as they were leaving the house walking back to his car.

"Yes, why?"

"We should go to the Hall of Justice."

"Any particular reason?"

"I want to check out their underground parking. If Dave's car is still there it gives us a place to start retracing his movements."

"Tomorrow," Jones said, opening the car door for her.

"We don't have much time before the whole world finds out he was a cop."

"They allow the public to park under the building during the day when the courts and offices are open," he said. "Unless you want to go visit Charlie Manson in jail or stop by the coroner's, I can't think of a good reason for us to be there tonight."

Josie sat back and was quiet while he drove. She didn't ask where they were going and was starting to worry they would never make any progress in finding Soriano's killer. As it got later and she grew weary, her confidence from earlier that day was beginning to erode. Neither of them had investigative experience. Maybe Murphy was right. They'd been pulled out of the field too soon and hadn't learned enough of the basics. In this assignment, they'd developed a keen eye for names and faces and a talent for making phony friends. They'd become highly efficient human recording devices, but knew very little about actual police work. She worried their inexperience would thwart any chance they had of finding the killer or even worse keep them from recognizing solid evidence when it was right under their noses. They should've told Murphy about the keys.

A feeling of urgency swept over her as she realized failure was not an option. There wasn't any chance she'd be able to reconcile her ego with the disappointment of leaving this assignment not knowing how and why Soriano died. Not to mention the department would probably never forgive her inability to do what the chief had asked. All the success she'd had over the last three years would be worth so much less if she failed to accomplish this final task.

Jones's calmness was becoming irritating too because she was concerned it might be an indication he was less committed than she was. Given his obsession about promoting, she could be reasonably certain that wasn't the case, but nevertheless the tension of the last few days was beginning to mess with her emotions, something she'd never experienced and didn't like.

"Is it just me or do you get the feeling something is not quite right with all this?" Jones asked, as he turned up the driveway and parked in front of their apartment. "It's like the department stirred up this whole Soriano mess and now they expect us to fix it, but they're not gonna give us what we need."

He turned off the engine, and they sat in the dark. She knew he was right. That's exactly what was bothering her. They'd been put in a position to fail.

TWELVE

The next morning, Josie was up and ready to go downtown by the time Jones returned from his run. Lying in their beds the night before, they had talked a long time before coming to the conclusion that no one in the department could understand or decipher Soriano's lifestyle better than they could and what they lacked in investigative experience and full disclosure from their superiors could be overcome by hard work. Sleeping had helped to further restore her energy and confidence.

Their plan had been to get to the Hall of Justice on Broadway and Temple as soon as the courts opened, but they were delayed when Manny and Alex drove up in Alex's truck and blocked the driveway as they were getting into her car.

Manny wanted to talk to Jones alone, but he refused, insisting Josie had to be part of any discussion. She offered to let them back into the apartment but Manny sat on the doorstep and Alex planted himself nearby. In the unfiltered early morning light, the WLM leader looked much older and weaker. He had a dead man's complexion, and what had been a hard, wiry body just weeks before, now was hunched over and emaciated. He coughed uncontrollably into a handkerchief before he was able to speak.

"You want to tell me what the fuck's going on?" Manny demanded in a thin voice, looking at Jones who was leaning against the side of the garage a few feet away. Josie was sitting on the retaining wall watching Alex. She expected some reaction from the big man but he stared silently at the ground. Manny's bodyguard had been at the camp and seemed to be very close to Quentin and Emily. Josie knew Alex was part of their plan, but obviously his boss wasn't.

"I'm not the one to ask," Jones said.

Josie could see Manny's jaw tighten, the veins on his neck bulging when he said in a hoarse whisper, "I'm fucking asking you," before he coughed and spit an ugly yellow glob of mucus on the sidewalk. He called Jones a name in Spanish she didn't understand, but it didn't take a linguist to know it probably wasn't a compliment.

Unfortunately her .38 revolver was in her purse under the front seat of the VW, but she knew Jones had shoved his semiauto weapon in his waistband under his shirt, so Manny wasn't a real threat at the moment. She wondered about Alex, but even if he had shifted his loyalties back to the leader of the WLM, he didn't appear to have a weapon and wasn't displaying any anger. It wouldn't be unusual for Manny to have a few of his people hiding around the corner so she kept an eye on their surroundings while they talked and had already calculated how long it would take to get to her gun if necessary.

"I'm not gonna speak for Josie, but it doesn't matter to me what you want," Jones said and added without emotion, "So go fuck with somebody who gives a shit."

Manny glanced up at Alex who reached down and helped him stand. He took time to steady himself a few feet from Josie before saying, "Something's not right about you, *tonta*. Just remember payback's a bitch, so don't be crying to me for no mercy when it comes."

Manny's parting threat was directed at her. She hadn't said a word, but the hate in his eyes told her everything she needed to know. Her instincts had been right; he never trusted her. Her days in the WLM were officially over.

They didn't move until Alex's truck backed out of the driveway and disappeared down the narrow street. She continued watching the rooftops and between houses and the alley, look-ing for anything suspicious, but apparently Manny's threats weren't meant to be imminent.

"You think Alex told him what Quentin's up to?" she asked.

"No, Alex wouldn't put Emily in danger. I don't know who's been talking to Manny. After that bomb fiasco at the Federal Building messed up his march, he should've figured somebody else was calling the shots . . . at his expense."

"Maybe, but I still wouldn't turn my back on Alex if I were you."

Jones shook his head and said, "Don't worry. I don't trust anybody."

THEY ARRIVED at the fourteen-story Hall of Justice before lunch but the underground parking was almost full. Josie drove down to the bottom level so they could work their way up moving slowly looking for Soriano's Ford Thunderbird. It took almost an hour but they found the dust-covered car on the second pass through the garage. It was parked on the top level in a dark corner under a dripping sewage pipe, with a ticket on the windshield. A concrete wall jutted out far enough to nearly conceal it. She parked nearby and when she got closer realized the car wasn't even in a legitimate parking space.

The ticket was dated five days earlier, but there was no way of knowing how long the car had been sitting in that spot before someone finally noticed it wasn't being moved. From the dirt on the windshield, Josie guessed it had been abandoned quite awhile. Jones took the car key from Soria-no's chain and opened the driver's door.

A musty metallic smell saturated the interior and Josie guessed dampness from the sewage line had somehow pen-etrated the roof or doors. The glove compartment contained nearly a dozen unpaid parking tickets. She took those and the one off the front window and put them in her purse. Jones searched the trunk while she looked under the visors and behind the seats. It was an older model but well maintained and much cleaner inside than she imagined it would be. They checked door panels and looked anywhere Soriano might've had a secret compartment or false bottom.

"I give up," Jones said, sitting on the driver's side. Having run out of new places to search, Josie was sitting in the passenger seat staring at drops of water creating dirt craters on the front window. "Other than those tickets, it's clean."

"Did you look underneath?" she asked.

"No, did you?"

"I have no idea what's supposed to be there. You should take a quick look."

He groaned and got out of the car again. "Do you have a blanket or something in your trunk I can put on the ground?"

She found a beach towel in the backseat of the VW, and he put it behind Soriano's car before lying on his back and shining his flashlight at the undercarriage.

It was quiet for several minutes and then she heard him shout, "Fuck me!" She leaned out of the car and saw him sit up quickly scraping his head on the bumper. He stood and moved the towel quickly to the passenger's side. He grabbed her arm and pulled her away from the vehicle, then knelt down again and looked under the car. Scrabbling to his feet, he said, "Get away from here," as he pushed her farther from the Ford. He gave her the towel and said, "Put this in your car. We'll take the stairs to the lobby."

"What's wrong?" she asked, throwing the towel in her car.

"I think it's wired with some kind of bomb under the driver's seat. We need to get as far away as fast as we can."

They hurried up the stairs and located a phone booth in the lobby. Jones called Murphy who immediately notified the bomb squad and LAPD's Central Division captain. She waited outside the booth listening to the conversation for a few seconds until she noticed the directory near the front desk. She got close enough to see that the District Attorney's Office was on the sixth floor. When she came back, Jones had finished the call.

"In the excitement, I forgot to tell you," he said, still sitting in the booth. "I found something duct-taped behind the rear wheel well."

"Where is it?"

"Still there, told Murphy so he can recover it when the bomb's dismantled."

"Did you at least see what it was?" she asked.

"Heroin . . . a plastic bag with dozens of tiny balloons filled with what I'm guessing is smack."

THIRTEEN

Murphy had told them to stay somewhere in or around the Hall of Justice for at least a couple of hours before returning to the parking level and retrieving Josie's VW. He estimated it would take at least that long to neutralize the device under Soriano's car, and he didn't want them anywhere near the emergency response teams.

He hadn't counted on the bomb squad ordering an evacuation of the building's lower floors, so hundreds of people including Josie and her partner were left standing on the corner of Broadway and Temple. The three top floors were detention facilities and either nobody was concerned about the prisoners or it was taking awhile to make arrangements for their transfer to another jail.

The Hall of Justice had been built in the 1920s with gold marble walls and gilded ceilings, so Josie thought it would be a shame if an explosion damaged the structure, not to mention blew up her only car. Before they were forced to leave, she had taken a long look at the directory in the lobby and was surprised to see that not only the district attorney, but the sheriff, public defender, tax collector, coroner, and superior and municipal courts were in the building.

"You don't suppose this bomb is part of Quentin's big plan . . . what he's setting up the next couple of days?" Josie asked as she and Jones stood on the sidewalk across the street from the Hall of Justice in front of the criminal courts building.

"It's possible, plenty of high-profile government targets inside."

"Might explain Soriano's reason for hanging around . . . maybe he intentionally left his car," she said, thinking out loud.

"For what, to blow up the sewage pipe?" he asked. "The bomb squad's always overly cautious. That bomb didn't look big enough to take down a fourteen-story building, but it might've done serious damage to anyone inside the car or nearby."

They didn't need to say what both of them were probably thinking—starting and moving the car had never come up, but what if it had. Josie felt a chill run down her spine remembering Charlie sitting in the driver's seat holding the ignition key.

"So you're saying somebody might've been trying to kill Soriano," she said and immediately hit her forehead with the palm of her hand. "Considering he's been murdered, I think that's pretty much a given."

Trying not to smile, Jones said, "I think you should take the detective's test as soon as you can. You're a natural."

She started to say something nasty about probably promoting faster than he would but stopped when she saw his expression change as he looked over her shoulder.

"What?" she asked, not wanting to turn around.

"Jacobson is coming toward us."

The judge was in a business suit, his tie undone, holding a cup of black coffee. He stopped beside Josie and said hello to her before shaking hands with Jones.

"This evacuation drill is getting to be part of my daily court routine," he said, smiling at her. "Have you heard what's going on this time?"

"Rumor is a possible bomb," she said and asked, "You've had a lot of false alarms?"

"One or two a week. This could take hours. Let me buy you guys lunch while we wait," he said, looking directly at her.

She accepted without asking Jones and the three of them walked north across Temple a short half block to a dingy-looking bar with chipped red brick and a bronze front door but no windows. The word "Docket" was embossed in gold lettering on a plaque to the right of the entry.

The name was a clear warning about what they would find inside, a den of jurisprudence. Her father had been an attorney and she and her brother grew up in his world of courtrooms and legal briefs, but they had both turned to a more exciting life in law enforcement. There was an aura of smug satisfaction that emanated from those stubborn few who endured and survived the rigors of law school. Josie could pick them out in any crowd and this place was crawling with Juris Doctorate arrogance. Their bulging expensive briefcases were stuffed under tables or leaning against bar-stools, and three-piece dark suits were the uniform of the day.

The judge led them to the least crowded section of the room. He let her slide into the booth first, then sat beside her with Jones across the table. They all ordered beer and sandwiches piled high with pastrami and coleslaw. She ate her sandwich and fries and most of Jones's leftovers before noticing Jacobson staring at her.

"Did I get something on me?" she asked, inspecting the front of her shirt.

"No, I was just wondering how you do that. I've never seen a woman finish one of those specials and almost two orders of fries. Don't you ever eat?"

"All the time," Jones said before she could answer.

"I'm curious. What is it you do, Miss Pastore, besides going to Larry Clarke's parties?"

"At the moment I work at the Sisters of Charity thrift shop."

"Charlie's told me he's studying at Santa Monica College," he said, nodding at Jones. "You must want something more than a thrift shop in your future," he said, sitting back and folding his arms. "You're a bit of a puzzle . . . bright young woman, sober, intelligent, well-informed with no apparent ambition or direction. I see so many young people who are . . . disillusioned with this country, but you're different somehow."

"I'm not happy with the way things are. I believe change will come, but it's not going to be easy," she said. Josie knew he was prying, goading her into talking about herself but it wasn't going to happen. She liked him, but he was in the middle of Quentin's world. It was critical that he believe she was exactly what she appeared to be. Maybe when this assignment was over, and she was out of the program and certain he had nothing to do with Soriano's death, she'd talk to him again, truthfully . . . if he still had any interest.

Jacobson seemed to realize pretty quickly she wasn't going to tell him much about her personal life, so he stopped trying and they chatted about books and movies, the state of the world, and people they knew. Josie was impressed with the range of subjects in which he had some knowledge or interest. Like Jones, he had fought in the war and had little patience with the antiwar movement. She could see the irritation in his eyes when she spewed doctrine decrying American imperialism and calling for a shift in power to the disenfranchised class.

"What do you think is the deal with Sandra Collins?" Josie asked, attempting to steer the conversation away from the war, not wanting him to completely dislike her.

"She's been poorly used," Jacobson said.

"What do you mean?"

"Sandra's a simple woman with a lovely face and a tiny brain who desperately wants to be relevant. She donates a lot of money to people like Quentin who pretend to care what she thinks. He writes her speeches. She recites them at demonstrations and like a well-trained actress she spews his nonsense as if it comes sincerely and directly from her heart."

"So you're not a fan," Josie said.

"I liked her movies; her theatrical politics not so much. She's lived in my neighborhood for years and I'm disappointed that someone with her influence can be so easily manipulated."

He paid the bill and they walked back across the street to the Hall of Justice. All the emergency vehicles had gone and the occupants of the building had apparently returned to their various offices.

Jones waited until they reached the front door before asking, "Do you suppose it would be all right to go up and say hello to Larry Clarke as long as we're here?"

"He's got a hearing in my court this afternoon, but I'm certain he'll make time for you. Besides I don't plan•to open my doors for another half hour at least. Better yet, stop by my courtroom if you like. You can see him in action. You'll be surprised. When he's working there's a pretty amazing transformation."

They thanked him and he disappeared inside an elevator. The same phone booth in the lobby was empty so she made a call to Murphy for an update. He told her the bomb squad had successfully dismantled the bomb. It was wired to the ignition and capable of seriously injuring anyone who'd started the car and anything within a few feet of the explosion.

"Did either of you wear gloves when you searched the car?" Murphy asked.

She looked at Jones and mouthed the word "gloves." He shook his head.

"Nope, sorry," she said.

"Don't sweat it. We'll eliminate your prints. How did you get into the car?"

She told him about the keys and how she got them. He was quiet for several seconds and she waited for the expletives, but instead he asked if she knew who might've left the keychain. Josie told him about her scavenger benefactor and the other items he'd deposited on her doorstep.

"We need to stake out your apartment and find this guy. There's a chance he might've seen the killer," Murphy said.

"Can we use the Shadow?" she asked. "Have him hang around for a few nights."

"We'll see . . . come out to the pier in a few hours and I should have analysis back on the drugs Charlie found."

"So it looks like whoever killed Soriano had a back-up plan to blow up his car in case they couldn't get him to Venice Beach," she said, watching Jones who was pacing outside the booth. "I gotta go. We're gonna check out the DA's office, where Dave worked. If he didn't take that car somebody had to drive him home or maybe to the beach. If we get lucky, he left a calendar or something to tell us who he was with, and I can sneak a peek when nobody's watching."

Murphy reminded her that the chief intended to make his public statement in another day telling the world Soriano was an undercover cop and everything would change. The killer would probably go underground and, like so many fugitives from the Black Panthers and Weather Underground, disappear forever. Even worse, every bit of intelligence Soriano had given PDID for the last three years would become worthless as his targets moved or changed their methods of operation. Murphy said he doubted the killer knew Soriano was a cop since none of the information they were receiving from any of the other UCs backed up the possibility that his cover had been blown.

They took the elevator to the sixth floor where the DA's office was located. The receptionist looked suspiciously at their clothes but called Clarke's number and he came out immediately. He was surprised to see them, but seemed to accept her lie that they were going to the clerk's office to check on the status of her court case just as the bomb threat cleared the building, and then they decided to stop by and say hello before making the trip back to the West Side.

This was a working office with stacks of case files piled in the hallway; mostly men in shirtsleeves sat behind desks covered with paperwork. Clarke led them through a bureaucratically designed maze to his workspace, only stopping to introduce them to one of the prettier secretaries. Even sober, he flirted.

He also pointed out the closed door to the district attorney's private office. Josie was grateful his boss wasn't there. She was afraid if they encountered the DA he might, with a careless word or facial expression, give away the fact that he'd already met them. Not everyone was as accomplished at lying as she and Jones.

There was barely enough time for Clarke to gather his paperwork before he had to leave for the courtroom.

"Where did Dave work?" she asked while the lawyer concentrated on stacking two boxes of case files on a small dolly.

"That was his cubbyhole," Clarke said, pointing without looking at a small desk tucked in the corner of the room under the window.

"Have you gone through his things yet?" she asked.

"I'm waiting for the police to tell us they notified his next of kin," Clarke said, straightening up and stretching his back. "I want somebody to claim his stuff so I can box it up and get my space back."

"We can box it up for you if you want. Doesn't look like there's too much," she said.

He squinted in her direction for a few seconds as if he were struggling to split his attention between what she was saying and the upcoming legal task at hand. His demeanor was different in this environment. Although his expensive suit needed pressing, his eyes seemed permanently bloodshot, and his hands were a little shaky, there was a sort of constrained seriousness about him. The alcohol and drugs had visibly taken their toll, but he seemed to be using all his sober energy to stay focused on the pending case.

"You can take a look if you want," he said shaking his head, "but I've got to get to David Jacobson's court on time. For such a mellow guy, he's a bloody dictator in that court."

As soon as Clarke disappeared down the hallway, Jones asked the pretty secretary if she'd locate an empty box for them. Josie was surprised the lawyer had agreed so easily to allow them access to Soriano's desk. She was afraid his cooperation meant there was nothing of importance left to find among the dead man's belongings.

They had everything packed away in a few minutes. The desk had obviously been resurrected from the county's ancient inventory of wooden relics, so the locked drawers were simple enough for Jones to open with a bent paperclip. In one of them, there was a copy of the complete case file on the Ruben Salazar death, the news director who had been killed a year earlier by a sheriff's deputy's errant tear-gas canister during an antiwar demonstration.

Nothing else of importance was found until Josie pulled the right side bottom drawer out too far and it came off its broken track, falling onto the floor. When she lifted it, she discovered two keys and a building blueprint taped under that drawer. They immediately checked under the other drawers in the desk but didn't find anything.

She put the keys and the blueprint in her purse and stuffed the bulky case file in Jones's belt behind his back, covering it with his shirt and jacket. The desk was empty now and Josie put the half-filled box with its contents on top, taped a note to it telling Clarke there were no personal items found so the space was his again.

They stepped out of the office as Jake Corsino was leaving his office across the hall. He hesitated just a moment, then turned, and walked away without a word or second glance.

"Good man," she whispered, closing the door.

Luckily no one paid much attention to them as they left the building. They took the stairs to the parking garage with two deputy sheriffs trailing a few steps behind, but the lawmen were laughing and talking and didn't seem to notice or care about the Quasimodo hump protruding from Jones's back.

There was an empty space where Soriano's car had been and pieces of yellow crime scene tape still remaining on some of the pillars. As soon as they got into the VW, Jones pulled his shirt out, removed the file, and started browsing through the pages as she drove.

"Did you know that after Ruben got his head blown up, Quentin and Emily were the ones who got the Brentwood crowd to put up money for the Salazar Center?" Jones asked.

"It was a tragedy but clearly an accident. From what I read he was drinking coffee in the wrong place at the wrong time. I don't understand why they've made such a big deal about it."

"Because Quentin knows it's a cause, something that'll make people angry. A respected Mexican guy is dead. The cops who killed him didn't get prosecuted, ergo the government is corrupt. In his mind that gets the masses to rise up, burn down the city, and kill everybody in charge . . . he wishes. This is his ideal formula to start a revolution," he said, holding up a copy of a grainy black-and-white picture of Salazar's bloody homicide scene.

"Then I don't get why Manny isn't part of it," she said.

"Manny doesn't want to destroy the city; he wants to run it."

"So Quentin uses him as a decoy to distract the police until his revolution gets started . . . clever little maniac. Here take a look at this," she said, taking the blueprint out of her purse and tossing it on top of the open file on his lap. She figured there had to be a reason Soriano was keeping it hidden.

Jones opened what looked like schematics for a very large multistory building and got quiet as he studied them. She asked what was so interesting but he didn't answer as he ran his finger along the lines of the plans and seemed to be tracing the interior space of one particular area. They didn't speak again until she parked in the garage at the Redondo Beach pier and was able to lean over and see for herself.

The drawings were blueprints for the Hall of Justice, and someone had drawn a circle in pencil around the sixth floor office of the district attorney. Another circle had been drawn on the top floor of the garage around a single parking space which, according to her estimate, was very close to where they had located Soriano's car. She folded the plans again, stuck them in the Salazar case folder, and gave everything back to Jones to deliver to Murphy.

They had to walk past the witch's store on the pier to get to the bar and she noticed it was dark inside and looked closed. Apparently Miss Satilla was still doing jail time. The more radical feminists embraced witches as their symbol of female power and uniqueness. Josie knew only someone with Murphy's weird sense of humor would've thought the location appropriate for an important meeting with Chief Perez and the DA.

A marine layer had covered the pier with a thick blanket of clouds making it difficult to see more than a few yards ahead and the distant, lonely wail of a foghorn was the only sound she heard as they stepped into the bar.

The bartender was sitting at one of the tables with a couple of unshaven men in worn army fatigues and didn't seem eager to get up until he recognized Jones. Murphy hadn't arrived yet, so he poured them a couple of tap beers and they sat in one of the empty booths. There was an open box of stale donuts on a nearby table. Josie reached over and took one covered with chocolate. She washed down a big bite of the greasy deep-fried dough with a gulp of beer.

"That's really disgusting," Jones said. "Besides how can you eat again after that lunch?"

"I think better when I'm eating."

"If that was true you'd be a genius."

She took another bite and showed him her middle finger before realizing Murphy was standing beside her. The sergeant didn't say anything but went behind the counter and got himself a bottle of Budweiser before coming back and sitting across the table from them.

Jones put the case file with the blueprint in front of him and Josie let him take a few minutes to look through it before she pointed out the two places that had been circled and gave him the keys she'd found taped under the drawer. She retrieved the pile of parking tickets from her purse and took a closer look at them while Murphy was examining the floor plans.

Most of the tickets had been written in front of Soriano's apartment in Mar Vista. He seemed to have had a problem remembering to move his car on street-cleaning day, but two tickets were from parking his T-Bird in a no-parking zone at an address in old Venice near Oakwood. It was interesting because that particular part of town hadn't come up before in their investigation. She jotted down the location on a bar napkin, then gave the tickets to Murphy.

"This is looking like the DA's office might be the target," Murphy said, finally glancing up at them.

Josie guessed he must've moved back home with his wife. He was in a better mood. His clothes were clean and he seemed rested. A few minutes later, Carlson came into the bar wearing new jeans and a silly smile and sat beside him. They exchanged an intimate look that changed Josie's assessment. The home he'd moved into most likely was not the one he'd shared with Angela and his sons. Brickhouse was on the prowl again and had found refuge with yet another woman who was lonely enough to tolerate his bad temper and sweaty nightmares . . . for a while at least. She guessed the physical injuries he'd suffered in the war had healed long ago but there seemed to be emotional scars making him a very unhappy man who didn't seem to take any satisfaction in the fact that he had a nice family and was really good at a difficult job.

Josie felt bad about his situation. She respected Brickhouse as a cop but had avoided spending prolonged periods

of time with him. His black mood was stifling and she sometimes found it so oppressive she needed to get away just to
take a deep breath.

"Maybe it's not a place but a person they're after," she
said.

"We'll give the DA and a few of the other high-profiles at
the Hall of Justice extra protection," Murphy said. "But we
can't watch all of them all the time."

"This must have something to do with the Salazar case. You
should provide protection for anyone who's connected . . .
especially the deputy who fired the tear-gas projectile and
whoever in that office decided not to prosecute," Josie said,
and could see the veins in Murphy's neck bulging. He never
liked being told what he should do.

"Wouldn't it be easier to have surveillance on Quentin?"
Jones asked.

Murphy looked at Carlson and hesitated before saying,
"It would if we knew where he was. He's gone underground.
None of our people can locate him."

"What about Emily?" Josie asked.

"She's still on the West Side but hasn't tried to make any
contact with him or Manny Contreras," Murphy said, motioning for the bartender.

"Unfortunately it appears Quentin has decided to cut
the two of you out of his revolution," Carlson said, with her
annoying sneer.

"We'll see," Josie said defensively, but she knew the irritating detective was probably right. It would be understand-
able if they wanted to ditch her since they didn't know her
very well, but she couldn't believe they'd leave Jones out. He
should've been valuable, their perfect soldier, a disgruntled
vet who was willing to fight for their cause and knew how.
"So now what?" she asked.

"Just stay available and see if Quentin contacts one of you,"
Murphy said, ordering whiskey for himself. Josie stopped the

bartender and told him to bring the same for everyone as Murphy added, "And if he does, you call me."

"The heroin under Soriano's car was Mexican brown, packaged for sale," Carlson said, as soon as the bartender walked away. "His autopsy didn't show any drugs in his system. So either he was transporting or selling."

"Or he didn't know it was under there," Josie said.

"Whoever planted the car bomb probably didn't realize it was in the wheel well, but it certainly opens the door to the possibility his death might've been connected to drug dealing," Carlson continued, ignoring Josie.

"Anybody could've put it there without Dave knowing," Jones said. "His girlfriend was a heroin addict; Quentin is a user . . . hell, half the population of Venice Beach is down on that cheap Mexican tar."

"Until somebody proves different, a drug-related killing remains a viable option," Carlson said, taking a sip of her drink before pushing her nearly full glass in front of Murphy.

Josie finished her whiskey and was ready to leave. The combination of beer, stale donut, and whiskey was making her stomach a little queasy. The stuffy room filled with cigarette smoke and the odor of Carlson's strong perfume didn't help. She needed to get out of there and into the cool ocean air to clear her head.

"After he makes his announcement about Soriano, the chief will decide whether or not to leave you two undercover," Murphy said. "But I want to know from this minute where you are and what you're doing. Stay in touch every day or I'll pull you out myself."

Josie had the napkin with the address she copied from the parking ticket in her pocket. As soon as they were out of the bar she gave it to Jones.

"You know where this is?" she asked, and explained where she got it.

"One of the shittier parts of Venice . . . second-, third-generation gangbangers . . . drugs, prostitution."

"Might be nothing but he was parked there long enough to get a ticket . . . twice," she said, already feeling better before they got to the parking structure.

She drove up Pacific Coast Highway to Venice, giving them time to think and plan.

"If Soriano was spending time in that neighborhood, maybe we shouldn't be so quick to take drug dealing off the table," Jones said, staring out the window. "There's nothing but drugs or sex bought and sold in that area."

"I know, but I hate it when Carlson's right. She's such an egotistical ass," Josie said, annoyed at herself for allowing the woman to get under her skin.

"Maybe, but she's just playing the odds . . . guys get killed a lot when they're dealing drugs, not so much for spying."

As they talked, Jones seemed distracted and was more interested in discussing Murphy's relationship with Carlson than Soriano's killer. He'd met the sergeant's wife, Angela, a tall Brazilian beauty who'd gained a few pounds but was still very pretty. He said he didn't understand how any man could possibly prefer Carlson.

Josie was convinced Angela never liked her, but she couldn't help admiring the outspoken woman who genuinely seemed to love her husband despite his faults. However she was certain the decision for Murphy to leave the family home hadn't been his. He'd been thrown out of his house on other occasions and she guessed Carlson was simply another temporary port in his stormy marriage, a place to sleep that wasn't the drafty dirty back room of the no-name bar until Angela relented, forgave him, and allowed him back into her bed.

"This job isn't designed for family life. I don't think it works unless two cops marry each other," she said.

"If you're both street cops, then you're gone or stressed out all the time and your kids get all screwed up. I'm going to wait until I promote high enough to get regular hours before I even think about marriage or kids."

"But by then you'll be old and ugly and no decent woman's gonna want you," she said, trying not to smile.

"At least I can promote," he said and added quickly, "Sorry, low blow. I'm sure in another twenty years, they'll allow you to become a management prick too . . . then working cops can bad-mouth you as much as any man."

He directed her from the coast highway to the Venice neighborhood a few miles from the beach where the ticket had been written on Soriano's car. His description of the area wasn't exaggerated. The houses had been neglected for a long time, most with yards covered by overgrown grass and weeds, filled with old mattresses, broken furniture, and rusted car parts behind chain-link fences. Several properties had big unfriendly looking dogs pacing the perimeter. A system of alleys ran throughout the neighborhood with barbed wire protecting the rear of those properties unfortunate enough to have access to one of those alleys.

Junk piled against graffiti-filled walls and strewn over the neglected potholed asphalt made it nearly impossible for a car any bigger than the VW to maneuver through most of the alleys. Josie spotted bloody syringes and used condoms thrown near overflowing dumpsters and other places where someone could take care of business without being seen by prying eyes from a patrolling police cruiser.

It was a depressing place, a breeding ground for criminals, and she worried whatever Soriano's reason for being there, it wasn't going to be helpful in convincing anyone the drugs found under his car didn't belong to him.

They located the house by using numbers painted on the curb. There wasn't a dog behind the fence, but a narrow dirt path from the gate to the porch was the only piece of the yard not cluttered with junk. A discarded baby crib filled with magazines, a toaster oven, and clothes was holding open the torn screen door. Old blankets and comforters covered what appeared to be furniture and a partly dismantled washing machine, leaving little space for visitors to walk anywhere but directly to the door.

There was extensive damage to the door and frame near the lock and deadbolt. It looked as if someone had kicked it several times and Josie's immediate thought was narcotics officers had served a search warrant and had to force entry. She knew drug dealers could do similar damage if a deal had gone bad, but either way it wouldn't be good.

The doorbell was an empty hole, so Josie knocked on the door. Jones tried to look in one of the front windows but there were too many obstacles blocking his view. After a few minutes, he knocked again. This time there was a barely audible voice from inside the house.

"What do you want?" a woman asked.

Josie couldn't hear very well but there was something familiar in that voice.

"We need to talk to you," she said. "It's important. Please open the door."

"Fuck off, I ain't opening no door."

"Kate?" Josie said, recognizing the singer's throaty sound. "It's Josie, Emily's friend. I need to talk to you."

It was quiet on the other side of the door. Jones shrugged, but Josie motioned for him to be patient. Although they hadn't known each other very long, she was confident she'd made a connection with Kate. She wasn't proud of it but creating phony bonds with people had become her special talent and she felt it had happened with Kate.

After a minute or so, the door opened wide and Kate stood there in her bare feet, dressed in sweatpants and what looked like a maternity top. She hugged Josie and gave Jones a hard unwelcoming glare.

"Come in," Kate said, grabbing Josie's arm and almost pulling her into the house. She looked over her shoulder at Jones who was trailing behind them and added, "I don't give a shit what the fuck you do. Just don't bother me."

The house was clean, but cluttered like the rest of her property. From what Kate told them, it had been her great-grandparents' home and passed on to her. Josie guessed nobody had thrown anything away for generations. An ancient upright piano and guitar were in the corner, inches from a kitchen table that at one time had probably been someone's patio furniture. A baby crib that looked old and handmade with simple carvings on the rail was set up in the living room with piles of baby clothes, a playpen, highchair, and packages of diapers. No doubt about it now, Josie thought. She's pregnant.

Nothing around the crib looked new, but clean and ready for use. Kate pushed aside a pillow and blanket on the couch to make room for them to sit. Jones wisely stayed at the kitchen table out of the way.

"Sorry for the mess. Can't sleep in bed no more," she said, scratching at her face and arms.

"When is your baby due?" Josie asked, but really wanted to know who the father was, hoping it wasn't Soriano's.

"Awhile . . . just started showing."

Josie looked in her eyes. Her pupils were pinpointed and her eyelids droopy, but beyond the effect of drugs, she seemed tired, worn out. Her skin was yellowish grey and her long brown hair dull and dry and needed brushing. She knew the woman was still using heroin, but asked anyway, "You off the needle?"

"No point . . . doc says don't matter what I do now; kid's gonna have shit in his veins." Kate looked at the pile of baby things across the room and said, "Thinking I might get rid of it, kill it . . . world don't need another fucked-up cotton shooter."

"What's the father say?" Josie asked, cringing at the casualness of her remark.

"He's a fucking dickhead. Fuck him," she mumbled.

"Is it Quentin?"

She gave Josie a what-do-you-think look, nodded, and said, "Kid's old man is the best damned reason not to let it breathe."

"Baby can't help who his father is," Josie said, relieved Soriano apparently hadn't deposited his protégé in the womb of Kate Sparks.

Kate groaned, held her side, and whispered, "Fucker's just like his old man, doing everything it can to make my life hell."

"I really need to ask you something about Dave Soriano," Josie said. She wondered what Quentin was doing to make her life miserable but could see Kate was getting increasingly agitated and probably not going to let them stay much longer.

She stopped fidgeting, looked up at the ceiling, and said with a sigh, "What about him?"

"Was he the one that copped the heroin for you?"

Her cheeks filled with air and she spit an explosive laugh, spraying Josie's face, "Who the hell told you that? Quentin?" she asked when she could talk.

"I heard Dave might've been dealing and that's why he got killed," Josie said, wiping her face with her jacket sleeve.

"Fucker hated drugs, never wanted me taking care of business around him . . . found a nickel bag here one time, swore he'd never come back 'til I flushed it . . . pretended to flush it."

"Any reason he might've had drugs in his car?"

"Hell no."

"Did anybody else drive his car?"

"I don't know . . . Quentin maybe after his truck got t-boned."

"Anybody else?"

"I don't know. Who cares? He's gone," Kate said, her drowsy eyes filling with tears.

"If not Dave, who'd you buy from?"

Kate stared at her, an empty emotionless gaze. She seemed to be searching deep inside her brain for a response, her survival instincts probably warning her not to reveal that information, but Josie seemed to be her friend . . . a sympathetic kind friend, someone who cared about her . . . she thought.

"Manny Contreras," she said. "He's everybody's contact."

"Everybody who?" Josie asked.

"You know, locals . . . mostly chippers, chicken-shit habits on the West Side, dip-and-dab needle junkies . . . his Mexican horse is such weak crap anyway."

"Did Manny have a beef with Dave?" Josie asked.

"Manny has a beef with anybody who hangs out with Quentin. He hates Quentin's guts."

"Why?"

"Because they're both shitty wannabe generals . . . Manny's a vicious sonofabitch. He'll get one of his apes to hurt you if he thinks you disrespected him or got in his way . . . Quentin's worse."

"You think Manny might've killed Dave?" Josie asked.

"No way, he didn't like him hanging with Quentin, but Manny treated Dave like a little brother cuz they both had family in El Salvador," Kate said. She got up and tried to stretch her back, but appeared to be in pain. Light beads of sweat were forming on her upper lip.

"You want us to take you to your doctor or emergency?" Josie asked, starting to worry about her.

"Fuck no. I want you both outta my house so I can get some rest," she said, walking slowly to the door and opening it.

Jones left first and waited for Josie on the sidewalk. He hadn't said a word and she had nearly forgotten he was there. Before leaving, she'd offered to help out but Kate refused and said the owner of O'Farrell's had promised to take care of her, loan her money to help handle most of the bills until she could get back to work.

"Now what?" Jones asked when they were sitting in the car. "Soriano came here, but he's not the father of Kate's baby; if she's telling the truth, he hated drugs but we still don't know what the heroin was doing under his car or who killed him."

"I think she might be really sick," Josie said, driving away, but watching the front of the house disappear in the rearview mirror.

"Not our problem. If Manny's the drug dealer, in my opinion he's suspect number one for planting dope under the car and killing Soriano."

"You heard what she said. Manny didn't have a problem with Dave. I wonder if she's telling the truth about who the baby's father is."

"I doubt Kate could tell you for sure . . . knowing her, it could've been anybody offering a couple of free dime bags."

"Manny liked Soriano because his family was from El Salvador. Quentin needed him for whatever his crazy plan was, and Kate loved him. So who's left with a reason to want him dead?" she asked, but didn't expect an answer. She said it out loud hoping an obvious name would pop into her head, but it didn't.

"We should probably go back to your apartment, make it easy for Quentin to find us if he's still looking," Jones said.

"What about dropping in on Emily and Burt? She seems pretty tight with Quentin, so I doubt he's going to do anything without contacting her. I can use the excuse that I'm concerned about Kate and wanted to ask their advice. She'll buy that . . . actually, it's true. I am a little worried about her."

They both figured Emily would be part of Quentin's plan so having an excuse to be around her was even better than waiting at the garage. Quentin was hiding now for reasons probably only he understood. If he was close to actually doing something, Josie knew his paranoia would be full blown, and he'd be seeing undercover police officers or informants around every corner. She believed the Hall of Justice had been his intended target, but Soriano got killed before the blueprints and keys could be delivered. There was no doubt in her mind that, given his need to blow things up, Quentin had already zeroed in on a new objective and Emily would be foolish enough to help him.

Josie was fairly certain Murphy had enough time to arrange protection for most of the high-profile people working in that building, but she was nervous about what Quentin intended to do now. She knew it was important that at least one of them, either she or Jones, made contact with him.

For the moment it had become her priority since their investigation into Soriano's death was going nowhere and Josie doubted CCS would come up with a viable suspect before the chief of police made his announcement the next afternoon. She'd try to get Murphy or Carlson to ask for more time but didn't believe that was likely.

Once the world knew Soriano was a cop, finding his killer would become a lot more difficult, but Josie feared that as much as she wanted and needed to be out of this assignment, she'd never get her life back on track and really enjoy normality unless she could find out who murdered him and why.

FOURTEEN

The shades were drawn but the lights were on in the Rice living room when Josie parked the VW in the carport near the guesthouse. They were welcomed by Emily and Burt who were both standing behind the front door when it opened. Emily squealed with excitement and hugged Josie, pulling her into the foyer.

"I'm so relieved we found you," Emily said. "Burt's been searching for hours. You really must get a telephone in that garage, Josie."

"I didn't know we were lost," Josie said, looking around the room, hoping Quentin would be there, but he wasn't.

"What's up?" Jones asked, walking over to the bar and pouring two shots of whiskey. He gave one to Josie and they touched glasses before taking a sip. "Thanks," he said, holding up his glass to Burt.

"My pleasure," Burt said, snatching the bottle and topping off his drink before asking, "Didn't Quentin get hold of you?" The empty bottle of single malt and Burt's slurred words told Josie the lawyer had been drinking awhile, but Emily seemed sober.

"Nope," Josie said. "We just left Kate Sparks's place. I'm worried about her. I thought you might come back with me and convince her to go to the emergency room."

"Not a chance," Emily said coldly and slid off the arm of the couch onto the seat cushion. "Drugs and psychosis aren't a great combination . . . love her voice but I've written her off as a total loser."

Josie didn't pursue it. Emily's disdain had to be about something more. She'd known her long enough to understand the childish woman's feelings operated on the extreme, irrational edges of love and hate. The people she adored who could do no wrong one day would become her enemy with as little provocation as a misspoken word or slight difference of opinion. There was an art to manipulating someone like Emily. Most people wouldn't even try, but so far Josie had managed to massage her ego and dance around her mood swings keeping her as a valuable resource for PDID.

"I need to talk to Quentin," Jones said, dropping onto an overstuffed chair near the fireplace. "If he's not gonna use us, we're taking a road trip north, do some damage in Santa Barbara again, big rally in Berkeley after that. Too much stuff going on. I'm not hanging around here anymore waiting for him to make up his mind."

Good move, Josie thought.

"That's why I was trying to find you," Emily whined. "We're meeting him tonight. I thought that's why you came. The car's all packed. Let's go," she said, bouncing like a little kid eager to leave for Disneyland.

"Where are we going?" Josie asked. "We can meet you there. I need to stop by my place and change."

"No, we have to go now," Emily insisted.

Josie exchanged a look with Jones. They were both armed but knew they shouldn't do this without letting Murphy or Carlson know. But there was no way to tell them.

"Isn't there anything we need to bring . . . weapons, equipment . . .?" Jones asked, his voice trailing off.

"Got everything," Emily said, grinning.

"Fine," he said, not looking at Josie, but she could hear in his voice he didn't think it was in any way fine. "Josie can wait for me back at the garage."

"No, we're all going," Emily said, "except Burt. He stays here to do what he does best . . . drink until he falls down." She gave her husband a look of disgust but he acted as if he hadn't heard her and left the living room without saying a word, clutching a full bottle of fifteen-year-old Glenfiddich. "If we didn't need his license . . ." she whispered, but stopped and looked at them as if she'd forgotten they were in the room. "Sorry," she said, her expression softening. "I know exactly what he is, but for now we've got to have a lawyer who does what he's told and keeps his mouth shut."

"And later," Josie said, thinking how much she wanted another taste of that expensive whiskey.

Emily made an ugly laughing sound but she looked deadly serious.

"Poor Burt," Jones mumbled.

They went through the kitchen door into the large garage. Emily told them she would drive the black Mercedes, so Jones got into the passenger side. Josie had noticed the license plate wasn't on the front of the car, so she walked all the way around to get into the backseat and saw the rear plate had been pushed up under the frame just far enough to make the numbers difficult to read.

There was nothing in the backseat so whatever they were bringing was in the trunk. Jones tried to get Emily to discuss what they were about to do but she wouldn't reveal any pertinent information, except to say that Quentin would tell them everything when they got to their destination.

"Can't you at least say who else will be there?" Josie asked as the car pulled onto the San Diego Freeway.

"No," Emily said, clearly annoyed. Her long blonde hair was in a single braid hanging down her back and a black headband held the loose ends away from her face. She wore boots, jeans, and a stylish leather bomber jacket that Josie guessed had come from one of the pricier shops on Rodeo Drive in Beverly Hills—Coco Chanel warrior gear. The road wasn't crowded but she stared straight ahead as she drove with a determined look that said, "I'm on a mission. Don't bother me."

Josie sat back wishing she'd had an opportunity to talk with Jones before they left, just a few seconds to come up with some sort of seat-of-the-pants strategy. Not telling Murphy wasn't their choice, but she knew they couldn't walk away and let Quentin destroy property or harm someone without trying to stop him. At the moment there were no options, but every one of her survival instincts was telling her what they were doing was a very bad idea.

When Charlie had suggested to Emily that Josie could wait for him back at the garage, she knew he was attempting to keep her out of danger and give her a chance to warn Murphy. It didn't work out and she wouldn't have left him alone anyway, but she had to admire the man's ability to think on his feet. She hoped he was clever enough to see a way for them to come out of this in one piece without killing anybody.

Twenty minutes later, they were in East LA. Emily parked the Mercedes in the lot behind the Salazar Center and told them to follow her down a narrow sidewalk on the north side of the building. It led to a basement door that Josie had never seen or even knew existed. Emily used a key to open it, and they climbed down creaky wooden stairs to a dimly lighted large room that smelled like a sewer pipe.

There was a workbench with a single 25-watt bulb directly overhead and metal shelves against two walls filled with assorted junk, dozens of empty coke bottles, and several cans of gasoline. Tools, coils of wire, and piles of rags were scattered throughout the space. A large furnace took up a whole section of the room with a banged-up refrigerator, a card table, and three folding chairs in another corner. The cement floor was partly covered with a stained wool carpet and on top of it there was one open sleeping bag and several others that had been rolled up and stacked together.

When Josie got closer to the table she could see what looked like two pipe bombs and a row of a half-dozen Molotov cocktails ready for use.

A few seconds later, Quentin came from around the furnace and Josie noticed there was another door behind the furnace that probably led to stairs that were a way to get to the main floor of the center where the gym and cafeteria were located. He was carrying a couple of handguns. Alex was a few steps behind him, and had an assault rifle slung over his shoulder.

Quentin put his arm around Jones before they shook hands, "This is it, comrade," he said, patting Jones on the back. "The time has come to wake up the sleeping masses." He gave Josie a hug and she could smell stale perspiration on his wrinkled clothes and alcohol on his breath. His eyes were glassy and his thinning hair and patchy beard needed washing, combing, and some serious trimming. The short-order cook was looking more like one of the bums on Fifth and Central than a revolutionary. He seemed agitated and jumpy, and his hands had a slight tremor. She tried to see his pupils and although they should've been a little bigger in the dim light she could tell they were much larger than Jones's or Alex's.

Great, she thought, our paranoid leader is probably on some kind of speed.

"So what's the plan?" Jones asked, moving things on the shelves and seeming to be looking for something.

"What the hell are you doing," Quentin asked, pushing strands of his thin stringy hair away from his eyes.

"Whiskey, where is it?" Jones asked.

Quentin laughed, a high-pitched shriek sounding like someone had stepped on a cat's tail and said, "That's my man . . . shelf under the table. Have to hide it from Burt."

"Thought Burt wasn't coming," Jones said, opening the bottle of Jack Daniel's and not seeing any glasses took a swallow and handed it to Josie. She started to do the same, but

Emily retrieved two plastic cups from the top of the refrigerator and Josie poured them each a drink.

"He isn't. Not yet," Quentin said, smiling at Emily and pushing the pipe bombs closer together.

"Don't mess with those," Alex ordered from across the room.

Quentin held up his hands and backed away, saying, "Just remember who's calling the shots here, comrade."

"Calling the shots for what? What the hell are we doing?" Jones asked. It was the first time Josie had heard him raise his voice. He seemed annoyed and was acting as if he were ready to walk away. Quentin sat on one of the folding chairs and seemed to be trying to focus.

"Dave was killed by the cops before he got keys and plans for the Hall of Justice, but that's our target," he said, pushing his hair back with both hands. "We can't get in there tonight and take out the DA's office and that judge's courtroom like I planned. They found the car bomb too, so that's out."

"Then what are we doing here?" Josie asked, thinking that at least in someone's mind Soriano's murder had been solved.

"We're gonna wait until the building opens in the morning, plant our bombs right under their noses, firebomb the shit outta anybody that had anything to do with killing Ruben Salazar. Motherfuckers killed him and nobody paid. Tomorrow we hand them the bill. When it's done, message sent, we go deep underground to fight another day."

Josie and Jones exchanged a look. They didn't need to talk. This guy was nuts.

"The sheriff has a whole floor full of officers in that building and the county marshals are in every courtroom. You really think we can do that and get away before they gun us down?" she asked.

Quentin stood and pulled a semiauto pistol from his waistband. Holding it up with a wild look in his eyes he shouted, "We got guns. We can kill a lotta fucking pigs with this and this," he said, attempting to take the assault rifle away from

Alex who wouldn't let go of it. "Real question is, you got the guts to do it?" He turned his back on them, bent over slightly, and seemed to be calming down, but with a sudden violent kick sent his chair crashing into the basement's cobweb-covered wall. He looked up at the ceiling and yelled, "I hate this fucking country; I hate the war; I hate imperialist pigs; I wanna kill them all, take everything they fucking stole from the sweat of working people."

He stopped suddenly and seemed a little confused about what he should do next, took a deep breath to compose himself, and then looked at Josie for a few seconds with eyes open wide like a cornered animal before calmly picking up the chair, sitting again, and carefully laying his gun on the card table in front of him. "Fight or don't fight, I don't give a shit, but nobody ain't leaving my sight until this is done."

Tension in the basement room was palpable, but as soon as Quentin put the gun on the table, Josie started to breathe normally again. She'd had her hand over her purse ready to draw the revolver and shoot if he pointed any weapon in her direction. No one had moved or uttered a sound during Quentin's tirade, but she believed everyone in the room had to realize his paranoia was reaching new levels.

Before they had an opportunity to speak or discuss his plan, there was loud banging on the outside door. Everyone got quiet until Quentin told them he'd been expecting Sandra Collins to join them.

"She's here? You've got to be joking," Emily said, as Alex went up the stairs to unlock the door.

"I let you come," Quentin said, with a nasty grin.

"What does that mean?" Emily asked.

"It means the wealthy contribute to the revolution in whatever way they can."

"Fuck you, you crazy bastard, I'm as much a part of this as you," Emily said, her cheeks crimson with anger. "This isn't a game for me. I'm giving up everything. You haven't got a fucking thing to lose."

"Hi," Sandra said in her cheeriest party voice from the middle of the staircase. "I made it. Sorry I'm late." She paused to look around before stepping down into the room. Emily didn't acknowledge her. Instead she walked around the furnace and out the other door. "Did I say something wrong?" Sandra asked, taking off her long black fur coat and looking around for a place to put it before deciding to keep it folded over her arm.

"Did you bring the cash?" Quentin asked, not getting up.

"Of course," she said, holding up her leather purse. "Are you sick? You look terrible."

"Just leave it on the table, then you'd better get outta here," Quentin said, not bothering to answer her question.

"Are you certain there's nothing more I can do?" Collins asked, pulling stacks of twenty-dollar bills out of her bag. "Five thousand as requested," she said, stepping back and coughing a little from the puffs of dust her money had created as it hit the table.

From a few feet away, Josie could smell a hint of her expensive perfume hopelessly battling the powerful odors of dankness and ingrained muck around them. The actress was wearing a pink long-sleeved silk blouse with black bell-bottom corduroy pants. A long white chiffon scarf was draped around her neck and she was making a valiant effort not to be too obvious about staying in a tiny clean spot on the rug in the middle of the room as far as she could from the filthiness around her.

"No, you'd better go. I'll contact you tomorrow," Quentin said. He was serious and doing his best imitation of the heavyhearted sane warrior again.

In dramatic matador fashion, the aging actress opened her coat and flung it around her shoulders before returning the way she had come, as quickly as she could. The grimy reality of basement politics was apparently more than she'd anticipated.

"Tell Emily . . . never mind," she shouted from the top of the stairs.

As soon as the outside door slammed shut, Quentin stood and put the gun back into his waistband. He walked over to the workbench and thumbed through the small stacks of money. Josie thought he almost looked like a rational little revolutionary again in his thrift-store army fatigues and high-top tennis shoes, unlike the whirling psychopathic dervish of a few minutes ago. She guessed he was coming out from under the influence of some potent stimulant, and the influx of substantial cash had given him a moment of clarity.

"Get some sleep," he ordered, stuffing the cash into a paper bag before pulling the only open sleeping bag across the floor to a spot near the stairs.

Emily came back from the upper floors of the center, her pockets stuffed with packages of junk food she'd taken from one of the cupboards in the kitchen. She tossed them on the workbench and saw the bag of money. A glance around the basement told her Collins had gone and she seemed to figure out money had been the sole reason for the actress to be there. Her impatience with Quentin was evident when she swiped the bag off the table onto the floor and mumbled, "Shithead," before taking a sleeping bag and opening it beside Alex.

Jones took two of the sleeping bags and put them near the furnace away from the others where he and Josie snuggled close enough to whisper without being overheard.

"When they look like they're sleeping, I'll use the phone in the lobby upstairs," Josie whispered into Charlie's ear.

"If that doesn't work, we'll have to warn security as soon as we get in the building tomorrow."

"He's really psycho enough to do this," she said, touching Charlie's ear with her lips as she spoke. She was so close she could smell his shaving cream, but the room was small and Josie wasn't certain the others were actually sleeping. Luckily no one had turned off the dim light, so it was easy to see if anyone got up and moved.

"Try to get some rest. I'll watch and wake you when it's safe to go upstairs. If you can't contact anyone, then we'll have to find a way to stop them ourselves," he said. She didn't answer but laid her head on his shoulder and he put his arm around her, pulling her closer. It was a good fit and the warmth from his body made her drift off immediately.

Gentle shaking woke her out of a deep sleep after what seemed like just a few wonderful minutes. When she was fully awake, Jones carefully helped her unzip the sleeping bag. She slipped out and tiptoed around the furnace, where it was darker, to get to the door. She slowly, carefully turned the knob but it wouldn't open. The deadbolt had been secured with a key.

"Damn," she whispered and turned, bumping into Emily who was standing directly behind her with an accusing frown.

"What are you doing?" Emily asked.

"I gotta pee. Somebody locked the door," Josie said, jiggling the knob and doing an improvised wiggle dance. Her bladder must've been gigantic because truthfully she never woke up to pee, but it was the first excuse that popped into her head.

"I locked it. You don't have to go upstairs. There's a toilet in that room," she said pointing at an unmarked door on the other side of the furnace.

"Great," Josie said, nudging her aside and moving quickly in that direction, but before she closed the door, Josie spotted Alex sitting up in his sleeping bag with the assault rifle on his lap.

After a decent amount of time, she flushed the toilet and came out of the bug-infested water closet that she'd never use even if she really had to go. She slid back into her sleeping bag and whispered in Charlie's ear, "It's me and you, partner."

FIFTEEN

Before Josie could get to sleep again, a portable radio went off. The music was loud and annoying enough to keep her awake as it blasted Jefferson Airplane's "White Rabbit."

"When logic and proportion have fallen sloppy dead . . ."

The others started stirring but she lay still, listening until the song finished, thinking Grace Slick might've been describing this basement hole . . . drugs, chasing rabbits, white knight talking backwards. Where's ten-foot Alice when you really need her, Josie wondered, rolling over onto her back.

"Get up warriors, rise and shine, time to ignite the fires of revolution," Quentin shouted in an almost giddy upbeat voice.

The Queen of Hearts appears to be sober again, but still wacky as a dormouse, she thought, looking at Quentin as she crawled out of the sleeping bag. Jones was already up and munching on some of the junk food Emily had taken from the kitchen last night.

"Can't we get something better to eat upstairs?" Josie asked, anticipating another opportunity to make that phone call.

"No time," Quentin said. "Besides the staff is up there by now and you might give away our safe house."

"Right," Josie said, taking a Snickers bar from the workbench, but before she could finish tearing off the wrapper, Alex came down the stairs carrying a large box filled with

Styrofoam cups of coffee, more than enough for everyone, and a dozen donuts from Winchell's.

"Listen up," Quentin said, using a tool box to step up and sit on the workbench as soon as the coffee and most of the donuts were gone. "This is how the mission's going down."

With the precision of a Napoleonic general, Quentin gave them his plan. He would carry the pipe bombs into the building in his backpack; Alex would stay with him and have the assault rifle covered by his overcoat to make certain no one interfered with the explosives getting to their destinations. Emily and Josie would bring the Molotov cocktails, and since Charlie was their best marksman, he would take out any security, and if he got lucky, the DA and Judge Jacobson too.

"What are the Molotov cocktails for?" Josie asked, starting to realize that even if this scheme was unsuccessful they could do a lot of damage, maybe kill a cop or two or even an innocent bystander who got in the way.

"When we're getting out of the building, you two start tossing those fireworks at anything that'll burn. Do as much damage as you can . . . offices, furniture, people . . . whatever, I don't give a fuck, but I better see flames."

At that moment Josie's path had become crystal clear, and she hoped Charlie was thinking the same. They couldn't wait until they got anywhere near the Hall of Justice before taking action. The best place was probably right here and now, but first they'd have to get the assault rifle and his sidearm away from Alex.

"Let Emily carry the cocktails. I'm a better shot than she is. I can help Charlie," Josie said, knowing exactly how her uptight buddy would respond to that putdown.

"You do what you're told," Emily said, obviously feeling slighted.

"It's fine for you, but I want to be in the middle of the fight, not setting fires after it's all over like some demented Girl Scout," Josie said with as much snarky attitude as she could muster.

"What? Then I'm not taking them either. I can fight as good as you or anybody here."

"Sure you can," Josie said sarcastically and mumbled loud enough for her to hear, "In your dreams."

"Both of you, shut your fucking mouths. This is my show. You're both taking them, end of argument," Quentin shouted.

"No, I'm not," Josie said, crossing her arms and glaring at him.

"I could use her help. Next to me, she is the best shot," Jones said, and added before Quentin could respond, "You know I should probably carry the assault rifle. I've used it before so I won't get excited and lose my head . . . screw it up," he said, glancing at Alex.

Now Josie was certain she and Charlie were thinking alike. It was too dangerous to allow this half-baked revolution out of the basement.

She had stirred up plenty of dissension with Emily and now Jones was poking at Alex's inflated ego and it was working. The big man left the assault rifle leaning against the wall and moved closer to Charlie like a stalking lion.

"What the fuck you saying, man. You think cuz you won some Mickey Mouse five-minute fight one time with a sucker punch you're better than me?"

"No . . . actually, it was five seconds, and I think I'm better than you for lots of reasons."

Trying to restore order in his usual manner, Quentin was reaching into his waistband for his semiauto when in one motion, Jones picked up a twelve-inch section of steel pipe left on the table from the bomb making and hit the smaller man across his left temple with such force it knocked him off the workbench.

Alex seemed dumbfounded and frozen in place by the unexpected blow to his leader. He looked from Quentin's crumpled body to Jones, still holding the pipe, and back. When he finally recovered and turned to reclaim the assault rifle, Josie had it pointed at him. Jones took the revolver out of Alex's waistband and Josie had snatched Emily's handgun before she could draw it and get the safety off.

Josie felt her muscles relax and took a deep breath. The moaning from Quentin told her he was still alive, but his comrades seemed preoccupied with their own predicament and didn't show the least bit of concern about his condition or make any attempt to assist him.

She and Charlie had secured all the weapons and explosives. There would be no deadly attack on the Hall of Justice today; the structure would remain intact, and the DA and Jacobson were safe, at least for this morning. That was the good news. The bad news—after she made a phone call, their cover would be completely and irretrievably blown.

SIXTEEN

The call to PDID brought not only Murphy and Carlson, but a squad of supervisors and the division's captain to the Salazar Center. Someone had made the decision to keep the local area's patrol officers and commanders in the dark for now. The three would-be revolutionaries were transported to the intelligence division's home base at the old Georgia Street station. They would be held in that jail until detectives could interview each of them and determine if there was probable cause to book them for conspiracy to commit any number of felonies including murder.

Paramedics examined Quentin and were satisfied all he'd have to show for his encounter with the steel pipe was a large ugly lump on the side of his head and a hellacious headache. He did break his nose on the belly-flop crash landing off the workbench, but refused any medical aid for that injury. Josie was certain he'd have Burt Rice take color Polaroids as soon as he got bailed out, so anything that made his nose look better or less damaged until then would hurt their inevitable police-abuse lawsuit.

Emily was subdued as one of the female detectives escorted her in handcuffs out of the basement. She wouldn't look at Josie and hadn't said a word after demanding to make a phone call to her lawyer. The only person she did seem concerned about was Alex. Josie saw her mouth the word, "sorry," to him as he was being handcuffed.

Josie was eager for the PDID detectives to interrogate Alex and delve into his past, which she suspected might provide some interesting information and a different background than the one he'd been describing. She always felt he wasn't exactly the person he pretended to be. He was a serious man who was obviously trusted and given a lot of respect by Manny, but he was loyal to crazy Quentin and seemed to be having an intimate relationship with Emily who, although dedicated to mayhem, wasn't in Josie's opinion a serious person. More importantly if he'd been Larry Clarke's bodyguard, he might've been in a position to know something about Soriano's murder.

When the evidence, arrestees, and all division personnel, including Carlson, were out of the building, and Murphy was upstairs making peace with the manager of the center, who couldn't understand why Emily Rice, one of his major benefactors, was being carted off in handcuffs, Josie realized she was exhausted. The bomb-making paraphernalia, except the gasoline, had been cleaned off the shelves, packaged, and taken to be booked at property division. Nothing of importance or value was left in the room except a pile of dirty sleeping bags and the few candy bars Emily had pilfered the night before. Jones was sitting on the floor with his back against the wall, eating a piece of what looked like a Mars bar and drinking from one of the plastic cups. She found the other cup on an empty shelf and sat beside him, holding it out with both hands in front of her like a beggar. He removed Quentin's whiskey bottle from his inside jacket pocket and emptied it into her cup.

"Want some?" he asked, holding up the other half of the candy bar still in the wrapper.

She shook her head, took a sip of whiskey, and leaned back against the wall. "I need some sleep," she said, closing her eyes.

"That ain't gonna happen," Murphy said, walking around the furnace from the direction of the interior door. "We got reports to write. You're about to learn the true mantra of police work—how many reports, with how many division record or DR numbers . . . in this particular barrel of puppy turds, the answer is too many." He stood in front of them for a few seconds before reaching down and taking her cup. He smelled it, drank what was left, and gave it back. "Come on, get up. I'll find real food and strong coffee before you have to face life outside Wonderland."

He drove them to a coffee shop on Olympic Boulevard just a few minutes southeast of downtown. They sat at the counter and ordered sandwiches and coffee. Murphy knew the owner's son, another veteran who'd served with him in Vietnam. Cory had a nasty scar over his right eye and walked with a limp, courtesy of a Huey helicopter crash in which the rest of his crew died. He used a cane to steady himself behind the counter as he carried food and drink with his free hand. He was wearing a stained T-shirt with an American flag emblem, but unlike Murphy, he was friendly and smiled a lot.

It felt strange to Josie when Murphy introduced her as a policewoman and called Charlie "Officer Jones." Her instant reaction was panic. She looked around to see if anyone heard before remembering it didn't matter any longer.

"Don't look like no police I ever seen. New kinda hippie cop . . . what'd they call them, Brickhouse . . . Mod Squad or something?" he asked and topping Josie's mug of coffee said, "But, you know girl, you're prettier than that skinny blonde hype on any show."

"Thanks . . . I think," Josie said, smiling at him.

They finished eating but she wasn't in a hurry to leave. Cory was good company and could recall so many details about the men he'd fought beside in the war. He remembered all their names, their families, and those strange places they had died. He'd kept his buddies alive in his stories, talked about them in the present but it was clear to her that although he had survived his injuries, his life had stalled, been put on permanent hold somewhere in a rice paddy years ago.

Murphy was doing everything he could to forget that war and the nightmares it had created, but in his way, Cory had embraced it to keep the warriors he'd loved and lost closer to him. Either way, she thought, it was sad.

The Georgia Street station was ten minutes from the coffee shop, just north off Pico Boulevard south of the civic center. Pulling into the driveway without lying down in the backseat hidden from view under a smelly blanket was a new experience for Josie. It was common knowledge among radicals that the Intelligence Division was housed somewhere in that station. On more than one occasion security guards had caught members of different leftist groups hiding on rooftops of nearby buildings taking 35 mm pictures of cars and people entering the station. Their intention was to out an undercover officer or spy or snitch who was stupid enough to walk through the front door. This was the first time in three years she'd been allowed to sit up and actually see the front of the handsome, multistory, turn-of-the-century, grey stone building.

Although it had been intended and built as a patrol division station, it shortly became a primary receiving hospital, but hadn't been used for either purpose in years. The police department commandeered most of the space, believing the out-of-the-way location would serve nicely as the supposed clandestine home of several specialized divisions including Intelligence. Cops are notoriously bad at keeping secrets so it didn't take long before a lot of people outside the department knew exactly where to find PDID.

Murphy told her the city would never have allowed the police department to take the building if it hadn't been run-down and a prime candidate for demolition. He was right at least about the condition of the structure with musty old rooms and creaky wood or broken concrete floors. He took her and Charlie upstairs to the third floor where a large well-lighted space served as the squad room for the PDID detectives. Wooden tables with drawers were pushed together serving as desks. It was a noisy crowded space sectioned off for teams of detectives working different groups of radicals— Weather Underground, Black Panthers, Symbionese Liberation Army, coalitions for or against dozens of different causes and grievances, as well as any organization in the city that advocated violence or the overthrow of the government.

About a dozen people were in the room and looked up when they walked in. They were greeted by everyone calling out their numbers, the only way they'd been known to these detectives for the entire time they'd been part of the division. She was S73, Jones S45. After shaking hands with everyone and being warmly welcomed, they followed Murphy across the hall to the captain's office.

Captain Williams and his adjutant were the only ones in the division wearing business suits. The others were dressed like she was in casual clothes. She guessed if some of these detectives had been standing on the street next to her during demonstrations, they'd have gone unnoticed. She had looked around the detective bay wondering which one was the Shadow but felt a little uncomfortable asking the question since no one had volunteered the information.

"You both did a fine job of containing a threat this morning," Captain Williams said as soon as they were sitting on the wobbly wooden chairs in front of his desk. "Too bad we had to bring you up, but the chief should be making his announcement in a minute or two, so any chance we had of finding Soriano's killer is diminishing anyway."

"We'll interrogate the arrestees from the Salazar Center, try to scare them into giving us something, but from what Josie and Charlie have told us, Soriano was on friendly terms with these nut jobs," Murphy said. "They had no motive to kill him."

"Actually his death screwed up Quentin's plan to get in to the Hall of Justice at night and plant the pipe bombs without anyone around," Josie said.

"Not having Dave's keys to the service door or the car bomb as a distraction, Quentin figured his only option was this morning's kamikaze commando raid," Charlie added. "I just don't think they killed him."

"Somebody did, but who or why seems elusive," Captain Williams said, standing, his cue that they were done. "Until everything settles down, you two will stay assigned to PDID, but work inside with detectives. Murphy will find something to keep you busy."

"For how long?" Josie blurted out. Standing on the edge of freedom, she just felt the cage door slam shut again.

"For as long as I say," Captain Williams said curtly. His demeanor had changed and Josie figured his honest feelings had finally emerged. He seemed disappointed, a little angry. They had failed him. Under his command, one of his under-cover officers had been killed, and soon the whole world would know. Even worse, he hadn't arrested anyone nor could he explain how it happened. She and Charlie were not so subtly being told they would have to do penance for not finding the killer and allowing a blemish to appear on their captain's record, perhaps damaging his chances for another promotion.

"We're fucked," Charlie mumbled when they were in the hallway again.

"I'm putting in my transfer papers. What can he do?" Josie asked.

Murphy gently pushed both of them into the corner at the end of the hallway near the stairs.

"Transfer where, Pastore, to the women's jail or commu-nications? Don't be stupid. He wants to keep you here . . . for whatever reason, so stay and work on Soriano's murder and learn something from these detectives. It's better than anywhere else you can go. And you," he said, looking at Charlie, "after making your own work hours and being inde-pendent for four years, are you biting at the bit for morn-ing-watch patrol in the projects, working every weekend and most holidays?"

Josie looked at the floor and knew he was right. Her choices were dismal. If she could stay here and do detective work until patrol was an option that would be pretty good, especially since her days as an undercover officer were finished.

"I was looking forward to wearing a uniform and working the streets; I don't care about the hours. I have to get the hang of patrol before I make sergeant. Remember, you guys took me out of the academy, and I never worked a black-and-white except weekends as a recruit," Jones said, clearly disappointed.

"Listen to me, Charlie. You're smart and tough; with your background, you'll pick up patrol faster than most, trust me on that one. I know it sucks, but use this time to learn something that'll help you down the road as a supervisor."

"Don't sweat it. We'll go along with the program," Charlie said, looking at Josie, and she nodded.

"But there better be a huge chunk of gratitude at the end of this loyalty maze and I don't mean the women's jail," she said, locking onto Murphy's stare.

WHEN THEY got back, the television in the detectives' squad room was tuned to the local news station. The chief of police was making his announcement about the death of Policeman David Soriano. Josie sat at one of the tables and heard him give only vague details about the murder reading from a press release which also stated the off-duty officer's body was found by transients on Venice Beach.

According to the statement, Soriano was assigned to Personnel Division at the time of his death. The chief asked anyone who might've seen or heard anything that night or the next morning to call a special number set up by detectives. He concluded by saying no suspects or possible motives were known at this time. Soriano's family was out of state and at their request his body had been transported there for a private funeral. There wouldn't be a police funeral in LA, but a memorial service would be planned for a later date.

That was it? She looked around the room and thought, am I the only one who's thinking this is bullshit. A man gave his life working this dangerous shitty assignment and they shipped his remains out of town in the middle of the night like they were ashamed of him.

"Makes you proud," someone said from the other side of the room.

"Protect and serve."

"Die and disappear."

"Essential but expendable."

"Once again, political ass survives and rises above all the shit."

The comments came like raindrops one at a time, then a deluge of disdain for the lack of respect and appreciation shown by their leader for one of his men. Before the chief finished his comments, a detective closest to the television got up and turned it off and everyone went back to work as if it had never happened.

Josie felt a little better knowing she wasn't the only one pissed off, but suddenly remembered her car and belongings were still at her apartment. Somehow she'd have to get back there and remove the few things she cared about before Manny or one of Quentin's followers broke in and took or destroyed all her stuff.

It wouldn't be terrible if she lost everything in the apartment, but hated the idea of Quentin or Emily getting the last defiant word. Murphy told her he and two other supervisors would take them back to Venice in a rental truck to retrieve her belongings and anything Jones might've left behind. He thought they'd have plenty of time because Burt and Manny should be preoccupied with getting their people out of jail.

She doubted Manny would have much to do with Alex any longer but also knew alliances among these radicals frequently survived worse betrayals in the name of a common cause.

A couple hours later, Murphy drove them in a small U-Haul truck, with a two-car escort, back to Venice Beach. It was quiet on the street in front of the garage, but the detectives made a tactical entry and searched the apartment before allowing her inside. Nothing had been touched or tampered with in the room. She had them load her dresser and table while she packed the few clothes and books. Jones threw his one bag in the truck and helped with the furniture.

As she folded the comforter on top of the bed, Josie thought about the young girl on the beach and wondered if she would use it. She doubted Murphy would want to hang around while she searched the boardwalk for the girl and suggested they take the truck back to Georgia Street and she could follow in her VW after either giving the comforter to the girl or, if she couldn't find her, leaving it at the thrift store.

After questioning her sanity, Murphy said he and Jones would go with her and the others could take the truck back. They walked to the boardwalk and as far as the pavilion before Josie gave up. The girl wasn't in any of her usual places and the regulars at the makeshift gym and small shops hadn't seen her for several days. Josie carried the comforter back to the VW and she drove to the thrift shop with Murphy in the passenger seat and Jones scrunched up behind him in the back. She told Sister Mary Margaret she'd have to quit, refused her last twelve dollars in pay, and left the blanket.

They were back in the office before dinner where they learned Burt Rice had already bailed his wife and the others out of jail. The evening news on the three major channels had a brief story on their arrest, but not many of the details. The chief's announcement about Soriano had been given even less time and attention.

One of the stations interviewed Burt outside the Central Jail where Quentin and Alex had been transferred after their interrogations. He was outraged that the police would spy on the Salazar Center and vowed to sue for false arrest.

"Police-agent provocateurs are responsible for entrapping my wife and her friends into doing something that was neither their idea nor intention; they were tricked by corrupt undercover cops. The city and the LAPD will pay dearly for this travesty," Burt said, sounding controlled but outraged. He appeared sober, clean, and well-dressed.

"Scumbag attorney has inhaled the elixir of deep pockets and looks reborn," Murphy said, dropping into the closest chair.

The room was empty; detectives had gone home for the day or were out meeting with their UCs. Josie and Charlie listened quietly until the news segment was over, then he turned off the television.

"What an asshole," Charlie said. "Pervert's half in the bag most of the time. If he's not pawing women he's sucking on a whiskey bottle. California Bar should've pulled his ticket years ago."

"What happened to the five thousand dollars Sandra gave Quentin?" Josie asked Murphy.

"Booked as evidence. She'll get interviewed tomorrow, but we all know that's going nowhere."

"She aided and abetted a felony," Josie said.

"The DA won't go after her."

"Why not?"

"Because she'll plead ignorance, and we can't prove she's not just a knucklehead who wants attention and can be talked into giving away her money as a way to do it," Murphy said.

"I'm glad," Charlie said. "She's harmless."

Josie didn't respond, but gave him a look that said she knew his feelings went deeper than charitable indifference. She guessed over the last four years there had been several women who'd slept with him and were not going to be happy when they found out their good-looking rebel Charlie Jones was actually a cop.

Murphy took two large manila envelopes out of his desk drawer and put one in front of each of them. She opened hers and dumped her badge, revolver, and police ID on the table. Policewoman was embossed on a banner across the top of the badge with a raised image of City Hall riveted below it and the lucky number 13 at the bottom. A smaller envelope had her bankbook and checkbook.

It only took a few seconds for Charlie to thread his belt with a holstered gun through the straps on his Levis and clip on the badge holder. Her gun was supposed to go into a special holster sewn into a saddlebag-sized black purse, but Murphy kept that and instead put a brown leather belt, holster, and badge holder on the table.

"Try this. It's a guy's belt but small enough for your waist and the holster will fit a .38 . . . unless you wanna carry this ugly black anchor around your neck," he said, holding up the purse. He waited until she was wearing the gun then slid a box of ammo across the table between them. "Load them, preferably without shooting me or each other."

She drew the gun, popped open the clean, freshly oiled cylinder, loaded six rounds, and slipped it back into the holster before picking up the badge and rubbing her fingers over the shiny silver ridges. Someone had polished it. She'd forgotten how heavy it was and how much she wanted it back. The ID card had a picture that had been taken in the academy early one morning after the drill instructor got pissed off. He had the recruits run on the street to the entrance of Dodger Stadium, about a quarter of a mile uphill, and back, minutes before they sat in front of the camera. She looked wide-eyed, sweaty, and tired, but otherwise it wasn't a bad photo.

"If you haven't been practicing, dry fire and go up to the range a few times. You'll have to start qualifying again this month," Murphy said, tossing her the purse. "Keep this with your other junk in case you have to wear a uniform again someday."

Josie groaned. The last thing she wanted was to put on that uniform skirt, shirt with the Girl Scout tie and high heels, and carry a purse that was designed to make it as difficult as possible to retrieve a gun or handcuffs.

Before turning off lights and locking the office door, Murphy gave them an address in Hermosa Beach, just a mile or so from his no-name bar in Redondo. The division had rented each of them an apartment there for two weeks, long enough to find a place. It was a secure area with cameras in the lobby and a locked front door. He told them the duffel bags with their uniforms and other police paraphernalia were already in their rooms and ordered them back to Georgia Street at nine the next morning ready to work.

"Where's all my furniture and clothes?" she asked as they followed Murphy downstairs to the garage.

"Still in the U-Haul; it's parked in the officers' lot at the Harbor police station . . . we'll help you move everything when you find a permanent place."

"But my clothes . . ."

"With all the cash you've squirreled away, Pastore, celebrate and buy some fancy new underwear and a pair of jeans. You finally got what you wanted," Murphy said with a smirk. She knew what he meant—that she'd been too dumb to know when she had it good.

SEVENTEEN

Rush hour had come and gone so it was only a thirty-minute drive to the South Bay. Murphy had described Hermosa Beach as the rich man's Venice. No jugglers, weight-lifters' pit, or the flood of tourists, but in a lot of ways that coastal city attracted some of the same odd characters, drugs, and free spirits that populated the sand a few miles north.

She followed Charlie's little sports car down the Harbor Freeway and he led her directly to the two-story Formosa Apartments on Pacific Coast Highway, walking distance from the beach. Parking was under the building and she used the code Murphy had given her to open the security gate. Her room was on the second floor at the end of the hallway, Charlie's at the other end and closer to the stairs.

It was small but clean. The first place she checked was the bathroom, and there was a functioning shower and big tub. She dumped everything out of the department-issued canvas duffel bag onto the bed and hung up the three uni-form skirts and long-sleeved shirts. The shoes were practically new, but she hadn't worn anything but sandals and boots for years and her feet must've grown. Her toes felt cramped in the tight matronly two-inch heels. If she'd had any linger-ing doubts about staying in PDID, they were resolved at that moment. She wouldn't budge until the chief gave his blessing for women to work in patrol cars, dressed in uniform pants, Sam Brownes, and comfortable shoes that were fit to wear all day and chase suspects without breaking an ankle. She'd heard horror stories of policewomen trying to run in these high heels and skirts while attempting to get their revolvers out from the death grip of that poorly designed purse holster. That was not how she pictured herself doing police work.

She opened her bankbook and was surprised at how much money she'd saved in three years, a sizable sum. There was a hundred-dollar bill folded behind the checks. A quick trip to the Thrifty drugstore down the street was all she needed to get toothpaste and other necessary sundries. She located a Sears department store a little more than a mile away in the city of Torrance and bought new Levis, boots, several sweaters, blouses, and enough underwear to last a couple of weeks.

When she got back to the apartment building, Charlie was coming into the lobby, sweaty and tired from his run down to the ocean. She had several large bags that he helped carry upstairs to her room.

"You took Murphy's advice," he said, putting the bags on her bed.

"What about you? Wasn't your stuff in the truck too?"

"It was only the one bag. He threw it in the trunk of his city car before they hauled everything to the Harbor."

"Great," she said. "At least he thought about one of us."

"Yours was too much. I don't think he knew what to pull off the truck."

"Doesn't matter. I need new clothes. What do you think he'll have us do tomorrow?"

"Don't know. Don't care," he said, sitting on the bed, clearly unhappy. "I'll do whatever he wants, but I'm not liking it."

She felt guilty. Staying in PDID would be her salvation from a life in high heels and a goofy uniform tie, but for him it meant an unwanted, indefinite delay in getting back to that job in patrol they were both so eager to do.

"Maybe we can convince them if I stay, there's no need for you to be there too," she offered.

"Maybe," he said, but they both knew from their conversation with Captain Williams that that wasn't likely to happen.

THE NEXT morning they had breakfast in the coffee shop next door and she drove them downtown. Josie knew her VW would eventually have to be sold. Too many people recognized that car and although she hadn't interacted with too many dangerous people during the last three years, there were a few like Quentin who'd probably take pleasure in rearranging the bug's design with a pipe bomb.

Carlson was the only one in the office when they arrived. She grunted some sort of greeting, but immediately went back to her paperwork.

"Is Murphy around?" Charlie asked.

"With the captain," Carlson mumbled.

Josie spotted a full pot of coffee on a table in the back corner of the room. There were Styrofoam cups nearby, so she took one, poured herself a cup, and sat across the table from Carlson who after a few minutes looked up at her.

"What do you want?" Carlson asked, clearly annoyed.

"Something to do," Josie said.

"When Murphy gets back he can entertain you; I'm busy."

"Is this the Soriano file?" Josie asked, touching the thick stack of reports in front of the grumpy woman. Carlson had been tasked with finding the UC so she had a lot of the information the CCS detectives had.

"Whether this is or isn't Soriano's file has nothing to do with either of you."

"Can't hurt if we take a look," Charlie said, sitting beside Josie with his coffee. "It's not like you or CCS is making much progress."

Carlson slammed the file closed without bothering to straighten the pages, but before she could say anything Murphy came into the room. She sat back, folded her arms, and glared at him, saying in her nastiest tone, "Would you find something to occupy your wards, so I can get some work done."

"Come on. We're going to Robbery-Homicide. A few of your friends are visiting this morning," he said, ignoring Carlson.

Josie figured the romance between Brickhouse and Carlson was over. It was a familiar pattern she'd seen over the years with him straying but always going back to his pretty Angela and his boys. She almost felt sorry for the obnoxious little detective because Carlson never understood there was no way he could or would abandon his family. His flirtations got him through the bad times, those insane drunken moments filled with night tremors brought on by terrible memories he wanted to keep away from the ones he truly loved. Carlson had provided comfort when he needed it, nothing more.

"How's Angela?" Josie asked when they were in the hallway.

"Shut up," Murphy said. He was back.

THE CCS and PDID detectives were conducting their interviews from Robbery-Homicide's third floor offices in Parker Center's police headquarters. Every effort was being made to keep the intelligence division's name and Georgia Street out of the murder investigation, but internally they had merged the arrests of the three radicals with the death of the UC; different investigators were sharing information. They were still trying to determine if Soriano's killing had something to do with Quentin and the others.

Murphy took them to a room that had one-way mirrors and would give them a clear view of the interrogation next door.

"They can't see or hear you but you'll be able to hear and see everything," Murphy said. "If you think of any questions the detectives should be asking, speak up. I'll make sure they get asked," he said.

There were two rows of chairs in front of the window. Josie sat in the front row, in the middle. Charlie and Murphy stood closer to the window. She could see Sandra Collins in the cramped interview room with an older distinguished-looking man and Burt Rice who sat as far as he could get from the actress.

When the tape was turned on, the older man identified himself as her attorney and Burt Rice said he was representing the interests of the accused, Quentin, Emily, and Alex. Whenever Burt spoke, Sandra turned away and looked disgusted.

"Does Mr. Rice represent you in any way?" the detective asked, noticing Sandra's not-too-subtle expressions.

"No," she said quickly.

The tape was stopped again and Rice was told he'd have to leave. He stood and whispered something in Sandra's ear. She leaned away from him at first but he persisted until she stopped squirming and listened for a few seconds. Her face softened and her shoulders slumped slightly before he straightened up and stepped away.

She cleared her throat and said in almost a whisper, "I was mistaken. Mr. Rice will be assisting me." She whispered something to the older man sitting beside her, and he got up and left the room.

"What's he got on her?" Murphy asked, looking back at Josie.

"He gets people out of trouble so they owe him," she said.

"Must be something big. She's still got bruises from when he jumped her at Clarke's house and she tells everybody she hates his guts," Charlie added.

The interview continued and as Murphy predicted, Collins pleaded ignorance. She claimed the cash given to Quentin was supposed to be a loan because she was fond of him. She knew nothing about any attack on the Hall of Justice and "didn't believe Quentin or Emily was capable of doing such a horrific thing."

She was asked where she was the night Soriano was murdered. After a quick look through her datebook, she said there was nothing on her calendar so she was probably at home.

"I hardly knew the man," Collins said when the detectives asked about their relationship. "He lived with Kate Sparks. She was crazy about him but they fought all the time . . . that much I do know."

"How do you know they fought all the time?"

"We went to the same parties, had the same friends. Frankly I think she was dipping into his profits."

"What does that mean?" the detective asked.

Collins got quiet and looked at Burt who shrugged.

"I didn't know he was a cop, but I do know he was a dealer and Kate couldn't get enough of the stuff."

"Soriano was a heroin dealer?" the detective asked. His tone said he didn't believe her.

"That's the way it was," she said.

"You saw him deal heroin?"

"No, but everybody knew," she said and started to turn toward Burt but didn't.

"Who's everybody?" the detective asked.

"I don't know . . . it was common knowledge."

"Did you buy from him?"

"Of course not," she said, with a lack of conviction.

Now she was lying. Josie knew it. Everybody around her knew it. The acting skills couldn't hide body language, the fidgeting, the looking away, all of it was screaming that she'd bought heroin . . . but was it from Soriano? It was easy for her to lie about the money she'd given Quentin, but this was personal. It was a serious flaw that lessened her Hollywood image. The few jobs she could get in Tinseltown at her age would evaporate if the studios even suspected she was an addict.

The interview was over a few minutes later, but she had given credence to another dimension in the murder investigation. Drug dealers get killed all the time.

"Didn't Kate tell you Manny was her supplier?" Murphy asked when the interview room next door was empty.

"Maybe she was protecting Soriano," Josie said.

"That would explain the heroin under his car," Charlie said. "Also tells me he didn't plant that pipe bomb. He's not gonna blow up his own product."

"He didn't drive himself when he left the Hall of Justice, so somebody had to take him home or wherever he was going after he left the DA's office that day. Wasn't Kate. She doesn't drive . . . Larry Clarke was his boss; he might know," Josie said. "Let's go talk to him."

They went back to Georgia Street to wait while Murphy tracked down the CCS detectives handling the Soriano murder. The investigation was so stagnant, he knew the detectives would be eager to get their assistance and probably only ask that they be kept informed and no arrests made without their consent.

The PDID office was bustling by the time they got back. Typewriters and telephones added to the noise level, and Josie wondered how anyone could concentrate and work with that amount of racket. While she waited, she looked around the room still trying to pick out the Shadow. She wanted to thank him for fixing her car. Actually she was curious to know what he looked like. When Murphy got back she had finally worked up the courage to ask.

"No big secret," he said, pointing at a small, slightly over-weight man wearing glasses and hunched over a pencil sharpener. "Alan, come here a minute," he shouted.

The man looked up. He had long thinning brown hair and wore a short-sleeved plaid shirt and dress pants. It took a moment but he put the pencil into a plastic holder in his shirt pocket and walked across the room.

"Sergeant Young, this is Josie Pastore and Charlie Jones; they wanted to meet you," Murphy said.

"Thank you for fixing my car," she said, thinking this man was nothing like the stealth, jack-of-all-trades she had imagined.

"I know who you are, all of you. I've been watching for years," he said, pushing his sliding glasses back up on the bridge of his nose.

Well that's pretty creepy, Josie thought, but said, "We're really grateful for all your help."

He blushed and straightened his glasses again before closing his eyes as if he were in pain and then said, "I almost forgot. Actually, I haven't had a chance to tell you . . . it might not be important because you've moved, but your pack rat came again last night, left something on the doorstep of your apartment."

"You saw him?" Charlie asked.

"I decided to stake it out one more night, and she came. I've got what she left on my desk."

"She?"

"Skinny, blonde, homeless-looking girl, really needs a bath . . . actually I saw her follow you partway home one night about a week ago when I first started watching the garage. I'm guessing she's harmless . . . just seems to like you."

"Did you see where she went when she left the garage?" Josie asked.

"Back toward the ocean, I didn't follow, but I got pictures."

He went to his desk, returned with an envelope full of black-and-white photos and gave her a small silver medal with the image of what looked like an angel in ancient warrior's breast plate and battle gear, holding a large sword while standing on the head of a dragon. Around the edge, it said, "Saint Michael the Archangel, Protect Us."

"Let me see that," Murphy said, taking the medal out of her hand. "You know who Saint Michael is, don't you?"

"Badass angel . . . drove Satan and the other losers out of heaven if I'm remembering my Saturday morning catechism," Josie said. She was Catholic but hadn't been to Mass in years. Her unstable mother's fanatical praying had driven her from the church as well as the family home.

"He's the patron saint of policemen," he said, giving it back. "If she left this, chances are she brought you Soriano's keys, too, unless you've got more than one admirer."

"You think this might've been Soriano's?" Charlie asked, taking the medal.

"Possibly . . . a lot of cops have them," Murphy said, pulling the heavy gold chain around his neck from under his T-shirt and revealing another larger pendant with a similar image of the warrior angel.

"Hope it works better for you. Didn't do him much good," Charlie said.

Sergeant Young spread the photos on the table in front of them. He had taken a roll of film showing the young girl sneaking up to the garage and leaving the medal on the front step then attempting to look in the window before leaving the way she came.

"She looks worse every time I see her," Josie said, flipping through the pictures.

"You know her?"

"I gave her stuff from the thrift shop. She's the one I was looking for yesterday. Maybe leaving the junk she found on the beach was her way of trying to thank me."

"You never saw Soriano wearing that?" Murphy asked, pointing at the medal.

They both shook their heads and he suggested they show it to Kate.

"The girl's a scavenger. She could've found this anywhere on the sand," Josie said.

"Or it could've been with Soriano's keys and who knows what else she hasn't given you yet. We need to talk to her and see how much she knows or might've seen," Murphy said. "We'll get to Clarke later. This girl could be our key witness."

EIGHTEEN

Although Josie had walked along the bike path in Venice Beach hundreds of times over the last few years, she could feel the vibes were different today. It had to be the gun and badge she wore under her jacket. There was a sense of purpose now in every step, but the magic of her make-believe world was gone. It was just another place to work, find the girl, get answers, and move on.

Charlie was quiet as they got closer to the pavilion. She wondered if being in this place again as a policeman felt strange to him too. They passed O'Farrell's; he hesitated a moment and seemed to be searching the environs for a familiar, friendly face, but it wasn't an establishment that would be welcoming them any longer. That life, including the more pleasant moments, was gone. How strange she thought to miss something she'd wanted to leave so badly.

The girl wasn't at the pavilion. They talked to several of the regulars and finally bullied one of them into revealing where she slept and kept her belongings. Her name was Sunny, at least that's what everyone called her, and she kept a makeshift shelter set up in the alley behind a kite shop. A path to the alley was a few yards away and the shop was located where it ended.

There were several crude cardboard structures and improvised tents made from dirty blankets and pieces of blue and clear plastic scattered throughout the alley. It looked as if someone had recently attempted to wash down the concrete and walls, but the smell of human waste and unwashed bodies overwhelmed the effort. Public restrooms and outdoor showers weren't far from this location but Josie could tell no one camping here made much of an effort to use them. There were a lot of younger people living here. They seemed to cherish their independence and lack of responsibility, which meant no job, no home, no possessions, and no desire to bow to conventions such as personal hygiene.

Charlie picked up a stick to lift or poke at the blankets, push aside the cardboard walls, but most of the structures were unoccupied. A young man sleeping under what looked like a shower curtain rolled over and pointed a pocketknife at them, but dropped it immediately, recoiling in fear when two revolvers were pointed at him.

"Where's Sunny?" Josie asked, kicking the knife out of his reach before putting her gun back in the holster.

"I didn't do nothing," the young man whined, trying to push his long matted hair out of his bloodshot eyes. "You got loose change you kin give me?"

"Never mind," she said, tapping Charlie on the arm. "Come on."

She saw the corner of a pink blanket like the one she'd given the young girl sticking out from a large appliance box at the end of the alley. The box was covered in a clear sheet of plastic splattered with green paint. Sunny was inside curled up and seemed to be sleeping. Josie knelt down and tried to rouse her, gently touching her shoulder, but there was no response. She shook a little harder. Sunny didn't move, so Josie told Charlie to help her get the girl away from the box. They tugged on the blanket until her body, holding its fetal position, was out far enough for them to pull her the rest of the way and confirm Josie's fear; she was dead and in full rigor. Her skin was cold and stiff to the touch, and Josie knew right away from the foamy pink vomit that had dried around her mouth, she had most likely overdosed.

Charlie walked around to the front of the kite store and used their phone to call for the Venice Division's homicide detectives and the station's narcotics officers. Sunny was wearing a bulky sweater and jeans and with her blonde hair still damp and pushed away from her face she looked about twelve years old. Her skin was pale yellow except the dark sunken shadows under both eyes, an old woman's eyes, Josie thought. She was puzzled because she no longer felt any connection to this person she had tried to help. All she could see now was a fragile, damaged young woman who had faltered and slipped through life without notice or purpose. Her death should've been sad, maybe even tragic, but instead Josie felt a sense of relief.

She moved the girl's left sleeve up and saw the familiar pattern of bluish-grey tracks on the inner arm. There was visible oozing from one site on a very large abscess; however, there seemed to be numerous fresh marks around it. If the division's narcotic detectives responded to the OD, she'd ask one of them to get a better look with the lighted magnifying glass they usually carried.

Guessing the detectives wouldn't arrive for a few minutes, Josie gently rolled the sleeve down again and crawled over the body into the box. The foul stench made her stomach turn, but she quickly found what she was looking for. A syringe with a bloody needle was lying on the urine-stained blanket dotted with rat droppings, in that area where Sunny's arm would've been before they moved her. It might've dislodged when they pulled her out of the box because Josie had never heard of an overdose where the user had time to remove the needle before dying. She covered her nose with the sleeve of her jacket and looked for some sort of packaging or paraphernalia for the heroin but couldn't find anything. Finally she had to back out and breathe fresh air or knew she would throw up all over what might be a crime scene.

Homicide detectives didn't take long to confirm the girl had died of what appeared to be an overdose, but the coroner would remove her body for an autopsy to actually establish the cause of death. The syringe would be tested to determine what kind of drug had been injected and toxicology tests would tell them if other drugs were in her system. There was nothing found on Sunny to help identify her. She was so small and skeletally thin that her corpse made barely a noticeable ripple under the coroner's blanket.

Murphy and Carlson arrived shortly before the body was removed. Venice Division's homicide detectives were more than willing to let CCS take responsibility for the investigation. This section of the Venice area was so overrun with gangs and drugs they had more than their share of drug-related deaths. Besides this looked like just another routine transient overdose, a familiar and frequent occurrence in the beach city.

Josie asked one of the narcotics detectives to take a closer look at Sunny's arm before the body was moved. With lighted magnification, he was better able to see the injection sites. He confirmed her suspicion that there were several holes covering the abscess, and they were still fresh and had oozed either blood or clear liquid.

"It's kind of odd," the detective said, moving away as the coroner rolled the gurney toward the back of his van. "There's a lot of recent activity . . . more than a man twice her size would need to stay under the influence."

"How do you know that?" Josie asked.

"Age of the puncture wounds . . . too many in the last ten to twelve hours. Some of those should've been scabbing if she'd been shooting up like a normal hype. I've never seen that many fresh ones at the same time on one skinny arm."

"I don't understand . . . what does it mean?"

"Have to wait for the post and toxicology, but my gut tells me she OD'd with somebody's help . . . or, on the other hand, she might've been a needle junkie."

"A what?"

"Keeps jabbing herself but doesn't take in enough drug to actually get down . . . addicted to the needle."

ONCE THE coroner was gone, it took Josie and Charlie several hours to go through Sunny's belongings. Murphy and Carlson stayed and watched for a few minutes before receiving a radio call to report back to the captain's office at Georgia Street.

The girl had packed her surroundings with enough trash from the beach to fill two large grocery bags, most of it junk and none of it, as far as they could tell, seemed to have any significance or connection to her death or Soriano's murder. Josie didn't mention anything but had to wonder if Sunny had stumbled onto not only his keys and the medal, but some of Soriano's heroin stash the night he was killed, and that had provided the endless supply of deadly poison she'd been pumping into her arm.

Charlie helped her interview the bums who slept in or around the alley, those who were coherent enough to answer questions. No one admitted to having seen or heard anything . . . ever. Whatever Sunny knew had apparently died with her. At least there was nothing among her fellow garbage dwellers that helped. The chemists could compare the drugs in her system with those found under Soriano's car to see if they could've come from the same batch, but Josie wasn't even certain what that would tell them.

It was getting late and they agreed they didn't want to face traffic congestion driving back to the office into downtown LA, so she called Murphy and asked if they could go home from Venice, a nice scenic route along the coast down to Hermosa Beach, and promised to be back early the next morning.

"Be here at eight, both of you," Murphy said. "We've got a meeting with the captain and the DA."

"Why?" she asked.

"Because they want to tell us what a great job we're doing fucking up this investigation."

NINETEEN

The next morning, Josie woke to find the front page of the *LA Times* shoved under her door. A red circle had been drawn around a story in the lower right corner, but the headline told her everything she needed to know—"Cops Accused of Plotting Terrorism." The rest was Burt Rice's version of how and why Quentin, Alex, and Emily got arrested for something that wasn't their idea. Josie and Charlie were named in the story as undercover police officers, agent provocateurs, who'd cajoled the others into attacking the Hall of Justice, but at the last moment got cold feet and made the arrests.

Burt promised that in the trial he would provide evidence to prove the idea and that training for the plan came from the police, and his clients naively went along.

She finished reading the story and crunched the paper into a tight ball before tossing it on one attempt into the trash can across the room. It was rubbish, but she knew in the city of LA both the city council and the police commission were dominated by left-leaning politicians and the ACLU. They would tend to be sympathetic toward Burt's fantasy version of events but she was confident her reports, corroborated by other UC documentation, would provide a very different account.

Charlie had already completed his morning run and was at her door shortly after she finished dressing.

"Thanks for the paper," she said, taking the cup of Winchell's coffee he offered. "Started my day off right."

"There's more good news," he said, sitting on her bed. "When I was coming back from the donut place, I heard on the radio that Georgia Street got firebombed last night and there's a demonstration planned for Parker Center later today to demand that we get prosecuted."

"So much for coming out of the program anonymously and quietly blending back into the police population," Josie said, remembering that's what her handler had promised when she transferred into PDID. He had further predicted that no one would ever know what she had done or acknowledge the contribution she'd made in keeping the city safe. That part might prove to be accurate if Burt had his way.

"I called Murphy. He wants to meet us at Parker Center instead of Georgia Street so we can get in the back way and take the service elevator up to the chief's conference room . . . keep away from the media," he said.

"Just when you think it's safe to jump out of the frying pan . . ."

THEY ARRIVED at the chief's conference room a few minutes before eight but Murphy, Captain Williams, and Carlson were already there. Murphy was talking to a lieutenant she didn't recognize, but she knew who he was immediately from his name tag. Lieutenant Harvey Mitchell was the chief's spokesman from Press Relations, but more importantly he was Quentin's snitch. Why he was still in his job and hadn't been fired or busted back to policeman was a mystery to Josie.

She waited until he finished his conversation with Murphy, and then ignoring her and Charlie, he left the room, concentrating on a folder full of papers.

"I don't understand. Why is that man still working and not facing a board of rights?" Josie asked as soon as he was gone.

"Conduits are useful in sending information both ways. For the moment, we need the sonofabitch exactly where he is. By the way, labs on your homeless girl found unadulterated China White. She had a pharmacy of drugs in her system, but the pure heroin killed her," Murphy said.

"Did they match any of the other drugs with the stuff under Soriano's car?" she asked.

"Didn't say . . . but the coup de grâce was definitely the white . . . dead as soon as it hit her vein. Narcs say they rarely see any on the street, but uncut it's always deadly. They won't even touch it without gloves."

"There's no way someone like her could afford China White," Charlie said. "It's mega bucks. I'm guessing someone fed her a steady diet of the cheap stuff before they slipped it in."

Josie sat at the conference table. She needed to think. Who would've known Sunny was a possible witness to Soriano's murder . . . maybe the killer? Everyone at PDID probably knew about the keys and the Saint Michael medal she'd left on Josie's doorstep, but no one outside the division. Unless . . . before she could say out loud what she was thinking, the DA came into the room with Assistant Chief Perez, but they weren't alone. Trailing a few feet behind were Deputy DAs Larry Clarke and Jake Corsino.

Clarke's long grey hair was tied back in a chaotic ponytail with strands hanging loose or tucked behind his ears, and his suit as usual needed a good dry cleaning. He nodded at her, but even his glassy bloodshot eyes couldn't hide his contempt. She didn't look away until he did, not wanting the man to have even an inkling that he could intimidate her.

Corsino touched her shoulder, leaned closer to shake hands, and whispered in her ear, "Showtime."

She knew what he meant but didn't react. Sometimes politics trumped good police work and it resembled performance art. Everyone in the room except Clarke had known long before the chief's announcement that Soriano was an undercover cop working in the District Attorney's Office. After the press release, the revelation should've been sobering, but everything about Clarke told Josie he'd been on a binge and was still suffering from the effects. His lifestyle might've finally caught up with him.

Josie remembered the district attorney from their first meeting at the witch's store in Redondo Beach. He was a no-nonsense, straightforward man. He had kept his word and had his deputy Corsino personally work with the detectives on the Soriano investigation and never revealed anything to Clarke.

"Larry Clarke is rightfully outraged that an undercover policeman would've been working in his office without my consent or knowledge," the DA began when everyone was sitting at the table. "I've explained to him the LAPD never sanctioned Officer Soriano's employment and the chief of police was as disturbed as all of us when he discovered what his UC had done. That being said, Officer Soriano is dead, so as far as I'm concerned there's an end to it," he said, staring at Clarke who looked away.

"But that doesn't excuse their continued covert presence at my home, spying on me and my friends at social gatherings for who knows how long," Clarke persisted, staring at the table in front of him.

"Unfortunately some of your closest friends are legitimate targets, so yes it does," the DA said with a shrug. "As far as I know you're the only one of my deputies who has or needs a bodyguard; even though I suspect, given your appetite for drugs and alcohol, it was simply to avoid DUI arrests."

Acting as if he hadn't heard his boss or didn't care what was said, Clarke pointed at Josie, spoke slowly, and, trying not to slur his words, said, "You deceived me. Made me believe we were friends . . . betrayed my trust . . . it's wrong to do that to someone."

She didn't respond. It would've been pointless. He had bragged about the rise of the proletariat and advocated violence in the abstract. He gave money and access to his home to people who viewed him and his excessive wealth as their primary target if or when their revolution ever materialized. Most of his so-called friends, including her and Charlie, were using him, lying to him. Maybe she should've felt bad, but didn't, because his money and naïveté allowed lunatics like Quentin to thrive.

"Obviously you're not going to support me in this matter," Clarke said, turning to the DA, his face a bright shade of pink. He stood a little unsteadily and picked up his briefcase.

"Sit down, Larry," the DA ordered.

Clarke hesitated but after a few seconds put his briefcase on the chair next to him and obeyed his boss.

"We can talk to you here, Mr. Clarke, with your supervisor present or take you to an interrogation room downstairs. It's your choice," Murphy said.

"Talk about what?" Clarke asked, looking confused.

"For starters, why was Officer Soriano in your office?"

"I thought he was a law student . . . an intern . . ."

"Who recommended him? How did he come to your attention?"

"I don't remember . . . someone. Maybe he lied to me like the rest of you," Clarke mumbled, shaking his head.

"What did he do?"

"Odds and ends . . . like all of them."

"Tell me one thing he did for you," Murphy said.

Josie could see Murphy was becoming impatient. Clarke was obviously suffering from the aftereffects of a hangover and having difficulty focusing, but it was clear to her he really had no desire to talk about any of this.

"I don't . . . I can't remember . . . he did go to court with me."

"How often?"

"Once, I think."

"Did Quentin Barnes tell you to give him the intern position?" Carlson asked.

"He might have recommended him. I told you I don't remember. I never pay attention to interns . . . they're worthless . . . mostly observers." Now a little nervous sweat was beading on Clarke's forehead. He wiped it off with the back of his hand. "What are you implying? Did your under-cover policeman have something to do with that plot in my building?"

"These so-called revolutionaries came to your home. You drank with them, partied with them, and did their bidding, and you expect anyone to believe you knew nothing about their intentions?" the DA asked, interrupting them. He was glaring at Clarke and Josie noticed his right fist was clenched, and he'd come up off his chair a little. Jake Corsino was sit-ting beside him and touched his boss's forearm, keeping his hand there until the DA seemed to calm down, the distrac-tion apparently diffusing his anger for the moment. "You're a disgrace, Larry. If you had anything to do with any of this, I'll personally prosecute you," he said, slumping back onto his seat, waving dismissively at Clarke.

"Who gave Soriano a ride from your office the night he was killed?" Murphy asked, after waiting a few seconds to be certain the DA had finished his outburst. "We know he didn't take his own car."

Clarke shook his head. "I don't . . ." he started to say, but stopped and cocked his head as if some pertinent thought had bobbed to the surface in his whiskey-soaked brain. "He got a call. I remember because he never got calls in the office . . . didn't see him again after that."

"Did anybody meet with him?"

"No, he was alone, but wait . . ." Clarke said, closing his eyes tight and grimacing as if he suddenly got a severe headache, before adding, "I do remember glancing out the window a few minutes later, saw him standing on the curb in front of the building like he might've been waiting for a ride."

"Did anyone pick him up?"

"I don't know. I didn't watch very long, but he wasn't there when I left the garage about ten minutes later."

Carlson said she would interview everyone who worked that day in the DA's office or at the front desk in the Hall of Justice. According to Clarke, it was late afternoon at the end of the business day and the courts were dark when Soriano received the call, so Carlson suspected it shouldn't be too difficult to zero in on the few remaining people who might've seen or heard something.

Assistant Chief Perez was unusually quiet until the DA and Larry Clarke left. He studied his paperwork or scribbled on a note pad and didn't seem to have much interest in anything any of them had to say. Josie watched him and had the same reaction she'd had the first time they'd met. He seemed pompous and self-absorbed. He was a big man but his uniform was too tight and had to be uncomfortable. The skin-tight blue shirt would be flattering for a fit figure but his prominent potbelly gave him a comical Tweedledum look.

"Captain Williams, what have you got to say about this Burt Rice, WLM lawsuit?" Perez asked, not looking up.

"Officers in PDID have documented every encounter and incident with that group. We are above reproach," Williams said, and when Perez didn't say anything, he added, "Their reports are thorough and their activities have been completely lawful and fully documented including anything related to Deputy DA Clarke."

"An intrusive discovery process cannot only destroy your division," Perez said, "but reflect very badly on the department and the chief. We all know how facts taken out of context can be very dangerous and damning."

Williams cleared his throat and said unconvincingly, "I don't agree. We have nothing to hide," he added, turning to Corsino.

"Not my call," Corsino said, shrugging.

The assistant chief finally closed his notebook and looked at Williams. "We will not give them any UC reports or internal correspondence. I want everything except official documents withheld . . . summaries are fine, best actually. I'll review everything."

"Can we do that?" Williams asked.

Perez didn't answer, but gave him a look that clearly said they weren't discussing it any longer. He turned to Josie and asked, "Did you or Officer Jones suggest or in any way organize the planned attack on the Hall of Justice?"

"No," she and Charlie answered quickly and together.

"After the WLM riot downtown, I've been told you participated in attorney-client meetings with the other arrestees. Is that true?" he asked.

"No," Josie said. "I intentionally missed every strategy meeting."

"I've talked to the public defender. He'll corroborate that. He claims she failed to contact him and ignored letters he sent to her address to attend those meetings. She should be fine," Corsino said, nodding at her.

"You on the other hand could be problematic," the deputy chief said.

"How's that, sir?" Charlie asked.

"You trained these morons with firearms and taught them martial arts. You can be very certain it won't go unnoticed that you traveled to Communist Cuba with Quentin Barnes and that Socialist actress."

"Anyone who's seen them shoot knows they haven't been trained," Josie said, before Charlie could answer, and got a dirty look from Carlson and Murphy. Corsino laughed softly. She hadn't intended to be funny but liked the fact that none of this seemed to overwhelm or frighten him.

"She's right and what they've learned from me in no way resembles martial arts. My trip to Cuba brought back valuable intelligence for our government. Ask the State Department . . . sir," Charlie said, not intimidated by the staff officer.

"Good, you'll do fine," Perez said, organizing his stack of papers. "You probably heard what happened at Georgia Street this morning. Do either of you want a protection detail now that you're likely targets?"

"No," they answered in unison again.

Perez pushed aside his paperwork and leaning with both hands on the table stared directly at Williams saying, "The chief expects to have the name of Officer Soriano's killer on his desk this week." With a nasty-looking smile he added, "I would think, Captain, you'd have a particular interest in making that happen." Then he straightened up, tucked the papers under his arm, and left the conference room.

No one spoke for several seconds. Finally Captain Williams stood, buttoned the jacket of his expensive business suit, and followed the assistant chief without comment or change in his frozen expression.

The two UCs, Carlson, Corsino, and Murphy were the only ones left now sitting at the huge over-polished mahogany conference table. Josie glanced around the room at framed charcoal portraits of former police chiefs that covered the walls. There was a lot of police history staring back at her, but at the moment she felt as if nothing that happened in this place really had much to do with actual police work.

"What did he mean I'd do fine?" Charlie asked.

"Burt Rice will probably depose both of you, but you'll talk to an attorney long before any deposition happens. My guess is the city will farm this out to some big downtown law firm," Corsino said.

"Not the city attorney?" Josie asked.

"Hell no, not unless they've already decided to lose," Murphy said.

"On that note, I'll get out of here before Brickhouse starts badmouthing the DA's office," Corsino said, grinning at Murphy. He looked at Josie, then Charlie, and added, seriously, "FYI, what Chief Perez was suggesting about not giving up all your reports in discovery . . . that's not in your best interests. It protects the decision makers like him, not you."

Josie watched him shake hands with Murphy and leave. He was confident and smart and she could see Murphy liked and respected him. She did too.

W<small>HEN HE</small> was gone, Murphy suggested they take the freight elevator down to the lobby and watch the coalition-fighting-police-abuse demonstration that should've already started. He figured the media would most likely be out of the building to cover it and they wouldn't be bothered with pesky reporters.

The lobby was crowded with officers and civilian personnel who'd come down to watch the protesters, so no one paid any attention to them. There were enough spectators gathered outside the front glass doors so Josie went out and stood behind them for a better view. She recognized most of the participants, at least those who seemed to be in leadership positions.

Manny Contreras was using his piece-of-junk bullhorn, so as usual, it was almost impossible to understand anything he said with the distortion of heavy static. He leaned on one of the marchers as they walked and looked very fragile. It was a large demonstration, about two hundred people from several different groups, but WLM didn't have the largest contingent this time.

It was unusual to see so many banners and placards with a similar theme. They demanded an end to police abuse and spying. There was a more militant angry tone to the chants and none of the levity or distraction that Josie had observed in so many demonstrations. Black power signs were side-by-side with the red bandanas of brown power and the WLM. These divergent groups—blacks, whites, Hispanics, gays, lesbians, Socialists, Marxists, Communists—had finally discovered a common enemy: the LAPD.

Platoons of officers in riot gear, batons, helmets with plastic face shields, and body armor lined the sidewalks outside Parker Center and kept protesters from moving up the long walkway to the front doors. The marchers were surrounded by hundreds of officers on both sides of Los Angeles Street and a skirmish line north and south. Josie saw paddy wagons and an ambulance parked near the Federal Building, but she believed the overwhelming presence of uniformed officers should discourage any violence.

"Recognize anyone?" Murphy asked, suddenly standing beside her.

"Yep."

"Good, remember them and give me a report tonight."

"I'm not a UC anymore," she said, trying to get a reaction, but he just gave her that familiar shrug that said he really didn't care what she was. He wanted a report. "You notice anyone conspicuously missing, today?" she asked him.

"Quentin, Alex, Burt, and Emily . . ." he said, looking up and down the street.

Murphy was still searching for familiar faces in the crowd when the demonstrators stopped moving and Burt Rice popped out in front of them like a pudgy gopher and climbed onto the bumper of a parked car with the help of two other men.

Someone handed him a megaphone that worked, and he began his speech in a loud clear voice with a condemnation of the LAPD and its Public Disorder Intelligence Division. Loud cheers came from the crowd every time he called for disbanding PDID or prosecuting everyone who worked there. He went through a litany of police shootings in South Central LA, calling for a federal investigation, removal of the chief of police, and jailing every officer connected to several dozen incidents, mostly controversial shootings, but the names included Josie and Charlie.

"He looks sober," Josie said. "Don't think I've ever seen him that way."

"He's a lawyer. The prospect of a big cash settlement is better than AA or any rehab center," Murphy said. "With our city council and police commission he's seeing dollar signs."

"You think they'll settle? We didn't do anything wrong."

"Most politicians in this city want what he wants, a neutered LAPD. If there's a way, they'll settle."

Josie stopped listening. She'd heard Murphy's theory more than once. He believed the dissidents of the sixties had smartened up and were working their way into the school system and government. They were going to take over from the inside and were willing to sacrifice the fringe people like Quentin and the others to raise awareness and cause chaos after which they'd step in and control the outcome.

According to Murphy, the LAPD didn't bow to political pressure and that had to change. He might be right but she wondered what difference it made. As far as she could tell, somebody's politics were going to rule, and they were all more or less corrupt. It was the nature of the beast.

The LAPD wasn't exactly supporting her that much anyway. Maybe a little change would be good. That was her last thought before a barrage of red bricks and rocks were hurled from somewhere on the crowded street toward the glass doors of Parker Center.

TWENTY

A small rock hit Josie's arm, but almost immediately something larger grazed the side of her head knocking her down and stunning her for a moment. Someone was there pulling on her arm helping her scramble to her feet. It was Jake Corsino. He made certain she wasn't badly hurt and tried to get her to go back inside with him and other civilians who'd been caught in the melee. She did until her head cleared and then left him in the lobby of Parker Center and ran back outside.

Her hair felt wet on the left side and drops of blood dotted the front of her jacket; surprisingly she didn't have any pain. The demonstrators were yelling and charging the front doors of the police building, but uniformed officers had quickly intercepted them. Men and women were shouting, swinging heavy sticks that had held their signs and placards just seconds before, but the blue vise was tightening, closing in on them from all directions.

She pushed over a man who was straddling a uniformed officer who'd been knocked to the ground. The policeman rolled onto his knees and jumped up, and Josie helped him subdue and handcuff the belligerent protester. They dragged him into the administration building where other officers took charge. She looked around for Corsino but he wasn't there any longer.

She hurried back outside to help, but the fight was pretty much over. Burt was sitting on the sidewalk with his hands secured behind his back. The others, some bloodied and injured, had dropped their sticks and were slowly being hand-cuffed and arrested by the army of officers. There were only about fifty of the original demonstrators remaining. Most of them, including Manny, had run away and escaped when the fighting began.

Parker Center had been nicknamed The Glass House by the criminal element in LA for good reason. It had a massive glass and stone facade, but the only damage she could see was a cracked front door. A ring of officers had protected the newly constructed and recently dedicated police memorial in front of the building and it survived unscathed. She guessed the red paint spilled in the street and on the sidewalk nearby had been intended to target the white marble monument honoring fallen officers.

It had become eerily quiet as officers methodically hand-cuffed, identified, and removed the protesters one or two at a time to an improvised booking area on the lawn adjacent to the sidewalk, where they would be processed and some sent on buses to other jails.

Burt had lifted himself up onto the curb now, his nice suit covered with dirt and splashes of what looked like the red paint. She watched him awhile. The guy seemed miserable, alone, and maybe a little vulnerable so she figured it might be a good time for a chat. She walked around and stood silently in the street in front of him until he looked up at her.

"What do you want?" he asked, not hiding his disgust. But he seemed to be staring at what was now dried blood in her hair and on the side of her face.

"Wanted to make sure you're okay," she said. Josie didn't really care about Burt but she was certain he knew more about Soriano than he was telling and she wanted to keep that line of communication open for as long as she possibly could.

"Yeah, sure you do."

"None of this was about you or Emily," she said . . . again not entirely true. "There's a dead cop and you're in the middle of the investigation. Despite what you think, I like Emily and we both know she's already in enough trouble. I don't want to see her get charged as an accessory to murder."

Burt shifted his considerable weight, attempting to get comfortable on the narrow concrete curb. "I don't know what you're talking about. She had nothing to do with that."

"I don't believe she did, but I think she knows who killed him. You're a lawyer. You've got to realize protecting that person might have serious consequences."

"Leave me alone. Go clean your own house before you come knocking at my door."

Two uniformed policemen arrived, helped Burt stand, and escorted him to the booking table. She stayed there a few seconds, still thinking about what he'd said. Maybe he was referring to her spying with his "clean your own house" reference, but she didn't think so.

She located Charlie in front of the memorial talking to Murphy and told them what Burt had said.

"I'm thinking maybe he's telling us we've got more dirty cops," she said.

"We don't even know Soriano was dirty yet," Murphy said.

"I think he was," Charlie countered.

"Nobody gives a fuck what you think. If he was dirty, prove it or shut the fuck up," Murphy said.

Charlie looked at Josie and knew she agreed with him, but arguing with Murphy wasn't something either of them wanted to do. Instead he asked her, "Do you think it could be another UC?"

"Maybe, but we do know Lieutenant Mitchell's a rat in our house. We should concentrate on him awhile . . . see what he's up to," she said.

"We're already monitoring all his communications," Murphy said.

Josie hesitated but lately she'd been thinking a lot about the Press Relations lieutenant.

"Don't you think it's strange Mitchell told Quentin that Soriano was dead but never told him he was a cop?" she asked.

"No," Murphy said. "If that information got out, it could have come back on him."

"How?"

"What difference does it make? He didn't tell them Soriano was a cop, so what. He probably didn't know. When you're deep cover, all your department files are pulled and kept at Georgia Street."

"Where did Soriano work before he went to PDID?" Charlie asked.

"Rampart patrol, but he was Spanish speaking so he got loaned to community relations just before he made probation," Murphy said, his voice trailing off and then he was quiet a few seconds as if that had triggered a new thought. He scratched his day-old beard and added, "I'll look at who he worked with before his transfer into Intelligence."

"Is Community Relations connected to Press Relations?" Charlie asked.

"Not really, but I can see where there might've been some crossover. I'll check it out," Murphy said. "You two are done for today. Do you want to go to Central Receiving and get medical treatment for that cut, Pastore?"

"No, all I want is a hot shower and a Band-Aid."

By late afternoon, Josie was feeling like herself again. The head wound had bled a lot but she only found a tiny cut above her ear, almost hidden by her hair. A short nap after the shower was refreshing and all it took to get her ready to go back to work. She walked down the hall to Charlie's room and knocked on the door. His dopey expression told her she'd gotten him up, but she didn't care.

When they got back from the downtown clash, she'd found a story on one of the local channels about the demonstration and riot. Once again it showed the worst violence and slammed the police department for being too heavy-handed, but that wasn't the problem. A shorter report followed it as a tag-on saying the culture of the LAPD might be changing soon since a consent decree had finally been signed and blessed by the court—preliminary testing would begin shortly for the first class of women to work patrol in the LAPD. She was determined to be in that class, but it was clear they weren't getting out of PDID until the chief had his killer.

She offered to buy Charlie dinner if he'd go with her to talk to Kate Sparks again. Josie had a nagging feeling Kate was protecting somebody and it wasn't Soriano.

"Are you gonna tell Murphy we're going?" he asked, before making any commitment.

"No."

"She's a junkie. What can she tell you? Half the time she doesn't know what time of day it is."

"She was living with Soriano. Maybe she knows who called and met him outside work that night . . . or if he was supposed to meet someone at Venice Beach."

"Last time we talked to her she said she didn't know anything, and if she did she wasn't telling us."

"I think she knows something," Josie said, handing him his jacket.

She couldn't sit in her room and do nothing even if Kate was another dead end. She had to keep digging, prying, and talking to anyone who might give her the tiniest clue that would lead to a killer.

The phone rang as they were about to leave. Charlie answered, sat on the bed, and listened for a few seconds before hanging up.

"That was Murphy. He says Alex and Emily didn't show up for court this afternoon. There's a felony warrant for both of them, but he's pretty certain they've gone underground. Nobody can locate them."

"What about Quentin?"

"He was in court but the case got continued. Burt's his lawyer, and he was getting booked at the time," Charlie said, grinning.

"There goes Burt's lawsuit. I wonder if he knew she would bolt," Josie said.

"He and Emily aren't exactly the perfect couple. He has to know she's using him. Besides he's still got the spying suit," Charlie said, locking the door behind them. "Manny and the others will jump into that one if it means getting a few bucks from the city."

They walked down the street to a seafood restaurant and market that was a parking lot away from the ocean. It had tables outside on a covered patio facing the water where they ate a plate of fried fish and greasy fries and almost finished a bottle of Pinot Grigio. The ocean breeze was cold and windy, so bundled in heavy jackets they had the entire area to themselves, and probably lingered longer than Josie had intended. She enjoyed Charlie's company, but the way she might enjoy being with a big brother. In her entire adult life, she'd only had two serious lovers, and both affairs had ended in disappointment. She enjoyed sex but it wasn't easy for her to be casually intimate with someone.

It was different with Charlie, and that puzzled her. He was everything she thought she wanted in a man. He was handsome, funny, and smart, but he never gave any indication that he thought of her as anything but a partner and a friend. She could tell when a man was interested and everything he did and said told her he wasn't, not in that way. At the moment he was her best friend and that meant a lot, but it wasn't enough. She wanted more in her life and her usually reliable intuition was telling her that Jake Corsino was a decent man who wanted to give her a lot more. They barely knew each other, but there was no denying they'd made a connection.

They finished and walked back to the apartment building, then Charlie drove them up the coast to Venice and Kate's run-down neighborhood. He parked the car across the street and a few houses away from her yard, as far as he could get from the street light and hidden in the shadows, behind overgrown bushes protruding from what looked like an abandoned property.

Lights were on in the front room and over the porch. Despite the stacks of junk blocking parts of the window, the curtains were open and Josie could see at least two people moving around inside the room.

"I'm gonna get a better look," she said. "Can you turn off your overhead light, so I can open the door?"

"This car doesn't have an overhead light," Charlie said, and grabbed her arm before she could get out. "Don't do anything stupid . . . never mind, just don't get caught."

"Good plan," she said, closing the door.

Almost everybody in this crime-ridden neighborhood had big dogs in their yards, so she had to find a circuitous route to the front porch that wouldn't alert the whole block. She knew this part of Venice was notorious for gangbangers and drug dealers. Her puny six-shot revolver wouldn't be any match for the sort of weapons they possessed, but she couldn't think of any other way to see what was going on in Kate's house.

The rottweiler next door barked a little as she crouched under the window facing the porch but apparently not enough to alarm anyone. The house next door stayed dark so she edged up a little to peek over the window ledge and see inside. Kate's living room was empty now. The crib filled with baby stuff that had been there on their last visit was gone. It could've been moved into the bedroom but Josie didn't think so. She'd had a feeling when they spoke to Kate she had no intention of having the baby. The abortion of another drug-addicted kid probably wasn't a tragedy, but Josie still felt a sense of loss for that unlucky life.

Any doubt about the fate of the baby was quickly dispelled when Kate came back into the living room. The maternity top was gone, and she was wearing tight-fitting jeans and a cropped sweater. Manny and Quentin were with her. They wore heavy parkas and she was carrying what looked like a fake rabbit fur jacket that she slipped on as they walked toward the front door.

Josie was trapped. She couldn't get off the porch before they came out of the house. The only choice she had was to hide among the piles of junk or be discovered peeking in the window. Luckily there was just enough room to squeeze between an old washing machine and stacked crates. The light over the door was burned out so unless they started some nocturnal cleaning project Josie figured she would remain hidden.

"I ain't sticking my neck out for no stuck-up white bitch," Kate said as the three of them stood on the porch while she locked the door.

Manny said something in Spanish that Josie couldn't understand, but it got an immediate, "Fuck you" from Kate.

"I helped you out. Now I'm asking you to do something for me," Quentin said, as they stepped off the porch.

"Helped me?" Kate snorted, swallowing a laugh. She stopped at the bottom of the porch stairs to confront him. "You give me money to have your bastard kid so I can't never get away from you. I killed it and done both of us a favor . . . your old man don't write you outta the will and I ain't puking all the time. Don't bullshit me, you crazy motherfucker. You never done nothing for me."

"This is bigger than your fucked-up life," Quentin said.

They were too far away now for Josie to hear them any longer, but she could tell Quentin was getting angrier and nastier. His Studebaker was parked on the street in front of the house. Still yelling at each other, they all got in and he drove away.

When the car turned the corner, Josie hurried from the porch and ran back to Charlie's MG.

"Did you see them?" she asked, as he pulled onto the street in the direction Quentin had gone.

"Yep, you get anything?"

Josie told him what she had heard.

"I'm guessing Quentin wants her to hide Emily," she said, trying to keep track of the taillights several blocks ahead of them. "You sure that's his car?"

"Two cars in front of that one," Charlie said, calmly.

"Where did you learn how to do surveillance?"

"*Adam-12, Dragnet*," he said, trying not to smile. "Truthfully, I don't know what the hell I'm doing, but I chased enough bad guys in Vietnam to know it's best if you see them and they don't see you."

It didn't take long for Josie to figure out exactly where they were going. Quentin took the route up Pacific Coast Highway toward West LA. As soon as they crossed Sunset Boulevard, she was certain they were headed into Brentwood and guessed either Larry Clarke's or Anthony Barnes's house. Quentin drove like Josie's grandmother so Charlie took side streets, got ahead of him, and managed to arrive and park down the street a few minutes before the ugly blue Studebaker pulled into the circular driveway of the Clarke mansion.

As usual the front door was open and Quentin and the others walked inside without knocking. A few minutes later a black Mercedes turned into the driveway and parked behind Quentin's car. Josie felt a jolt of adrenaline as she recognized Emily's car, but Burt was driving and Sandra Collins was the only passenger.

"Now there's an unlikely couple," she said as Burt and Sandra went into the house.

"He's got to have something really bad on her," Charlie said.

"Maybe not," she said, but didn't pursue it. Charlie seemed upset and she guessed she had underestimated how much he cared for the aging actress.

She had barely finished speaking when a newer Cadillac arrived and parked in the street in front of the house. They slumped down as far as they could in the roadster to avoid being seen and peered over the dashboard to watch his honor David Jacobson get out of his car and go inside.

"Gang's all here," Charlie said, sitting up again. "Maybe we'll get lucky and Emily will show."

Headlights turned onto the street from behind them, but this car parked several houses away. She kept watching in the rearview mirror and saw a man cross the street and walk in the direction of Clarke's house. She warned Charlie and they slid down in the seats, hidden again, until he walked up the driveway, deliberately seeming to stay in the shadows until he got inside.

Neither of them could make out the man's face so Josie slipped out of the MG's passenger door, crouching down as she jogged back to where he had parked. This particular road was narrow and paved but didn't have sidewalks or streetlights. The only illumination came from the private properties, but Josie had watched carefully and was certain she could locate the right vehicle and get the license plate number. She stood on the parkway near the four-door Plymouth and said out loud, "You've got to be kidding."

It was a late-model police utility vehicle with red and blue emergency lights in the corner of the back window. There was just enough light from the adjacent property to see the radio and microphone on the dashboard and an empty space where the shotgun should've been bolted to the floor. She couldn't make out the exterior color in the dim light but memorized the license plate number and used her keychain flashlight to read the shop number stuck on the inside of the gas cap cover with a Dymo label . . . finding shop numbers was another useless piece of information policewomen were taught so they could do fleet inventories. However in this case, that shop number should tell them who had checked out and driven the car tonight.

She hurried back to Charlie's car and quickly jotted down the memorized numbers on the back of an old piece of mail before telling him what she'd seen.

"The car looks new," she said, folding the envelope and sticking it into the back pocket of her jeans. "Anybody else go in while I was gone?"

"No," Charlie said, turning in the seat toward her. "If one of them is a cop, how are we gonna know who to trust?"

"The person I saw walk across the street was big, but too short to be Mitchell. When we were in the chief's conference room he looked to be over six feet tall. We'll give it to Murphy. He'll find out who drives that shop number." Josie knew she wasn't answering his question. There wasn't any good way to know whom to trust, so she'd go with her usually reliable instincts, which told her Murphy might be an emotional time bomb but otherwise he was completely trustworthy.

It was after midnight when the visitors began leaving Clarke's house. They departed in practically the same order they had arrived except David Jacobson. He was the last and stood outside arguing with Clarke for several minutes before Anthony Barnes came onto the porch, said a few words, then escorted the judge to his car. Quentin's father must've already been in the house or went in another way because Josie never saw him arrive. The older man waited until Jacobson had driven away and then, without saying a word to Clarke, he walked across the lawn in the direction of the house next door.

The headlights came on from the police car parked behind them. It made a U-turn and was out of sight in a few seconds.

Josie was surprised because she hadn't seen anyone come out of the house or get into that car. Clarke was still standing on the porch so they couldn't follow right away without letting him know they'd been parked there watching, but as soon as he stepped back inside and closed the door, Charlie started the MG and went after the car, but it was too late. At the end of the block, he stopped at the intersection and they looked in all directions, but the street was deserted.

WHEN JOSIE got back to her room, she called Murphy's house to give him the information on the police car, but Angela answered.

"Do you know what time it is?" Angela asked. "My kids gotta get up for school tomorrow. This ain't no damned police station you can call all hours of the night."

"Sorry," Josie said, looking at the clock on the nightstand. She had forgotten it was so late, but asked, "Is Sergeant Murphy home?"

There was silence on the other end of the line for several seconds then Angela exhaled and said in a calmer voice, "No, try his play wife," and hung up.

The testy interaction between Murphy and Carlson told Josie the chances of them being back together were slim. Either he'd found another lonely woman or he was at the no-name bar. She wasn't sleepy and thought a trip down the coast to Redondo Beach might be a great opportunity to be alone and do some serious thinking.

She wouldn't bother Charlie, more for her sake than his. She needed time alone. Something was bothering her about the players who got together tonight but she couldn't quite bring the big picture into focus. Driving always cleared her head, so ten minutes later she was in the VW Bug on Pacific Coast Highway.

The night was clear and out the passenger window she could see moonlight covering the ocean with a delicate shimmering blanket of silver. She stopped for a few minutes and got out of the car to look down from the side of the road at waves tumbling onto the shore. It was peaceful and magnificent. Josie realized she hadn't taken enough time to actually enjoy this view all those years she'd spent living in Venice. The work had consumed her. She'd never had a job before that became her life, the reason she got up in the morning and all she thought about until falling asleep exhausted at night. Was this what her entire career in the LAPD would be like, she wondered.

"Damn, I hope so," she said, getting back into her car.

THE PARKING garage at Redondo pier was nearly empty so it was easy to locate Murphy's old T/A-damaged Mercury sitting in the space closest to the walkway. His city car didn't look any better than the abandoned ones she'd seen men sleeping in around Venice. PDID got its vehicles as hand-me-downs from other more prominent detective divisions such as Robbery-Homicide and immediately removed anything resembling police equipment.

She hurried to the closest shops and restaurants hoping the buildings would act as a barrier to protect her from the biting wind off the ocean. Everything appeared to be closed but she could see a thin stream of light coming from under the door of the no-name bar. It had been left ajar just enough to let the local beach bums know it was still available for business. She doubted a two A.M. mandatory closing time meant much to this crowd since their best customer was a police sergeant.

There wasn't much more light inside, but enough to see Murphy sitting alone at a table across from the bar. A small neon Budweiser beer sign flashed on and off above his head as he scribbled on a yellow legal pad. The bartender was playing chess with an older, scantily clad woman at the other end of the bar. No one seemed to notice Josie until she sat at

Murphy's table. He didn't look up but said, "Get a glass," and pushed a half-empty bottle of Jim Beam toward her.

She went behind the bar and found what looked like the cleanest glass. The bartender ignored her. He was concentrating on the chessboard, but mostly gawking at the low-cut neckline of his aging adversary.

"I called your house. Angie was angry," she said, pouring enough whiskey in both their glasses.

He stopped writing and sat back.

"Angie was born angry . . . beautiful, sexy and pissed off," he said, emptying the glass. "What do you want?"

She wanted to tell him his wife was pissed off all the time because it was impossible to live with a drunk, but she knew that was pointless. It was becoming clear to her that except in a structured work environment, Brickhouse didn't have a lot of control over what happened in his life. He was a lot like his city car; it kept running but usually looked like shit on the outside and everything under the hood was barely held together with spare parts and wire. Instead she told him what they'd seen at Larry Clarke's house and gave him the numbers she'd taken off the police car.

"Whoever it was stayed in the shadows. We never got a good look at him, but I'm pretty sure it wasn't Lieutenant Mitchell . . . too short and heavier."

He pushed the legal tablet in front of her. It was a flow-chart with all the people who had been linked to Soriano's life.

"Do you see anyone who has an unusual number of connections?" he asked, filling their glasses again.

"Not really, except . . . you're not talking about Charlie?" she asked, realizing nearly every line on the paper led back to her partner. "That was his job to get close to all of them."

"Charlie admitted to you he told Quentin that Kate was cheating with Soriano . . . He'd already guessed Soriano was a cop and had to know Quentin just being Quentin might do something crazy. So why tell him?"

She didn't have a good answer because she had thought about it and also wondered why he would do that.

"Maybe Charlie knew Quentin well enough to know he wouldn't hurt Dave . . . not over a woman like Kate. Besides, what possible reason would Charlie have to kill him or even want him dead?" she asked.

"He thought Soriano was a dirty cop, confronted him, and it got out of hand."

"No," she said shaking her head. "I know him. He wouldn't do that."

"How do you know? You saw what he did to Alex over practically nothing and how he beat the crap out of Burt," he said, and hesitated before adding, "Yeah, I know the truth about that one too. Look, all I'm saying is be careful and keep your eyes open. I'm not accusing him of anything . . . just telling you to watch your back."

"You're wrong."

"I hope so, but I wanna know before you two have any more midnight excursions, okay?"

Josie nodded, but they both knew she probably didn't mean it. She also knew Brickhouse well enough to surmise that his stupid flowchart was the reason he was here instead of at home with his beautiful, cranky wife. Murphy liked and respected Charlie, a fellow marine. The possibility Charlie might be a cop killer, even a bad cop, was most likely eating at him. Together with all his other demons it had derailed his domestic life again.

"How soon before you know who our mystery cop is?" she asked, splitting the last few drops in the bottle between them.

"I'll give the shop number to Motor Transport. They can tell me which division was assigned the car, then we'll see who checked it out . . . mystery solved."

She got up and slid the tablet back across the table to him. "Walk me back to my car," she said, hoping to lure him out of the bar and onto the road home. Even drunk, Murphy was a better driver than most and she had no fear of him crashing. If she could get him into his car, he'd make it home and pass out until morning.

Josie was certain he'd sleep better than she would. That flowchart was definitely going to keep her mind churning like an eggbeater all night.

TWENTY-ONE

The alarm went off at seven, but Josie was already awake, lying on her side in bed staring at dark storm clouds forming over the ocean. She'd forgotten to close the curtains last night but it didn't matter. Sleep had come in short bursts between moments of worrying about Charlie and Brickhouse and anxiety over . . . she wasn't certain, maybe everything. Charlie had left a note under her door saying he wanted to make his morning run in the Elysian Park hills surrounding the police academy and that he'd catch up with her later at the PDID office.

Her usual route into Los Angeles was the Harbor Freeway north, but when she got to the downtown exits, she kept driving, and went past Dodger Stadium on the Pasadena Freeway to Academy Road. She hadn't intended to go to the police academy and didn't really know why or what she wanted to say to Charlie. It just seemed important to confront him. Maybe it was foolish, but she thought she'd know if he was lying to her.

This was the first time she'd been back to the training facility in three years, since graduation day. She drove up the narrow driveway, under the arch built in 1934 when some Olympic events were held there, and found a parking space across from the PT field and reasonably close to the café. Nobody ran at the academy without stopping for breakfast. A recruit class was lined up in squads on the large assembly area near the flagpole. The class drill instructor, or DI, was screaming at a young man who didn't have the proper hair-cut. In seconds the entire class was on the ground in their business suits doing push-ups. She walked past and smiled at one of the instructors she recognized. He smiled back—a gesture she hadn't experienced her last time through here.

"Pastore, isn't it?" he asked.

"Yes," she said and caught herself before saying "sir." They were equals now . . . sort of.

"Been reading about you. Good work," he said and turned away to yell at another recruit.

"Thanks," she said and kept walking. It wouldn't be easy to come back here and get retrained even if it meant being able to work in a patrol car. The chief would make it difficult for those few women who were willing and able to do it. She wondered if it were even possible now to subject herself to that kind of treatment, to tolerate the mental and physical indignities that were certain to come with additional training.

Josie laughed softly and said under her breath, "Fuck, yeah."

She located Charlie sitting at the counter in the café by himself. The recruits were the primary customers for break-fast here and most of them were in classes now so the place was nearly empty. He looked up when she walked in and seemed happy to see her.

"I'm starving," she said, sitting on the stool next to him.

"How unusual," he said, grinning.

She ordered bacon and eggs with her coffee and it was placed in front of her in seconds.

"What's wrong?" he asked, as she stuffed a big forkful of eggs in her mouth.

"Nothing, wanted breakfast," she answered, still chewing.

"You hate the academy and you can get better food closer to your apartment."

Josie stopped chewing and swallowed, took a sip of coffee, then swiveled around just enough to face him.

"I've got a question."

He shrugged, "So ask."

"Did you have anything to do with Soriano's death?"

"If you mean did I kill him, no."

"That's not what I asked."

His expression could've been a photograph—not a blink, not a twitch, or tightened jaw muscle. He stared directly, calmly into her eyes and said, "I swear I had nothing to do with Dave's death."

She pushed her half-full plate away and put six dollars on the counter. "I'll see you back at Georgia Street," she said, sliding off the stool. He nodded and she started to leave but came back and said, "Don't you want to know why I asked?"

"Not really. I figure Carlson put the idea in Murphy's head and he probably ran it by you like he always does."

"Why would she do that?"

"I scare her . . . actually, you scare her."

"What're you talking about?"

Charlie paid his bill, and he walked with her out of the café. They stood in an alcove away from the door where the newspaper racks were bolted to the cement and waited while a group of fifty or so recruits ran past them to their next class.

"I'll admit Carlson's got a grip on the technicalities of police work, but she'll never have the heart or mind of a warrior," he said.

"Okay, so what scares her?"

"You and me, we thrive in life-and-death situations, main-line the adrenaline rush, and are willing to accept the consequences. She doesn't understand any of that and it scares the hell out of her. She's like a lot of cops who are desperate for desk jobs. They wake up one morning and realize how dangerous this job is, so they're afraid most of the time and try to hide somewhere safe, away from the action," he said, as they started toward their cars.

"I know she doesn't like me," Josie said. "I'm not sure that's the reason, but I do believe you about Soriano's death."

Her gut feeling told her he was being truthful. She might be wrong but was willing to trust him for now.

THE SHADOW, aka Sergeant Young, was waiting for her when Josie arrived at the intelligence division. He told her Murphy was still at Motor Transport and there hadn't been any word on the shop number yet.

Young was dressed in a dated business suit that was slightly too small for him and stood out more than usual in the raucous squad room. The other detectives kidded him about having a promotional oral for the lieutenant's list, but he insisted he was going to a funeral. More raunchy jokes followed about the possible demise of several unpopular staff officers.

"It's for that homeless girl," Young said, seemingly tired of the relentless taunting.

"Sunny?" Josie asked.

"The coroner said some guy claimed her body and I found out the funeral's today. I figure she's not gonna have too many people who cared enough to go. Wanna come?" he asked. Then he added, with the obvious intent of making her feel guilty, "She did show some fondness toward you."

Josie looked down at her jeans and wool jacket, not exactly what she would normally wear to a funeral.

"I'd have to change . . ."

"The woman was homeless. I don't think they're gonna judge your appearance," Charlie said, interrupting her.

"It's in Hollywood. We could be back in an hour," Young said.

He had a city car so he drove Josie and Charlie to the Hollywood cemetery located on Santa Monica Boulevard in one of the seedier parts of Tinseltown. The area had declined over the years with gangs and prostitutes setting up shop in nearby neighborhoods. Although the likes of Rudolph Valentino and Cecil B. DeMille were interred on the grounds, the modern Hollywood crowd had more or less abandoned the place.

As she entered the front gate, Josie could see the landscape and buildings needed some attention but the cemetery still had that aura of glitzy bygone years. She could almost imagine a procession of glamorous movie stars stepping around ornate headstones, following the coffin of Tyrone Power to its final resting spot.

The grounds were deserted except for three figures hovering over a freshly dug grave close to the Gower Street wall, a particularly ugly location with overgrown grass and weeds. When she got closer, Josie saw the taller man was dressed in a black suit and wearing a priest's collar. Standing on either side of him were Sandra Collins, in a full-length mink coat, and the handsome young man who had driven her RV up to the Santa Clarita campsite.

The actress didn't notice them until they were a few feet away. She looked up and at first seemed puzzled, but her expression hardened quickly and she crossed her arms glaring at them.

"What are you doing here?" she asked bitterly, and then turned to the young man standing beside her as if she expected him to do something. He looked down and was silent.

"She was my friend," Josie said, knowing that was probably another lie, but then again she might've been the closest thing to a friend the girl had.

"Laura did not have friends," Collins said, putting on the dark sunglasses she'd been holding.

"Not true; you're here," Sergeant Young said, as the cemetery workers lowered the simple coffin into the hole.

"You people have no shame," Collins whispered, dabbing under the glasses with a handkerchief. She gently tossed a single rose onto the coffin, made the sign of the cross, and walked away from the grave. They watched as she maneuvered unsteadily in high spiked heels over the uneven patches of dirt and around the headstones until she reached the paved road and got in to a limo that drove toward the front gate.

The young man took a deep breath, exhaled, and started to follow her, but stopped near Charlie.

"This is really hard for my mother and you're making it so much worse. Laura never had . . ." He started to say, but stopped, shook his head and said, "Never mind," before walking away.

"Sandra's your mother?" Charlie asked, and the young man hesitated before coming back.

"Yes, she trusted you and like all the others . . . oh, what's the difference."

"Laura, this girl, was your sister," Josie said, finally realizing how much he looked like the homeless girl.

He nodded and watched quietly, his face frozen in grief as workers lowered the vault cover into the hole over the coffin and began filling it with dirt. Josie felt sorry for him and tried to gently distract him with simple conversation. His name was Peter and Laura was his twin sister. She was diagnosed as bipolar in high school and left home three years ago when she was nineteen. Susan Collins refused to have her daughter institutionalized but couldn't convince her to come home. Without medication her behavior became erratic. She was easy prey on the Venice boardwalk and, before she died, didn't seem to recognize either her mother or brother, refusing any help from them or anyone.

"It was the heroin and other drugs that finally pushed her over the edge," Peter said, wiping tears from his eyes with the back of his hand. "I blame that dead cop."

"Soriano?" she asked.

"He gave it to her."

"How do you know that?"

"I know," Peter insisted.

"Because that's what your mother told you?" Josie asked, walking beside him away from the grave. Sergeant Young and Charlie went ahead of them, talking quietly while trying to stay on the narrow strip of tall grass and dirt between graves.

When they reached the paved road, Josie stepped in front of Peter and he stopped.

"You realize you've just given me a strong motive for you and your mother to want Officer Soriano dead," Josie said.

"I didn't kill him and I certainly didn't want him dead," Peter said, shaking his head. "I just wanted him to leave Laura alone. As for my mother . . . do you honestly believe she could harm anyone? She's vain and foolish but hardly a killer, unless she drives over someone in a drunken stupor."

"Where's your father?" Charlie asked. He was sitting on the hood of Sergeant Young's car a few feet away.

"What difference does that make?" Peter asked.

"Do you know?" Charlie persisted.

"Yes, I know, but I think that's a question better answered by my mother," he said with a wry smile and walked around Josie toward a white Porsche 911. It had been parked on a dirt patch several yards away under the shade of a massive old oak.

SERGEANT YOUNG had them back at the Georgia Street office in a little over an hour but Murphy still wasn't there. They hadn't talked much on the return trip but Josie was starting to agree with Murphy that the homeless girl might be a key piece in the murder puzzle. Laura apparently knew Soriano and had items that belonged to him. The question was, did she find those things in the sand or was she there that night and see who killed the undercover officer. Her overdose was suspicious and gave credence to Josie's suspicion she had seen something the killer was afraid she might reveal.

Charlie told her he had asked about Peter's father because if he was in any way involved in his children's lives he might've had a motive to kill Soriano too. The county birth certificates should show the father's name. With his contacts, Sergeant Young thought he could get that information quickly.

They were talking about what to get for lunch when Sergeant Carlson told them Murphy had called and wanted them to meet him in the captain's office at Internal Affairs. He had tentatively identified the driver of the police car.

Internal Affairs was on the fifth floor of Parker Center, one floor below the office of the chief of police. The captain's office was a few steps from the elevator. The door was open and Josie saw Murphy standing by the secretary's desk when she, Charlie, and Carlson stepped out into the hallway.

The IA captain ushered them into his private office where Captain Williams from PDID was already waiting, and he closed the door. Six chairs had been placed around a worktable across from his large messy desk, and he told everyone to sit.

"Who was driving the car?" Josie asked, after describing in detail at the IA captain's request what she and Charlie had seen the previous night at Larry Clarke's house.

Josie noticed Carlson scowl and Murphy look down when she asked the question and knew they thought she was too bold for a lowly three-year policewoman, but she was tired of the secrecy.

"That shop number belongs to Deputy Chief Perez of the Office of Special Services. I think you're familiar with him," the IA captain said.

"Does he admit being there?" she asked.

"Yes, he lives in Brentwood and has known the Clarke family for years. Judge Jacobson is a personal friend who also lives in the area. They asked him to stop by," the captain said.

Josie shook her head. "No, that doesn't make any sense . . . why did he hide in the shadows? Why park half a block away?"

Captain Williams cleared his throat and said, "Chief Perez said he never parks close because Clarke always has so many people visiting he can't get his car out if he's in or near the driveway . . . he denies hiding in the shadows."

"Why did Clarke want him there?" Murphy asked.

"He had a dilemma," the IA captain said. "Anthony Barnes's son, Quentin, his girlfriend, Kate Sparks, and Manny Contreras with WLM were coming to his house with an ultimatum and Clarke wanted Perez to be there."

"What ultimatum?" Murphy persisted. Josie could see he was starting to fidget which meant he wasn't buying any of this.

"Quentin showed them a communiqué he claimed was mailed to him from Emily and Alex saying if the DA and judge didn't prosecute the sheriff's deputies who killed Ruben Salazar they'd bomb more government buildings and start executing cops."

Josie sighed and whispered, "Salazar again."

"Did Perez confiscate the letter?" Charlie asked.

Williams cleared his throat again and said, "Chief Perez wasn't there in an official capacity . . ."

"He's still a damned cop, isn't he?" Murphy asked.

"Internal Affairs will be interviewing everyone who was at Clarke's house," the IA captain said. "Hopefully we can still retrieve the letter, but I assure you we will determine if there was any unbecoming conduct or neglect of duty by Chief Perez and deal with it."

It was common knowledge among the rank and file that staff officers rarely got held accountable and Murphy expressed that skepticism with a barely audible groan. The captain added, perhaps as an appeasement, "You're welcome to sit in on the interviews, Sergeant, or any of you."

The meeting lasted twenty minutes and Captain Williams left without speaking to any of his subordinates. The IA captain shook their hands and told his secretary to notify Murphy when the interviews were scheduled.

"So they haven't given up on their crazy mission to avenge the Salazar accident," Josie said, as they stood in the hallway waiting for the elevator.

"Quentin probably wrote that communiqué," Charlie said. "Alex and Emily are about as politically illiterate as you can get."

"One time Emily tried to convince me Karl Marx had brothers in show business," Josie said with a straight face because it was true.

"But they're still dangerous, and I'm sure the two of you are high on their list of targets, so watch your backs," Murphy said, squinting at Josie as if he was trying to decide if she was serious about Emily.

Now that Murphy was sober, she wondered if he still harbored suspicions about Charlie. She figured Charlie was right and Carlson had most likely planted those ideas in his head, but Josie hoped he was thinking more clearly today and had thrown away his stupid yellow pad with the flowchart.

It wasn't easy to tell what Murphy was thinking. He was a master at hiding his feelings, which might've explained a lot of his personal problems.

On the elevator ride, Josie told him what they'd learned at the homeless girl's funeral and how Sergeant Young should have the birth certificate information by the time they got back to Georgia Street.

When they arrived at the PDID office, Sergeant Young was waiting at Murphy's desk and jumped up waving a piece of paper as soon as he spotted them. Murphy grabbed the paper out of his hand. Josie and Charlie crowded close to read it.

There were several seconds of silence as they continued staring at the barely legible fax copy. The revelation about the father of Sandra Collins's twins was a bigger surprise than even Josie imagined it would be.

TWENTY-TWO

In Josie's mind, Anthony Barnes was the least likely candidate to have fathered the movie star's children, but his name was clearly listed on the birth certificates. He was close to Collins in age but unlike her he was known to be a sober, intelligent man. Although they were two people who seemed to have nothing in common, Josie knew that before Quentin's father had his encounter with the Commie-hating HUAC and turned to a lucrative career in real estate, he'd been a screenwriter. It was a period of time when he and Collins could've met.

"Quentin's got a half-brother. How scary is that?" Murphy said, giving the fax back to Sergeant Young.

"Peter isn't anything like him," Josie said. Then added, "For one thing, he seems sane."

"Anthony Barnes had a motive to kill Soriano if he knew Dave was feeding drugs to his daughter," Charlie said. "I wonder if Quentin knew the girl was his half-sister."

"All of a sudden we've got lots of people who might've had an issue with Soriano," Murphy said, glancing around the squad room as if he were looking for someone. "Come with me; we gotta talk somewhere else."

Carlson, Josie, and Charlie followed him into the empty captain's office and he closed the door. He kept the blinds open. Josie guessed to watch for Captain Williams's return.

"What is it?" Carlson asked, curtly. She still seemed angry with the way Murphy had treated her and not ready to forgive or forget.

"Did any of you believe that bullshit story Perez told IA?" he asked.

"Not really," Charlie said.

Josie shrugged and said, "I'm certain of one thing. Perez was sneaking in and out of Clarke's house. It was pretty obvious there wasn't a party. He could've easily parked in the driveway or in front of the place."

"Let's face it. IA's not gonna do a thorough investigation. They don't give a fuck about some dead cop . . . they're not detectives and their careers will always get in the way of asking tough or embarrassing questions of the guys who might sit on their promotion boards," Murphy said.

"So what can we do?" Josie asked.

"We interrogate Anthony Barnes and that judge ourselves. They may not be blowing up buildings but they're hanging around these idiots and can probably give us an educated guess about who had the best motive to kill our UC."

"They've got reputations and positions to lose; they can be intimidated," Carlson said, caught up in the moment.

Murphy grinned and said, "That's my girl."

"Fuck you, Brickhouse; I'm not your girl. As soon as we catch those assholes I'm out of this division," she said and returned to the squad room.

For the first time since she met her, Josie actually admired Carlson a little, but she also knew it was easy to find fault with Murphy who couldn't be diplomatic or sensitive to other people's feelings if he tried.

It was another routine task for Sergeant Young to find addresses for both Jacobson and Barnes. They lived in Brentwood on Clarke's street. Barnes was in the house next door and the judge lived at the end of the block in the corner house. After some discussion, they decided it might be better to confront the judge at work in his chambers, hoping the man would find it difficult to lie to them while wearing his black robe and surrounded by other reminders of his oath to administer justice.

In an attempt to save time, Murphy told Charlie and Carlson to go to Anthony Barnes's house and talk to the older man while he and Josie went to the Hall of Justice and confronted his honor.

"Check out the area before you go into that house," Murphy said, cornering Charlie as he and Carlson were getting ready to leave. "Pull back and call me if you see Quentin's car or anything suspicious that makes you think Alex or Emily might be in there. I want to know what Anthony Barnes has to say, but that's all. Do not engage his wacko son and those fugitives. Got it?"

"Ten-four, boss," Charlie said, giving Murphy a perfect salute before catching up with Carlson who didn't care what Murphy had to say.

Josie could see Murphy wasn't comfortable letting the two of them go alone. Charlie was a good cop but inexperienced. Carlson had time on the job but was untested in field situations. It was a fairly uncomplicated task but, like her boss, she knew Quentin and his buddies could pop up anywhere, and they were human land mines ready to go off with little provocation.

She and Murphy got to the Hall of Justice late enough that all the courts were close to the end of sessions for the day. As they walked through the nearly empty hallways, the sounds of their boot heels echoed off the marble floors. Josie looked up at the gilded ceilings and knew saving this building from Quentin and Emily's lunacy had been the right thing to do. She still found it difficult to believe a policeman like Soriano could've been involved in planning its destruction. What was the point, she wondered, if ending the war and bringing about revolution meant destroying everything we've built? She understood this building was a symbol of injustice and government oppression in the minds of Quentin and others, but there had to be a better way to be heard and bring about change. Once again she had to remind herself not to try to make sense out of crazy.

When they got to Jacobson's courtroom, he was still on the bench, finishing the last case on his docket. His bailiff was hovering over the shoulder of a black defendant who was handcuffed to a chair. The defense attorney was comparing schedules with a young female deputy DA attempting to set the date for a continuance, and it wasn't until the bailiff escorted the defendant back to the holding cells that Jacobson looked up and noticed them sitting in the back row.

Josie was curious to see how the judge would react to her now that he knew she was a cop. He'd only known her as someone she wasn't and had been subjected to all sorts of far-left rhetoric from her. She liked him and had enjoyed his company, but wouldn't be surprised if he was a little testy about her deception.

As soon as the lawyers finished business and packed up their briefcases, Jacobson stood, tugged on the collar of his black robe, and said, "Officers, we can talk in my chambers." He stepped down from the bench, and whispered a few words to the court clerk before disappearing through a doorway behind the witness chair.

The office was big, a man's space with sumptuous dark colors and heavy furniture. Floor-to-ceiling mahogany bookshelves filled with volumes of case law and criminal statutes lined the walls. His walnut desk was enormous with hand-carved decorative legs and piled high with thick folders. It was set in front of a picture window looking down on Broadway. He took off his robe, hung it in an armoire in a corner of the room, loosened his tie, and sat in his shirtsleeves behind his desk. When he was settled in, Murphy pulled two wooden chairs closer to the desk and they sat.

"Miss Pastore, are you happy to be back among your own kind?" Jacobson asked, breaking the silence. He hadn't said a word or acknowledged them since leaving the courtroom. Josie thought he appeared nervous and maybe a little annoyed, but he avoided looking directly at her.

"Yes, sir," she said curtly, not wanting the meeting to become about her.

"Not quite as talkative as our last encounter . . . too bad," he said, smiling at her before turning toward Murphy. "What can I do for you, Sergeant?"

"Internal Affairs has spoken to Chief Perez about your get-together at Larry Clarke's house last night," Murphy said.

"One of your IA investigators already called me this morning about that, so I'm a little puzzled why I'd be talking to you . . . if that's the only reason you're here."

"IA's primary concern is possible misconduct by an assistant chief. I'm investigating your involvement in Officer Dave Soriano's murder."

"Me," Jacobson said, forcing a laugh. "I barely knew the young man and I certainly had nothing to do with his death. Why would you even think such a thing?" he asked, and looked directly at Josie.

"Your association with Quentin Barnes, Emily Rice, and others not only makes you suspect, but a reasonable person might argue it compromises your position on the bench," Murphy said.

"In the first place, I'm not associating with any of them except Anthony Barnes. I've been at neighborhood parties with the others but that's all. I assure you I have no knowledge of criminal activities."

"What happened last night?" Josie asked. "Why did you go to Clarke's house?" She knew Murphy wanted to conduct the interview but she could talk to this man and believed he'd be more likely to respond to her questions.

"Larry called, said he'd heard from Emily and Alex, and he needed to talk to me. I told him to call the police. He said he already had, and Chief Perez was coming to the house and had requested I be there. Of course it was all a fabrication."

"In what way?" Murphy asked.

"It was a ploy to get me there. He said Burt had received a letter from Emily, but he wouldn't show it to anybody,"

Jacobson said, shaking his head. "Burt wanted Clarke to convince the DA to file murder charges against that police officer who killed Ruben Salazar and he wanted me to try the criminal case in my courtroom. Clarke is about to get fired and has no influence with the DA. I got angry, told him his request was improper, and left."

"Why was Chief Perez there?" Josie asked.

"Burt wanted him to bring misconduct charges against everyone in PDID for spying on innocent citizens and to order the division disbanded. In return he promised to get Emily and Alex to turn themselves in."

"What did Perez say?"

"He'd try, but couldn't make any promises."

"Asshole," Murphy said, and quickly added, "Sorry. Did you tell all that to IA?"

"Yes, of course I did."

"How did Perez get involved with these guys?"

"From what I understand, Perez, Manny Contreras, and your dead officer were all from a town in El Salvador and knew each other's families."

"So did Manny know Soriano was a cop?" she asked.

"I don't know about any of that," Jacobson said, shifting in his leather chair. "But I'm positive your Chief Perez has divided loyalties and like too many people in this city, he's beholden to Burt Rice."

"You mean Burt's got dirt on him," Murphy said.

"Your words not mine, but as you people say, it is suspicious," the judge said, and stood. "Anything else?"

"Did you know Anthony Barnes was the father of Sandra Collins's twins?" Josie asked.

Jacobson sighed and stretched his back a little before saying, "He told me years ago, and despite Sandra's influence, Peter has become a pretty decent young man. Poor Laura's dead, but what does that have to do with any of this?"

"If Officer Soriano gave drugs to Laura, her father and twin brother might've had a reason to want him dead."

Jacobson laughed. "If Peter or his father killed everyone who gave or sold drugs to Laura, they wouldn't have had time to do anything else. They knew she was a lost cause. It broke Anthony's heart but he and Peter stayed away from her. As far as I know there were only two people Laura ever let get close—her mother and Emily Rice."

"Emily?"

"She's beautiful and Laura in her fantasy world was fascinated with beautiful or shiny things."

They talked for a few more minutes but Josie had stopped listening. Her mind was immersed in a Scrabble board of ideas. She could feel something starting to take form—the drugs, the demonstrations and terrorists' acts, the network of people inside and outside the police department, and a spider web tying them all together.

She was beginning to wonder if Soriano had figured it out and had to be killed before he could tell anyone. Sandra's accusations of his drug dealing, the heroin stashed under his booby-trapped car, it was all too convenient and tidy.

One thing was certain—he had been killed and his body dumped into the ocean. Josie had a gut feeling Laura had seen it happen, recognized the killer, and had to be eliminated too. She knew after years of being undercover and observing human nature that politics frequently took a backseat to personal relationships, and too often ego trumped altruism. So it wouldn't be a big surprise if his death had nothing to do with his assignment and everything to do with his affair with Kate. No matter how many times she thought about the pool of possible murder suspects, Kate Sparks's name kept popping into her head. Kate was there right in the middle of everything. She had to know and be a party to what happened.

"Josie."

She heard her name and looked up. Murphy was waiting by the door with the judge.

"Sorry," she said, getting up. "I was thinking about something."

"I've had people doze off in my courtroom before, but never while I was talking to them," Jacobson said, with a slight smile. She liked his smile. "Maybe you'll let me take you to lunch again sometime and I can talk to the real Josie Pastore," he said, escorting them back into the courtroom and unlocking the door to the hallway.

Josie didn't respond to his offer, but felt stupid because she knew she was blushing.

"What was that about?" Murphy asked when they reached the elevators.

"Nothing," she said, but knew when a guy was coming on to her. She really hadn't been attracted to any man for a long time and the strong vibes coming from his honor were flattering. But she knew it would've meant so much more if Jake Corsino had been the one making the offer. "Did you believe him?" she asked, wanting to change the subject.

"Yeah, he confirmed Perez is a lying piece of shit."

"So now what?" she asked.

"I checked the time books for those few weeks during probation when Soriano was loaned to Community Relations. He spent several days in Press Relations helping as a Spanish speaker. Lieutenant Mitchell had to know he was a cop. We're gonna talk to him before we meet up with Charlie and Carlson."

"But then he'll know we're watching him," she said, as they drove out of the garage.

"I've got a gut feeling he's known that since the minute we told Perez."

Press Relations was on the sixth floor of Parker Center just down the hall from the office of the chief of police and directly across the hall from his chief of staff. Assistant Chief

Perez had his office on this floor too, but on the other side of the building.

Mitchell was sitting at the secretary's desk facing the open door when they entered. He looked up and Josie could've sworn his face drained of color as soon as he saw them.

"Sergeant Murphy, how can I help you?" Mitchell asked with forced nonchalance.

"Need to talk to you in your office, Harvey," Murphy ordered, not showing any deference to the man who out-ranked him and not bothering to wait for his compliance but walking directly across the room to the glass-enclosed space with Mitchell's name in bold letters on the door.

Josie waited until the lieutenant got up and followed him, closing the door behind them. There were two uniformed officers in the outer room but they were talking on telephones and didn't seem to care what was happening around them.

Mitchell immediately slipped behind his desk and sat. It was almost as if he wanted a safe barrier between him and Murphy.

"What is it? What do you want?" he asked, blinking as if something was in his eyes. Josie guessed it was a nervous tic that seemed to be getting worse.

"I want to know why you were leaking confidential police information to Quentin Barnes and Burt Rice," Murphy said. When Mitchell tried to deny it, he interrupted, leaned over the desk, and in a low threatening voice, said, "Don't fucking lie to me, Harvey. Quentin gave you up and I managed to find more than enough proof before you or Perez had an opportunity to destroy it."

Being a city girl, Josie had always wondered what cops meant when they said "deer in the headlights look" but after today she definitely understood the condition. Mitchell's eyes seemed to glaze over with a frozen vacant stare. He didn't move or attempt to speak. After a few seconds, she worried he might've had some kind of seizure, but finally he slumped back in his chair.

"You didn't actually believe an assistant chief would risk his career to protect you, did you?" Murphy asked.

Mitchell didn't answer right away, concentrating instead on pulling apart a paper clip from the top of his desk. Josie tried to fade quietly into the corner out of sight, afraid anything she did or said would interfere with whatever Murphy was doing here. She had no idea what he was talking about since Quentin hadn't given them anything and they had no proof of what this lieutenant was doing, but Mitchell seemed to believe him.

"I never told them Soriano was a cop, but they must've found out somehow," Mitchell admitted, tossing the mangled clip into the trash.

"How?"

He looked up at Murphy, enough for her to see his indecision and fear. A battle was clearly waging in his head. Whatever he knew was going to be difficult for him to say. Murphy seemed to recognize the internal struggle; he pulled a chair closer to the desk and sat.

"What is Burt Rice holding over your head?" Murphy asked, in a gentler tone.

Mitchell shook his head, before nervously covering his face with both hands.

"I barely know Rice. Look, do I need an attorney . . . or a union rep?" he asked.

Murphy's fist pounded on the desk, startling Mitchell and Josie, before he asked, "Do I look like a fucking IA geek? I don't give a fuck about your rights. A cop is dead and you're already up to your balls in shit. Just tell me what you know."

"And if I don't . . ."

"Then you've got my word I'll do everything I can to make sure you not only lose your cushy job and pension but get sent to the worst prison in California."

"Prison?" he blurted out and put his head back, staring at the ceiling, before saying, "I haven't done anything illegal. I only do what Perez tells me."

After that, Mitchell was like a broken faucet. He couldn't stop the flow of words, admitting that Chief Perez would feed him embarrassing department information which he then released not only to some of the news outlets but to certain ACLU lawyers such as Burt Rice or people he designated such as Quentin Barnes.

"Perez says he only wants the department to be transparent and completely up front about everything we do, so he tells me sensitive information the old man is trying to keep in-house, and I leak it. He doesn't believe we should have secrets," Mitchell said.

"And you believe that crap?" Murphy asked.

"He hates your division . . . calls PDID the Gestapo . . . says what you do is what they did to his friends and family in El Salvador."

"Did he ask you to tell Quentin that Soriano was a cop?" Josie asked.

"No," Mitchell said, his features contorting as if the thought were repugnant. "Besides, Perez didn't know he was a cop. I knew but I never told him. I was afraid . . ." He didn't finish, hesitated a few seconds, started to say something, and finally the blinking slowed down and he worked up the courage to say, "Look, the police commission told Perez they would never make him chief of police. He's bitter and wants the department to look bad because he thinks we're all a bunch of white racists."

"They made him an assistant chief. That's not bad for a bunch of racists," Murphy said.

"The old man keeps him at arm's length, and Perez resents it. He's an outsider. I think he's hoping if things get bad enough . . . demonstrations, riots, bombings . . . the commission might dump the old man and reconsider," Mitchell said. "I leak everything he gives me, but I swear I never told anybody Soriano was a cop. I confirmed to Quentin he was dead . . . that's all."

"Are you the reason WLM knows so much about our deployment and police-shooting boards . . . what goes on at every disciplinary hearing?" Josie asked.

Mitchell nodded. "Manny Contreras and Burt Rice have their reasons for creating chaos; Perez has his. I'm just the messenger."

"When IA's done with you, I hope you're just a civilian," Josie said, getting up and leaving the office.

The outer room was empty now, but she went into the hallway to get as far as she could from the lieutenant and wait for Murphy to finish. Josie believed Mitchell had told them mostly the truth, which meant he and Perez had violated the chief's trust, but they hadn't let anyone know Soriano was a cop.

A few minutes later, Murphy came out, didn't look up, but as he shot past her, said, "Let's go, Pastore."

"Now what?" she asked as they got into the elevator.

"Now we get out of here before I choke out that weasel Perez too."

TWENTY-THREE

Charlie was waiting at the PDID office when they returned, but most of the other detectives, including Carlson, had gone for the day. He told Murphy that Anthony Barnes hadn't been at his house. They waited in the car for more than an hour but he never showed up.

"So are we done here?" Josie asked, tired of hearing her stomach rumbling and thinking how good Italian food would taste right now. She was about to ask if anyone wanted to go to Little Joe's in Chinatown when Murphy said, "We're not done."

"Are we going back to Brentwood?" Charlie asked.

"Yeah," Murphy said.

"You'd better feed her first," Charlie said, after Josie's stomach growled again, much louder this time. "Before she shoots some small animal in the street and devours it."

The most Murphy was willing to do was stop at a hotdog stand on First Street across from the courthouse. It was a run-down shack but known citywide for the best chili dogs and cheese fries in LA. She glanced at the chalkboard menu and ordered the biggest messiest concoction they had, loaded with onions, peppers, and a special hot sauce created by the owner, Mr. Doggie. Four stools were bolted to the ground in front of the counter and to get her food Josie had to reach between two smelly homeless men who were perched there sharing an order of fries, but she didn't care. Not even the odor of human flesh that hadn't touched bath water in months could prevent her from claiming her meal. Both Charlie and Murphy had passed on getting food, but once she got back in to the car and the spicy aroma filled the close quarters, they regretted their decision. After Murphy got onto the freeway, she let them have a couple of fries . . . to stop the whining.

As their car turned onto Barnes's street, Josie looked at the corner house. Jacobson's Cadillac was parked in the driveway behind the gate. Floodlights came on as they drove by, illuminating his expansive lawn and most of the street. She knew from past conversations the judge wasn't one of the neighbors who supported Quentin's radical ideas, but she wondered if he was being truthful about how much he knew. She really wanted to believe him.

Down the street, Anthony Barnes's house was on a bigger piece of property than Larry Clarke's mansion next door. It seemed as if every light in or around the place had been turned on. There were cars in the driveway and several parked in a separate garage, but not Quentin's old Studebaker. Josie saw a motor home next to the garage and thought it closely resembled the one Peter had driven with his mother to the Santa Clarita campsite.

There was no gate or wall around the Barnes property, so Murphy pulled up the driveway and parked in front of the entry. Josie could barely see Clarke's house from there. Actually it was difficult to see anything outside the ring of bright lights.

An older woman in a maid's uniform answered the door and asked them to wait in the library off the foyer. Josie thought the interior of the house was magnificent, with the huge entryway opening to a circular staircase centered on a crystal chandelier. Anthony Barnes was obviously a very wealthy man, and she wondered why Quentin always looked as if he got his clothes off the Sisters of Charity thrift-store rack. He had completely bought into the hippie lifestyle with his shaggy thinning hair and his aversion to personal cleanliness. Josie knew if her parents had this kind of money she'd have no qualms about spending it on expensive clothes and all the trimmings. She certainly wouldn't be driving an ancient Studebaker and working as a short-order cook in some run-down beach diner.

While they waited, Josie looked around at the oil paintings covering nearly every inch of wall space. They were mostly family portraits. There was a large picture of a younger Anthony and a beautiful woman. Josie guessed she might've been his second wife and maybe Quentin's mother, since his nose and eyes resembled hers. There were several renditions of Quentin as a baby, a young man and student, but not one as an adult.

She was surprised to see a painting of a youthful, glamorous Sandra Collins in a movie-star pose hung in a place of prominence over the fireplace, and one of Peter and Laura as children. She wouldn't have recognized Peter, but the young girl was definitely the homeless Laura with that unmistakable detached stare. Her body was there but her mind engaged somewhere only she could go. It seemed as if Anthony did have a connection and genuine attachment to his children with Collins.

The books in his library were mostly classics. He had an extensive collection of the Greek philosophers and poets, as well as Shakespeare, European and American novelists and playwrights, and one whole section with shelves devoted to historical and political writing. When Anthony finally came in, she'd been thumbing through a copy of *The Anarchist Cookbook*, a newly published user's manual on drugs and weapons and advocating violence to bring about political change. Josie put the book back on the shelf and thought, like father like son.

"What can I do for you officers?" Anthony asked. He was wearing black pajamas, a matching silk bathrobe, and slippers and looked very tired. Josie guessed he had to be in his seventies, but he shuffled unsteadily and moved like a man twenty years older.

"We want to ask you a few questions about Dave Soriano," Murphy said.

Anthony didn't respond but asked them to follow him to his den where they could sit comfortably and talk. He led them down a hallway past the dining room and kitchen and into a cozy wood-paneled room with another fireplace and more pictures on the walls, but these were less personal landscapes framed like museum pieces.

"Now, who did you want to ask about?" Anthony asked, seeming a little confused.

"Officer Dave Soriano, the policeman who was killed on Venice Beach," Murphy said and paused as if he'd heard something. "Is your son home, Mr. Barnes?" he asked.

"Peter?"

"Quentin."

"I don't think so. I'm sorry, but I don't believe I know your policeman. Am I supposed to have met him?"

"You and I had a discussion with him at Larry Clarke's house about the need for violence in bringing about change," Charlie said.

"Was I for or against?" Barnes asked.

"Strongly in favor."

Anthony chuckled and said, "It's easy for rich old men to support quick violent fixes. Two reasons—we want to be around to see the results and we probably won't be doing any of the fighting. I do remember him now . . . handsome, fairly articulate young man."

"Do you know why someone might've wanted him dead?" Josie asked.

"He was a police spy," Anthony offered indifferently.

"Did you want him dead?"

"No, all I want is him and you out of my private affairs. My involvement in political or social causes or even the fact that I use recreational drugs in my own home is my business and I resent Charlie and you misrepresenting yourselves to spy on me."

"Do your private affairs include promoting and funding criminals who blow up buildings and injure innocent people?" Josie asked.

"I give my money to causes and people I believe in."

"Did you give someone money to kill Soriano?"

"Why would I do that? I had no idea he was a policeman until after he was dead."

"Kate Sparks told me you were driving her and Quentin to Palm Springs to meet with Soriano just before he was found murdered. Was that true?" Josie asked.

Anthony got up and went to a wet bar where he took a bottle of brandy off the shelf. He held it up and asked, "Would anyone care for some?" They all declined so he poured a little into a snifter and came back, sat again, then took a sip before answering. "We drove most of the way to Palm Springs, but not to see your policeman."

"Then why?" Josie persisted.

Anthony hesitated. It was clear he didn't want to talk about this. Finally he put the glass down on the table near his chair.

"The woman was pregnant, perhaps by my son, or so she claimed. I was taking them somewhere to deal with it . . . at my expense of course."

"You took her to the desert for an abortion?"

"That was the plan but on the way my son changed her mind, so we came back . . . I understand she did it later on her own."

"You wanted your grandbaby dead?" Josie asked. She was trying to get him emotional, angry enough to say things without calculating his words so much.

"I wanted that fetus dead. The woman is a heroin addict. I have no objection to occasional marijuana, but . . ." He stopped as if he'd caught himself in an ideological dilemma.

"Do you have any idea who killed Officer Soriano?" Murphy asked. He was getting impatient with the old man.

"No."

Josie was watching Murphy and understood his body language well enough to know he had decided it was time to change course. She worried because with him that might mean something weird, but then again the old man obviously wasn't going to volunteer information, so what did they have to lose. She didn't have to wait long for the new direction.

"Okay, you leave me no choice but to arrest your son Quentin for murder," Murphy said, standing. It was time to scare the old man.

Anthony's eyes widened and he said, "You have no proof my son killed anyone."

"I can arrest and prosecute him on circumstantial evidence. Your son had motive—jealousy. His pregnant girlfriend left him for Soriano. He had opportunity and means. He's shown a propensity toward violence, publicly calling for the death of cops, and he has no alibi for the night our officer was killed. Besides, I think it's a safe bet he's gone underground with his pals by now, so he's a fugitive on top of all that," Murphy said, without taking a breath.

"I know the law. That's still not enough to charge him."

"Maybe not, but we also have his prints on the heroin and pipe bomb he planted under Soriano's car. His prints are on the bags of heroin he left at the murder scene to make it look like a drug deal gone bad," Josie said, but couldn't look at Murphy or Charlie because they knew she was bluffing.

Anthony was shaking his head but not speaking. He didn't want to believe any of it but, after three years of lying, Josie had become quite proficient. She sensed, however, he might need a touch more persuasion so she added, "Poor Laura was there the night Soriano got killed. She saw everything and knew the killer. We know that because he came back and gave her enough pure heroin to be certain she'd never talk to anyone again."

She stopped and waited, hoping he cared enough about his daughter to get angry. Charlie and Murphy were quiet. She still didn't dare look at either of them but kept staring at Anthony. He stared back as if he were attempting to read her mind. Was she telling the truth? He wasn't good at hiding his emotions and the mention of his dead daughter had unsettled him.

"That can't be right. He couldn't do that," Anthony finally whispered, but without much conviction.

"But he did," Murphy insisted.

"No . . ." Anthony said and hesitated before asking, "Is it true? Was Laura killed?" Josie noticed a little palsy in his hands now, and worried they might've pushed too hard and he was about to have a stroke, but he said in a firm voice, "Please, sit down Sergeant." He picked up his glass and gulped the rest of the brandy. Suddenly he looked angry.

Murphy sat directly across from him, leaned toward the old man, and said, "Don't waste my time Mr. Barnes."

"Sandra Collins is my ex-wife and mother of our twins. She was always beautiful and a little naive, but she's become a vain, stupid woman who can easily be manipulated by most men. Burt Rice is the worst. He uses her ignorance to bleed her for a lot of money."

"What does that have to do with Soriano's murder?" Murphy asked.

"During one of her drunken binges, Sandra got hysterical and admitted to me that she and Emily Rice drove your policeman from downtown LA to Venice Beach the night he was killed. She's terrified Burt will tell the police she did that."

"Did she see what happened?" Josie asked.

"When they got there, Sandra left Emily and your officer on the beach to talk; they were arguing and she went to the pavilion to look for our daughter. Laura wasn't there, so Sandra said she came back along the bike path where she found Emily pacing and shouting Laura's name as if she were looking for some lost dog."

"Was Soriano there?"

"No, but Sandra told me Emily was frantic and sweating as if she'd been running. She grabbed Sandra's arm and pulled her away, yelling at her they had to go and not to 'f'ing' worry about her daughter. Nobody saw your policeman alive again after that night . . . they found his body twenty yards from where Sandra left him and Emily."

TWENTY-FOUR

I t wasn't easy, but Murphy convinced Anthony Barnes to call his ex-wife and she reluctantly agreed to come to the house. After Murphy's gentle prodding, a technique Josie had rarely seen him use, Sandra Collins told them essentially an identical story. The only difference was she embellished her narrative with a number of expletives whenever she mentioned Burt Rice or his wife. She said the lawyer had convinced her she couldn't talk about that night without incriminating herself, and he promised if she were to say anything, he and Emily would swear to a very different story.

She signed a statement Josie had quickly typed in Anthony's office, and they were standing in the foyer getting ready to leave when Charlie suddenly touched Collins's shoulder and asked, "Has Quentin called you again for money, Sandra?"

She moved away from him and didn't answer, but gave Anthony a sheepish look.

"Stupid woman," Anthony said after a long sigh. "How much did you give him?"

"I'm his mother. He needed money."

"You're his stepmother and he's a grown man. I told you not to give him any more. How much this time?"

"Ten thousand," she whispered.

"Where did you bring it?" Murphy asked. He had already been out the front door standing on the porch when Charlie asked if she had given Quentin money again.

She hesitated but Anthony ordered her to speak and she mumbled, "Kremlin basement," and added quickly, "But they're not there anymore. It was just for that one night."

"Who's not there anymore?" Josie asked. "Were Emily and Alex with him?"

Collins nodded and Josie felt a jolt of adrenaline at the prospect of maybe catching them.

"He's going after the Hall of Justice again," Charlie said. "I know this guy. He's obsessed with bombing that building."

"Fuck," Murphy said, and, hurrying back into the house, told Anthony, "I've got to use your phone."

They followed Barnes back to his office where Murphy dialed Captain Williams's home number. Murphy told them the PDID captain would contact the chief of police and he would call the sheriff to arrange security for the county building when it opened. She heard Murphy suggesting to Williams that the downtown area go on tactical alert which would keep the morning watch officers from going home and then additional officers could be brought in to guard as many public buildings as possible. None of the government offices or courts would open for several hours so they had plenty of time to set up.

"What can we do?" Josie asked, while Murphy was on hold waiting for the captain to arrange a conference call.

"Nothing right now," Murphy said. "Actually, we're so close to your apartments right now why don't you take the car and get a few hours sleep. I'll have one of the West LA patrol guys take me back to the office and you can meet me there in about four hours."

"We'd rather stay with you," Charlie said.

"I'd rather not have you falling asleep in the morning when I really need you, so do what I say and I promise you won't miss any of the action. Trust me nothing's gonna happen until morning. They're not going to bomb or shoot up the outside of buildings, and they can't get inside until after eight. You'll be there."

He tossed Charlie the car keys, but they didn't move until Murphy gently pushed them out the front door and closed it behind them.

"He's probably right," Josie said, getting into the passenger seat of the junky city car. "At this hour, we're twenty minutes from Hermosa Beach. We can sleep until six and be back downtown before rush hour."

"I don't want to miss anything," Charlie said.

She felt the same, but knew Murphy didn't really need them now and they'd only be hanging around watching him work. As Charlie drove slowly past the judge's house at the end of the block, the floodlights over his front gate and driveway came on again. What Josie thought she saw was so surprising she couldn't get the words out right away.

"S . . . Stop!" she ordered. "Turn around, go back."

Charlie didn't say anything but parked on the other side of the cross street where Josie could still see Jacobson's house in the rearview mirror. She watched until the lights around the property dimmed and a few seconds later went off.

"What are we doing?" Charlie asked.

"I saw Quentin's Studebaker in the driveway. It wasn't there when we went by the first time. We need to go back and tell Murphy," she said.

"Shit," Charlie mumbled, starting the car again.

"No, no, shut it off," she said, putting her hand over his to stop the key from turning.

"What the fuck is wrong now?"

"Headlights, a car's coming out the gate."

They both slid down a little in their seats. She adjusted the mirror and could see it moving slowly in their direction, but it wasn't the Studebaker. Jacobson's Cadillac passed them and the judge was driving with Quentin clearly visible in the passenger seat and she could make out at least three more people in the backseat. Josie sat up as the car drove through the gantlet of more security lights, and she caught a flash of blonde hair in the rear passenger seat.

"Follow them," she ordered, but Charlie had already started the car and pulled away from the curb with his headlights off. There was no time to go back and tell Murphy. She was certain Emily was in the car, and with the judge's assistance, they didn't have to wait for the Justice building to open. If that's where they were going, Jacobson could probably get them inside anytime he wanted.

"You got extra ammo?" Charlie asked.

"Same as you, two speedy loaders on my belt, twelve rounds."

She opened the glove compartment and found a box of .38-caliber lead-slug ammo with a stub stamped "passed" from Murphy's monthly qualification. Josie was grateful he hadn't replaced his city-issued ammo yet. She showed it to Charlie before taking half the bullets and putting them in his jacket pocket and the rest in her pocket.

"I know Murphy's got a shotgun in the trunk, but if Collins gave Quentin another ten thousand dollars he probably picked up some automatic or semiauto weapons," he said, concentrating on staying as far as he could from the Cadillac while still keeping it in sight.

"We're screwed unless we can call in the cavalry when they get to wherever they're going . . . or we can flag down a black-and-white."

"Does this piece of junk have a radio?" he asked.

"In the glove box," she said, opening it again and turning on the police radio. "Voilà." She put the volume higher, picked up the microphone, and broadcast, attempting to reach anyone who might be in the PDID office or on the frequency. There was no response. She turned to the Tac-2 frequency but got heavy static. "I don't understand; why can't I get the emergency channel?"

"Equipment failure . . . don't worry about it. The West Side's notorious for dead spots. They're getting on the freeway; buckle up," he said, slowing down so the Cadillac could access the onramp without seeing their car behind it. When it was out of sight, he raced up the ramp and onto the freeway and quickly had the car in view again.

There were other vehicles on the freeway so Charlie put on his headlights but stayed so far back Josie worried he might start following the wrong car. He assured her the taillights on that model were unique which made it easy to follow. It took her a few minutes to understand what he meant but before they got close to the downtown area she could pick out the unusual pattern better than he could.

When the car made a quick lane change, Charlie lost it for a second, but she spotted the lights immediately and said, "We make a good team."

"Yeah, too bad I'm gonna promote and you'll still be a lowly patrol officer. We're coming up on the downtown exits, try the radio again."

She did with the same result.

"We need a plan," she said, closing the glove box. "I haven't seen a police car since we started."

"The streets are so quiet at this hour most morning-watch coppers find a hole and sleep. I'm thinking unless a pay phone is nearby when we finally stop, we're on our own with our puny six-shot revolvers and one shotgun."

"As soon as we get close, you stop, and I'll snatch the shotgun and extra shells from the trunk."

Charlie looked at her. "You ever fired a shotgun?"

"LAPD academy trained," she said with a shrug.

"Why is that not reassuring?"

"Maybe because of the big hole some policewoman blew in the range instructor's booth when her shotgun accidentally discharged."

"That could be it."

"Wasn't me. I love shooting big guns," she said.

"Somehow Josie, I knew that. He's onto the interchange and off at Broadway. Looks like we're heading back to Justice."

"Are we going to let them get inside?" she said, knowing what his answer would be.

"Don't think so. What about you?"

"Nope, but we should let them get out of the car . . . they'll be more vulnerable that way and maybe smart enough to give up." She really didn't believe they'd give up and knew Charlie didn't either. She was guessing they wouldn't park under the building since that would make it harder for a quick getaway. It made more sense for one of them to stay in the car, but if past experience was any indicator, Quentin and Emily rarely did anything that made sense.

Her biggest disappointment was Jacobson. She had believed him and didn't think he knew about or condoned any of the dangerous things Quentin was doing. It was frustrating to be that wrong about someone she liked.

Charlie stopped before the Cadillac arrived at the Hall of Justice. Josie got out, grabbed the shotgun and shells, and jumped back into the car. The gun was loaded but she'd wait until they were outside the car again to chamber a round.

It was nearly dawn, and the homeless were drifting south from their overnight encampments among the weeds and overgrown shrubbery beside the freeway exits. Others were stirring inside the shelter of doorsteps and on sidewalks where boxes and tents were crowded together for warmth and protection. They got up early to be first in line at the missions and shelters for a hot shower and breakfast. The Cadillac drove past them and pulled in to the service road off Temple just east of and adjacent to the Hall of Justice.

"Good," Charlie whispered, as they watched from across the street, sitting in the Plymouth and hidden behind heavy equipment in a Department of Water and Power lot. "Any wild rounds should be contained between the block wall and the Justice building. Now we just gotta hope there's no homeless camp at the other end of that alley."

The Cadillac had stopped near what looked like the building's service door, and a few feet from the loading dock. The trunk popped open, but no one got out of the car.

"What are they waiting for?" she asked, after what seemed like a long time. She could feel her palms getting sweaty and her breathing accelerate. She envied her Vietnam, battle-tested partner. He seemed calm and detached from all the terrible things she imagined were about to happen.

"Take a deep breath," Charlie said. "You're doing great. Just remember that training day in the mountains. None of these idiots can hit the side of a barn. As soon as they're out of the car I'm pulling in behind them. Use your door for cover and don't chamber a shotgun round until they can hear it . . . very unnerving sound. Okay?"

"Roger that," she said and wasn't nervous anymore. They had a plan.

Finally the front passenger door opened, and Quentin got out, walked around the Cadillac, opened the driver's door, leaned in, and said a few words to Jacobson, then moved aside his jacket and showed him something in his waistband. After a few seconds, he reached in with both hands and yanked the judge out of the car, causing him to stumble onto the ground.

The back doors opened and Alex got out on Quentin's side; Emily and Burt climbed out the other door.

"Clown car's empty. You ready?" Charlie asked, but didn't wait for an answer. He floored the accelerator and drove the beat-up Plymouth straight across the street as fast as the old car could go into the service alley, stopping a couple of car lengths behind the Cadillac.

Josie flung open her door and immediately pumped a round into the shotgun and pointed it at Emily and Burt. Charlie yelled "police" and ordered them to put their hands up and not move. Burt froze, dropped to his knees, and then fell face down onto the ground with his hands covering his head. Emily reached into the backseat of the Cadillac and produced an AR 15 automatic rifle. When she pointed it toward the police car, Josie fired one round from the shotgun that hit the edge of the Cadillac's open trunk blowing pieces of metal into the air. Alex leaped into the backseat of the Cadillac and disappeared from view. Emily was momentarily distracted by the metal shower, but raised the rifle a second time as the next shotgun blast hit her torso. She fell backward so violently the AR15 discharged a burst of gunfire into the asphalt as her head hit the open door and the weapon flew from her hands landing ten feet away. Josie heard Alex screaming Emily's name from inside the car, but he didn't venture out to help her.

Quentin fired wildly from behind the Cadillac. The rounds from his semiauto were hitting the Plymouth's hood and had shattered the police car's windshield and the driver's door window as he returned Charlie's gunfire. Josie was watching Burt and waiting for Alex to charge out of the car with guns blazing, but at the same time couldn't stop staring at Emily's motionless body, hoping to see some sign of life. She thought she'd heard Charlie shouting her name, but could barely hear anything with her ears ringing from the deafening sound of live rounds. She'd never been this close to so much gunfire without earplugs or protectors; it was painful. She saw Jacobson had rolled behind the loading dock and was wisely hunkered down.

"Josie," Charlie called again from the other side of their car. She looked over the seats and saw blood on the right sleeve of his jacket. He was still using the door for cover but had been hit and was gingerly holding his revolver in his left hand. "Reload the shotgun and cover me, keep firing, keep Quentin down so I can move behind that loading dock. Keep an eye out for Alex. Don't let him get out of the car."

She was loading shells into the shotgun preparing to bombard Quentin with a hailstorm of shotgun pellets when she heard it—that beautiful piercing sound of police sirens. Seconds later, black-and-white patrol cars with sirens blaring and emergency lights flashing screeched into the service road behind their car. She yanked the badge off her belt, held it up, and saw Charlie do the same with his good hand. A uniformed sergeant yelled at them to keep their heads down and within seconds he had officers in positions of advantage around Quentin where all he could do was surrender or get killed. Josie wasn't surprised he gave up so quickly. Quentin was crazy, not stupid. As soon as the shooting stopped, Alex crawled out from the backseat of the Cadillac and dropped to his knees with his hands over his head.

After the sergeant had everyone safely in custody, Josie placed the loaded shotgun with the safety on, in the open trunk of Murphy's car. She'd never been in a shooting but remembered hearing in the academy that the shooting team would want it that way. She checked on Charlie. His wound was painful but superficial and the paramedics were there in minutes to clean and bandage it.

Emily wasn't as fortunate. The second shotgun blast had killed her instantly. Her face was splattered with small ugly cuts from the metal pieces and pellets that hit the Cadillac's trunk, but Josie's next shot was a direct hit, a tight blast of twelve deadly pellets, tiny holes in her clothing covering her chest and stomach. Josie was surprised how little blood there was.

"Senseless," she said, shaking her head and turning her back on the body. She watched one of the uniformed officers assist Alex into the backseat of a patrol car. He seemed devastated by her death and had meekly given up without a fight.

This wasn't what Josie had wanted, even though she knew Emily hadn't given her any other choice. The back floor of the Cadillac had enough ammo for a small army and the trunk was filled with more, another AR 15, and two crates packed with homemade pipe bombs. They had intended to do some significant damage.

Although his wife's body was only a few feet away, Burt made no attempt to look at her or get any closer. He seemed terrified and had tremors in his hands and face. He'd probably gone too long without alcohol and whined to the paramedics about painful stomach cramps too before he was taken to central jail for medical treatment. Based on her experience with jail doctors, Josie figured he wasn't going to feel much better anytime soon.

Murphy arrived as the uniformed officers were handcuffing Quentin, who wouldn't stop yelling about police abuse and threatening fiery death and destruction for every "pig" in the city. The PDID sergeant listened for a few seconds, then took him aside, and whispered something in his ear. The shouting stopped immediately and Quentin sat quietly in the backseat of the black-and-white until he was taken away to Parker Center.

"What did you say to him?" Josie asked, after Murphy made certain she was all right.

"I told him if he didn't shut up, I'd take him to jail by myself and promised on the way he'd get shot trying to escape," Murphy said, before they sat next to Jacobson and Charlie on the loading dock. They watched silently as the homicide detectives and the coroner examined and photographed Emily's body and the surrounding area before lifting her corpse onto a gurney and depositing it inside the van.

The officer-involved shooting team arrived seconds later and wanted to take Josie and Charlie back to their offices to be interviewed. She wasn't ready to leave and face that ordeal so she convinced Murphy to tell the OIS detectives he would be responsible for getting them to Parker Center within the hour. The shooting had happened in milliseconds, but everything she did, every instinct, thought, and movement would be dissected and evaluated to decide if she'd made the right decision. Josie understood and was willing to go through the process, just not right now.

In the grey light of morning, she could see swelling and bruises beginning to turn dark purple on Jacobson's face and under both eyes. He was chain smoking but sounded steady and composed as he told them his story about the night of horrors he'd endured. His hands, however, betrayed him, trembling as he lit a new cigarette off the old one.

Unwilling to give in to Quentin's bullying, Jacobson said he'd been hit repeatedly with the barrel of a gun before he'd agreed to drive to the Hall of Justice and get them inside.

"I knew they were going to kill me anyway, but Quentin made it clear he preferred to do the execution in my own courtroom," the judge said. "I convinced him I could get them in through the service door and past the security guards because I hoped it would keep me alive longer . . . I needed time to figure out what to do."

"Why was he in your house?" Josie asked.

"The Ruben Salazar fiasco . . . he blames me and the DA for not prosecuting that deputy who accidentally killed Salazar. He intended to plant pipe bombs in my courtroom, the DA's office, and the sheriff's office and then kill me and anyone he saw to send a message." Jacobson tried to smile at Josie but winced from the pain and said, "To answer your question, he forced his way into my home with Alex and Burt. Emily and Kate showed up later."

"Kate? Where's she?"

"I don't know. He dragged her down to my wine cellar and came back alone ten minutes later. I'm afraid . . ." He didn't finish.

"Why would he harm her?" Josie asked.

Jacobson shook his head. It was difficult for him to talk about it.

"Emily killed Kate's lover . . . your undercover officer," he said and looked around at their faces. "You already knew."

"But we don't know why," Murphy said.

"From what I heard last night, I'm guessing your officer found out about Emily's drug trafficking and demanded a piece of the action."

"They told you that?"

"They intended to kill me; there was no reason to lie or not to talk in front of me."

"Did she know he was a cop?"

Jacobson rubbed his neck and shoulder and shifted his weight uncomfortably on the cold cement before saying, "I don't think so, but apparently Emily and Burt with Manny's contacts are making a lot of money transporting heroin and marijuana from Central America. Most of the profit's going into their pockets and the rest funds arsenals and safe houses. From what they said, I'm guessing Kate's the one who told Soriano and he threatened to tell the police unless they cut him in, so Emily killed him and tried to make it look like a drug deal. She got pissed at Kate last night and spilled the whole story."

"What did Kate do?" Josie asked.

"She got hysterical and that's when Quentin took her down to the cellar."

They stopped talking and watched as the coroner's van backed out of the service driveway, maneuvering around evidence tags and police cars.

"There was no way to let you know," Josie said, looking at Murphy and feeling a little guilty. "It happened too fast. We tried the radio, but nobody answered."

"Don't sweat it. You did exactly the right thing," Murphy said, sliding off the dock. "You're going home in one piece and the bad guys are going to jail or the morgue." He borrowed Jacobson's keys and directed two uniformed officers to go to Brentwood and check his wine cellar. "You saved his honor's life and maybe a lot of other innocent people," he said as he walked slowly around his bullet-riddled city car surveying the damage. "Assholes destroyed my fucking car."

After the shooting team removed the shotgun from the trunk, Charlie helped Murphy salvage whatever he could from the wreck before a tow truck dragged it to the city impound yard for further examination. Murphy figured he wouldn't see it again for months . . . if ever.

Josie sat quietly beside the judge watching them. After the paramedics checked him out, she looked at his bruised face and asked, "How are you feeling, your honor?"

"Call me David . . . sore, angry about too many things."

"Sorry I had to lie to you."

"I understand and don't blame you, Josie," he said and hesitated before adding, "It's the rest of it. I want change, an end to the war . . . but not this way. This is . . . it's anarchy."

"It's just starting; there're a lot more Quentins and Emilys out there waiting for the right moment to torch the city."

He nodded and was quiet for several seconds before asking, "When my face heals and I can be seen in public without scaring small children, will you have dinner with me? I promise no politics, strictly personal stuff. You're an intelligent, beautiful woman and I'd like to know you better. What do you think?"

"I admire you a lot and I'd like you as a friend. Let's start there," she said.

TWENTY-FIVE

The Officer-Involved Shooting team made it easy for Josie to tell her story. They guided her through the statement and the final document she signed made her and Charlie sound a lot more competent and experienced than she thought they had been. Everyone including Jake Corsino, who was called in from home and helped edit the statement, assured her that the shooting would be found "in policy" by the District Attorney's Office and the department's Shooting Review Board. Murphy warned her the board always included some negative comment to prevent charges of leniency and it always resulted in additional training. Her training might be prompted by the initial round that hit the lid of the Cadillac's open trunk.

Josie told everyone she hurried that first shot and missed. Truth was she had her finger on the trigger and it went off accidentally. There was no way she'd ever admit that to anyone. She'd rather be a bad shot than too dumb to keep her finger off the trigger.

It took several hours to finish all the reports and interviews, but Officer Soriano's death investigation would finally be closed, "cleared other, suspect deceased," based on circumstantial evidence with the suspect identified as Emily Rice. Uniformed officers located Kate Sparks's battered body in Jacobson's wine cellar. With the judge's eyewitness statement, detectives had more than enough probable cause to arrest Quentin for her murder. Anthony Barnes said he wasn't surprised by his son's actions. He admitted Quentin had never really forgiven Kate for aborting their baby.

Jake Corsino stayed all night helping with the reports to be certain everything would be acceptable to the DA's office. He was especially attentive to Josie and she realized, in the informal environment of the PDID squad room, there was another attractive side to this man. He was not only funny and smart but could hold his own with the cop banter. The detectives welcomed him as one of their own and she felt as if she'd known him much longer than a few days.

"What happened to the allegations Soriano was trying to horn in on the drug trafficking?" Josie asked Murphy after she finished reading the homicide summary. It was nearly dawn, and Corsino had to leave for a court hearing, but she and the others were still in the Georgia Street office sharing a bag of the greasiest chicken and fries she'd ever eaten. The only way to tolerate the taste was to bathe each piece in hot sauce.

"Until somebody can prove he wasn't intending to pass that drug information on to us, it's a nonissue," Murphy said.

"But we all know he was a drug dealer," Charlie said and grinned when Murphy glared at him.

"Asshole," Murphy said, reaching into his desk drawer and removing a full pint of whiskey. He poured some in his coffee cup and, holding it up, asked, "Anybody thirsty?"

They immediately dumped any trace of coffee from their cups into the trash cans and lined up for shots. Carlson was first and from the come-hither smile she gave Murphy, Josie guessed Miss Angela and the kids were sleeping alone tonight.

"What's the occasion?" Charlie asked.

"You're going back to patrol. That's reason enough for me to celebrate."

"What about me?" Josie asked.

"You're staying to help with the lawsuits," he said and must've seen her disappointment because he added, "Unless you have a burning desire to work at Harbor Jail because that's where personnel wants to send you."

"Guess I'll stay," she whispered, cheering up a little when she remembered helping with the lawsuits meant working with Jake Corsino.

"Good decision," Murphy said. "From what I've heard, the first academy class to train patrol women will probably be scheduled sometime next year. I'd think you've got a better chance of getting in from here. Don't you? Not to mention, given enough time, you might actually learn something from me and that DA who's falling all over you."

She knew he was right but shrugged. She was tired and didn't want to talk about it anymore. The division's detectives would be coming in any minute and her body was telling her to go home and sleep, but her mind refused to shut down. The image of Emily's dead mutilated body kept popping into her head. Somehow she knew the department's shrink she'd be forced to visit in the next day or two wouldn't understand or make her feel any better. The shooting really didn't bother her. That was the problem.

"I'm afraid this job is changing me," she confided in Charlie as they stood outside their cars in the apartment building parking lot in the early morning hours. They'd just gotten home and had to be up in a few hours to go back to work. Even sunglasses weren't helping to keep the rising sun from hurting her eyes.

"What do you mean?" he asked.

"I just took a woman's life. A few years ago, I know I would've been devastated, sick to my stomach."

"It'll hit you; trust me."

"I'm not certain I like this side of me."

"You knew when you took the job that killing somebody was a possibility; it may never happen again. Most cops go through their whole careers without firing their weapons, but if you can't handle it, then quit."

"Not a chance," Josie said.

She knew she could handle it the way she handled everything in life . . . her way. First thing tomorrow she'd buy a new pair of running shoes and start jogging in Elysian Park. She'd get through the academy again, work in patrol, and get promoted to detective, lieutenant, maybe even higher. She loved being a cop and had a plan for her career path in the LAPD. Quitting definitely wasn't part of that plan.